THE COUNTERFEIT
MISTRESS

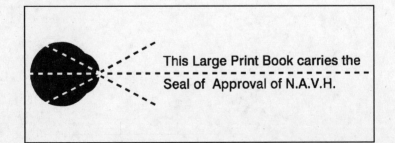

This Large Print Book carries the
Seal of Approval of N.A.V.H.

THE COUNTERFEIT MISTRESS

MADELINE HUNTER

THORNDIKE PRESS
A part of Gale, Cengage Learning

Detroit • New York • San Francisco • New Haven, Conn • Waterville, Maine • London

GALE
CENGAGE Learning®

LIBRARY OF CONGRESS CATALOGING-IN-PUBLICATION DATA

Hunter, Madeline.
    The Counterfeit Mistress / By Madeline Hunter. — Large Print edition.
        pages cm. — (Thorndike Press Large Print Romance)
    ISBN 978-1-4104-6484-2 (hardcover) — ISBN 1-4104-6484-9 (hardcover)
    1. Large type books. I. Title.
PS3608.U5946C68 2013
813'.6—dc23   2013036227

Published in 2013 by arrangement with The Berkley Publishing Group, a member of Penguin (USA) LLC, a Penguin Random House Company

Printed in the United States of America
1 2 3 4 5 6 7 17 16 15 14 13

This book is dedicated to the memory of my aunt Rose and aunt Madeline

CHAPTER 1

Handsome Stupid Man was following her again.

Marielle noticed him as she turned at the crossroads near her house. She clutched the roll of papers that she carried closer to her chest and hurried on, dodging her way around the people crowding the lane.

It had been months since she had seen him. She thought he had given up last spring after she let him know that she was aware that he watched her.

It had been a game to her while it lasted. She had enjoyed leading him around London while she addressed the most mundane aspects of her life. When more significant activities occupied her, she always managed to evade his attention.

She stole a glance over her shoulder to see if he had also made the turn, and smiled at the absurdity that he believed she might not detect him. A man who looked like this one would always be noticed.

An agent who followed spies needed an unremarkable appearance, not a presence that commanded attention. Subtle activities required an average countenance, not one that makes women sigh. Sharply hewn and masculine in its beauty, his face compelled one's gaze despite its severity — and perhaps because of it. His lack of understanding of his unsuitability for this duty, and how obvious he became in executing it, led her to name him Handsome Stupid Man.

How annoying for him to choose today to bother with her again. The people she had to meet would not appreciate his attendance, that was certain. She needed to escape his shadow before she reached her destination.

Changing course, she turned down the next street, then made a right on the one after that. She fell into step in front of a wagon drawn by a lumbering horse, so she might be less visible in the crowd. Spying a milliner's shop several doors away, she darted inside when the wagon came to it. Positioning herself near the window, she watched the street she had just left.

Eventually Handsome Stupid Man came into view, pacing his horse slowly. The steed paused in the crossroads. Peering around a bonnet displayed in the window, she stole a glance at the man in the saddle.

He gazed down the lane, frowning. Perplexed, he raked his dark, cropped hair with his fingers, and twisted in his saddle to look back up the street. His emerald gaze darted right and left, forward and back. He even looked right at her window but the bonnet and small wavy panes of glass surely obscured his view. Finally, he turned his horse. Riding like a field marshal, he retraced his path.

She swallowed a giggle. What a Stupid Man.

She waited for the horse's tail to disappear, then began counting to mark time before she should leave.

A warmth on her shoulder startled her. The shop's owner loomed at her back, wearing a frown as severe as Handsome Stupid Man's.

"Would you like to try that bonnet? You have been admiring it for a *very* long time," she said. Pale blue eyes peered suspiciously at the long, full shawl that had admittedly hidden more than a bonnet at times.

Looking down, Marielle noticed that the top of the roll of papers that she grasped to her chest now peeked above the shawl's patterned silk, appearing much like a hidden, stolen item.

She picked at a ribbon on the bonnet behind which she had hid. Such a luxury was not for her, even if she had enough money squirreled away. She saved for something far more important than bonnets.

"I thought I might like to buy this, but I do not care for some details now that I see it closely."

The woman's lids lowered on hearing her voice. "Ah, you are French. One of our *guests.* That explains — well —" Her gaze meandered down Marielle's garments, pausing on the tattered lace around the dress's neckline, then on the faded glory of the pale, patterned Venetian shawl, then on the full skirt that announced how old-fashioned the dress was. That gaze finally settled on the paint smudge that marred Marielle's gloveless hand.

Marielle stared the shopkeeper down. "*Oui,* one of your country's guests. My clothing may be old, madame, but so is my blood and that is what matters, no? As it happens I am purchasing a new wardrobe with funds recently brought out of my country. I thought your shop was one recommended to me by my friend the Viscountess Ambury, but it appears I misunderstood. Your wares, I fear, do not have the quality necessary to secure her patronage."

Posture rigid, she left the shop and walked back to the crossroad. There she angled her head around the corner to see if Handsome Stupid Man had gone.

He was nowhere to be seen. She hurried in the other direction, down the shop's lane to the prior street. Moving indirectly, she made her way toward her rendezvous.

As she darted out of a small lane onto a busy street, she spied a hackney leaving off a patron. She always knew exactly how much coin she had in her purse, and today it would be enough. Cursing the time and money that Handsome Stupid Man had cost her, she jumped into the coach.

Where in hell had the French bitch gone?

Gavin Norwood, Viscount Kendale, surveyed the heads bobbing along the street, looking for one with long golden brown curls that fell down a woman's slender shoulders.

He could spot Marielle Lyon from several blocks away without any trouble. It was not so much her lithe form that marked her, or even that hair. Her garments were old-fashioned and she usually swathed herself in a long shawl, but even knowing her wardrobe in detail was not how his eyes sought her.

Rather, her walk made her stand out. It did something to her body. Caused it to sway a little, and give the impression that she dared take only small steps. The resulting elegance of movement contrasted with the broad strides and purposeful gaits of others on these lanes filled with working people and men of trade. She walked like a queen, and it negated all her attempts to look poor.

When he followed her regularly last spring, she often thought she had outsmarted him and gotten away. He let her believe that, but he almost never lost sight of her. However, perhaps he had today. That oasis of elegance had disappeared. If so, today's reckoning would have to be put off. The notion did nothing for his humor. He had a month at most to settle this nettlesome business before he undertook his next mission.

He paced his horse slowly, gauging the distance to the next crossroad. He would check the alleys between the buildings on the right before he gave up. When running away, Marielle Lyon always aimed right.

He had just begun his slow progress when something caught his eye. The driver of a hackney twisted around and spoke to his passenger. A thin arm stretched forward from the window as the driver's arm stretched back. Coin passed between them. The driver lifted the reins.

Marielle must be in a hurry. She had never used a coach before. He did not doubt that had been her arm. The stain of blue paint on its snowy skin, and the hand's long, slender fingers said it was.

He followed in the coach's wake, keeping his distance. The advantage of being on horseback was that he could watch an entire street from the higher perspective. He had followed men on foot through crowds thicker than this, from as far back as four hundred yards.

The coach made several turns, but he always found it when he turned himself. After the last turn, he found it too easily. It had stopped a hundred feet down the street. The driver set his whip into its stand, pulled an apple out of his coat, and bit.

He paced up and alongside so he could see in. Empty. He rose off his saddle and looked down the street.

"The woman you brought here — where did she go?" he asked the coachman.

The fellow gave him and his horse a good look. Mouth full and jaws working, he jerked his thumb toward a narrow alley across the street that ran between a stationer's shop and a grocer.

He dismounted and tied his horse to a post. He walked to the grocer shop, then along its front to where he could spy down the alley's length.

Three forms moved in the shadows halfway to the next street. Two men faced him, although the shadows proved too dark to see anything specific about them. Marielle Lyon walked toward them, her slender body swaying within the cocoon of her long shawl.

He waited. This was not the first time she had met men in alleys, that he knew. He debated how to interrupt the rendezvous. She had a roll of documents with her. He had seen it beneath the shawl as she hurried from her house. He could not let her hand it off the way she planned.

Light showed at the end of the alley as surely as the exit to a tunnel. He doubted he could stop those men from escaping, but he would be damned if she could. Before the hour was out, if he had his way, the mystery of Marielle Lyon would finally be over.

Marielle peered into the shadows. At first the alley appeared empty, which displeased her. It would be a fine thing if she had paid for that coach only to have Luc and Éduard

14

arrive late, or not at all.

She should have replaced them months ago. It was never wise to use the same people too long. Patterns start being noticed then. Questions start being asked. Worse, with time comes comfort and carelessness.

She could not afford the latter on anyone's part. Luc and Éduard risked nothing in this. It was only a chore to them, for which they were paid. She was the one who could face a reckoning that involved more than money. If the English decided she was a spy, her fate would be unpleasant. If her enemies attached her name to these papers, she could end up dead.

A movement deep in the alley caused the shadows to move. A man reached out and beckoned. Relieved, she walked toward him.

"Why are you hiding?" she asked as she drew nearer. "Were you followed?" She did not trust Luc or Éduard to know how to handle that. They were only messengers.

He did not reply. That was odd. In a swift series of impressions, she absorbed other oddities. The man wore a tricornered hat. Luc and Éduard considered them old-fashioned. As her eyes adjusted to the dark, the man's form thickened. He was too wide. Too short. Another man joined him, and caution tightened her throat. He did not look right either.

Alarm screamed through her. She stopped in her tracks. They must have smelled her fear, because they strode forward.

"Attendez-vous," the thick one said in a hoarse whisper.

She turned on her heel and ran back toward the street she had left.

Boots pounded behind her. Terror split her mind. She kicked off her shoes so she might run faster, but it was already too late. A vise of a hand gripped her shoulder. She spun and flew until her back slammed against the stones of the building flanking the alley. Pain stole her breath and darkened her sight.

Desperate, she groped for her purse while she steadied herself. She gritted her teeth against an impulse to sink to the ground in surrender. Her attackers crowded her so closely she could smell the beer the thick one had drunk with his last meal.

"Here. It is all I have." She threw the purse on the ground.

The thick man looked down at the purse, then at her. "We are not here for that." He spoke in French. Native French. That gave voice to her worst fear. They were not mere thieves.

If they did not seek money, they were here

16

for her. The truth chilled her. She would die in this alley today.

The two of them looked at her while a horrible tension poured out of them. Her stomach sickened. She knew why they paused. It was not easy to kill. Even a hardened man needs to draw on something inside himself before he does that.

She sensed the determination forming in them. It came first to the other, not the thick man. An animal light entered his eyes.

As soon as he moved, she did too. She lunged at him, pushing away from the wall with all her strength, ignoring how her bruised back burned. She turned and twisted to create confusion and avoid his grasp. If she could break past them, perhaps she could run and —

His arm slashed forward and up and the faintest light glinted off metal. She twisted again and her shawl caught the blade. Silk makes a poor shield, however. The fabric deflected the knife's thrust, but it connected anyway. A line of raw pain shocked her hip.

She dared not let it stop her. Thrashing, twisting, refusing to accept her fate, she dropped the papers and clawed at his face. A blow landed on her head in punishment. Then another on her shoulder.

More shadows now, gathering around her

vision and in her head. Black ones, closing in. She barely felt the next blow that sent her flying against the wall again.

Drifting now, unable to fight, she swayed on her legs while chaos surrounded her. Then she saw nothing and heard nothing as she floated toward the darkness.

She accepted the inevitable. It was over. Done. She had lost. Perhaps she had been a fool to ever think she would not. *Je suis désolée. I am sorry I failed you.*

Kendale used his fists and tried to avoid the dagger swinging in his direction. He should have brought his pistol when he got off his horse.

The two men seemed to think they would win this fight. When the blade split through his coat and connected with flesh, he wondered if they might be right.

The wound brought out the warrior in him, the man who had once single-handedly battled his way through five trained soldiers. Primal instincts snapped alert, in ways even the welcomed action of this fight had not resurrected them.

He waited for the dagger to slice again, and this time caught the arm wielding it. Gripping hard, he forced that arm back until he could grab it at another spot. With a jerk he twisted it around until he heard the snap of a bone breaking.

His victim cried out and turned limp. He threw him toward the other man. That one, the fat one, had finally fumbled his own knife from its sheath, but the sound of that cry stopped him in mid action.

Kendale eyed him. "Don't lose your nerve now. Or does one-on-one with a man scare you? Only a coward would attack a woman, and need an accomplice to do so at that." His blood was up and he hoped the fool would try to use that knife.

The fat one backed away, pointing the knife in front of him for protection. His companion staggered after him. Halfway to the far light the fat one turned and ran.

Catching his breath, Kendale walked to the wall and looked down. Marielle Lyon sat on the ground where her body had settled as she fell under their blows. Her bare feet stuck out from the rumpled skirt of her dress. Her head lolled down on her chest.

She had spoken as she sank. He wondered if he had heard her words correctly.

She made no sound now. Nor did she move. She could be dead.

Crouching down, he lifted the shawl and laid his palm on her chest, below her left breast. He felt the movement of her breath and heartbeat but his hand touched moisture. Blood. She was alive now, but if the wound was bad she soon might not be.

His own cut burned hotly now. The excitement of the fight drifted away, leaving him sore and tired. He spied her shoes and fetched them, then returned and reached down for her. Glad that she would not feel the pain, he lifted her to her feet and propped her against the wall. Something rolled against his boot and he looked down. The documents.

Holding her upright with one arm, he bent and picked them up. Then he slung her limp body over his shoulder and carried her out of the alley and toward the same hackney that had brought her here.

The driver turned in surprise when Kendale opened the coach door.

"I hope she's not sick. I'll not be having my coach dirtied by her puke."

"You will drive where I tell you and you will not disobey my orders."

"Orders! I'll be damned if I — See here, you are bleeding! It is all over your waistcoat. Hell, so is she! I'll not be taking you any—"

"I am Viscount Kendale. If your damned coach gets dirty or bloody, I will buy you a damned new one." He opened the door and dumped Marielle onto the seat and threw the documents and shoes after her. He untied his horse and tethered it to the coach's rear. "Now use those ribbons smartly and get us to Hertford Street as fast as you can," he said as he climbed in. "It is worth your while to serve me well today, because there will be hell to pay if you do not."

CHAPTER 2

"You look like hell," Anderson said upon entering the library of Kendale's town chambers. "I can see you were in a fight, but it looks as if you got the worst of it."

"I broke his arm. Although since I was stabbed, at best it can be called a draw."

"Stabbed! Get that shirt off and we will see what is what beneath all that blood. It's a wonder you are still standing."

"Not all of the blood is mine. A good deal is hers." Kendale stripped off the shirt as if it did not hurt to move, but the twist and stretch of his torso induced a deep, sharp disturbance in his side. He already knew how bad it was — bad enough to hurt like hell, but not bad enough to bring a man down. It was not easy to kill with a knife. Even a bayonet or sword rarely did the job with one jab.

Anderson, a regimental surgeon who had left the army and established himself among the ton of London, examined the wound in the raking afternoon light coming in the window. Edinburgh trained, he knew his business as few surgeons did. Scots were the best at this because, Anderson had explained, they studied medicine at university, and did not make the distinction between surgeons and physicians that the English did. Scottish surgeons were not tricked-up barbers. The army had been damned lucky to have him.

"Deep, and a puncture, not a cut," Anderson said, peering and pressing. "Best lie down on that divan while I purify it. Is your man here? We should call for some towels."

"I didn't bring him up from the country this time. There are towels in the dressing room somewhere." He sank down onto the divan, which made the wound feel as if the knife were still in it. "Damnation."

"Are you cursing my suggestion that you lie, or that I will purify?" Anderson called from the dressing room. "If it is the latter, what is a bit more pain after this? It is not natural for the human body to be skewered thus. What comes next is a small thing."

"I am cursing that the fool managed to stab me."

"You mean fools, don't you. You indicated there was more than one. You are not

23

Hercules, my friend." Anderson returned with a large folded sheet and two towels. He draped the sheet on the divan and placed a towel on top. "Now, lie on your good side, and I'll be finished with you quickly."

Kendale obeyed. He gritted his teeth as Anderson hovered over him with the potion bottle. Whatever it contained hurt like hell as it dripped onto and into his wound. He suffered the deep scorching stoically.

"It is fortunate you did not have to do this to her." He would have heard Marielle scream if Anderson used this firewater on her.

"Oh, I did, although her wound is not like yours. More a bad scrape. The blade hit her obliquely and cut long and shallow, high on her hip. A good deal of blood, but it did not have to be sewn." Anderson set aside the bottle and folded the other towel for a bandage.

"It was a good thing she was still out when you tended her."

"She was not out. She was aware of it all. I daresay she is listening to every word we say in here now."

So she had been subjected to that purification and had not cried out. Good for her. Of course one would expect a spy to be brave. She would not be much use if she weren't.

"Stand now," Anderson ordered. When Kendale did the surgeon wrapped a long strip of cloth around his torso to hold the bandage in place. "I will leave some of that cleanser. A vial for you and one for her. It must be used each day for three days. If you see or smell any corruption, you are to send for me."

"I will give her the vial and the instructions."

"She will not be staying here?"

"Except for the attack, she would not be here in the first place."

"Ah. Then she is not your . . ." Anderson raised his eyebrows quizzically.

Kendale glared his response.

"Pity," Anderson muttered as he set the two vials on the table. "She is a pretty little thing."

"Too pretty and too French to trust."

"You bothered to save her life. Will you now throw her out the minute I am gone? She should not be walking about town for at least a week, and should remain abed for a few days until it is clear that beating she took did not do more damage than is initially visible. As should you. Remain

25

abed, that is. Separate beds, if that is how it is."

Anderson helped Kendale slide his arms into a long banyan, then pulled on his own coat. "I rarely deal with knife wounds anymore. This afternoon made me nostalgic. Be sure to send for me should you get sliced or skewered again. It has been a refreshing two hours."

After Anderson departed, Kendale listened for sounds in the bedchamber. Only silence came to him. Marielle had probably fallen asleep after her ordeal.

Deciding to let her rest a spell, he retrieved the papers from the chair where he had dumped them. He set the thick roll on the library table, untied the ribbon that held it together, and spread the documents out.

The voices stopped. Marielle waited. Surely someone would come now to send her on her way. People who lived in houses such as this might do a good deed, but they would not want the object of their charity to remain long.

She took stock again of her chamber. A man usually slept in this bed. The drapes and hangings said he had money but little style. Colors and decoration such as these had been popular in France over a generation ago and no longer found favor in England either. Too much gilt. Too aristocratic and pale. Classical would be better, especially for a man. With all the emphasis in the world on égalité, it would be safer too, perhaps.

The sheet felt cool against her skin. That leech had stripped her so he could see all her wounds. There had been nothing untoward in his manner, even though he was not very old. Perhaps her bruises had checked him. She found his bland manner and expression comforting, and spent her time while he dabbed and poked contemplating how he would look when his receding blond hair finally disappeared. She had been a specimen to him, and nothing more, although he had tried to avoid hurting her. That had not been possible, especially when he poured that potion over the knife's cut.

That was how she had woken, to that fire. Never before had she welcomed pain, but today she had. Even before she opened her eyes, she knew the pain meant she was not dead. What a relief to see that leech, and discover the pain was not torture but an attempt to help her.

More pain now. On her shoulder and back, and on her face. Her right cheek throbbed. She could see its swell from the bottom of her eye. Well, no matter how badly she hurt and how odd she would look, despite how comfortable she found this bed and how she yearned to sleep for a week, she needed to thank her benefactors and leave. There was much to do, and decisions to make. Today had changed many things.

Knowing it would be unpleasant, she forced herself to sit. Her back rebelled violently enough to steal her breath. Moving slower, she turned her body and sat on the side of the bed. Her chemise and dress, streaked with blood, lay in a heap on a chair near the door.

Standing, she walked carefully to the chair. She laid her ear against the door. A curse seemed to leak through the wood.

Slowly and silently she opened the door and peeked out.

She did not see the leech, but she saw a man across the room. It looked to be a library. His back was to her and he angled away, bent over a table piled with books. He wore an expensive robe, the sort that mimics a greatcoat but made out of green silk brocade, not wool.

He straightened, and she recognized him. Handsome Stupid Man.

She carefully closed the door and pressed her good shoulder against it while her thoughts raced.

Had she misunderstood today completely? Was it possible those men had been sent by this one, to waylay her and bring her here? To what purpose? She looked down on her nakedness, then pictured his robe. Lady Cassandra had told her that he was a lord and his real name was Viscount Kendale. There were such men who believed they could have whatever they wanted, even women. Especially women.

Was he one of them? If so, in playing games with him, she had played with fire.

She fingered her ruined dress and forced the rush of panic down. If he had sent those men to abduct her, he surely had not expected them to bring him a woman beaten and sore and not even conscious. No, her initial thoughts were the right ones. He had interfered and saved her. Whatever his intentions had been, she was safe now. Unless he was a monster. His friendship with Emma's and Cassandra's husbands said he was not, but one never knew for certain.

She took her dress and chemise to the washing stand. Some water remained in the pitcher. She poured it in the basin, and soaked and scrubbed the blood out as best she could. Then she laid the dress out over a chair so it might dry.

She returned to the bed and pulled off the soft blue blanket. It would cover her better than her torn garments, but also remind him that she was badly wounded. Her vulnerability would both appeal and discourage. That would give her an advantage when they faced each other. That and the fact that Handsome Stupid Man wanted her.

Oh, yes, he wanted her. She had known that for months.

With one glance at the papers Kendale's triumph turned to confusion, then annoyance. These were not documents or letters, such as he assumed. He flipped through. None of them contained a spy's secrets. Instead each sheet of the stack of thick paper displayed the same engraving.

It was a satirical image, such as the bookshops and print shops display in their windows. In a crude drawing filled with exaggerated faces and poses, accompanied by dialogue filling bubbles exuded by various mouths, a little scene from a farce unfolded.

The words were in French, however. He bent down and studied the caricatures. He always recognized the ones showing British political figures or members of the peerage or ton. He could not identify any of these men.

It did not appear to be an image ridiculing British policies for propaganda purposes. Rather, it looked to be a satire of a French official. His French was not the best, but the engraving accused this official of stealing funds from the government. He sat on a throne composed of farmers and workers while he doled out part of the taxes they paid to himself.

Why would Marielle Lyon be meeting men in an alley to hand these over? Perhaps she had discovered who made them, and obtained these as proof to be sent to France as evidence. If so, the artist might be in danger if his name became known to the French.

"Ah, it is *you.* I expected to thank the good soul who found me, but if this is your home, perhaps it is more complicated than I guessed."

The lilting voice startled him. He resisted the impulse to pivot toward it. Instead he moved several folio-sized books to cover the papers strewn on the table. These engravings were the least of it. It would be a hell of a thing to bring a French spy into these chambers and leave maps of France's coast out for view.

He turned around. Marielle Lyon stood at the doorway to the bedchamber. Her loose golden brown hair fell around her shoulders in a cloud of disarray. Her dirty bare feet showed at the other end of her body. In between she had cocooned herself in a blanket much as she normally wore a shawl.

She appeared naked under that drape of soft wool. She clutched it closed above her breasts, but a good deal of skin showed around her neck and upper chest anyway. A bruise besmirched one snowy shoulder, and another defiled the side of her normally flawless face. She had to be in pain from the blows alone, plus the knife wound. She showed no indication of it, however.

Her cool gaze drifted down his body, reminding him that he was barely in better dress than she. He resisted the impulse to button his robe so his naked chest would not show. Marielle Lyon would be impossible to handle if she thought herself bolder and more worldly than he was.

"It is not more complicated," he said. "It is very simple. I chased them away and I brought you here so you could be tended."

"You hardly came upon me by accident."

"However it happened, you are alive because of it. Your allies appeared intent on killing you. You can still thank me."

"They were not my allies. They were common thieves setting upon a woman."

"Thieves take purses and shoes and even garments and leave. They do not take the time to beat and cut."

She gave a little shrug that was eloquent in conveying her indifference. *If you want to think so, it is all the same to me.* He assumed it also meant there would be no thanks. Ungrateful bitch.

Her attention drifted around the library, to the shelves of bindings and the fabrics at the windows. Her gaze paused on the fireplace, and the musket and sword held to the wall above it by iron arms. She took a few steps and fingered the wood of a chair with interest.

"You are rich," she said. "I was told you are a viscount, but they are not always rich."

"Better came before me who did well by the estate."

"How modest. Or, more perhaps, a statement that your interest lies elsewhere." Her gaze now found him. She walked over until she stood very close. Humor and challenge showed in her eyes. "You undressed. Even if you hoped for pleasure due to my gratitude, that is very bold."

Pleasure had been the last thing on his mind. Until now. The flirtation of her demeanor and provocation of her words caused his body to heat and tighten. She saw it in him. Smiling sweetly, triumphantly, she stepped closer yet. Her eyes sparkled with humor and delight.

She had looked at him like this once before, from far away. He had come upon her unexpectedly, sitting in a garden with Emma Fairbourne and Lady Cassandra. Seeing his spy chatting with those ladies had taken him aback. While he decided what to do, she had noticed him. Boldly, smugly, she had stared at him.

Then she had smiled. Just like this. It turned her into a girl. An innocent. It was as if time reversed, and he was seeing Marielle Lyon years before she came to England.

Desire and confusion had assaulted him then. And now. Confounded him. Even knowing all too well that Frenchwomen were experts at coquettish charm did not help. Nor did knowing that she was wounded even beyond the damage he saw. He began calculating a seduction that ended hard and slow.

She slid her hand to where the robe parted, then ventured under its silk. Warmth penetrated his skin and chest. Desire roared dangerously. To hell with the seduction part. It was all he could do not to grab that blanket and tear it off her. With effort he kept his jaw firm and his eyes clear.

A caress, like a teasing flow of velvet, drifted tentatively. He must have reacted more than he thought because she smiled again. Then her fingers touched the bandage. A skimming sensation assessed the size and placement of the dressing. No longer flirtatious, but her hand still had him clenching his teeth.

"You also felt the knife," she said. "You did not chase them away. You fought them."

"It is not too bad. No worse than yours."

She strolled away. "It complicates today even more."

"If by that you mean it makes neither one of us fit for finishing this game you are starting, you underestimate me."

Her glance acknowledged the game, and that she had miscalculated. "I thought perhaps you had sent those men for me. However, if you are wounded . . ."

"Why would I send them?"

"Perhaps to abduct me."

"I do not need to abduct you in order to investigate your activities. Better to leave you to continue as you were, in fact. And should I ever send men to grab a woman, they would not beat her first."

Her head tilted back while she perused

the bindings on a high shelf. "You do not follow me only to investigate the rumors about me."

Her blanket slipped a bit on one shoulder, revealing more skin and making her appear as naked beneath as she was. She was thin. Too thin, but soft enough. Her body would suit her face and that walk — lithe and delicate. She probably used her femininity the way she used her mind, with dangerous and worldly cunning.

She was wrong, however. He did not follow her in anticipation of pleasure or seduction. Even if she really were whom she claimed and not the charlatan he suspected, he would never pursue a Frenchwoman for her favors. Even the best of them were not to be trusted.

Her gaze scanned the chamber, searching. "I had some papers with me. Did you find them?"

"No. Were they important?"

"Not so much." She hitched up the blanket so it covered her shoulder again. "I need to go home."

Not yet. "I will send someone to retrieve some clothes for you first. You cannot go like that."

"I will wear what I have. I cannot wait."

"Your dress is covered in blood."

"I have washed out much. My shawl will hide the rest." She strode toward the bed-chamber.

"Your wrap is sliced to shreds."

"Then I will look as poor as I am. The world will not care."

It hurt to move more than he liked, but he reached her before she opened the door. Weight braced on a hand placed on the door above her, he barred her escape. "I cannot let you leave until we have the conversation I sought you out for today."

She turned and leaned against the door. "What could we have to say to each other?"

"I know why you were in that alley. I know about the papers that make their way to the coast."

"You know nothing. The best in your government have had these conversations with me, and admit they know nothing too."

Not for certain, but suspicions ran rampant about her. In the government, and even among the French émigrés. She had to know that. Her show of indifference and impatience was a feint.

"I know because two times now the papers have been followed from the moment you carried them from your home to the moment they were given to smugglers on the coast."

"You are lying. If you followed me these last months I would have known."

"Not if I did not want you to."

She stretched so her face came closer to his, belligerently. "A waving flag would be more subtle than you are. I always know when you are there. I let you follow while it amuses me, and end it when it grows tedious.

"Like today?"

"Yes."

"And yet you were surprised to learn it was I who interfered in that alley. If you always know when I follow you, you should have expected me to at least witness that attack."

She pondered his logic. She looked down at herself. "May I dress before this conversation? Or do you prefer that I remain naked so I am more vulnerable?"

"I much prefer you naked and vulnerable. However —" He removed his hand from the door.

She yanked the door open and strode in. "I will be fast so you can say what you must. I must go home soon, so I pray that you be quick."

He would be quick enough. Eventually she might even return home. Soon, however, this particular shrewd, pretty Frenchwoman would be going to gaol, and that was the best outcome she could expect.

CHAPTER 3

She dressed quickly, and ignored how the damp garments felt like iron pressing against those places she had been hit. Her shawl displayed two long slices, but otherwise had fared well enough. At least it was not covered in blood. Wrapping it around her, she assessed that few would even notice the tears with the way the silk flowed.

This viscount would see it all, however. The blood and the tears. He would know it was all there. Maybe he would pity her. That would be useful.

Returning to that library, she sat on the divan next to a damp towel that smelled of the fire potion. He had taken it without a sound. She guessed he had been stabbed more successfully than she had, considering that heavy bandage.

He did not sit too. Perhaps the wound made that uncomfortable. The silk robe hung off his shoulders like it dared not crease or float. Even in pain and dishabille he remained straight as iron, as if he rode a horse in parade. No one could sway such a man when his mind was made up.

He intended to interrogate her now. She needed to convince him that while he suspected many things, he knew nothing for certain. One doubt, just one, would buy her some time. She needed it. His suspicions had become small worries compared to the larger ones looming now.

He hovered and made her feel small and helpless. And naked. Oh, yes, she saw that in him, the awareness that while she had dressed, her garments barely covered her decently now. The knife had done its damage to her dress and the physician had done more, and if not for her long shawl, much of her skin would be exposed. That interested him. *She* interested him. A woman knows such things.

She had learned that for sure last spring on the same day that she let him know that she knew of his surveillance. It had ended then, both the following and the interest. Or so she had thought. Now he implied that he had kept the surveillance going, but so cleverly that she remained unaware of it. That was not good news. She did not need trouble coming from two directions.

"What are in the papers you pass off to messengers?" he asked.

"Letters. Some to a lawyer of my family, who tries to obtain money from the properties for me. Others are attempts to contact family members who might be alive. I keep sending them, and wait and hope."

"You go to a lot of trouble to send letters out of the country."

"Family is worth a lot of trouble, don't you agree?"

Apparently not. He did not even nod an acknowledgment.

"You have not only sent letters. Sometimes you have sent unsealed papers. Documents. Stacks of them in rolls such as you carried today."

"Today I carried only some items from my business, to bring to a printer who asked for coloring. That is what we do in my home. Color pictures. Ask Lady Cassandra or Emma. Ask that other viscount whom Cassandra married. All have been there and seen the women coloring." She trusted that would divert him, in the event he had seen that roll today after all.

His eyes flashed and his face found its most severe expression. "This will be faster if you do not treat me like a fool. I have told you that those men you meet have been

42

followed all the way to the coast. Those rolls have been seen leaving England on smugglers' boats. I doubt the printers who hire you to color are in France."

Regrettably, Handsome Stupid Man was not stupid enough to be easily hoodwinked. She tried anyway. "Did you see this yourself?"

"Those whom I trust did."

So that was how he had followed her without her knowing. He had set others to the task. How unfair. "They erred. Or the men the printers send to meet me stole and sold my work to those smugglers. Or your trusted men never left London, but spent your coin on ale and told you what you wanted to hear. You know nothing at all and you can prove nothing."

He folded his arms and glared down at her. The vaguest wince accompanied the movement. His pose caused that robe to open enough for her to see his chest but he seemed oblivious to that. A nice chest. Lean and hard and evident of an active life. A military man, she assumed. Everything about him suggested that. Not an agent, however. A viscount would not be a lowly agent.

"Your English is very good," he said.

She tried to look flattered by the compliment, but alarm rang in her head. "I have much cause to practice since I came here. I do not only spend my days with my own people."

"Did you learn English in France?"

"I learned what I could. It amused me to do so."

His gaze locked on hers. "Even your accent —"

"I imitate those I hear who are of the better classes." He appeared merely curious, but she did not like the way he pressed on this. Her head began pounding. "Those who speak a foreign language with a heavy accent are lazy. One need only imitate what one hears, with little effort."

He strolled back and forth thoughtfully, casting her glances. "Do you think in English? Have you learned the language that well?"

A chill passed through her. "Rarely." She raised a hand to her head. "*Pardon,* m'sieur, but —" She closed her eyes and fought to conquer the panic shaking through her.

"Are you ill?"

His voice startled her. It sounded truly concerned. She opened her eyes to find him right in front of her, down on one knee, peering at her face.

"Only a little faint. It is passing."

"You lost blood today. I expect it was enough to make you faint. And those blows." His fingertips hovered above the bruise on her face while he examined it.

"I will be better once I return home and rest."

"That is out of the question."

Her heart sank. "Because you do not like my half of this conversation?"

"Because you are too weak." He stood and lifted her to her feet. "It was ignoble of me to force this talk on you now. Go and rest. We will find another time."

He eased her toward the door to the bed-chamber.

"It would feel much better in my own bed. If you would send for a hired coach, I would appreciate it. I will have the coin to pay when I arrive home."

"I will not hear of it. The physician said you should not move from here for several days. I should have insisted you return to bed as soon as I saw you and not imposed on you with my questions at this time."

He was not going to give in. What a nuisance he could be. She would have to sneak out later.

"Will the servants not — ?"

"I am here alone right now. No one will know. I will send for food in a couple of hours. I will let you know when it arrives and you can eat something."

It was a small apartment then, with no other bedchamber. If he remained in this library, the bedchamber would become her prison.

She did not undress again, but lay on the bed fully clothed. It still felt delicious. She had truly become a little light-headed, and resting held great appeal. She would indulge herself until that food came. Then she would get away, before he returned to that interrogation.

Kendale set about arranging a meal for his invalid. He leaned out the window and hailed a boy in the street. Young Harry always loitered there, hoping for errands and a few pence as payment.

"What can I do for you now, m'lord?" he called up upon hearing his name. "Do you need the leech again?"

"Go to the White Knight and tell old Percy to send over whatever had been cooked today. Enough for two."

"Two, eh? She's come to then, has she? She looked dead when you carried her in."

Kendale flicked one of the pennies he had in his hand. It flew and landed on the stones below with a high note. "That is for forget-

46

ting that you saw me carry anyone, lad. And this is for taking my message to the tavern." He flipped another three pence.

Harry collected them all. "You want ale with that food?"

"Wine." He told himself that he did not choose wine because a Frenchwoman had flirted with him. Rather he felt churlish for having harassed her with questions when she was wounded and sore and sick. He merely sought to make amends.

He opened cabinets to see where his manservant stored the china and crystal. He should have brought Mr. Pottsward with him on this visit to town, but he almost never did on short journeys. The day he could not wash and dress and care for himself for a week was the day he would know he had lost the battle to remain the man he was, instead of the man this damned title said he should be.

He found the plates and glassware, and a cloth and silver too. Good of Pottsward to keep it all together. He would have forgotten about the cloth otherwise. Not really sure he was doing it right, trying to remember just where those forks rested all these years when he sat to dinner, he set a service on the library table. To do so he had to remove the large tomes, and the engravings and maps beneath them. Rolling and tying them again, he hid them safely on one of the high shelves of the glassed-in bookcase.

Then he waited for Marielle Lyon to awaken, and wondered about those engravings again, and the men who had attacked her, and how close she had come to dying over some pictures. She claimed she was on her way to hand those to a print publisher who hired her women to color them. Only these were not colored.

She said the attack had been a typical alley attempt at theft. He thought that unlikely, but he could not rule it out completely, considering the disappointing contents of that roll of paper.

His mind turned to the last words she had spoken as she sank to the ground in the alley. *Je suis désolée. I am sorry I failed you.*

She had said it in French, then in English. Good English. Too good, now that he had spoken to her. She had been well groomed for this role she played. No doubt she understood English even better.

He had never trained spies, but if he ever did, that would be one thing he would require — that they spoke the language well and understood it even better. There was no point in having ears and eyes among the enemy unless those ears understood all that

48

they overheard, no matter whether spoken by a schoolmaster or by the worst user of popular slang.

She had an answer for everything, and had not been at all cowed by his questions and accusations. Even on hearing that her documents had been traced to the coast and into the hands of smugglers known to row across the channel, she had not blinked. What had she said? Ah, yes. That better than he had interrogated her, and they knew nothing now either.

He shifted uncomfortably on the divan. His side hurt worse than when Anderson had been here. He had been wounded before and knew that was normal. Tomorrow would be worse yet. Then slowly, day by day, it would pass until the morning came when he forgot the wound was there. He eyed the divan on which he would sleep tonight.

A scratch came at the door. He got to his feet and let in the tavern's servant. The man bore a tray covered with dishes, each in turn covered with upturned pewter bowls. Two bottles of wine emerged from a sack the servant had slung around his body.

"Here. Take what is left for yourself." He handed over some coin, more than enough to cover the meal. The servant had already tucked some away before he left the apartment.

As long as he was up, he went to the bedchamber door. There were sounds on the other side. "Come and eat something." He spoke quietly enough that if he were wrong and she still slept, she would not hear.

The door opened and Marielle emerged, carrying her shawl. Without it the damage to her dress showed. It appeared she had used the morning's washing water to blot out the worst of the blood. That side of her dress clung close to her body from the resulting damp. The dress was one of those old-fashioned ones with a low waist and lacing up the front. He guessed that when new it had been lovely, but now its fawn color had turned to something akin to the hue of very dry dirt on a country road and its wilted white lace trimmings had taken on a gray tinge.

"I do not have time to eat." Even so she walked over and lifted the pewter covers and sniffed.

"I insist. You were faint. If you eat proper meals, you will heal faster."

"It is wrong of you to make me your prisoner."

"Not a prisoner. A guest. I got skewered while saving your life and I am not about to

50

risk having it all be for nothing because you will not use good sense and rest a day or so."

"You only want to ask more annoying questions."

"Gentlemen do not impose on ill or wounded women with questions. I would have to keep you here a week before you were fit enough for me to interrogate you further. I do not think of it as imprisoning you, but if you insist on doing so —"

"A week would be most inappropriate. Impossible. I could not allow it."

"The thing about being a prisoner is that there is no choice. However, as I said, you will remain here and rest only as long as the physician ordered. After that, you will be free to go."

She smiled to herself, as if she saw through a bald lie. Then she gave one of those shrugs. "Sit. I will serve, since you have no proper help here."

He sat and went to work opening the wine. She stood and spooned out the chicken stew and potatoes, then took the bread, broke it neatly, and set some at his place.

She settled on the chair at the end of the table. With him seated on the side, she was close enough to touch. He probably should have set the places across from each other. He had not really thought about that. She did not seem to mind or notice how close they sat to each other.

"Please pretend I do not smell of an alley and blood, and my hair is not a rat's nest in need of a brush. It embarrasses me to be in such a state while dining with a gentleman."

"We are neither of us in good condition today. However, your hair looks slept in, not a rat's nest, and all I am smelling is this stew." He ate some of it, to reassure her.

"How gallant of you to say so. I think my friend Lady Cassandra is wrong about you."

"How so?"

"She says you are not one to flatter even when it is wise to do so. That you are not" — she puzzled over the right words — "in sympathy with polite society."

More likely she said he was *not fit* for polite society. "She has noticed that I cannot abide all the chatter over insignificant things. The scandals. The fashions. Why anyone gives a damn about it all is beyond me. Always was." He wondered if Lady Cassandra, now Lady Ambury, had offered the information about his lack of social skills as part of that insignificant chatter. Perhaps Marielle had been probing for it instead.

The latter notion pleased him. That made

him curse inwardly. Hell, he could be an ass at times.

She ate some food before turning her attention on him again. The bruise on her face was turning ugly, but it really did not detract as much from her delicate countenance as it should. Her eyes appeared clearer than they had all day. "You are a soldier, no? An officer."

"Did Cassandra tell you that too?"

"No. It is in you, however. The way you stand, the way you ride. It is in your face and your eyes. I have seen many soldiers in my life."

"If you mean the rabble that is now the French army, I must ask that you not insult me."

"Not all the current officers are such rabble. But I speak of the past, from when I was a girl."

If she had left France when a girl, how would she know who was rabble in the army now or not? "I was an officer. When I received the title, I sold out my commission. There are some peers who are army officers, but very few."

"It is the same everywhere. The duties do not allow for this other life too, I think."

"No."

She cocked her head and looked directly

53

and deeply. "You miss it."

Did he? He missed the higher purpose, that was certain. Fighting to protect a nation possessed a clarity that poring over the account books of an estate never would. Or that sitting through interminable arguments in parliament, while small-minded men jockeyed to protect their own interests, could match.

He missed other things too. The easy camaraderie of men. The simplicity of life in the field. The whites and blacks of honor and dishonor. He missed the physicality of the life and the waking at dawn.

Mostly he missed the certainty of knowing he was doing what he had been born to do.

"I miss some things. Not others." Not the deaths, or the betrayals.

He would be wise to remember the latter now, especially the worst betrayal, and the lessons learned from it. Foremost had been not to trust pretty Frenchwomen who can make men into fools with a smile.

He concentrated on eating his meal, trying to ignore the lovely Frenchwoman sitting so close he could smell her. She did not carry only the scent of that alley and of blood. Musk and flowers drifted to his nose distinctly. She wore clothes that were decades old, but she also wore perfume. Probably French perfume. Probably smuggled in. Possibly it was part of her payments from whomever sent her orders, and to whom she sent rolls of documents.

He did not have to look up from his plate to see her, they were so close. So he noticed when she set down her fork. Her pale, small hand rested on the table near the dish. A soft hand, as he knew from her touch earlier. She probably lathered creams on them at night. French creams.

His mind began itemizing the evidence against her, stacking each detail like a stone in a wall. It did not fortify his resolve about her as much as he assumed it would. Her wounds and bruises and the role he had played today encouraged tendencies to feel protective and sympathetic. Her bright eyes and flirtatious smiles and that scent tempted him to feel other things.

Finally the meal ended. He drank some wine and waited for her to excuse herself and retreat to the other chamber. Instead she relaxed in her chair and drank wine too, glancing over its rim at him while her lips pursed along the edge of the glass.

"So, m'sieur le vicomte, I am fed. Evening falls and I am still here, as you required.

May I ask now — what are your intentions?"

A few ignoble ones entered his mind. "I told you. I intend to see that you follow the physician's orders and rest a few days. There may be other wounds from those blows. Internal ones."

"That is all you want?" She favored him with one of her coquettish, worldly smiles.

It demolished the wall in a flash. *Hell, no. I also want to take you on this table, on the floor, against the wall, on the divan, and everywhere else I can think of.* "You are too clever for me. The truth then. I intend to see you follow those orders, and after it is clear you have suffered no as yet unseen damage, I want to continue my interrogation."

"Do you intend to torture me during this interrogation?"

"Of course not." What kind of woman even asks such a question, or considers torture likely? Not a normal one, but a spy taught that it could happen.

"You are insulted. I am sorry. It is not unheard of," she said.

"You know that, do you? Is that another memory from the past, when you were a girl, or a more recent one, from your alliance with that rabble?"

Her expression froze. Her bright eyes turned icy. "I have no such alliance."

He downed the rest of his wine. *The hell you don't.*

It was time to leave this place and this man.

Oh, he would not torture her. Not in the normal ways at least. But he would be intrusive and relentless and pick away at whatever she said. She would have no relief from being careful with every word and nuance.

Worse, he would interfere with her sorting through what today meant to her life and safety too. He would delay action when time might be critical. Right now other things needed her attention, like deciding if she needed to flee London entirely, and if so how obscure she should become.

His questions would have to wait. With luck, she might never answer them.

Nor would staying here be comfortable. To remain here, even if she locked herself into that chamber, would mean having to worry about him. The lack of servants made it all too intimate. Too domestic. Even this simple meal had begun making them too familiar.

She doubted he would allow her to walk out the door. He had imprisoned her, no matter how he chose to cast it. She calculated how to escape. Despite her resolve, a feather bed beckoned. Her head hurt and her back had stiffened and that bed held appeal. She guessed tomorrow she would have trouble moving, however, and then escape would be impossible for a while. She had to leave now.

"I will return to the chamber and see you in the morning," she said. "There is still clean water from the morning there for me to use. Without a servant here, who will provide for you?"

"There are boys in the street who will bring up whatever I want in return for a coin." He gestured at the tray and plates.

"Who does for you in other ways when you have no servants with you?"

"I do for myself, as most men do."

She angled and examined his side, from head to toe. "Today you have a bad stab wound in your side. I do not think you will enjoy removing those high boots on your own. Is it even possible in your condition?"

He thought about that, then shrugged. "I will sleep with boots on, it appears."

"You should have had that physician aid you while he was here. As he did with your coats and shirt." She stood. "I will do it. It is a small payment for my life. Sit over there, on the divan and I will pull them off."

He began to object. She walked away before he could. "Do not argue, m'sieur. I have done this before, for my father. It is a small thing."

She heard him stand, then pause. She assumed that wound was taking its toll on him as the hours passed. Any movement of his torso would pull at the injury. She kept her back to him, so he could collect himself without her seeing his pain.

He walked to the divan and lowered himself slowly, pushing aside her shawl. Expression stoic and hard, he eased back against the divan's cushion.

"I would have thought your father had a valet to remove his boots," he said. "He was the brother of a comte, wasn't he?"

She managed to keep her face impassive, but inwardly she cursed herself. "And you are a viscount, but here you are without *your* valet. Such inconvenience occurred for him too at times."

Looking up at her with some amusement, he raised his left leg. She bent, grabbed the back of the boot's heel and its toe, and yanked it off.

Impressed, he began raising the other foot. It did not get far before he tensed, grimaced, and lowered it. He closed his eyes a moment and did not move a hair. When he opened them again, the pain had passed. "It appears I will sleep with one boot on after all."

"Nonsense." She knelt in front of him. "I will get it off."

It passed in his eyes then, his awareness of her proximity and the suggestiveness of her position. Other than his jaw tightening he gave no reaction, however.

She assessed the boot's tightness with her hands, skimming up the sides of the leather. He watched her and did not notice how she made sure her finger hooked her shawl. The patterned silk slid off the divan onto the floor beside his foot.

It was not easy getting that boot off with him only angling his leg out. She worked from the bottom and eventually felt his foot slide up. Then she pulled the boot away and held it up triumphantly. He took it from her and set it aside on the floor.

She sat back on her legs and admired him in his dishabille. He had managed to button most of that robe, but without a shirt beneath it a good deal of his neck and upper chest still showed.

"I might as well do this too." She began sliding her hands up his leg, to release his hose.

He did not stop her. He did not object. He just watched.

The air between them filled with the soundless chords that played when a man wanted a woman. This might be dangerous if not for his wound. Even earlier in the day, before his body rebelled at the injury, he might have given her trouble.

He truly sat in dishabille now, his legs bare from the knees down. Nice legs, she decided. Shaped by action and exercise, as was the rest of him. Trusting that she had not misjudged his interest, she once more slid her hands up, this time on skin. A subtle flexing tightened through him. When she looked at his face again his eyes were like embers burning in the darkest forest.

"You should stop that," he said.

She continued caressing the skin on his legs, feathering up to his knees. "Do the bruises make me ugly and stop you from wanting me? Or perhaps I misunderstood about that."

"You misunderstood nothing, and you could never be ugly. You know that, as all beautiful women do."

"Then why should I stop? It is no imposition by you." She skimmed higher, over his knees and the fabric of the pantaloons buttoned there. Never taking her eyes from his, she unfastened the buttons.

He closed his eyes for a moment. She could see how he forced some control on himself during that long blink.

"It will make no difference," he said. "There is nothing for you to win with this."

She knelt high and leaned against his legs so her body pressed his shins and her breasts rested on his knees. "There is pleasure to win. I expect nothing more." Down, out of view between his legs and her body, she lifted her shawl. With her right hand she caressed higher on his thigh while her left hand smoothed the shawl's silk over his lower legs' skin, again and again.

He looked ready to grab her, so fierce his eyes had become. "You forget that we are both wounded, and ill suited for pleasure now."

"You are charming. And very English." She caressed higher, along his inner thighs. The evidence of his arousal bulged against the fabric of his garment. She did not think he would stop her now. She did not think he could even if he wanted to. "I, on the other hand, am French. Remember? We know ways to pleasure that will not aggravate our wounds."

He understood. The mere suggestion caused his lips to part and his teeth to clench. He watched her, and she guessed he felt only her right hand on his thigh, not the other one working the shawl.

"Close your eyes," she said softly. "I am still shy with you on some things."

He did not close them right away. Not until her hand ventured to the buttons over that bulge. Then he did, and his jaw squared so hard it might have been chiseled in stone.

She loosened the buttons, trying to ignore how her fingers skimmed against the hardness of his arousal. She forced herself to suppress a deep stirring that this game had incited in her too. She would not mind knowing pleasure with this man, even if that would be all it could ever be. They could both close their eyes, and pretend whatever they chose for a while.

With his pantaloons unfastened, she had to move fast. She allowed herself a caress of his bare chest, just to see if it felt as she expected, hard and warm and so alluringly male. Then she looked down at his legs and her shawl. Satisfied, she stood and quickly walked away, refusing to allow the stiffness in her back and limbs or the throbbing in her head to delay her.

What the hell —

She had taken ten steps, no more, before his voice rose in fury. She glanced over her shoulder as she began to run.

"Damnation. *You bitch.*" The viscount glared at her while he bent over, grimacing while he tried to untie her shawl and free his legs from the silken chain she had made for them. His furious expression raised the hairs on the back of her neck.

She threw the door latch, swung the door, and fled. Kendale's curses followed her all the way down to the street.

CHAPTER 4

"It is a wonder you are alive," Dominique said while she dipped a rag, then gently squeezed warm water over Marielle's shoulders. She clucked her tongue while she assessed the bruises, evident in all their mottled darkness as Marielle bathed in the house's kitchen.

Marielle and Dominique had been together since leaving France six years ago. No one, not even the other women who sometimes took refuge in this house, knew how close they were and how she relied on Dominique for advice and sometimes sympathy.

"Will he be looking for you now, this lord you escaped after he saved you? You said he was angry that you left. No doubt he expected a show of gratitude first."

She had not explained *everything* to Dominique. Not that Kendale had expected only what she appeared to be offering. As for his anger, a man both thwarted in his expectations of pleasure and hoodwinked by an adversary at the same time would not be happy, now would he?

"Hopefully he will wash his hands of me. We must put that aside and think about the rest of it. About how those two men replaced Luc and Éduard today, and knew about me."

Dominique poured water over her hair, then took some soft soap and began washing. "I suppose Luc and Éduard will take another's coin as quickly as yours, and sold you out."

"But how did anyone even know to offer them coin?"

"The images were traced back, it seems. You knew that was a danger — that Lamberte would look for whoever made those prints and might realize they came from England."

She had known that. She had hoped that if Antoine Lamberte suspected that, he would assume it was the English government behind it, trying to undermine him. Lamberte was conceited enough to believe himself worthy of such attention.

How well had those men seen her in that dark alley? It had all happened very fast, and after Kendale was done with them they might not remember much at all. "I do not think they knew whom they met. Éduard and Luc did not know who I was, other than a woman who handed them something to bring to the coast."

"You can be described to Lamberte by these men, if he sent them."

"I no longer look like anyone he ever knew. I am no longer a young girl. A description will tell him nothing."

"It is never wise to count on your enemy being a fool, or less shrewd than you want to believe him to be."

It was a lesson she believed she had learned today and would never forget. She doubted she could think of Kendale as Stupid Man again.

"Lamberte has survived where most others would have fallen long ago. He is bolder than most, and smarter, and he will eventually wonder if there is a connection. You must take care now. More than before," Dominique admonished.

Marielle did not argue. The older woman possessed the kind of wisdom that only comes from seeing the world at its best and its worst, and realizing that a thin border separates the two. Born into an aristocratic family, Dominique had escaped the guillotine by using her body to bargain with men susceptible to such things. It had been Marielle's good fortune to share a boat across the sea with Dominique, and to receive her motherly affection and help ever since.

She looked up at Dominique, whose round face wore no paint and appeared softly creased beneath the edge of her white cap. She always dressed and looked like a servant now. Most people thought she was one, what with the way she answered the door each time a visitor came. Those visitors did not know that this woman of mature years would never feel safe again, and carried a knife in a special pocket sewn into the deep folds of her skirted dress. She answered the door so that she would know who entered, and could be ready to kill the wrong person should he ever come.

"I wonder if I should move to another city. Not one far away. Just not stay in London."

"I would sleep better if you did."

"What of the other women? They depend on the work here, and most of the printers are here."

"We will find a way to get the work from the printers. As for the women here, Madame LaTour can continue this group. She has been doing it for three years now, and has a good head on her."

Marielle weighed it all while water poured over her, washing out the soap from her hair. The day's attack had shaken her confidence, and her sense of safety. The latter had perhaps always been an illusion. Now she doubted that she would ever leave this house without watching the eyes of each person she passed, searching for the ones that took too much interest in her.

If she left London, she needed to choose a place not too far away, and close to the coast. She needed to remain among the émigrés too, so she would learn what news they brought from France and would hear if Antoine Lamberte still thrived, and what executions if any took place in his region. These qualifications had always limited her choices and decisions. Now they pointed to the only good option.

"Brighton," she said. "I will move to Brighton."

To say that Marielle Lyon had ruined Kendale's mood was an understatement. As a man who had little to do with women socially, he was not accustomed to being led along like that only to have no satisfaction in the end. It never happened at the brothels he visited.

He spent the next two days in a surly

69

humor, thinking he should visit just such a place and pay for that which Miss Lyon had promised. Only it was not some nameless bawd that he wanted. It was Marielle herself. On her knees, on her back, he did not really care how. Only that would settle this particular score and level the field again.

Only then would he stop imagining her hands on him, caressing his legs and body and gazing at him with lights of passion in her eyes. He had not mistaken that part, he reminded himself. Desire had not compromised his good sense entirely.

Two evenings later he dressed to attend dinner at his friend Viscount Ambury's house. He did not do for himself because he had called for his valet, Mr. Pottsward, to come up to town. The hole in his side said he would stay in London longer than he expected, and his old batman's attendance would be needed. He also needed to stay here because a woman who lived in London could hardly be called to task while he rusticated in Buckinghamshire.

He always tried to be on his best behavior when dining with Ambury. Not because Ambury demanded it. Rather Ambury had married Lady Cassandra Vernham and the new Lady Ambury did not much like her husband's friend Viscount Kendale. Nor did he much like her, although Ambury's apparent happiness had softened his views considerably. Not wanting to cause trouble for a friend, he always made an effort to avoid doing the sorts of things that would cause Lady Ambury to complain to her husband long into the night after the party ended.

The good news this particular night was that Southwaite and his wife Emma would also be there. As for the sixth member of what was to be an intimate meal, Kendale hoped the ladies had not dug up some cousin who needed a husband and who would even put up with him if it meant becoming a viscountess. That would turn what might be an enjoyable few hours among friends into a night from hell.

He was relieved when he arrived to see that the third woman sitting in the drawing room was Cassandra's old Aunt Sophie. Colorful, witty, and a little dotty, Lady Sophie Vernham, at over age sixty, was not, he assumed, looking for a husband. Furthermore it was unlikely that his bad behavior would be criticized since Lady Sophie had a reputation for besting him in that area.

No sooner were the greetings exchanged than Ambury and Southwaite maneuvered him to the far end of the drawing room.

Ambury smiled the smile that he normally used when he was up to no good, which was often. Southwaite on the other hand appeared a little sheepish, but determined.

"We need to warn you about something," Southwaite said, in the tone of a man who expected trouble for his efforts.

"Not *warn*. How dramatic that sounds. *Inform*," Ambury said.

Kendale waited, his gaze on Southwaite, who was more likely to have guessed the correct reaction to this *something.*

"There will be another member of our party tonight," Ambury said. "The invitation was given late, after you accepted. I saw no reason to mention it."

"Who is she?"

"The she who will join us to balance the table is Southwaite's sister Lydia. Her presence was required because I found myself at the club yesterday in conversation with Penthurst and decided to ask him to come tonight too."

"Penthurst?"

"Now, Kendale —"

"You did not mention it because you knew I would not come. I cannot believe that you have schemed to have me sit at a table with him. I cannot believe that you will offer him the hospitality of your home either."

Ambury rolled his eyes, which made Kendale want to punch him. Southwaite spoke lowly, and with sympathy. "He should have mentioned it. I said so, didn't I, Ambury? However, in his sunny state of mind since his marriage he sees no clouds, even when they are threatening to rain on him. And, let us be honest, the break between us and Penthurst — the evidence mounts that it was not as we thought. Ambury and I have both explained our thinking on this. You, however —"

You, however, won't see reason. You are the only holdout, and we decided to reconcile whether you agreed or not. You have been rigid, so we chose to force you to bend.

He wanted to have it out with them both now, but that would hardly do. Even he knew not to create that kind of scene in a drawing room where three women waited. And, he admitted, while he still held it against the Duke of Penthurst that he had killed one of their friends in a duel, he knew it had indeed not been as they had thought — the why of it, at least — not that the new ambiguity absolved the man.

Mostly he did not lose his temper or take his leave because the notion of talking to Penthurst tonight held some appeal. With his close ties to the government ministers, there were questions Penthurst might be able to answer as neither Ambury nor Southwaite could. Questions about Marielle Lyon, for example. Kendale would have never sought him out to ask those questions, but if the duke were being imposed on him like this . . .

"Fine."

Southwaite blinked, astonished. He glanced cautiously over at Ambury whose smile did not waiver but whose eyes turned curious. "Fine? You do not mind?"

"It is your house and your food. I trust you do not think I am so rude as to object to the guests you invite, or curse them for their sins while sitting with them at your table."

"No. Of course not. That goes without saying," Southwaite muttered. "I assure you, no one thought that you —"

"I told Southwaite here that you did not have to be *warned.*" Ambury looked down the room and caught his wife's eye. Something passed between them in that look that made Lady Ambury visibly exhale with relief.

Lady Ambury had worried about the wrong guest, Kendale noted with satisfaction toward the end of dinner. She spent so much time keeping the other members of her own family from embarrassing her that she barely knew he was there.

Lady Sophie concluded early on that Lydia had been invited for the eligible viscount in the party, which meant she, Sophie, was expected to be the eligible Penthurst's partner. Her graying hair, dressed in the curls of her youth, dipped toward Penthurst while she plied him with wine and innuendo.

Since they did not sit far from Kendale he overheard much of their conversation. To say that Lady Sophie flirted with a duke who at thirty-two was half her age would not be an exaggeration. Penthurst took it in stride and after his third glass of wine even flattered her back.

"I have no idea why I am here, and invited on such short notice. Do you?" Lady Lydia asked softly. She sat beside him on his left looking her normal pale, remote, soulful self. Dark hair and eyes drew attention to her face, but her eternally impassive expression discouraged any intimacy. Indeed, in the last few years talking to Lady Lydia had become a chore, much like dragging a cart up a muddy hill.

He had therefore neglected her, so entertaining did he find the conversation across the table and down two places.

He gave her his attention now, lest she add to the rumors that said he lacked social polish. "You are here to balance the table. This meal is not about you, or me, but about him." He gestured to Penthurst.

"That is a relief. I thought perhaps my brother had convinced Cassandra to do some matchmaking."

"If so, I was not told of it. I doubt they would ever try to match us. I knew you when you were a child, and could never think of you in that way."

"Not matchmaking with *you,* Kendale. What a notion. That would be a match fit for hell."

Indeed it would be, but even he thought it rude of her to say so outright. As a schoolgirl Lydia had been an impish and spirited bright-eyed, dark-haired child. Now in her twenties, she had retreated into herself with maturity in this peculiar way. Like a sphinx, she watched the world, and wore the smile of a statue if she reacted at all.

She worried Southwaite to no end with this behavior, although Kendale sometimes wondered if it was all a feint. There had been other worries in the last year regarding her that had to do with gambling and other behavior that indicated Lady Lydia could be most impish still. Kendale had reason to know that when Lydia had an accomplice that brought out the worst — one like Cassandra, the new Lady Ambury — Lydia surrendered to the impulse to be very naughty.

"You mean Penthurst, then," he said. "I would be surprised if your brother has such designs. They may be friends of sorts again, but there is some bad business between them still." There should be, at least.

"I hope it is bad enough to keep my brother from getting ideas. I do not like Penthurst. I do not like any dukes, now that I think about it, and I have reason to think that this one, for all his grace and condescension, is very cruel. At least he finally cropped his hair, I will give him that. He must be the last man younger than forty to do so. He also appears to have ordered coats in the current fashion as well. It was about time. He is too young to look like an antiquity."

"He waited to adopt the new styles deliberately, and not for lack of fashion sense or because he did not care for the changes." If anything, Penthurst fit the new styles well, and vice versa, and his dark cropped hair, which Kendale was glad to see he did not fuss with overmuch, flattered his countenance.

"It was perverse arrogance, is what you mean," Lydia said. "A way to say he was above it all, and does not need anyone's approval."

Lady Sophie had rather suddenly remembered her age. "I knew your mother," she said to the duke in a voice amplified by wine. "She owned some lovely jewels, as I recall."

"My father was fond of giving her gifts."

"I recall one brooch in particular. She often wore it on a mantle of deepest scarlet. It had pearls on it. Many small ones around one so large — well, I have never seen the likes since. I expect you still have it."

"I am sure I do, although I have not counted the family jewels in some years."

"It was gorgeous. Unique. She preferred town, as I remember. I expect it is still in the jewel box she used here before she passed."

"Most likely."

"She also wore an emerald, set in a gold ring, surrounded by tiny diamonds. Stunning."

"You have a better memory of my mother's jewelry than I do, I must confess."

"I make a study of jewels. I find them fascinating. I always have. It is a pity that hers sit there in that box, never seeing the

78

light of day or night." She sent her attention down the table. "Cassandra, we must call on the duke when next we are out."

Penthurst nodded kindly. Cassandra's blue eyes narrowed on her aunt with curiosity and an inexplicable caution. "Certainly, if he requests it."

"I would be honored," he was good enough to say.

"When we visit, you can show me the jewels, Your Grace."

Cassandra's face reddened. "Jewels?"

"His mother's," Sophie said. "They languish unseen and unloved. I think they are lonely."

"His Grace does not want to have us pawing through his mother's jewel box, I am sure."

"Lady Sophie, you are welcome to visit the jewels whenever you like. I will tell the butler to bring them down to you, should I not be at home when you call," Penthurst said.

Lady Ambury caught her husband's eye. Again something passed between them. She stood abruptly, signaling the ladies that it was time to leave the gentlemen.

The cigars were half smoked before Kendale found himself talking alone with Penthurst.

Southwaite and Ambury arranged it to happen. They drifted away five minutes after luring him into a discussion about the war. He realized that quite likely the only matchmaking intended by this dinner was that between the two men now pretending that social conversation remained normal for them.

If they did not mention the reason that was not true, the next ten minutes might go well. If Penthurst had the sense not to allude to it, let alone name it, there would be no row.

"Your opinions about the war are insightful," Penthurst said. "No doubt your time in uniform gives you a special perspective."

"The War Office has men in uniform, or who used to be. Generals. I doubt my perspective is better than theirs."

"Theirs is colored by ambition. That always qualifies the value of such things. It can fog the perspective badly."

He was supposed to be flattered. He was, although the reaction carried a good deal of resentment that his pride could betray him so easily.

"And of course you actually have seen some action in this war, when so few in the army have," Penthurst added. "None of those generals have, that is certain, least of all on French soil."

Penthurst did not allude to that which might cause a row, but he touched on a topic that Kendale did not discuss with anyone. "That was a mistake. A costly accident at best."

Penthurst acknowledged the truth of that with a nod. "Such experiences can scar a man."

"Not me." Yet his mind had already filled with images of that horrible day, vivid ones that could be summoned forth by less direct calls than this one. The merry confidence of comrades on a mission — the shock at realizing Feversham's mistress had betrayed him — the carnage that followed, and the desperation of fighting for their lives — then blood everywhere, and pain, and holding a friend as he breathed his last words. *Avenge me. Promise it.*

He had promised. The man was dying. He did not argue that revenge would be impossible. The temptress who had lured Feversham would not even be on the same continent soon.

In his own way he was making good on that promise. He might never be able to kill all the people who had betrayed them, but he did his part to ensure there were fewer betrayals in the future. He may have sold out his commission, but every citizen of the realm needed to be a soldier these days.

"They know that you are still in uniform, in a manner of speaking," Penthurst said, as if reading his thoughts. The duke was not stupid, of course, and, as he now proved, he remained very well informed. It was his only value at the moment, in Kendale's opinion. "They know that you still have missions and have not truly retired from the field."

"Who are *they*?"

"Those generals. The ministers. It worries them at times. The surveillance on the coast that you, Southwaite, and Ambury set up — that was less troubling. Your self-appointment as an agent, however, is not looked on with favor."

"That is too damned bad." He itched to ask how they knew and how much they knew, but he would not give Penthurst the satisfaction. Nor did it matter what the ministers and generals liked or thought.

Penthurst chuckled. "That is exactly what I told one of them that you would say when he asked me to talk reason with you, and encourage restraint."

"I would think they would be glad that someone is keeping an eye out."

"Not if that someone is not a man they control. Not if that someone has a little army of servants who aid him, whom they also don't control. Not if that someone occasionally turns his attention to English citizens."

It seemed those generals knew quite a bit. Perhaps as he followed others, they followed him.

"It smells of vigilantism, I suppose," Penthurst drawled. "I explained that you would never take it on yourself to act as judge and jury, let alone executioner, if you uncovered an intrigue." He looked over, a smile half forming. "I was correct, was I not?"

"Good of you to speak on my behalf. Would it not make more sense for them to air their concerns about me *to* me? I could reassure them. Perhaps they could convince me to stop."

"I asked myself the same question. I concluded that they must not want you to stop, even if you worry them."

"You might tell them that I have no interest in any English citizens at the moment."

"Pitt at least will be glad to know that. As for the others — I expect they will be curious as to whom is of interest now."

So there it was. The opening he needed, handed to him as plain as could be. He had tolerated this conversation in order to ask questions. It appeared Penthurst had as

83

well. "It is my intention to unmask Marielle Lyon. Have you heard of her?" He was up to much more than that, and was glad he had Miss Lyon to throw into the pot to confuse matters.

"Yes. I am told she is very pretty. Is that true?"

Kendale did not honor such an irrelevant question with an answer. "Have you heard the rumors about her?"

"Most everyone has by now. I can think of several members of the Home Office who will find your pursuit of her interesting. After two years they gave up their own quest to unmask her, but not happily. Have you had more luck?"

I have proof that she delivers papers to men in alleys, who then carry them to the coast, where they are put on boats to leave the realm. It would get her arrested if he mentioned it. Other men who were paid for the task would take care of the rest. "Not enough to hand her over. Did they ever seek to prove she is not the niece of the Comte de Vence as she claims?"

"Some of her own people tried to do that. Those who knew the comte and his family would quiz her, to show she was a charlatan. It went on for several years after she arrived here. No one was able to trip her up. She calls up detailed memories of a childhood in Provence and of visiting the comte's manor. A line of old hens tried to peck away at her, but she convinced them she did not lie."

Of course she knew about the comte. She would hardly be given the identity of his niece and not schooled in how to respond to those hens. "You seem to know a lot about it."

"Well, as I said, she is considered very pretty. Those who think so tend to talk about her more than they would an ugly spy."

No wonder she had been living in London right under everyone's noses, acting with impunity. Those Home Office agents were too bedazzled by her face to think straight. Clearly they had not done their job well as a result. It was a damned good thing that he had taken up the cause.

"Have you ever heard of a man named Lamberte? He is in the government there, I think."

Penthurst shook his head. "If he is, he is not significant enough to be discussed."

"At least not by ministers and generals, you mean. Perhaps I need to ask men who hold less elevated conversations."

"Is he in Paris?"

"I do not know. Right now he is just a name to me."

Penthurst thought that over. "Best to ask our French guests then. There is a writer who came a year ago when his pamphlets got him denounced. He knows most of those in politics who survived the worst of it. I will see if he will meet with you."

"That would be useful." He did not offer thanks. Penthurst would be doing this for England, not him.

Ambury and Southwaite drifted over, smiling like indulgent parents glad to see two belligerent boys playing nicely together. They all wandered toward the drawing room, and the ladies.

"Now, that wasn't so unpleasant, was it?" Ambury asked as he sidled alongside. "It looked like the two of you enjoyed a friendly, civil conversation."

"He wanted something and so did I. Don't expect us to be making social calls on each other."

"The day you make social calls on *anyone,* Kendale, I may need smelling salts."

CHAPTER 5

The next morning Kendale woke to the itching stiffness that said his wound was healing quickly. He had his valet change the dressing and pour on the fire potion, but he could tell that the puncture had begun to close.

After Mr. Pottsward helped him to dress, he picked up the other vial of potion. In her haste to leave, Miss Lyon had not taken it, of course. She had also left her long silk wrap. He lifted it so the two slits showed. Perhaps she no longer had use for it, in this condition. He would return it anyway.

He disliked carriages, but he called for his anyway so Anderson would not scold him for riding so soon. Bearing Marielle Lyon's property, he rode like a gentleman in his state coach to the house where she lived near a section of the old north wall of the City.

The blue door remained resolutely closed

despite his knocking. A movement at one of the flanking long windows caught his eye. A white cap moved behind the glass. He angled so he could see inside and held up the wrap. Anyone who knew Miss Lyon would recognize it.

A few moments later the door opened and a formidable woman of regal bearing faced him. She wore a sumptuous dress of the old regime that had seen better days. She also wore an unfashionable wig with a festoon of curls on one side of her face. She was a lady, her appearance announced. One who maintained standards as she saw them.

He handed her his card. "I would like to see Miss Lyon."

She lifted a monocle on a silk cord and squinted at his card. She looked up in astonishment, then angled so she could view his coach. *"Un vicomte? Mon dieu!"* She stood aside so he could enter. *"Bienvenue."* She curtsied.

She noticed the silk shawl in his hand. One eyebrow rose. *"Venez avec moi, s'il vous plaît."*

She led him through a passage and into a large room. It looked like it would be the dining room if anyone else lived here. In Marielle Lyon's house, however, it served as a workroom. Rows of tables filled it, where women sat dabbing with cloths at papers.

When Marielle had said the women in her house colored engravings for printers, she had not lied.

"Germaine! Antoinette! *Ici, ici!*" the woman beckoned, then turned back to him. "The situation does not allow for the proper formalities, M'sieur le vicomte. I must need introduce myself and require your forgiveness. I am Jeanne LaTour, late of Rouen, before the disgrace that befell my country. I am distressed that Marielle did not forewarn us that you would visit, so we could prepare and dress." She made an apologetic gesture at her garments with a resigned expression on her face.

"I did not write to say I would call," he explained. "I would very much like to speak with Miss Lyon if she will receive me, however."

"Certainement," she muttered, tapping her mouth with her fingertips.

The other two women closed in. Madame LaTour huddled with them and spoke lowly. They did not intend him to hear, so he picked up little of the rapid French conversation. He heard Marielle's name mentioned several times by Madame LaTour, and not happily. It appeared these other women debated what to do with him.

Finally Madame LaTour again took center stage. "I regret that Mam'selle Lyon is not at home. I am sure she will feel great disappointment that she was not here when you came."

She might be lying. There was no way to know, since he had not had this house watched since the day before he followed Marielle to the alley. "Is there a chance she will return soon? If so I will come back this afternoon."

"Unfortunately, I am very certain she will not return this afternoon. She has left town for a few days." Madame held out her hands in a gesture of helpless regret.

Damnation. Wounded or not, beaten or not, Marielle Lyon had bolted. He should have come here immediately, or the next day, to make sure he could finish his business with her. All of it.

Where had she gone? To the coast? Back to France? He cursed himself for falling for her ploy at his apartment and for losing his hold on her.

"Ah, you are not pleased." Madame La-Tour clucked her tongue. "You did not know. She did not tell you. I promise the decision was sudden, milord Kendale. Still, if she anticipated your visit she should have written to you. Marielle has a good heart and means well, and is too generous by far, but sometimes her actions are — *pas normal. Her experience amoureuse* with gentlemen are not . . ." She groped for a word, but gave up and resorted to French again. *"Ample."*

One of the other women touched Madame LaTour's sleeve. Madame bent her curls to listen to the confidence offered. When she straightened again, she looked less distressed. "Madame says that she overheard them talking and knows where they went."

"Them?"

"She left with Dominique — Madame Bertrand. She is Marielle's woman servant. It is normal for her to open the door, of course, not I."

"Of course. It was good of you to permit me entry at all."

"I only delayed while I overcame my surprise that you had unexpectedly honored us. I did not expect a man like yourself to call. Your card only confirmed the fact I had already guessed. I know a person's high birth immediately, milord."

"As do I, Madame LaTour." He made a vague bow, as acknowledgment that he saw it now. "Since we have this in common, would you consider trusting me with what this other woman here overheard? Miss

Lyon and I have some friends in common. Perhaps she went to visit them."

Brighton could be delightful in the summer, when society enjoyed its sun and sparkling coast and when lovely breezes wafted into windows. Marielle always enjoyed her visits to the town in July and August.

March showed her a very different environment. The wind off the water carried an icy bite. Gray clouds hung low. The sea appeared the color of steel. A fine rain fell.

She walked down the lane flanked by houses, wishing she had brought a wool shawl and not the dark silk one that she now clutched to her body. She peered at buildings that appeared of recent construction. She consulted a list that she carried, noted the third address, and forged on. She spied the small To Let sign in a low window of a house two doors away from the next crossroad.

She knocked. Mr. Tilbury, the estate agent, opened the door.

He beamed a smile at her. His thick spectacles caused his eyes to appear like tiny black dots in his very pale face. His blond hair was so light as to be mistaken for aged white. "You are a little late, Miss Lyon."

"I had several other houses to see."

"Alas, you are alone again too. Your cousin did not make it down from town, I see."

The cousin he referred to had been a fiction created so that Mr. Tilbury would accommodate her. Estate agents did not take well to women on their own, least of all French ones of questionable fortune. "He must have been delayed. I would wait for him, but men do not know much about hiring a house anyway."

"He will be here to sign the papers, I am sure." His inflection made it a question.

"Of course." If a man had to sign the lease, she would provide a man to do so.

Mr. Tilbury showed her into the dining room. While he extolled the moldings and prospects, she assessed how many tables it would hold for print work. She paced it off, taking a rough measurement. She checked the windows to be sure that trees would not dim the natural light too much in summer. She studied the garden outside to determine if the plantings would give her the necessary privacy, but not too easily hide an intruder.

Mr. Tilbury grew restless after a quarter hour had passed. He pulled out his watch and made a face. "Miss Lyon, could we tour the rest of the house more quickly? I have another meeting several blocks away and should leave soon. The steward of a most illustrious man requires that I show him several suitable domiciles for his lord."

"My cousin would have grown impatient by now too. It is just as well he was delayed. As for your meeting, go to it, m'sieur. Your efficiency indicates that you will be done with those other two houses before I am done with this one."

The two points of his eyes grew smaller yet while he frowned over that idea.

"M'sieur, I am hardly going to steal something. The house is empty. There is not so much as a pillow to take."

"I was not thinking — that is, I am responsible for —" He flushed. "No doubt you are correct and I will return before you are done, at this pace. Are you sure that you will be comfortable alone here?"

"I doubt that, since there is not even a stool on which to sit. I will be safe, however. All the thieves know by now that there is nothing to be had inside this house."

He lingered awhile anyway, fretting and glancing at his watch. Finally he could wait no longer. "I will return soon. If you finish and choose to leave, write to me and let me know what you have decided."

She saw him off with some relief. There

was nothing worse than a man hovering, watch in hand, when she wanted to take her time and do something well and correctly. This house had possibilities, but she would not know if it would do unless she inspected it from attics to cellars. She needed to picture it in use by Dominique and herself and the women who would come here to earn a few shillings very discreetly, in order to keep body and soul together.

The cellars proved to be shallow, perhaps due to the nearby sea. The kitchen was not below as a result, but in a small outbuilding snug alongside the garden entrance to the home. The inconvenience of that arrangement did not discourage her. She assumed it meant she could get the lease for less money, since members of good society would not want a kitchen right off the veranda where they might entertain guests.

Her spirits rose on the thought. If she let a house here, she would still also be responsible for the one in London. If something went wrong and her trade did not expand to cover both, her savings would be depleted fast. She could ill afford that. She saved that money for a reason. She had for years and did not want her great goal set back now.

She made her way up to the attic, and its chambers for storage and servants. It would be a long day before she had many of the latter again, but it was nice to know there would be room should that day ever come. Descending to the next level, she threw open doors to inspect the bedchambers.

It was a good house, she decided, and much nicer than the one in London. She had taken that one before she had any income, and its neighborhood required vigilance. By the time she earned enough to consider leaving and finding a house more suitable to the niece of a comte, it had become home to her.

Home. The emotions conjured up by that word, of respite and safety and comfort, had been ruined now. She hated how she felt vulnerable in her home now. She resented that the past might have found *her* after she had planned for years to have it go the other way.

A chill shivered through her as she considered how that attack had changed her world. Her nape prickled much the way it had in the alley when she realized the men who waited were not Luc and Éduard. She knew in her soul that she no longer could count on having more time to make herself ready for her quest.

How long before other men came looking for her? How long before they did not have to wait in an alley, but learned her name and could show up at her door? If they had the engravings, not long at all. Even if they ran off empty-handed, it might not take much thought to deduce her identity.

Maybe it would not happen like that. Perhaps they would not come here, but lure her back to France. They had the best bait in the world, after all.

She studied the bedchamber in which she stood with new eyes, those of a knight assessing fortifications. If she needed to take refuge in here, would the door latch and lock hold? If she had to —

Another chill. The worst alarm filled her head. She did not move a hair while she listened.

There had been footsteps below, she was certain. No, not certain, but — perhaps the fearful turn her thoughts had taken had her hearing that which was not there. Perhaps —

Again. Clearer, this time. Had Mr. Tilbury returned so soon? It sounded like the man wore boots, and Mr. Tilbury had not been wearing boots. Nor did he walk with the sure, clear footfalls pacing down there now.

She looked around desperately, but indeed there was nothing in this house to steal, or to use as a weapon.

She was being a goose. No one had tracked her here to do her harm. Even so her breaths shortened when those boots began a slow climb up the stairs. She slipped to the wall behind the open door and pressed against it. With luck, whoever's curiosity had brought him here would glance in and move on.

The steps stopped right outside. Logic said it would not matter if he entered or not, but her blood pulsed hard and her soul prayed he would not. It had been years since such irrational terror had owned her, and she hated that even now, as a grown woman who had braved much, she could not conquer it.

A step. Then another. Finally he was inside. She examined the back of the lean, broad-shouldered man wearing a fine dark blue coat and fawn breeches and high boots. Her breath caught in surprise, then she exhaled annoyance. What was *he* doing here?

She did not move. Hopefully he would turn and leave the way he had come. She might not be seen. There was a chance she could avoid even greeting this man.

To her horror, not only did he not leave. He walked farther into the chamber. Then he turned and looked her right in the eyes.

"Are you hiding, Miss Lyon? Not from me, I hope."

"Not from you. From an intruder who should not be here." She left the wall and walked with studied indifference while she put more space between them. Feigning boredom, she kept him in view out of the corner of her eye, looking for signs of anger or even potential violence. She did not think he had forgiven her for what she did to him the last time they had seen each other.

He stood there, tall, handsome, and formidable, looking at her as if he debated what to do with her. A very different shiver ran through her, and an oddly compelling kind of fear. She tried to think of him as Handsome Stupid Man, but that trick no longer worked to block his dangerous appeal. She knew him too well now to pretend he was stupid.

"How did you know I was here?" she asked.

"I followed your scent." He reached into his coat and pulled out a neatly folded square of patterned silk. With a flick of his wrist it grew and flowed. He held the shawl to his nose. "Lavender. I caught a whiff of it near the stairs."

She grabbed the shawl and passed it by her nose. "It does not only smell of lavender." She picked up more primal odors, lying in a musky depth beneath the floral one. The sweat and fear and, yes, even notes of that day's arousal permeated the silk.

"True. Not only lavender."

She began folding the shawl again. "I do not mean how did you come up to this chamber. I wonder how you found me in this town and this house."

"The ladies at your house told me the town. Madame Betrand told me the estate agent. The estate agent's clerk told me the house. So here I am."

Madame Betrand? Dominique had betrayed her? She would have some strong words for her old friend when she returned to the inn. "Does everyone always tell you what you want?"

"No. You don't."

She did not respond. Better to try to keep that door closed now.

He paced around the chamber like a man taking its measure. "Sometimes they do not know that they have told me what I want. The estate agent's clerk, for example. He assumed — I have no idea why — that I was your cousin as soon as I asked after you and whether you were using that firm's services. I did not realize you had a cousin in England."

"I do not know why you followed me at all, and put yourself to such trouble. Surely a viscount has better ways to spend his time."

He stopped his pacing. "You know why. There is unfinished business between us."

She hoped he referred to those questions he wanted to ask. Only the rest was in his eyes — the anger at how she had weakened him with the promise of pleasure, then run away. He probably thought she owed him more than words now.

"Why are you letting a house here in Brighton? Are you thinking to live here?"

"I thought I might. I love the sea air."

"You will have to put off such a change. Later, perhaps. But now — I cannot allow it."

He had a talent for vexing her. If he thought she was impressed or frightened by his stature and birth, like Dominique or that clerk, he did not know the cut of her. "Perhaps you forget that you are not really my cousin, even if you were mistaken for him today. Nor are you an official of the government."

"I am a peer. It does not get much more official than that."

"You cannot tell me where I will live."

"I just did. You will remain in London for

now. Brighton is too inconvenient for me."

"Inconvenient to this unfinished business you claim we have, you mean."

"I have my coach here. Come, I will return you to the inn. In the morning I will bring you and your woman back to town." He stepped toward the door and gestured for her to lead the way out and down.

"I prefer to find my own way to the inn, and to London, but thank you."

"There is no reason to be afraid. I am not going to impose on you."

What an odd thing to say. She had not suggested fear of either him or imposition. True, her instincts warned her that it would not be wise to allow this man close proximity, let alone in such privacy. And, she had to admit, he did frighten her a little, in part because of the score he might think he had to settle and in part because his presence filled this large chamber without his appearing to even try to exert any power. She could be excused if she stirred in response to his masculinity too. They had shared a type of intimacy the day she was attacked. She was a normal woman and he a man in whom much simmered below the surface.

"I do not fear you," she lied. "I merely refuse to be escorted by you. I am accustomed to making my own way. Furthermore, I am not done with my reason for coming to this town, and I intend to finish."

He moved toward her. Not threatening. Not even unfriendly. She took a step back anyway. Having him near her proved a little intimidating.

"Perhaps you did not understand," he said, taking the final step that brought him much too close. "You are very finished already. This estate agent will show you no more houses. Nor will the others in Brighton. No one will let to you here, even if you offer to pay double the rent in advance."

She looked up at the confidence reflected in his eyes. Of course she knew that such men could make others conform to their wishes by simply stating their aristocratic names. She had seen that too often in her life. It was enough to make one sympathize with the revolutionaries in France who had believed in more equality.

Except — looking at him, feeling the command his body and mind sent into the air, she doubted it was only his title that made him so sure his will would be obeyed. He was the sort of man one felt inclined to follow without even knowing his name. That would be useful in war, or any battle. The army had lost a leader when he left it.

She should move away again, so that his

aura did not surround her so completely. She should look to the window, her shawl, anywhere except in his eyes. In the very least she needed to respond to his high-handed announcement of how he had removed control of her decisions from her own choices. She must not allow his assumptions to stand unchecked.

Instead she remained in place, feeling small and frail and unexpectedly safe. There could be comfort in his power too, her soul said. He had saved her once, and might again. She need only ask for protection, or invite him to give it.

It required effort to grope her way back to the truth. Lord Kendale did not want to protect her, but to expose her.

She needed to discourage his suspicions, or else convert him into a friend. She doubted she could do the former without telling him every detail of her life from the time she was a child. As for an alliance . . .

A silent thrumming existed between them, full of possibilities. He might be in that robe again, and she in nothing more than a blanket, their mutual awareness of each other was so complete. The chamber echoed with their breaths. A visceral thrill trembled in her full of primal feminine reactions of fear and desire and aching anticipation. She allowed herself to feel what it did to her, so that she would have the courage to be bold once more.

"You do not need to interfere with my plans," she said while she smiled at him. "I will return to London often after I move here. I will need to bring items to Emma's auction house. I serve as go-between with the recent émigrés from my country. If you ask her, Emma will explain this is true." She reached up to touch his face. Her fingertips hovered near his skin, trembling. "There will be enough opportunity to finish that business you speak of."

She did not have to force herself to caress his jaw. She wanted to feel him again and bridge the small distance still between them.

A blur. A shock of movement stole her breath. Suddenly her back pressed the wall. She faced a force of masculine intensity hovering closely, straining against its reins.

He cupped her chin in his hand, firmly. "I will not impose on you, but I'll be damned if I will be your fool again," he said through clenched teeth.

"A friend, not a fool," she began to say.

He pressed a hard kiss on her that silenced the words even as they formed.

Did she struggle at all, even instinctively? She doubted she did. She succumbed to the power in that kiss. She hoped that she did not unleash a force larger than she calculated.

He kissed her harder, if that were possible, as if punishing her for the flirtations and teasing. He claimed her mouth possessively. She gasped for breath when she could and an onslaught of sensations poured through her.

Finally he stopped. Still holding her face, he gazed at her with hot eyes. She saw much in him, all combined. Desire for certain. Also curiosity and fury. And, for an instant only, indecision.

"Hell," he muttered. He pulled her into an embrace and kissed her again.

This was not a gentle or artful lover. To her surprise the tight way he held her, the manner in which he controlled her, made her arousal soar. When he moved his mouth to her neck and chest she stretched her fingers through his hair and held tight, not worrying about being gentle in turn.

His embracing arm almost lifted her off her feet when his kisses and bites moved lower yet, to the top of her breasts. His left arm held her while he caressed her firmly, pressing through her garments all over her body, finally sliding his hand up to her breast.

Against the wall again. His knee pressed between her thighs, high and hard to where she pulsed. It raised her off her feet so she pressed down, deliciously. It felt too good to bear, both easing and deepening the furious need bursting in her. Deliberately, almost cruelly, he used his hands on her breasts, not in admiration but purposeful titillation.

She began losing sense of anything else. Maddened, helpless to the pleasure, she hoped he would strip her. She could barely breathe let alone talk, but she scandalously begged in her mind for him to finish it. She did not care if it was on the bare floor.

He came close. She felt it in him. She saw it through the slits beneath her lowered lids. She waited for him to turn her and lift her skirt. Instead he lifted her whole body in a new embrace. He held her to him, high, so that his mouth could close on her breast. She pressed his head closer yet and lost herself in the exquisite pleasure of his sucks and bites.

Then, suddenly, she felt the floor beneath her feet again, and the wool of his coat against her cheek. His embrace circled her shoulders. No kisses now. No sounds. He held her while her body trembled and punished her for allowing such an incomplete passion to happen.

He released her and stepped away. She snuck a glance at his face, wondering what she would see. Smug satisfaction, that he had now done to her what she had done to him? Disgust, that she so easily allowed such behavior? Calculation, as he plotted how to continue this in a place more conducive to his intentions.

He appeared serious. Thoughtful. Stern, too, but that part was nothing new when it came to her.

Without a word he took her arm and led her to the door. They descended the stairs. He took her arm again, and did not release it until he handed her into his coach out in the street.

He closed the door and looked at her through the window. "The coachman will take you to your inn. Tomorrow morning you will return to London with me. And you will not be moving here to Brighton."

He walked away in one direction while the coach rolled in the other.

CHAPTER 6

Two days later Kendale still could not decide if he had won or lost the skirmish with Marielle that had taken place in the empty house in Brighton. She had returned to London, that was true. It had been a silent, long, and awkward ride. If not for his healing wound he would have ridden down to start with, and ridden back beside a hired coach, but he was not such an idiot as to spend hours in a saddle until the tender mending underway had taken securely.

As for the rest — damned if he knew if he had again been her fool or not. Perhaps he had reacted exactly as she intended. Her lack of resistance suggested as much. He knew Frenchwomen to be very wily in their ways with men. A smart man would have nothing to do with them.

Any chance of choosing that path had now become complicated.

He wanted her. Hell, but she knew it,

didn't she? She was probably the enemy, and she would undoubtedly use it against him again and again, as she had already. Stopping himself in that bedchamber had taken more strength of will than he normally exerted these days. He never did with women, that was certain. Whores promised a useful simplicity. One never wondered for days on end about motivations and compromises, the way he did now.

He ruminated over the situation as he left his chambers and rode to Brooks's. He resisted the temptation to ride on to a blue door near the old City wall instead. His mind had taken him there many times since his coach had left Marielle and Dominique there. He had a man watching again, so that he would not use the need to remain aware of her movements as an excuse to pant after her like a randy, green boy.

Southwaite and Ambury sat where he expected them. Southwaite studied a letter in his hand. When he noticed Kendale approaching, he waved it. "News from the coast."

Kendale kicked out a chair and sank into it. "I am not going this time."

"How suspicious you are."

"It is a well-founded suspicion. You sent a message for me to meet you here, and now

I learn you received a missive from our friends on the coast. Every time that has happened since your wedding, I have found my ass in a saddle for days. Well, you or Ambury can go this time."

Ambury dared to look wounded. "We thought you enjoyed a bit of action and getting out of town. I am dismayed that you think we have been taking advantage of you."

"You know very well that you have been taking advantage of me. And spare me your next breath, on which you will explain how I am much better at dealing with our watchers than either of you, et cetera, et cetera, et cetera. I am not going."

Ambury glanced at Southwaite, who peered across the top of the letter. "It may actually be worthwhile this time. Two men were found dead in Dover. Frenchmen. They had been knifed."

Kendale fought the curiosity that spiked on that tidbit. "The local magistrate can handle it."

"But surely you would want —"

"The truth is I cannot go unless I want to spend days in a coach. I have a wound that is healing and I should not ride that far." He signaled for one of the club's servants and sent him for some beer.

He returned his attention to the table to find two friends frowning at him.

"A wound? Where? How? When?" Ambury demanded.

"Several days ago. Two days before Southwaite's party."

"You did not appear in pain from a wound at the party," Southwaite said.

"To show discomfort would have been rude. It was only a stab to my side. It does not affect my walking or sitting in ways that are normal if I intend to appear such. However, it means I cannot be your lackey and do all the work on the coast for now."

"He is maintaining an unusually rigid pose right now," Ambury said to Southwaite. "He did appear to move carefully at the dinner party, now that I think about it."

"A stab wound is not something one can suffer and show no effects a few days later," Southwaite said.

"If any man could, it would be him."

"Perhaps it was a very small stab."

"I would appreciate if you did not discuss me as if I am not here. It was a good-sized stab, thank you. As for what a man can do after, how would either of you know? You have not been stabbed."

Southwaite acknowledged that with a chagrined nod. "How did it happen? I am offended that you did not inform me at once."

Kendale downed some beer. "It was a small skirmish with some thieves in an alley. One had a knife."

"I trust you laid down information about it."

"I do not know the thieves, or where they went. I am not in the habit of announcing when I am wounded either."

"I am shocked that thieves are stabbing lords in London's alleys," Ambury said. "What were you doing in one in the first place?"

This was why he had not told them about it before. "I was helping a woman who was being attacked."

Their attentions focused more. Both now appeared truly impressed and shocked. "Zeus, man. How like you to rush in and how unfair to then get stabbed for your bravery. I trust this woman at least laid down information even if you did not. These ruffians must be found and stopped," Southwaite said.

"I do not know if she did. Perhaps so." Not damned likely.

"Of course you can't be riding to the coast. Fortunately, this does not require that any of us do so. We will have someone keep eyes on the magistrate, to see if anything is discovered that we need to know." Southwaite set the letter aside with a certain firmness.

Kendale looked around the chamber to see who else had taken refuge at the club. He saw Penthurst near one wall, reading. Normally when Penthurst came here he enjoyed the company of ministers. It was how he knew so much. Today no such luminaries graced Brooks's.

He jerked a finger in Penthurst's direction. "Did you tell him I was coming, so he could not join you?"

Southwaite flushed. "Not exactly. That is —"

"No one wants to rush matters," Ambury said, soothingly.

When it came to Penthurst, these two had begun to treat him like a woman. He did not like it.

"Do not deny him on my account. If I do not want his company, I will find yours at another time."

They mumbled and nodded and looked here and there but not at him. He might be a girl who had been thrown over by His Grace, and had to be handled delicately.

He decided to move the conversation to a more productive topic before he found himself wanting to knock their heads together. "Do any of you know any of the French refugees here in London?"

Southwaite thought the question odd. Ambury found it a welcomed diversion from a growing awkwardness that they all seemed to feel. "I know several of the ladies."

"You would," Southwaite muttered.

"I have not spoken to any of them in some time," Ambury added, pointedly.

"I hope so, or your new wife will cut off your head if not something else," Southwaite replied, just as firmly.

"Would they receive me if I carried a letter of introduction from you?" Kendale asked.

"You want to call on some French ladies, when you never bother to call on English ones?" Ambury asked.

"I have something I am curious about, and they may be able to enlighten me."

Again his two friends exchanged meaningful glances. They did that a lot. Did they think he did not notice?

"Who are you after?" Southwaite asked. "Do not deny that you are after someone. We know you too well."

"I would rather not say at this point. If I am wrong, voicing suspicions would be slanderous."

115

Southwaite's brow furrowed. His face turned stern. "Not an English citizen, I trust. I have not forgotten how you turned your sights on Emma. I won't have it, Kendale. I will go to Pitt myself to stop you if you ever subject one of our own to your surveillance."

Southwaite may never forget about Emma, but it appeared he had already forgotten that the suspicions about her had been proven more than appropriate. It was not something one reminded a friend if one wanted to avoid a duel, however.

"No one who is English," he reassured.

Ambury called for some paper and a pen and ink. "I will give you their names, then. And a note from me that both introduces you and explains your purpose."

"Hell, don't explain my purpose. When you do one of your investigations, do you start your conversation by saying, *I am Ambury and despite my title I have a hobby of sticking my nose into others' business and I want to trick you into saying compromising things about my current victim?*"

"I cannot send you there without some explanation. They may assume that you — that is, at least one may think that I have sent you for rather different purposes than you intend." He stopped writing and looked up. "Unless you would like me to allow that assumption to stand — ?"

"No."

Again they exchanged glances. And this time, little smiles.

"Forgive me," Ambury said. "Hope springs eternal. You know I believe you need a woman."

"I have women whenever I want them."

"You know that I mean for more than ten minutes a fortnight."

"Ten minutes? Is it only supposed to take that long? If so, one wonders why the whores cry, *More, more, my lord,* instead of, *Your time is done, you lout.*" He cocked his head, puzzling over it. "Or perhaps it only takes *you* that long. I have said for years now that you need to exercise more, Ambury."

Southwaite howled. Ambury just stared. "Did you just make a joke, Kendale? Are you unwell? Drunk? I swear he showed some wit just now, Southwaite. My world has suddenly tilted in the least expected way."

Southwaite caught his breath. "Was it a joke? I assumed he was serious. Now, Kendale, as to knowing any French types — Emma still has some dealings with that woman who dabs at prints, Marielle Lyon. I

117

am sure she would arrange a meeting so that you can ask your questions."

"Cassandra could too. I don't know why I did not think of her. She did us some good turns not long ago, so I believe you could trust her information."

"Do you indeed? That is convenient. I would be glad for either of your wives to arrange that Miss Lyon and I meet."

The conversation moved on to some boring bill being proposed for parliament. Kendale half listened. The ways in which Marielle had inserted herself into the lives of two ladies married to peers of the realm were among the reasons she needed to be stopped.

Soon he took his leave so that his mind would not turn to porridge under the onslaught of political gossip and speculations. While he walked out, a voice hailed him. He turned to see Penthurst beckoning.

Their estrangement was well enough known that heads turned. Annoyed by this public display of a ducal whim, he walked over.

Penthurst barely looked up from his book. He reached in his pocket and withdrew a folded paper. He held it forward. "The man I mentioned. Here is his name. He is out of town for another week, but will receive you upon his return."

Kendale fingered the paper. There were men who would not hand this over until he either begged or forgave or apologized, and England be damned if their pride interfered with catching a spy. He had to give Penthurst credit for putting country first, much as he did not want to think good of the man.

He stuck the paper in his coat and walked away.

Dominique fussed with her cap, tweaking its lace this way and that while she peered at her moon face in the looking glass. "I do not see why I must come."

"I should not go alone. Madame LaTour made that very clear. They will be of the old blood. They will expect me to have a woman with me, if not a male relative," Marielle said.

She picked through her meager wardrobe. Normally she did not mind wearing these old clothes. She intended her money for a bigger cause than passing fashions. Some of her current garments were Dominique's old dresses from many years ago, and others she had bought used from newly arrived aristocrats. Such women never sold their newer things, however. They would give up the long-waisted dresses of yesteryear, but not anything that might be called à la mode.

She doubted anyone other than Madame LaTour would be so poorly dressed today, however. Before leaving France the women who had come over would have had dresses made and delivered, even if they did not pay for them.

She settled on a dress with lavender flowers sprinkled over a cream background. Its lace displayed very little mending and had kept its freshness. It was her best dress, she supposed, as she slipped it on. Made for a shorter woman, it would hang too high except that she owned no thick petticoats to pouf out the skirt. She took a brush to her unruly hair.

"I do not understand why they cannot come here, as most do," Dominique said. Dominique did not want to attend this salon. She did not like even leaving the house.

"A whole boat came. There will be many new faces, and the chance to bring Emma many old items to sell. I can hardly ask them to line up in the street here." For a year now she had served as an agent for Fairbourne's auction house. She convinced the émigrés to put their treasures on consignment there if they wanted to convert the books and jewels and art that they smuggled out of France into money. In return Emma gave her part of Fairbourne's fee. Begun almost by accident, it had turned into an employment that helped feed her savings for her great cause. It also had proven useful for other reasons.

As she queried the newcomers about their possessions in need of sale, she would also converse about other things. News from all over France might come her way today.

If one of this new group had come from the Vendée or a nearby region, she might even learn how things fared there and if Antoine Lamberte still lorded over everyone. She would hope for information that might give her a hint whether the attack on her had been at Lamberte's bidding, and if so how much he knew. She could also discover if he had arranged any executions too.

Her brush stopped halfway down her hair. That was a piece of news she hoped she did not learn. She would ask, however, no matter how much she dreaded hearing the answer.

"You be careful," Dominique said. "You make sure you can trust them before you ask after Lamberte. He may well have sent one of them on this boat to find you, and your own interest will pique curiosity. Better if you left the questions to me."

"You cannot play the servant and ask highborn women about the news of their country. Will you present yourself as their equal so they will confide in you?"

Dominique shook her head. "You just be careful."

Two hours later Marielle and her maid entered a handsome townhome on a street behind Bedford Square. She wondered if the family who lived here owned it, or if it was only let. If the latter, she wondered if the rent had been paid.

Most of the émigrés lived a precarious existence. Few of them would work, not that the aristocrats among them had skills to sell. They were gentlemen and gentlewomen after all. Her own print work was tolerated since it was better than whoring, but unkind comments still came her way, even from families who sent one of their women to sit and dab paint at her tables. A good many families relied entirely on debt to survive, and on the credit offered by tradesmen who counted on the old ways and estates eventually returning to France.

As she mounted the stairs to the drawing room, she assessed the furnishings. Either Monsieur Perdot had property in England from long ago, or the porcelains and hangings had indeed been bought by his expectations. There was too much here to have been brought over when he escaped.

The drawing room hardly soared the way they did in France's best houses, but its decorations were tasteful, and its occupants merry. Seven men and nine women sat on chairs and divans, drinking champagne and celebrating their escape.

Madame LaTour sat among them. She noticed Marielle, beckoned her over, and introduced her. One of the newcomers, Madame Toupin, a woman of senior years with white hair and very dark eyes, took particular note. She peered through spectacles mounted on a long wand, eyeing every inch of Marielle's person and deportment.

Marielle faced her down, mustering as much hauteur as what came her way. Lips pursed and eyebrows high, this woman did not hide her skepticism regarding what she saw.

"So you are the niece of the Comte de Vence. I knew him well, and am delighted to make your acquaintance." She patted the bench beside her chair. "Come, sit with me, so we can reminisce about that good man."

Sabine Peltier lived in a small apartment at a good address on the edge of Mayfair.

When Kendale presented himself at the door, a maid ushered him into a tiny sitting room before she walked off with his card and Ambury's letter. She did not return for a good while.

He amused himself while he waited by perusing the books in a cabinet tucked discreetly in one corner. Not only French books rested there, but also new ones in English. That fit with the little he knew about the woman. Ambury had explained that the Peltiers had moved in the highest circles in Paris before Monsieur Peltier, an academically inclined younger son of a baron, had paid for his conservative philosophies with his life.

The chamber itself possessed a feminine, elegant décor that he assumed cost a bit of money. Madame Peltier bought sparingly but well. The few chairs appeared well made. The upholstered divan would be at home in the best drawing room.

Madame Peltier looked much the same when she finally entered and greeted him. Dark haired, slender, and tall, she was a beautiful woman of middle years. He guessed she was about forty, but it was hard to tell. Her ensemble and style inclined toward the exotic, as was the fashion among some ladies. The high-waist dress looked to have layers of thin fabric, all of which floated as if she flew just above the ground when she moved.

She still held the letter in her hand, and after they sat she perused it again. "Ambury is very charming. He writes that you want a favor from me, but not my favors."

"Perhaps other men are so rude as to call on a lady as a stranger in hopes of the latter, but I am not." It was an insult to suspect he would do that. Perhaps, however, there was a reason why it did not insult *her*.

She gave him a good examination. "I expect you are not."

"What else does he say?" It did not appear to be a brief letter.

"He thanks me for writing to wish him well on his marriage, but very subtly and kindly discourages me from writing again in the future." She made a sad little smile, then laughed. "Of course he must marry the daughter of one equal to himself. And English, of course. It is normal."

It was not his place to explain that there had been little normal about Ambury's choice of wife, nor that if he had wanted to marry a Frenchwoman whom strange men called on for favors of a special kind, he was the sort to do so. "Very normal."

"And you, milord. Do you have such a

normal marriage?"

Madame Peltier had broached an intimate topic with alarming speed. He decided to discourage her from spinning any webs. "I intend to one day. Very soon." He added the last part in response to a rapacious gleam that entered Madame Peltier's far too interested dark eyes. It reminded him of the lights in the eyes of men who view a horse at Tattersalls that they would not mind owning.

"Bien." The word sighed out of her. It signaled resignation, from the tone and from the less flirtatious way she gazed at him. "Tell me what you want. I will try to help you and one day, perhaps you will help me."

He had not expected this to be without cost, but her bluntness surprised him. He noticed that she spoke very good English as she clearly articulated the bargain. Almost as good as Marielle. Unlike Marielle, however, she had lost little of her accent and it caused the sentences to inflect oddly, and to rise when native English might fall. She was one of those whom Marielle considered lazy for not listening and trying to imitate. Of course Madame Peltier had never been trained to listen and imitate. Either that or her accent lent her charm in London so she had little incentive to lose it.

"I have come to ask you to tell me what you know about Marielle Lyon."

"Ahh." She looked toward the window, thinking. "Little Marielle." She tsked her tongue lightly. She returned her attention to him. "I know her, of course. We all know each other."

"Do you believe her story?"

"I have no reason not to. And yet . . . all is not right there, to me."

He hoped his silence would encourage her to continue. Eventually it did.

"It is too much," she said. "The old dresses that make her appear both lovely and helpless. I picture her carefully tearing the lace just so, for effect. The long shawls — they become her too well. How convenient that she owned them and was able to bring them out with her. The way she dirties her hands with that odd studio. There are ways to make one's way beyond starting a little factory, no?"

"I expect so."

"I know the suspicions that she is a charlatan. I have been there when she is put to the test. She makes no mistakes." She leaned toward him like a conspirator. "None at all. It is not normal. We all forget things from our youths. But poor Marielle, she remembers it all. The name of the comte's

127

horse. That he liked currants in his porridge. Little things that his own daughter might not remember, Marielle can recite like a lesson."

"I admire your perception."

"Then there is the way she speaks," she added, ignoring his flattery.

"Her English?"

"Her French. Usually it is most correct. The language of Paris, as would be taught to her in a good home of a comte's niece. One day, however, not long after she arrived, I was at the home of a family with three children when she visited. She was still much of a child herself then, and she went to play with them. When I went into the garden, I heard her. No longer did she speak like a Parisienne, but with an accent most provincial. I recognized it as a voice from the west. I had family who lived in Nantes, and she spoke like them."

She locked her gaze on his meaningfully. He missed whatever significance she gave to this discovery. He never thought Marielle had come to London from Paris.

She rolled her eyes at his stupidity. "Milord, she does not claim to come from the *west*, but from the *south*. The comte lived in Provence, and Marielle says she lived nearby. That at least is not true, I think."

And if one detail were untrue, how much else?

"Do you know her well? Have you seen her among us?" Madame Peltier asked.

"I have only seen her among English people." Mostly he had seen her as a lone figure in the distance. Of course recently he had been face-to-face with her, and very close. Too damned close.

Madame Peltier lowered her eyelids and gazed down in thought. "You are not the first to wonder. Not even the first to ask me about her. Your government has shown interest before. You, however, are the first who did not threaten me before you asked your question. And the first to come with a letter of introduction, as a sign of respect."

"Did you tell the others what you told me?"

"I only answered their questions. They did not ask about her speech, or ask for my opinions."

"I am glad you decided to receive me. I have learned something new from you it seems." Damned if he knew what to do with it, though.

He rose to take his leave. She stood too, but paced over to the window overlooking

129

the street. Abruptly she turned.

"Would you like to see her among her own? There is a gathering right now to welcome some new arrivals. She may be there. She likes to learn if they brought things to sell. She gives them to that auction house and takes a piece for her efforts. Our little Marielle is most shrewd in going between the English and us."

"It would be useful to see her being shrewd, but I would not like to intrude."

"There are often English friends at such assemblies, so introductions can be made that might be of use. You can escort me."

"If I escort you, will there not be talk?"

She laughed musically. "How gallant of you to worry for me. There is always some talk. What else do we have to do, but talk and wait and pray, and talk some more?"

CHAPTER 7

Marielle avoided the quizzing by Madame Toupin as long as she could. She engaged the others sitting nearby in conversation. Before the hour was out she knew the identities of all of the new arrivals, and from where they had hailed.

One man in particular held a special interest to her. A native of La Rochelle, he had visited his home before slipping away. La Rochelle was not Savenay, where Lamberte wielded power, but both were in the west.

She contemplated how to escape Madame Toupin so she could pull that man aside. Deciding to be direct, she began rising from the bench, excusing herself. Unfortunately that brought Madame's attention on her.

"My dear, you must not go so soon. We have not had time to talk."

"Of course, Madame." She sat again, but turned her head in the direction away from Madame. Dominique stood right behind her, and moved close when she gestured. Dominique bent low to hear her whisper. "Monsieur Marion, over there with the green waistcoat. Ask him to meet me in the garden in half an hour."

Dominique nodded and eased away. Marielle collected her wits and turned to face Madame.

"I was so sad, hearing about your uncle. It makes me grieve even now, all these years later," Madame said, patting her hand.

"We all have much to grieve, Madame. I thank you for remembering him in your prayers."

"I expect the house was taken. And the lands."

"Of course."

"How sad and unfair. Your family's land was stolen too, no doubt. Was your father executed as well, after his brother?"

Such matter-of-fact discussions of death were normal in their community, but Marielle found them disconcerting. Death had become so commonplace during the revolution that no one treated the losses as deserving special reverence anymore.

"Our property also was taken and my father indeed died soon after my uncle, but of a long illness. I think that you have misunderstood my relationship too. My

132

father was not the comte's brother. Rather my mother was his sister. The comte's only brother passed away years before the unpleasantness started." *You will have to do better than that, Madame.*

"I do not think I ever met your mother."

"Most likely not. She did not make an approved marriage, and did not get invited to my uncle's balls and house parties. She was not disowned, however. My uncle allowed us to visit privately, and he purchased for her the house in which we lived."

"How fortunate that you could have the advantages of visiting that magnificent home. My memories of it are full of light and beautiful gardens. There was a maze in one. It took me over an hour to make it to the center, and the statue of Apollo there."

Marielle began to respond, but a ripple of excitement distracted her. Heads turned and whispers buzzed. She looked to the drawing room's entrance and saw the reason. Madame Peltier had arrived. Late, of course, so she would make a grand entrance.

This entrance appeared grander than most. While Madame Peltier presented a lovely face and figure, and one more stylish than most in the chamber due to suspicious sources of support, the attention she now garnered seemed extreme.

The crowd parted and Marielle saw why. The whore was on the arm of Viscount Kendale!

Madame Peltier made sure she and her escort secured glasses of the champagne that had been smuggled out of France with the émigrés. Then she surveyed the chamber. Her gaze came to rest on Madame Toupin. No doubt she considered Madame Toupin the most impressive woman among the newcomers.

With Kendale in tow, she moved in their direction, introducing Kendale to all she passed. For a man reputed to have no interest in social affairs, Kendale appeared gracious enough about the fawning attention coming his way.

Marielle refused to watch. Such a display was gauche. If Sabine wanted to play the courtesan for the nobility of England, that was her business. One might hope she would be more tactful, however, and not parade her lovers about like this, interfering with important business that Marielle had to conduct.

Madame angled so she could see around Marielle while she tipped her head to whispers pouring in her ear. "A viscount? How wonderful. I must be sure to meet him," she said. "I am told it is impossible to get anyone in the government here to listen to a petition. He is very handsome, isn't he? Although perhaps not amiable. Of course I knew he was of the blood as soon as I saw him."

Since Madame Toupin had lost interest in her, Marielle decided to escape and go wait in the garden for the man in the green waistcoat. She took her leave but no one heard her repeatedly excusing herself. All attention in their little circle had fixed on the space right in front of her bench. She looked up to see Viscount Kendale standing right in front of her.

Short of pushing him to the side, she would not be able to leave now. She settled back on the bench.

"We do not interrupt, I hope," Sabine said. "Lord Kendale was good enough to agree to meet our new friends and I could not deny them the introduction. Marielle, would you be kind enough to do the honors."

She introduced Madame Toupin and the others sitting nearby. Pleasantries and blandishments flew through the air. Kendale might be the prince, for all the eager claims on his attention. Then conversation lagged.

"I fear we did interrupt," Kendale said to Sabine, in English.

"It was no interruption," Madame Toupin said, turning to English as well. "I was reminiscing with Mademoiselle Lyon about her family."

"Then I am glad we arrived just now. I would be happy to know more about Mademoiselle's childhood."

"What? Do you know each other?" Madame Toupin asked.

"We have only had two conversations, very brief ones," Marielle said.

"Too brief," Kendale said. "Although Mademoiselle Lyon did teach me a few things about some differences between French customs and ours."

Marielle hoped she did not flush at his oblique reference to that afternoon in his chambers.

"How nostalgic it must be for you, Marielle, to meet someone who knew your family well. Did you have a long history with the comte, Madame?" Sabine asked.

Madame launched into an explanation of how the two families knew each other. Each breath improved her own family's stature. Marielle let her chatter on. She turned her attention to the other guests and tried to see if the green waistcoat remained in the chamber. From a nearby corner Dominique caught her eye and gestured to the window and the world outside.

"I was describing my delight in the maze in the comte's garden when you arrived," Madame said. She speared Marielle with a sidelong glance of suspicion. "There was a statue in its center."

"That is correct," Marielle said, impatient with this game now. Another time she would let this woman quiz her for hours. "I am afraid your memory is a little faulty, however. The statue depicted Neptune, not Apollo. He rose up from a fountain, as if it were the sea. Remember?"

"I do now. Thank you." Madame appeared disappointed that Marielle did too.

"I always thought the little lake more fun than the maze. The maze frightened me, but I could float a little boat on the lake. Mama would sit under the large tree on its edge and watch. A very old tree with a trunk too thick for a man to embrace completely." She scoured her brain for some detail to end this latest interrogation. "I was so sad that summer when lightning hit it and sheared off the branches that overhung the water."

Madame retreated into silence. Sabine did not. "Your memories are so clear. It is a wonder to me that anyone has such detail in their mind."

"My memories are all that I have from that happy time. Therefore I take care of them like the treasures they are. Now, you all must excuse me. I need some air." Pretending to be a little light-headed, she stood, ready to push Kendale out of the way if necessary. He stepped aside and bowed.

She sought out Dominique. "You must come with me. Eyes are watching and I claimed to need some air. It will appear odd if I go down alone."

Dominique fell into step, making a display of concern while she fanned Marielle's face with her hand. "What is the viscount doing here?"

"Perhaps hoping for an excuse to buy Madame Peltier a fur mantle for next winter's cold."

"Do you think so? That is too bad."

Marielle hurried down the stairs once they escaped the drawing room. "Why too bad? It is good news. She will distract him from trailing me. She will also make him available to others who need help. You remember how useful it was when Viscount Ambury was her dear friend for a few months, don't you? We must all pray that Madame Peltier never loses her appeal to the lords of England."

Dominique huffed down after her. "True,

true. I just thought . . ."

Marielle stopped at the bottom of the stairs and turned on her. "You just thought what?"

She shrugged. "He seemed somewhat taken with you, enough that if you over-looked a few failings that he possesses, the fur mantle might well be yours."

"What a stupid notion! First, I am not a whore," she said, speaking with whispered annoyance. "Second, and I would think this would drive such ideas away at once, he has decided I am the enemy. He does not want me as his mistress. He wants me on a gallows."

She strode through the house's first level, sticking her head into chambers as they passed, seeking a garden door.

Dominique hustled alongside. "Do not be angry with me for considering the possibility, and do not be so stubborn as to ignore it yourself. If a liaison with him helps you win the final prize, what do you care if he does not trust you? It is certain that you will be needing what protection you can find now. There is none better than an English lord who, from the looks of him and the telling of others, is still as battle ready as when he was an officer."

Marielle spied the garden through a window in the library. Nipping inside she found a door as well. She reached out and grabbed Dominique and dragged her into the chamber. "Do not speak this nonsense again."

"If you insist. Pity for that Peltier woman to get him, but as you say, maybe it will distract him from hunting you."

She imagined just how he would be distracted. It did nothing for her mood. Sabine lived well, it was said. Her furniture did not show frayed fabric any more than her dresses showed long waists and front lacing. She was a goddess, a picture of fashion and elegance, and imbued with the worldly sophistication that made Frenchwomen of good breeding so alluring. In comparison, Marielle looked like a shepherdess to Kendale, she was sure.

Well, if Sabine Peltier were going to seduce Lord Kendale, one could only hope that she did so thoroughly. She probably would soften his hardness some. When she was done with him, those edges would be smoothed and rounded. Sabine would train him how to flatter and charm and tolerate society too. After an affair with Sabine, he would be just like all the other gentlemen in the drawing rooms of Mayfair most likely.

How sad.

She stood at the edge of the terrace, looking for a green waistcoat amid the plantings. When she did not see it, she cursed. "He is gone. I will have to write to him and ask him to call on me now, and who knows if he will bother."

Dominique grasped her shoulder and pointed with the other hand. "There. He is sitting in front of that shrubbery."

Indeed he was. Monsieur Marion appeared to be in a reverie while he admired the tulips blooming nearby. Relieved, Marielle walked down the stone steps into the garden and headed toward him.

"I must go. I will leave the coach to take you home," Kendale said.

Madame Peltier smiled up at him while she stood a fraction too close. She had been drinking a good deal of champagne. "Do not."

"Do not leave the coach?"

"Do not go." Her eyes promised much if he obeyed. Since others could see her looking at him like that, there would definitely be talk.

"I must." If he did not leave he would go mad. It was bad enough to suffer parties like this with his own countrymen. Doing so with forty French persons made it unbearable. He understood what they said well

enough, but speaking French beyond rudi-
mentary sentences was not a skill he possessed. Not that he had anything to say in
any language at such affairs.

He had never understood the appeal of
these gatherings. So much talk, and so little
actually said. So much falsehood and flattery and so much unkindness. Marielle had
barely left the chamber before the group
where she had sat began savaging her. Not
because she might be a spy. From what he
could tell, no one here suspected her of that.
Not even because she might be a charlatan.
Her handling of Madame Toupin left that at
least an open question. No, the ladies tore
her down for her dress, her hair, her trade,
her independence. They found each other
very witty as they did it too.

Now one of those ladies cajoled him to
stay. Nothing she could offer would keep
him here another five minutes.

She pouted. "Then take your coach too. I
will hire one, or find another guest who is
more sympathetic."

"As you like. Again, thank you for receiving me today." He bowed and went to look
for the host.

It took a good ten minutes to make a clean
escape. No one wanted the English lord
with good connections to go. Remaining

vague about his willingness to help, inwardly groaning at the line of callers he could expect in the coming weeks, he fought his way out like a soldier retreating from overwhelming forces.

He was not really free until he started down the stairs. He took his time then, assessing the orientation of the house and the likely plan of the chambers above and below. He had noticed that the drawing room overlooked the garden. Perhaps down here the library did as well. He turned and made his way to the back of the house. The few servants who noticed him did not question his presence.

Out on the veranda the late afternoon breeze refreshed him. Little fields of spring flowers gave some color to a landscape still showing barren trees. The scent of the changing season could not be mistaken, however. It reminded him of his youth in Buckinghamshire, when so much on the land promised renewal at this time of year.

A white spot caught his eye. A cap. Marielle's woman stood near some shrubbery near the back of the garden, half obscured by the branches of a tree that interfered with his line of sight. He moved to the left and saw Marielle herself. She sat on a bench next to a man who had been upstairs. Some boxwood half hid them, but he saw them speaking intently, heads bent close together and hands moving. They looked like intimate friends discussing a matter of great importance.

Or like lovers having a row.

The man made a gesture of resignation and apology with his hands, holding them open. Then he stood, bowed, and walked toward the terrace. Kendale noted his face as he passed back into the house.

Down in the garden Marielle remained on the bench. She sat there, not moving at all. Her woman stepped over and placed a hand on her shoulder. The touch seemed to call her back from wherever her thoughts had led her. She turned her body toward the older woman and embraced her, burying her face in the woman's dress. She remained thus for a long count before standing, smoothing her skirt, and strolling back with a slow, listless gait.

She noticed him when she was halfway through the garden. That put some iron in her spine and stride in her walk. Head high and eyes alight with mockery, she came up to the terrace.

"Madame Peltier has allowed you to leave her side? I am surprised. She depends on friends like you to make her important with our countrymen."

"Regrettably, I do not care for small talk in any language and had to take my leave before I went mad."

"If you are drinking champagne, what do you care how big the talk may be?"

"I do not care for champagne either."

"Do you prefer beer, ale, gin, and tea, like most of your kind?"

"I like wine too. Just not champagne."

"Madame Peltier will change your mind about that."

"I do not think so. Women do not influence me much."

She wagged her finger at him. "Beware, Lord Kendale. A woman who knows what she is about can influence a man and he does not even realize it."

Did she warn him about Madame Peltier, or herself? "Who was that man you were sitting with?"

"One of the new arrivals. I came out for some air and he had as well."

"I was not introduced to him, as I was to the others."

"Perhaps he left before you were brought around."

Perhaps. Then again, maybe Marielle now lied. She did that sometimes. "You appeared distressed by whatever he was saying."

"Were you spying on me? I will not have it."

"I have been spying on you for over a year. Do not act shocked now, especially after —" *After I have come within a hairsbreadth of possessing you, damn it.* "You went through some effort to meet that man. It was no accident, but a rendezvous. Who is he? What did he say to make you distraught?"

Is he your lover? Your partner in crime? He wanted to know, badly. Too much. He hated to admit he would prefer the second explanation to the first, even if it confirmed his worst suspicions.

Her expression hardened. "He described the suffering he has known the last few years since his father's property was confiscated. The hunger and the humiliation and fear. Yes, I was distressed, as any person would be to hear such things. Up there they drink champagne to celebrate their deliverance, but they all know the life they once had is gone, perhaps forever, and they are paupers begging at England's door."

He had not seen sympathy, but real worry, and emotion that required a friend's embrace to contain. He would not argue with her now, however. To do so would make him more of an ass than he had already been. Kissing a woman a few times does not give a man the right to demand explanations, even if he battled a primal anger at seeing that woman in an intimate conversation with another man.

"My coach is here. I will take you back to your house."

"No, thank you. I am not inclined to be questioned and tested more today, and cannot risk that you will attempt to do so."

"It is not safe. You must take better care. You take the coach and I will walk."

"No, milord. Dominique and I will walk and enjoy the fair weather, and then work long into the night to make up for this afternoon's entertainment. Go back to Madame Peltier. She has all the time in the world to waste with men like you."

Marielle's mind raced. Dominique walked alongside.

"You might have accepted his offer of his coach, for my sake," Dominique muttered after half an hour.

"When you want to ride in a coach, we will hire one. We will not accept his gifts of any kind. It will only let him think he can intrude whenever he likes, in whatever he likes, as he did today." She screwed up her face to imitate Kendale's frown when he spoke on the terrace. "Who is he? What did he say?" She rolled her eyes. "I was right in how I named him the first time. What a stupid man."

Dominique trudged on, not happy. "He is not one to be put off, that is certain." She turned her head and looked back. "He has been following us all the while."

Marielle refused to look. How like Kendale to enforce his will. Her exasperation did not entirely conquer her relief that she would indeed be safe at least today.

"Nor is he so stupid," Dominique said, pausing by an iron fence to catch her breath. She was neither young nor slender, and she rarely walked this much. Marielle debated whether to hail the coach following them.

Dominique pushed away from the fence and walked on. "He saw well enough what he saw today. You are annoyed he was not stupid enough to believe you asked after a stranger's history and nothing more. He may have misunderstood the reasons, but he saw your sadness and worry."

Those words did not do justice to her reactions on that bench as Monsieur Marion gave her news of the region around Savenay.

"What am I to do? What? For all I know Lamberte is here in England if he has not

148

been seen in Savenay for two weeks and is known to not be in residence in the château."

"Monsieur Marion said it is rumored he went to Paris. That he is hoping for a position there, and has gone to make his case."

Had it come to that? Had Lamberte risen so far and so well that he might find himself in the government's inner circle? She did not think it was so simple. Monsieur Marion had revealed more than that, too.

"The images have affected him, he said. There have been questions. Suspicions."

"It is what you intended. You should be relieved."

"If he thinks he can rise further, he will want to make sure such accusations do not continue. He cannot afford for the ministers in Paris to investigate possible financial irregularities. If I were him, I would want to make sure my house were very clean before inviting such attention. I would do what I must to see that only the best parts of my record could be read."

"He can never be certain of that, after all he has done."

"He can perhaps if he tears out the bad parts of the record and burns them."

They walked in silence then. Marielle guessed that Dominique's thoughts went to the same place as hers. Lamberte had sent men to track the engravings back to their source and remove that problem. She could only hope that he had not realized that Marielle Lyon was the source of that dangerous nuisance.

"He said there has been no word of your father." Dominique reached over and squeezed Marielle's hand.

"It has become harder to execute without good cause. Harder to be a power that answers to no one, as he was during the chaos six years ago. To do that now might bring the wrong kind of attention to him." She hoped so. She prayed so.

"And, he knows I could be alive. He may have surmised that only his hold on Papa keeps me from denouncing him outright, and with more than satirical images." Her mind took her back to that alley, and to how close she had come to having long plans come to naught. It would be sadly ironic if Lamberte killed her without even knowing who it was that he killed. "Perhaps that is what I should do now."

"Do you think to go back?" Dominique shook her head. "No, no, no. Whom would you trust? To whom would you present your evidence? The government is busy fighting wars. No one will care about a crime from long ago. No one will listen and if they do, they will not believe you."

Marielle knew that. She had never alluded to the worst crimes in her engravings. With so many deaths, a few more became meaningless.

Instead the prints showed Lamberte stealing from the government. They would care about that, perhaps, if enough of those prints made their way to Paris.

Twilight had fallen by the time they turned onto their street. Footsore and tired, they both hobbled up the steps.

Before Marielle could open the door it flung open. Nicole the cook faced them, her eyes wide with fear and relief. She began crying.

"What is it?" Dominique demanded. When Nicole did not answer she gave the woman a shake.

"Thieves!" Nicole exclaimed when she caught a breath. "We have had thieves intrude while you were gone. I thank God I was below and heard nothing. Had I come up, I might have been killed."

"If you heard nothing, how do you know someone intruded?" Marielle asked.

"You will see, mam'selle. Such desecration — I may never sleep well again." She stood aside so Dominique and Marielle

151

could enter.

Sounds from the street pulled at Marielle's attention. Those of horse hooves clipping slowly on stones and of wheels crying as they stopped turning. She glanced back and saw Kendale's coach in the street. He sat near the window and looked out at her.

She turned away quickly. *Go away, go away, you stubborn, intruding man,* her mind urged. Her heart swelled with relief, however, when she heard the carriage door open.

"What has happened?" Kendale asked as he mounted the step to the blue door.

"The cook says we had housebreakers. Thieves." Marielle did not bar his entry, so he followed her over the threshold.

Evidence of the intrusion spread across the studio. Papers had been tossed haphazardly on the tables and floor. Marielle flushed and covered her eyes with her hand, then began gathering the prints into a stack. "We will have to go over each one most carefully, to see if there is damage."

"And if there is?"

"I must pay for them, of course." Her slender finger plucked more off the floor.

He bent and helped, trying to avoid being more harm than help. It took half an hour to pick them all up.

"Why were no women here working?" he asked.

"I chose to go to that party. Madame La-Tour can be my eyes here when I am gone, but she too attended. So we all took a little holiday." She smiled sourly at the workroom. "Such a cost for so little gain."

"Marielle," the old woman said from the doorway. She gestured for Marielle to follow her. Kendale tagged along.

A small chamber at the back of the house overlooked the garden. He peered out. There was not much property, and what they had was planted. Not flowers. No tulips here. The ground had been worked in rows. He guessed it would fill with greenery and vegetables in a few months.

The old woman pulled back a drapery to reveal a broken shutter and sash. A small pane of glass had been smashed too. Kendale pulled the window open. It was large enough for a man to enter.

"What did they take?" he asked.

"If you will wait here, we will go and see if anything of value is gone," Marielle said. Huddled close and whispering, they left him.

He sat on one of the chairs and took stock of this house. Although modest, it was larger

153

than many. Marielle's print coloring business probably paid the rents. Her industry provided a modicum of comfort at least, but he supposed it was a precarious existence. One unexpected problem, such as having to pay an engraver for prints one could never sell, might tip the balance.

He caught his own thoughts up short. How easily he was willing to worry for her, and forget that she probably had other income besides that from those prints. She may not have even signed the lease to this house, if it had been provided to her so that she had a home while she collected information. He would have to check to see whose name was on the paper.

Marielle returned alone and sank into another chair. "They were above. Our chambers are overturned. Mattresses, clothing, all over. However, we can find nothing gone."

"They were looking for something, from what you describe. Why else overturn a mattress?"

"To see if coin is hidden beneath it, of course."

"Do people really do that? Hide money beneath their mattresses, tied to the ropes?"

"Some do, although if I were a thief, I would look there first, so better places should be found."

"Where do you hide yours?"

She patted her hip. "Here. It is a benefit of being unfashionable. One can sew a pocket into these skirts." Her hand slipped between two folds and the fabric swallowed her arm almost to the elbow.

He wondered if that were the real reason she wore such styles now. Like the long shawls, those pockets allowed all kinds of things to be carried invisibly. "First men try to kill you. Now this. I do not think it is a coincidence."

"They are not related, except to show London has many thieves in it."

She smiled at him, putting on a brave face. He saw how concerned she was, however. That had never happened before with a woman. Females remained ciphers to him for which he possessed no solution. They all wore masks of one kind or another, playing this role or that on life's stage. They confounded him when he noticed them at all.

This one, however — for good or bad he had come to know her. Right now, he knew she was afraid.

"If you tell me what this is all about, perhaps I could help you."

He braced himself for mocking Marielle or self-possessed Marielle, and maybe he even hoped for seductress Marielle. Instead she looked at him so directly that he thought he could see right into her mind.

"That is kind," she said. "You have already helped me enough. I am alive, aren't I?"

"The men in the alley — they spoke French. I heard enough. Are your own people after you? If so, the Home Office will protect you if you cooperate with them."

"Do you mean if I turn? If I tell them all about the spies sent here, and what I know of France's intentions? They will make sure I am not harmed if I agree to this?"

"Yes."

She reached over and placed her hand on his. Her touch felt cool, too cool, and unbearably soft and fragile.

"Then it is a great pity that I am not a spy, and have nothing to sell in such a bargain." She stood. "I must push you out now. There is much to do above and I should not leave it all to Dominique and Nicole."

She walked him to the front door. He waited for the door to close behind him, then went to his coach and retrieved a pistol. He walked down two blocks, turned the corner, and circled back through the alleys and gardens behind the buildings on the other side of Marielle's lane.

He let himself into a building across the way and two doors down from hers. Up one level he knocked on a door.

A short, wiry, fair-haired man with gray eyes opened the door. "Milord!" He hurried inside to grab his coat and slip it on.

Kendale stepped in and inspected the bedsitting chamber that had been let a few days ago. Its occupant had carved areas for the bed at one end and a little library at the other. "Are you comfortable here, Mr. Pratt?"

"Fair enough, milord. I slip out to the tavern for food, or they will bring it if needs be. It is not so nice as Ravenswood Park, but better than a barracks, so I am content."

"Good. Today, did you remain on duty all day?"

"Of course, milord."

"Even after the lady left her home? Did you watch all afternoon?"

"Had to, didn't I? No way to know when she came back if I was not watching. Not to say I would have been derelict if there had been a way. You know me, sir. I obey orders."

Richard Pratt obeyed orders with singular diligence. If his commander told him to hold the crossroad and let no one pass alive, he would kill every man who approached. If told to watch that blue door, he would sit at

157

the window from dawn to midnight staring at it.

"Did you see anyone suspicious lurking around, Mr. Pratt? Anyone taking a particular interest in the house?"

Pratt thought hard, frowning. He shook his head. "Nah. Was very quiet. No visitors. No women coming. Course most of them don't go right up to that front door, do they? Too proud, I suppose. They enter that little portal in the alley between that house and the one beside it, and pretend they are just cutting through to the street behind. Not unusual for folks to do that. I expect those women then go into the house through the kitchen."

"Did anyone at all go into that alley and use the portal?"

"One man. Not too tall. Fat fellow. Dark hair. That is all I remember."

The man in the alley had been dark-haired and fat. Kendale placed the pistol on the table that served for eating and writing and whatever else Pratt might need it for. "I am going to leave this. Someone intruded there this afternoon. I need you to be extra vigilant now, and to watch for ne'er-do-wells who might be around. If you have cause for concern, send me a message. I will be sending Jacob to join you, so you can take turns and remain alert."

Pratt picked up the pistol and inspected it. "I'm trusting that if I use this, milord, that you will be explaining matters to the magistrate on my behalf."

"I do not think you will use it. But with today's event, I want to know you have it should it be needed." He set out some coin. "Once Jacob arrives, go out and buy powder and balls."

"I understand, sir. Just to be prepared in the unlikely case, as you said."

"Be sure to alert me to anything odd."

"Such as what, sir?"

Hell if he knew. Belligerent visitors. Men creeping along the roof. Marielle Lyon walking out with something hidden in her deep pockets and under her long shawl.

"Just use your judgment, Pratt, and let no harm come to the women in that house."

Marielle pushed her mattress back onto its ropes. She pulled the sheets into place and tucked them. Standing back, she examined her chamber. All had returned to its normal order now. Nothing showed of the violation of her home.

Whoever intruded had torn this space apart, emptying drawers and wardrobe, dumping the contents of an old trunk on the floor. He had even turned over her dressing table, as if he expected to find something of value tied beneath it. He had learned to his sorrow that no treasures hid in these bedchambers.

Which was not to say that none could be found in the house elsewhere.

Night had fallen. Dominique slept in the chamber next door, her soft snores sounding their familiar rhythm. Tomorrow would be a long day. Before the women arrived to work, the engravings had to be inspected to see which had damage and which could still be colored. Marielle did not look forward to calculating the cost of the ones she could not return to their printer.

The day had exhausted her and left her sore. Her bed beckoned, but she lifted the candelabra and left the chamber. She descended the stairs and moved through the silent house to the studio. Three times she froze, to listen to sounds that made terrible fear shoot through her blood. She had always felt safe in this house, but she no longer did. If they came once, they could come again.

She set the candelabra on the worktable closest to the paneled wall that flanked the long windows at the rear of the chamber. Feeling along the molding on the left panel, she found a metal hook. When she pressed it, the panel swung open to reveal a hidden cupboard.

They had lived in this house for three years before she accidentally found this hiding place while dusting. It was the sort of secret one expected to have in fine homes and châteaus, not in cottages hugging the London wall. The normal thief would never guess to look for it.

She set aside a box of burins and other tools that lay on a shelf, and a sack of jewelry waiting to go to Fairbourne's auction house. She grabbed the heavy sack of coin that she had painstakingly collected over the years. Its undiminished weight gave her heart.

Then she lifted out a stack of copper plates. The ones on top were unused and new and she set them aside. She laid out each of the others to make sure none had been taken.

Several depicted London views. Upon first casting about for some employment, she thought engraving pretty pictures would feed her. Even after adopting a fictitious male name, however, they had not sold enough to justify continuing. She still made them out of vanity, but often they did not sell well enough to be worth the cost of hiring the press to print them.

The others proved more lucrative. Satirical prints, they poked fun at the powerful and famous. Such images had helped bring down the monarchy in France. The people of London had an insatiable appetite for them too.

They did not display the careful technique of the views. She deliberately made them cruder, so no one would think the same hand had made them. The name on them — Citizen John — would never be thought the real name of the artist. They bore no address.

She lifted a special one, made not for London but for export. "Citoyen Jean" this time claimed credit and all the words were in French. In it a man sat on a throne composed of farmers and tradesmen who strained under his weight. A line of people placed coins on a table in front of him. With one hand he slid two coins into a strongbox labeled "taxes." With the other hand he pocketed every third coin. The words he spoke said, "One for Savenay, one for Paris, one for me."

Was this what the intruders today looked for? Either to take it, or to discover if she was responsible for its creation? Or had they merely been thieves who saw an empty house on a fair day, ready for the picking?

Most likely the latter. Kendale had a suspicious mind in general, and she should not give his judgment on such things too much weight.

And yet — She thought about the news she received today from Monsieur Marion. Lamberte had departed Savenay, presumably to visit Paris. He saw the chance to rise, and would want to cleanse any old stains on his reputation. He would not want the past to interfere with his ambitions now.

She turned to the cupboard once again, and felt along its side. High up her fingers touched a little interference. She clawed at it, and pulled a little book from where it hid behind the wooden framing.

Flipping its pages, she scanned the numbers and, at the back, the names. *Run, and take this to Papa. Tell him to use it to bring this bastard down.* She looked at the little book, then at the plates. Did Lamberte just assume that whoever made the images had seen this book that contained the proof of his thefts? In the least, perhaps he hoped so, and might get it back. He could not sleep well knowing it was somewhere, waiting to reveal everything.

She returned the book to its hiding place. She stacked the plates, and put them back in the cupboard. She could either sit here and wait for whatever might happen, or she could try to discover whether Lamberte had sent those men to that alley. She should determine whether he pursued her, either to stop a nuisance of an engraver, or to silence a witness to his crimes. Her own plans depended on it. She might not have the time to save the rest of the money she needed. If not, she wanted to know so she could find another way.

It was time to learn what she could, so she would not be a sitting goose.

CHAPTER 8

"I am curious about something," Kendale said. He rode beside Ambury in Hyde Park, and had allowed some time to pass before casually broaching his subject. "You are probably the best person to consult."

"It is rare of you to flatter me, or anyone," Ambury said. "Your curiosity must be intense."

"Not at all. It is a passing question that came to me as I watched those women back there gossiping."

"They may have only been chatting. The subject could have been art or literature, not gossip."

"The way they whispered and laughed after another woman passed indicated otherwise."

"You do have a talent for noticing the least favorable sides of people. What question did this inspire in you?"

Kendale hoped he appeared nonchalant.

"If a man has intimate relations with an innocent, he is a scoundrel and honor requires him to redeem himself and the female with marriage. And if a man has relations with a whore, he is guilty only of a sin that none take too seriously and he owes the female nothing but the price agreed to. What, however, are the expectations if he has relations with a woman who is not an innocent but also not a whore?"

"A fallen woman?"

"An experienced woman."

"Like a widow, you mean."

A nod seemed the best response, even if the widow status did not fit, to his awareness at least.

"Is there a particular reason that you are asking me this question?" Ambury's voice and face hardened. "If you are in any way alluding to my wife, you risk our friendship. I know of the talk about her and I know you believed all of it, but I'll be damned if
—"

"Hell, it has nothing to do with that. Are conversations about women now impossible because you will see insult around every corner?"

"You have never invited conversations about women, Kendale, so this one is very peculiar to me. I must conclude that Madame Peltier impressed you more than I expected. I even warned her off, lest she cast covetous eyes on you. I know how that annoys you."

"Madame Peltier is looking for a husband, I think, not a liaison."

"Let us say that she anticipates one day having a liaison that turns into a marriage. That is not uncommon in the situation you described. However, if the arrangement is clear and such expectations firmly discouraged, it is not required of a gentleman to wed an experienced woman should there be — how did you put it — intimate relations. I suggest with Madame Peltier that you clarify that before embarking on an affair, however. Make sure that she understands at the outset. No, *before* the outset."

"Did you?"

"I did."

Kendale wondered how Ambury had raised such a delicate point with the woman, especially before having true cause to do so. He could think of no words appropriate to opening such negotiations. Did he just come out and say, *Madame, I want to share your bed and enjoy your favors, but I must be sure you understand that afterward there will be no marriage?*

And Ambury accused *him* of being hard

and coarse.

"I also made clear that I would be generous in other ways," Ambury said, warming to the lesson. "That is also customary."

"How generous?"

"You cannot be serious. Even you are not so ignorant."

"Only on the nuances. I have seen men driven to ruin from being generous to women. I am trying to determine how much less would suffice."

"With Madame Peltier, I would think expensive but not ruinous jewels are required. A few gowns. The occasional delicacy for her table. The use of a coach would ensure a longer liaison than I enjoyed."

"Ah. I see. She threw you over for being *un*generous."

"No. I threw her over for thinking she might get a wedding after all. She is not for you, Kendale. Truly. I am delighted you are showing interest. However, you are not equipped for such as she. To start you should find some quiet, modest woman who is not too jaded and who does not have memories of the grand life of Paris in her head. Madame Peltier should not be engaged by anyone but a general, and in this war you are a raw recruit."

Since he had no interest in Madame

Peltier, he would not lose a single battle to her. Unfortunately, on his own, for all his words, Ambury had not told him what he really wanted to know.

"In such an arrangement, what else is owed? Loyalty? Constancy?" He tried to sound very casual indeed.

It did not work. Ambury stopped his horse, turned in his saddle and scrutinized his face. "I should have known these were not idle questions. There is someone, isn't there? And it is not the woman in question."

Kendale tried to demur. Ambury would have none of it.

"Who? I demand to know. I won't tell anyone. Not even Southwaite, who would only lecture you on discretion and not contribute anything useful, the way I have."

Kendale moved his horse forward. "You are boring me. I can ask a simple question without having you leap to stupid conclusions, I hope."

Ambury paced on too, then stopped again. "The Lyon woman?"

"Who?"

"Is it Marielle Lyon? Madame Peltier would move in similar circles. You might have recently met her in your quest to meet French émigrés. Miss Lyon is quite lovely.

Perhaps lovely enough even to get you to notice."

"She is French."

Ambury smiled. "All the better. And she is one of the good French."

"You are mistaken. I have no designs on her, or anyone else."

"That is disheartening. However, you did want to meet her, as I remember. Say! Let us ride to Albemarle Street, and I can introduce you. I just remembered that this afternoon she will be at Fairbourne's. Cassandra mentioned in passing that Miss Lyon will be bringing in a consignment of jewelry. Cassandra will be joining them to help Emma appraise its value."

Fairbourne's auction house graced Albemarle Street with its stone façade and heavy oak door. Here Emma Fairbourne continued the business begun by her father. The world thought her brother the mind behind the business's success, but Kendale had seen and heard enough to know that Emma, now the Countess Southwaite, gave so much advice that the true captain of the ship had become at best ambiguous.

He was the last person to criticize Southwaite for permitting this secret vocation. Emma Fairbourne had been born to this trade and felt estranged from her own life and person without it. Why shouldn't she exercise her God-given abilities the way nature intended? He knew what it was like when that happened, and how nothing really filled that void.

He expected she avoided gossip about it by never publicly taking the role she played. At the auctions last fall her brother oversaw everything, while she attended only as a potential patron on her husband's arm. Today he saw the other reasons why she could maintain such discretion. An auction house was not like a typical shop. It only opened to the public when an auction loomed. Otherwise no one entered. Even if they did, they would have to seek out the private office in order to witness Emma at work.

That is where Ambury took him, their bootsteps echoing in the empty exhibition hall. They found Emma and Cassandra in the office, head-to-head, examining a small cache of jewelry and debating values.

Cassandra looked up. "Ambury, what a surprise." Her blue eyes sparked with happiness at the sight of her husband. The lights dimmed considerably when she greeted Kendale in turn.

Ambury looked down at the jewels on the

desk. "Did Marielle bring these? Has she already gone?"

Emma swept her hand in a gesture over the glittering objects. "She arrived with them at my home last night. It was most peculiar. I did not mind, but after arranging last week for her to come here today, it seemed a mysterious thing to do."

"Most irregular," Ambury said.

"That is Marielle however," Cassandra said with a laugh. "She works very hard at it, I think. Being mysterious."

"Surely she gave an explanation for intruding so late and unexpectedly," Kendale said. "I do not know our French guests well, but I have never heard them described as deliberately rude."

"She said that due to an unexpected meeting elsewhere, she could not come today and wanted me to have these now."

Kendale lifted one of the earrings. If Marielle had arranged last week to deliver these, she had them two days ago when intruders entered her house. She must have had them very well hidden if they were not taken. Perhaps she kept them on her person.

"Did Marielle mention where she was going for this meeting?" he asked while he judged whether a bag with these jewels would fit in deep pockets.

Silence pulled his attention away from the desk surface. Three pairs of eyes looked at him with curiosity. He realized he had spoken of her with intimate familiarity. He attempted to appear merely curious himself. "To intrude on an earl's household at night — the reason would have to be very important for the niece of a comte to do that."

"I thought so too," Emma said. "It worried me and she appeared very distracted and that worried me more. I asked if I could be of any assistance to her but Marielle is not one to confide or to request help. She only said that she had to leave early in the morning. It sounded like she intended a journey of some kind."

That was not what he wanted to hear. She had been attacked and her home ransacked, and now she had probably left London. For good? He had asked if her own people might be after her. All it would take was one enemy denouncing her to the right ear and that could happen.

"She is probably only visiting some friends," Cassandra soothed.

"Perhaps, but seeing her last night was too odd. Lord Kendale thinks so too, so I am not being dramatic."

"Ambury, have you learned or heard anything to suggest she is . . . in trouble,"

Cassandra asked. "What with the stupid rumors about her, perhaps some fool in the government decided to threaten her and she has run away out of fear."

There were times when being a man not known for conversation had its benefits. This was such a time. Since he might be the fool in question, he did nothing to draw attention to himself.

"I have heard nothing," Ambury said. "I will ask and see what I can learn, however, if it will relieve your concern."

"Please do," Emma said. "I will talk to Darius and have him quiz a few men as well."

"If you learn the names of the knaves, please tell me first," Cassandra said. "When I think of the kindness and help she showed my aunt, I want to have first go at anyone who drove her out of London."

Kendale doubted that Cassandra would care much that in truth he had tried to obligate Marielle to remain in London. If she learned of his recent involvement in Marielle's life, she would blame him for frightening her away.

He took his leave of them all and went out to his horse. While he rode to the City, and the remnants of its north wall, he assessed if he had healed well enough for a night in the saddle.

If Marielle had left London, he thought he knew the direction she would take. She was heading east or south, to the coast. It should not be hard to learn which. He would ask at the coaching inns that served those routes. If Marielle Lyon had paid a fare and boarded a stagecoach, she would be remembered by any man who witnessed it.

CHAPTER 9

Marielle knew only one person in Dover. After a teeth-chattering ride that took forever, she stretched herself in the yard of the coaching inn and debated how to find him.

She did not like to visit the eastern coast. She did not care for the damp of it, nor the mix of people in the towns. Dover in particular always seemed gray to her, and its houses appeared bitten by the sea. Too many men loitered about, many of them sailors waiting for a ship.

Fewer could be seen this time. The press gangs must have come through recently. A smart sailor made himself scarce when unemployed, else he might find himself serving His Majesty under conditions little better than that of a galley slave. Thus did England remain a power at sea. Of course, with conscription into the army allowed now, France was no better.

She walked to the shop she sought, trying to battle the emotions provoked by these streets. Mostly she disliked Dover because it was the first English town she set foot in after climbing off a longboat up the coast some miles. Her first knowledge of Dover had been full of fear and exhaustion and the kind of cold that only wet shoes in winter can create. She had been past gratitude for being alive by then, and devoid of the alertness that comes when death tracks you. Numb and alone and sick at heart, she had lagged behind the others and found a doorway where she sat down and cried.

Dominique, who had been on the same boat, had noticed and taken pity on her. It had been the first kindness anyone had shown her in over a month. She felt that motherly arm around her now, as if Dominique once more walked beside her, helping her take the steps to safety.

There was no Dominique with her now, however. After the intrusion on the house, they dared not risk another by having only Nicole be there at night. She hoped the intruders did not come back while she was gone. It would be self-defense when Dominique killed them, but that would not avoid the attention and disruption of a magistrate's inquiry.

She found the stationer's shop that she sought. The proprietor recognized her at once. He returned to his patron while she stood back and pretended interest in his fancy papers. When the patron left, the shop owner barred the door so there could be no unexpected interruptions.

"It has been a long time," he said. "Over a year."

Had it really been that long? She had perhaps been negligent in her duties, and lacked constancy in her goals. The life she had built distracted her with its many details. She had become Marielle Lyon, French refugee, perhaps too thoroughly.

"Éduard and Luc did not meet me as planned last time, Monsieur Farmen," she said. "So I have brought my things to you to pass on to the men with the boat." She set down a roll of prints that she had carried with her. Not a fat roll, like the one she lost in the alley. Even paying the printer for the use of his press all night, she had only been able to make a dozen good impressions.

Monsieur Farmen looked out his window, as if checking to make sure no one peeked in. "I'll see they get it. You have the coin for them?"

She set down over four shillings. They

would sell the prints in France to a book-seller or print shop, and make more money yet. The smugglers did well for their efforts, but they also took the risks.

"Do you know where I can find Éduard or Luc? I want to know if they have chosen not to come to London in the future. If so, I must find others."

"I do not think they will be doing this anymore. I think — I do not know for certain, but I think they are dead." He watched her carefully. Perhaps he thought she would swoon. "There's two men laid out in that French tailor's house — Lebois is his name. He took them, since no one knew their families. That is what I heard at least. Also that one is named Éduard. I think it is our Éduard, see."

"You have not gone to check?"

"Would be odd if I did. How do I explain it? Say I have come to pay my respects to a man I hired to transport goods to and from smugglers up the coast?"

"You could say you had become friends with him, and shared some ale at times at the tavern. No one will question you, least of all a tailor who is not his family."

"Best if that is not commonly known that we had a friendship or business together, I think. Others probably know what he was

179

up to. And there is more to it that says best to stay away."

"Where is this tailor? I will go and see if it is the Éduard we knew. I will say . . . something. I will be one more French-woman with whom he flirted if necessary."

"Best you stay away too. See, like I said, there is more. It was no accident, how these two died. They were knifed up, and beaten badly I hear. Maybe they helped themselves to someone's goods and he came looking for them. Anyway, you stay away if you are smart. I'll be finding others to take their place. English this time, I think. Safer. Three weeks from now you go to the meeting as you used to, and they will be there."

He appeared resolute. He would be no help. Marielle left, still carrying her prints and her shillings. She would find this tailor on her own. Then she would find the smug-glers too. She would not go back to London and wait three weeks. If Éduard and Luc had been killed, she might not have that long.

Kendale swung off his horse in front of the tailor's shop. Beechem the magistrate did the same.

"He has them in a shed in the back. Wants them out soon, though. No one claimed them, and they are getting very ripe," Beechem said. "We'll be planting them today, so it was fortuitous you came now."

Kendale had not come for this. However, as long as he made the ride to the coast, he had called on the magistrate to learn about these murders that had been reported by their watchers. He would look, find nothing, and carry on with his real mission.

The tailor greeted them in the shop. A short, slightly built man with an unexpected mustache, he did not hide his disappointment that the bell had been rung by Beechem instead of a patron looking for a coat.

Beechem explained that the bodies would be gone in a few hours. The tailor appeared relieved.

"Did anyone come to pay their respects?" Kendale asked.

"A few the first days. Then nothing until one of the bigger man's cousins asked after him. Seems his name was Éduard Villon. She thinks the smaller one's name was Luc, but she did not know his surname."

"Éduard Villon. Well, that is something," Beechem said. "Why did it take her so long to come here?"

"She said she lives west of here, and only learned of these deaths several days ago.

Her cousin had gone missing, so she thought to come and see if he was here." The tailor shook his head. "Pretty lady. So sad she was when she saw him. Despite the smell she stayed in there a half hour. I left her to her grief. Eventually she came out and sat outside for a long while. Many hours." He shrugged. "Perhaps she knew those others would come, and waited for them."

"Others?" Beechem asked, suddenly interested. "Other relatives?"

"I do not think so. They were English and these two here — well, from their garments they were French, and some on this lane had seen them about and heard them speak, so . . ."

"Did these men go inside the shed?" Kendale asked.

"*Oui.* A moment only. It is foul inside, of course, and —"

"Did she speak with them?"

"I do not know. Perhaps. I think so. The men did not leave the garden at once."

"But she did soon after them?"

"It was getting dark."

"Describe these men," Beechem said.

"No, describe the woman," Kendale interrupted.

The tailor described both. His memory of

the woman far exceeded that of the men. The latter had been rough, with the appearance of laborers, and of no interest. The woman, however, had been pretty enough to be memorable down to the shape of her nose.

Medium height, very slender, golden brown hair down around her shoulders, elegant fingers and face, and a long, old, patterned silk shawl that hung to her knees — the tailor all but glowed as he painted a picture of Marielle Lyon.

"So sad she was," he said again. "So sad and pretty as she sat in that garden, so still, as if lost in her memories of her dear cousin."

Cousin, hell.

"Wish he had noticed more about those chaps who came by," Beechem said after they left the shop. "Sounds a bit like West and Garrett, but not so close as to be able to do much with it. They do a bit of smuggling, and I'm thinking they were wondering what happened to their runners who bring it inland. The two rotting corpses in there were known here in Dover, sounds like, but did not seem to have ties to this town, so they may have been in the employ of West and Garrett, seems to me."

With no one to swear down information,

least of all the pretty cousin, there was nothing Beechem would do with his suspicions, Kendale knew. If anything the disruption of a smuggling ring would be welcomed by the authorities, even if it were brief and two men got murdered in the process.

As for the mourning cousin . . .

"Where would I find West or Garrett?" Kendale asked. "Since I am not an official, I can ask questions that you cannot."

Marielle wished Monsieur Garrett would hurry up. He took forever to tie his horse. He walked slowly down the quiet lane with a loose but tired gait. A wiry man with sandy hair, he still had a bit of youth in him that showed in the way he moved his body.

She waited for him in front of a weathered house covered in graying whitewash at the southern edges of Dover's outskirts. He noticed her and stopped while he examined her, his body suddenly tight and alert. Then recognition unwound him again and he walked on with a big, flirtatious smile.

"You don't take your time," he said. "I said I'd be here today, but you arrived first. You must be very eager to see me." His thick eyebrows wiggled with insinuation while he opened the door. "Have you been waiting since sunrise?"

184

"I have not been here long. Let us talk out here." She would be stupid to enter this house alone with a man she knew to be a criminal, especially one with such a hungry look in his blue eyes. "I need to know this will get to the boat." She slid her shawl away to reveal the roll of prints.

"More of those, eh? I looked once. Seems to be an odd thing to pay to get into France. But maybe there are secrets in 'em that I can't see."

"Would it matter to you if there were?"

"Not to me. To some, perhaps. This ain't my war, and it is bad for trade, is how I see it." He reached for the roll. "Tomorrow it will be on the boat."

"You need to bring it to its destination. They will not know to meet you this time."

"Well, now, that makes it more danger-ous, don't it? I'm not fond of staying there overlong. Will cost you."

"I will pay. If you put in north of Granville, the bookseller is only a few blocks away at the end of the main lane." She gave him the shop's location and name.

"I'll not be walking even a few blocks until night."

"He will not care if you rouse him at night." At least she hoped not. She dug into her pocket and withdrew six shillings. "This is twice what I would pay Éduard and Luc, and they in turn kept much of it before paying you, so it should be more than enough."

Garrett laughed while he took the coins and prints. "Must be some secrets after all, if you pay that much not to mention the cost of the journey here."

"I am paying for more than your transporting those papers. I also want information."

He leaned against the door frame, curious and cautious. "Men in my trade don't last long if they talk too much."

"I do not care about your trade, or about who helps you. I seek other information. Do you know who did that to Éduard and Luc?"

He shook his head. "I've a mind to return the favor if I find out. They had their uses and could be trusted. Not easy to find honest men. I felt real bad when I saw what is left of them and knew it was them for sure."

"Did you ever see two other Frenchmen with them? One fat and dark haired and the other tall and lean."

"Not with them, but I may have seen the ones you mean. A few weeks ago a French boat came over with some of those fancy types. We keep an eye on those. Don't want it to become a habit on our coast and don't want 'em taking goods back and stealing our trade, do we? Those two were with them, as I remember. Not so fancy as the others, so they stuck out."

"Were they alone, or with another man?" She tried to keep the desperate worry out of her voice. "Maybe a fancy one."

She held her breath while she waited for his reply.

"Nah. We watched them get out and walk up the beach. Those two were alone then. Not talking to others, or even walking alongside another man."

A heaviness lifted off her heart. It was not proof that Lamberte had not come to England, but it was enough to allow hope that he had not.

"I wonder if —" She sought the right words for her next query. "The fancy man I speak of may have come before or after. He is noticeable. Taller than most, with thick dark hair." She tried to picture Lamberte now, years after she had last seen him. Had he thickened? Had he cropped his hair? "He is very fond of wearing coats with a military cut. He might have a beard, but well groomed in its shape and length. Have you seen such a man on other boats, or in any villages or taverns?"

"Nah." He wiggled those eyebrows again.

"If I do, should I let him know that you seek him?"

"No." She said it too forcefully. Garrett raised his eyebrows. "I would like to know if you see him, however. I will pay well for the information."

He looked at her differently, as if she presented some risk he had not realized before. "If I see him, I'll send word with whoever comes to get your next roll of images. We should have the net repaired by the next time that is due."

"Three weeks. Monsieur Farmen said you were going to use English in the future."

"We use who we can trust. Those two weren't killed on our account, that I know. There should be no danger for any others." He began to open his door, but stopped. He held up the prints. "You give your word there are no secrets in these?"

"No secrets. They are only what they appear to be."

"I hope so. 'Cause someone beat those two good, for a reason, probably for information. I'd not like to think I am helping a spy with these."

"I am not a spy. Do I look like one?"

He laughed. "You look like a woman who is pretty enough to have me doing something my gut says I shouldn't." With a little wave of the roll of prints, he crossed his threshold.

Kendale watched Marielle speak earnestly to the man outside the house. That would be Garrett, whom Beechem said lived here when he wasn't on a galley crossing the channel. Fortune had led Kendale to seek out this man instead of the other. He had remained in this alley since noticing Marielle waiting in front of the door.

Their conversation ended. Marielle took a step away from the door and man. Garrett laughed and gestured farewell with the roll of papers in his hand. The door closed on him.

Marielle walked only a few steps before stopping. She stood still, lost in thought, her shawl wrapped close to her body beneath her crossed arms.

He wished he had seen those papers better. Had it been another roll of prints? He could not be sure they contained nothing suspicious, of course, but at least then it would not be maps or letters or the sort of information that a spy might send across the water.

Worse, she had paid Garrett, not the other way around. That implied nothing of value to Garrett had changed hands. She was not a source for goods he smuggled. Garrett was a packhorse who carried what she required.

The evidence against Marielle had just ceased to be ambiguous.

He should inform Beechem at least. He should really alert the Home Office. One of their agents monitored affairs right here in Dover. If he described what he had just seen, both Marielle and Garrett would be in gaol being questioned within an hour.

He had always known what she was. He had not spent a year without good cause proving it. Now he had as much proof as was needed to have her arrested. This was one duplicitous Frenchwoman who would not ply her lies and deceptions. He had won.

He felt no triumph. Seeing her at Garrett's house had sickened him. Watching the exchange of money and documents dulled his mind and wit, rather than sharpened it. Now he watched her standing on a deserted street, out of sight of Garrett's house, looking so alone. She appeared a person who did not know where to go now. She looked lost and very frail.

Images forced themselves into his head, of what was done sometimes to encourage spies to talk. He did not know if they violated women the same way. Probably so, if necessary. His mind recoiled from picturing Marielle subjected to those pains. There was no point in contemplating it overmuch. Such things happened in war, along with so much else that debased humanity.

She moved finally. She came alive and strode on with a determined expression. He moved too.

He wished she had not come here. He wished he had not followed. He would have liked many things about the last weeks to have been different. They were what they were, however, and it had all led to this lane and this day. Now his duty was clear, and he could not pretend it was not.

While she walked back into Dover, Marielle listed the things she must do.

Garrett had not seen Lamberte, as best she could determine. She would go to that tailor and ask him as well. Then she would find a way to meet others who lived on the streets where the French congregated, and quiz them. As long as she had come all this way, she would use the inconvenience to her benefit.

Even if no one had seen Lamberte in England — and she prayed not — some of them might know more of his recent actions and movements in France. A lot of gossip made its way over the water, as if it traveled on the wind.

Then she would return to London. Three weeks, both Farmen and Garrett had said. The schedule of handoffs would resume then, on the day used before, in the same alley. She would prefer not to go there again, after what had happened. Once she returned home she would write to Monsieur Farmen and give him another meeting place.

She had time to make more prints. A new image was in order now. She would make it quickly, and arrange to hire out the press at night.

Having plans always gave her heart. How much better than being Lamberte's victim, and being paralyzed by fear. She had outsmarted him once, when only a child. She would do so again, as often as necessary.

Knowing some relief, and even a bit of joy, she smiled to herself as she turned a corner.

Abruptly she could move no more. Not one step. She almost bumped right into a wall of blue superfine and white linen. She looked up into green eyes on fire with righteous fury.

She did not have to ask why he was here. She did not think much at all. He had followed somehow. He had just seen her with

Garrett. He thought he knew everything and he now had the proof he had long sought.

It had been a mistake to forget who he was. *What* he was, and why he pursued her.

"Lord Kendale! Such a coincidence to see you here in Dover." She tried a flirtatious smile. It did not soften his expression one bit.

She pivoted and started to run. He was upon her at once, his arms closing around her body like iron clamps. He lifted her up and the lane moved past her eyes while he carried her away.

Squirm though she might, she could not break his hold. She kicked the legs behind her, but he seemed not to care. She managed one scream but then his hand sealed her mouth. She saw his coach waiting down the lane and bucked and squirmed more.

His coachman held the door open as calmly as if Lord Kendale dragged unwilling women into his carriage all the time. Kendale threw her in and slammed the door shut. She scrambled up from the floor, sat on the bench, and glared at his face on the other side of the window.

"Coward," she spit while she righted herself.

"Do not try to get out," he warned.

"Cochon."

"If you do, I will tie you up."

"Imbecile!"

"Give me no trouble and you will not be hurt, I promise."

Her head wanted to burst. "And when you hand me to them? Will you stay and watch, to be sure your word is kept?" She turned her head so he would not have the satisfaction of seeing that she wept. *"Go away,* Stupid Man. Do not try to ride in here with me. I will tear your eyes out if I have the chance."

CHAPTER 10

Lord Kendale was not taking her to London. She realized that when in the morning they made a stop at a coaching inn south of the city. It was not one her coach had used on its way to the coast. They were taking another route that circled around through the countryside.

He rode his horse alongside. She could see him out there, his back straight and his command of his animal complete. He did not look in the carriage window. Not once. Silent and stern, he transported her like a criminal.

He waited outside the necessary when she used it. He brought her food and waited while she ate it. He did not let her out of his sight, but he refused to acknowledge she existed as anything more than baggage that happened to possess human needs.

"You must promise to let Dominique know what has happened," she said when they stopped again near midday. "She will worry. She may as well worry about the truth than whatever her imagination creates."

He did not even nod. He merely took the crockery on which he had brought some stew and bread, and turned away.

She spent the rest of the day wondering what she would say to her inquisitors once they arrived at whatever prison he took her to. It would be someplace obscure, no doubt. Far from a village or farms, so that its prisoners would be lost should they ever escape.

Perhaps she would explain it all and tell them the truth. Would anyone believe her? She sifted through her story, deciding what could be proven, if anything.

The coach-and-four moved at a good speed. The land sped past. In such a conveyance, with such an escort, she might have been a princess, not a prisoner suspected of a crime punishable by death.

Another stop came in the middle of the night. The coachman changed the horses. This time Kendale climbed into the coach after she entered. He sat across from her and said not a word. She noticed that he favored his side while he settled in.

"Is your wound hurting you?"

"It is rebelling at so much riding. Go to sleep. I will not bother you."

She had not thought he would bother her, or bother with her. "I should have remembered your wound and let you ride in here."

"Your preference had nothing to do with it. I chose not to ride with you. Now, go to sleep, Marielle."

Be silent. Do not speak to me. Do not make me aware of you. He acted as if she had betrayed him. As if he had a reason to be wounded in other ways, and disappointed in her. She could not imagine why.

She did sleep, however. When she burst back to consciousness the sun shone overhead and tree branches formed a bower outside the window. Lord Kendale no longer sat in the coach.

She peered outside and saw him standing amid five dogs and three men. The dogs all looked at him like he was a god visiting earth. The men all looked at the carriage.

Past them the lane ended in a wide drive and circle. A very large house loomed beyond that. Its broken roofline said it had grown over the years. She judged it to be very old. It reminded her a little bit of the châteaus in France.

Kendale noticed the men were distracted from whatever he told them. He turned and saw her at the coach window. He walked over with his canine entourage and opened the door. Dog noses poked in at her, sniffing. He ordered the hounds away and they obediently trotted off.

He offered his hand so she could step down.

"Where are we?"

"This is Ravenswood Park. It is my family estate. I brought you here while I decide what to do with you."

"And where is Ravenswood Park?"

"Too far from anywhere else for you to run away. Come with me now. We will try to make you comfortable."

She followed him to the house. The dogs followed her. The three men followed the dogs. She examined the façade of the big house as they approached.

As prisons went, she could do much worse.

"Where should we put her, sir?" Angus posed the query while he tried to act as valet. Mr. Pottsward would not be down until tomorrow, and they had to make do.

The problem was young, fair Angus was not a valet. He was a Scot swordsman of great talent who knew how to use his height and breadth to advantage. He possessed a good deal of intelligence but, when it came to women, no more understanding than his master. Kendale liked him a lot.

"For now just choose a chamber on this level, so she is not bothered by the noise you fellows make up above and down below. There must be one that is suitable," he said while he stripped off his upper garments.

Angus poured the warmed water into the bowl. "There's those that are clean enough, I guess, if that makes one suitable."

"Then stick her in one. When Mr. Pottsward gets here he will reorder matters if that is necessary."

Angus picked up the razor and sharpened it on the stone. "Who is to do for her? There's no women here. I suppose Old Pete can —"

"Hell if I know who is to do for her. Tell her to do for herself until we find some woman to bring here. I do for myself often enough." To make his point, he took the razor from Angus and bent close to the looking glass.

Marielle had turned the household on its head without saying a word. It had been a mistake to bring her here. He only had come because as they approached London he admitted he could not give her into the hands of the sort who dealt with spies. Men died at those hands sometimes.

He could hardly bring her to his chambers in London either. Nor would his honor allow him to let her move freely after what he had seen. So here she was, until he sorted out his thoughts and finally, at last, had that long due conversation with her.

And if after that he concluded the worst was true of her, then . . .

He scraped away the hard stubble of beard. Angus stood there like he assumed a valet would, holding a cloth at the ready. Out of the corner of his eye Kendale noted Angus's frown.

"What is it?" he asked while the blade skimmed his neck.

"Nothing. Not really. Just, we all could not but notice that . . . she is French, from the sounds of her, such as we heard when she spoke out on the drive. Not too French, but French."

"What do you mean, not too French? One either is or is not."

"She is understandable, not like some of them who talk through the back of their noses. Incomprehensible they are."

"The way you are incomprehensible with your thick brogue?"

Angus flushed. "Not the same at all. I am a Scot. She is French."

"Just not too French."

Angus nodded. "Like she has worked hard to sound more normal to us. I expect with time one could even forget she was French, that accent is subtle enough."

He set down the razor, took the cloth, and wiped off the soap. "One could, but I would not. I never forget the French are the French. If you are worried she will learn something about our mission and word will get out to other French guests, or back to —"

"No. Of course not, sir. Not a man here will reveal anything, and there is nothing much for her to see that is telling. Just she has worked very hard at it, though, the way she talks not too French. I tried once to talk not too Scot, and my brain would never accept the oddness of it."

"Get me some fresh water. I need to wash."

"Have some right here still." Angus dealt with the dirty shaving water in a manner no valet would approve. He carried the bowl over to the window and tossed the contents out. "I expect she will be wanting to wash too. Or bathe. Should I tell the others to start heating water to carry up to her?" He poured clean water into the bowl.

An image invaded, of a naked Marielle

stepping into a metal tub set in front of a fire. Pale, soft, and lithe, she balanced on one foot while the other tested the heat of the water before settling in it. She bent to hold the edge while swinging the other leg in, and her hair fell forward, revealing the elegant and erotic lines of her back and bottom.

He shook the fantasy away and picked up the soap to wash away the journey's dust. "Put old Pete in charge, as you suggested. Tell him to show her to that chamber with the blue bedclothes. Tell him to offer her water to bathe and to follow her instructions on the rest. Then tell the cook to make a decent dinner tonight."

Angus nodded, and walked to the door. "It will be odd, having a woman here."

"Don't worry, it will not be for long."

Angus looked back and smiled. "I didna say it would be odd in a bad way, sir."

There were no women in this house. Not a one.

Marielle realized that when an ancient man who introduced himself as Old Pete came to her and escorted her up the stairs. Small wonder she had waited so long to be shown her prison. All of these men had probably spent an hour discussing how to manage her intrusion.

In the chamber Old Pete chose, he set about rolling a tub out of a dressing room. "My lord said to bring you water to bathe. It will be some time to heat it. He said you would not mind doing for yourself after that."

"If there are no women servants, of course I will do for myself."

He grinned, revealing three missing teeth. "My lord finds women a nuisance. When he came back he pensioned off the ones still here. The last was sent away a few months ago. Seems that housekeeper kept telling him what to do and not do, and his mother's lady's maid kept complaining about us who he brought in to serve him, so he just paid them all off one by one. There's a few women on the estate, of course. Wives of farmers and milkmaids and such."

"It is generous of him to allow them to remain, and not insist all his tenants live the monastic life he has chosen."

"Monastic?" Old Pete appeared startled, then laughed. "Oh, I see. You've a wit about you. We're none of us monks, miss. 'Tis more a barracks than a monastery."

In their essential characteristics, she could not see much difference. Except, perhaps, monks — the good ones at least — did not have any knowledge of women of the carnal kind. Soldiers, on the other hand . . .

Perhaps periodically they imported bawds so these soldiers could sate themselves, to better concentrate on their duties afterward.

After Old Pete left, she examined her quarters. She began with the window, to see just how hard it would be to leave. Very hard. She overlooked a hill, and any descent from this window would be a straight drop that could hurt her badly. She would have to find another way. She could not remain here long, that was certain.

The rest of the chamber appeared comfortable. Very much so. Much larger and better appointed than her own in London, it held good furniture and hangings. The bed felt almost new and unused and very soft. Although she resented that Kendale had abducted her, she had to admit some gratitude that she would not be sleeping on straw in some dungeon tonight. This house probably had one, if he decided he needed it.

The water arrived by way of a parade of men carrying steaming buckets. Quite an assortment they presented as each in turn poured, bowed, and left. Except for Old Pete they all had a physicality that reminded her of Kendale himself. This was indeed a barracks of sorts from the look of them.

She held Old Pete back after the others departed. "Will I be eating here?"

"I don't know."

"If not, if I am to go below and eat with Lord Kendale, please make sure I am told an hour before I must go down."

"My lord said we was to do what you want, and if you want to be called an hour before, that is how it will be."

She bolted the door behind him, then began shedding her garments, eager to submerge herself in that hot water. It would be heavenly. Delicious. And tonight she would sleep in that soft bed with its expensive sheets and linens.

With a prison like this, a woman might be tempted to never let Lord Kendale set her free.

After the manner Kendale had adopted on the journey to this house, Marielle expected she would in fact be eating in her chamber. She even moved a little table near the window in preparation for the tray that would arrive.

Instead Old Pete came to tell her that his lord expected her below in an hour. At the appointed time she draped her shawl around her and walked down the stairs. She wished he had not chosen to dine this way. If he remained stern and aloof, it would be a poor hour or two. On the other hand, if he chose to talk, she doubted she would want to hear what he would likely say.

He already sat in the dining room when she entered. He rose until she was seated across from him. It was a wide table. The distance between them spanned considerably more than that day in his chambers. She wondered if he thought about that when he gazed across at her. How formal this was in comparison too. The lord sat in his castle now, and one could not mistake his power.

"Old Pete said you told them to do what I wanted done," she said after they had the soup. "I want them to bring me back to London."

"They will accommodate your wishes *here*."

"Then I am telling you, not them. I want to return to London."

"You may instruct them. Not me."

His tone brooked no argument. She gave none while they ate some fish served by a strapping young man with fair hair. He looked like he should be wielding a battle ax and his coats should be replaced by animal skins. What a very peculiar household.

"I have nothing with me," she said after a long silence. "Not even a comb. All that I brought with me to Dover was left at the inn where I stayed when you kidnapped me."

The young footman glanced sharply at Kendale. Kendale gestured for the young man to leave. When he was gone, her host settled his attention on her fully. "Do not accuse me of kidnapping in front of my people."

"What should I call it instead?"

"Arresting."

That took her aback. "You have arrested me? On what authority?"

"On the authority of being a British citizen, a member of the House of Lords, and a confidante and ally of all of the Home Office agents who monitor the eastern coast. You are here, instead of with them, because I did not want to err with you if there is an explanation other than the obvious one. So be glad for the respite, and do not insult me in front of my men."

She nibbled at the beef that had been served before the footman left. She waited for Kendale's ill humor to ease at least a bit.

"I still have nothing with me," she said.

"We will get you a comb, and whatever else you need."

"I have no garments, Lord Kendale."

"Then wrap yourself in a blanket," he snapped. "You have done it before."

Again an allusion to that day. It seemed to make him less friendly, not more so.

"If you write to Dominique, she will come too, and bring some clothes and such."

"Is she your ally in all things? Should she be here with you?"

She realized his meaning to her shock. "You are not to arrest her too, if that is what you mean. Do not be more cruel and horrible than you are already."

He glared at her, then ate his food. When he put down his fork, he sat back in his chair. "I already wrote to inform her that you are safe, as you requested when we arrived. I also made arrangements for her to send you some things, being the cruel and horrible man that I am."

She regretted the insult, especially since he had considered her comfort even before she had demanded he do so. She also regretted saying something else to make him hard and unmoving. The fullness of her vulnerability overwhelmed her and she held on to her composure with effort.

"My apologies. This is not a situation that encourages happiness or calm. You dragged me here and have now told me that I am under your arrest. I would be a fool not to be afraid, or concerned about the decisions you will make."

The severity left him. He gazed with different eyes all of a sudden. Their lights were not sparks struck off flint, but warmer ones such as she had seen before. In his chambers. In Brighton. In a London garden. He looked so intently that it stole her breath. The lure of pleasure and the demands of desire rapidly arced between them, creating an exciting, primal understanding.

She expected him to rise up and come over and pull her into a rough embrace. Instead he leaned toward her over the table and held her gaze with his own. "Go upstairs now. Remain there until morning. If you want a book from the library, stop and get one, but do not wander the house tonight. And do not try to leave. The doors will be watched all night."

She rose. "I give my word that I will not try to leave. You can allow your men to sleep."

"Thank you, but I have no reason to know if your word is worth anything, do I? And the evidence thus far says that everything about you is a lie."

CHAPTER 11

Kendale spent long hours that night battling a chaos of anger, desire, and exasperation. Only one rational thought survived it all. Honor required that he learn the truth about Marielle, and be rid of her soon if his worst suspicions were confirmed.

The other thought to survive began with a curse and ended with the fury of wanting a woman he should not have. Never before in his life had his judgment been so compromised and he admonished himself for being weak with her. He should have directed the coach straight to London today, not talked himself into learning the truth before delivering her to her fate. Her face had softened him too much. So had her fear. It was his own hunger that really made the decision, though.

Nor had the resolve he reestablished on that long ride lasted. As soon as he looked at her across that table tonight her sad eyes had him wanting to comfort, to kiss, to caress.

He was a hell of a soldier, wasn't he? One sniff from her pretty nose and he was ready to put aside everything that mattered.

He paced his chambers, his body tight and needing action to relieve the effect she had left in him. The only good thing, if it could be called that, was that as the night passed he finally understood part of that disaster in France.

He had never comprehended how Feversham had been so easily lured into trusting Jeannette. Feversham had sound judgment. He was a damned mountain of rationality. They had all followed his lead on using Jeannette's information regarding the position of French troops around Toulon. Feversham was not a man to have his head turned by a pretty face.

Except Jeannette had an exceptionally pretty face, and a way about her that left men stupid. Even Feversham it turned out. All of them, really. A whole unit had set aside good sense that night and believed what Feversham wanted to believe.

Something similar had happened in the dining room tonight. One more minute and he would have convinced himself to believe anything she wanted him to believe.

He opened his window and gazed out at the grounds below. An enclosed garden stretched for an acre toward woods and farms beyond. The cool air refreshed him as it flowed over the skin of his face and chest. With any luck it would relieve this infernal agitation that had him pacing like a caged animal. If he could avoid thinking about Marielle in her bed down the hall, he might even sleep.

A distant sound reached his ears. He set his ear to the open window. Voices. Then silence.

He looked out again. Someone moved in the garden. Marielle. It had to be her. Men did not walk so soundlessly. The moonlight picked up subtle golden shines off her hair. She aimed directly through the garden toward the far end, probably hoping to find a back portal.

Damnation. He had given orders to his men that she was not to leave the house. He pulled on his shirt and strode out of his chambers. There would be hell to pay for whoever was on duty at the garden doors.

He strode through the house to its back, and first checked the doors in the morning room that gave out to the terrace. A tall silhouette darkened one of them. He walked over and tapped Angus's shoulder.

Startled, Angus spun around, battle ready. He relaxed when he saw who had joined him. "You are still awake, sir?"

"I am. What were you watching out there?"

"Nothing much." Angus shifted from foot to foot, then took a firm stance and crossed his arms.

"I said she was not to leave the house."

"That you did, sir. Only she said she felt a little faint and needed air, and the garden has a wall, doesn't it? Not likely she will be able to climb over it."

If Marielle Lyon decided she wanted to climb a ten-foot wall, Kendale did not doubt she would find a way to do so.

"You must learn to obey orders even when a pretty woman says she needs some air."

"Yes, sir. I know, sir. I will go and get her." Angus reached for the door latch.

"No, I will. Go and get some sleep."

"Are you sure, sir? She may try to leave again after —"

"She will not try to leave the house again. Go."

Angus walked away. Kendale turned the latch and stepped out into the cool night. Too cool, even for that shawl.

He wandered down the central path, listening and looking. No wind broke the night's stillness. The half moon gave vague form to the plantings and trees, and deep shadows.

One of those shadows breathed. Up ahead, to the right, Marielle sat on a bench beneath the dense tangle of a young elm tree's barren umbrella of branches. He walked over until he could see her clearly. Her bench rested in a river of ivy that churned around the tree in dense growth.

"Do not blame that guard you had at the door," she said. "He is young and easily flattered."

"He is no younger than you." He had no idea how young she was, or how old. She possessed a maturity that made the question insignificant. Yet he found his head calculating the little he had heard, about her flight from France and her loss during the Terror. Early twenties?

"He only tried to be kind. I told him I was feeling faint."

"Were you?"

"No. It was a lie."

"You must have been disappointed to learn there was no portal in the back."

"Isn't there? That is odd. However, I did not look for one. I told you I would not try to leave. That was *not* a lie."

He walked through the ivy and sat on the

bench. She had used a blanket as her shawl. It wrapped her from neck to ankles.

"You have no coat," she said.

"You have seen worse." They might be there again, in his chamber, both in dishabille, he in a banyan and she naked beneath a blanket. He angled his head to see if the hem of her dress showed. A bit of white poked out.

Side by side they looked into the night. The silence filled with messages that needed no words. A large loop of rope might have slid down around them and now it tightened, tightened, until he felt her presence more completely than if they touched.

"Who are you?" he asked. "What are you?"

"You know who I am. As for what — I am not a spy."

He wanted to believe that. With her right next to him and her delicate profile softly outlined by the moonlight, he almost did. She lied when it was convenient, however. She even admitted that she did.

"What was it that you handed off to that man Garrett today?"

She swung her foot up and down, slowly kicking through the end of the blanket. "Engravings. They are made in London, then I send them over through men like him."

216

"You pay to send engravings into France? That is an odd trade. No profit and all loss."

She laughed. "It is a peculiar business. I cannot deny that." She turned her head and looked at him. "The engravings are to encourage others to investigate crimes against the people. This new order there was born in much blood, but it should not be lawless. France deserves that. Her people do too."

"Are you using those engravings to denounce the people?"

"We trust the engravings might encourage others to investigate certain crimes, that is all."

He thought about the engravings in his chambers, the ones he had rescued in the alley.

"It could be dangerous," he said. "For the engraver and printer, and for you."

"Not too much."

"It almost got you killed in an alley, I think." He knew for certain now that those men would have killed her. Now he had a reason why. If she were telling the truth.

Right now he believed her. In the morning, when her scent did not fill his head and his blood did not burn and the exquisite torture of lust did not preoccupy his body and soul, he might well conclude this had been one more lie, and one more move in a long game played by an expert agent.

"You do not have to believe me," she said, hearing his thoughts somehow. "Too much is made of the need for trust in friendships. We can never really know who and what another person is. You do not dissemble at all, and yet much of who you are is a mystery to others."

"I doubt that."

"It is true."

The notion was bizarre. Perhaps she thought it flattered him, much as she had found a way to flatter young Angus.

"For example," she said. "A great mystery to me is why you have been sitting here so long and have not even tried to kiss me a single time. Do you think you would dishonor yourself? Dishonor me?"

"Nothing so noble as that." Now who was lying? And yet, with her so close that he could hear her breathe, honor retreated as a consideration. "I am not interested in kissing you a single time. I contemplate far more than that."

"Ah. I see."

"You cannot blame me. It was you who put the idea in my head."

She laughed quietly. "Now you are the one who lies. The idea was in your head before we ever spoke. It has been in your head, and elsewhere, for months."

"You think so, do you?"

"*Oui, m'sieur.* A woman knows these things." She leaned toward him until her large eyes looked directly into his. "It is good, perhaps, that you have chosen to not be so noble. I will not think that I corrupt a saint when I do this now." She kissed him lightly. "Or this." She laid her hand on his face and kissed him again.

The first kiss unlocked the restraints on his desire. The second one threw the door wide.

Raw and real and determined, the want owned him then. He trusted that she invited more than kisses. If she denied him now, he would go insane.

He held her face in his hands and kissed hard, imagining her body vividly, claiming, owning her mouth the way he would do the rest of her. She did not resist at all, but lifted her face in offering, and sighed on the musical gasps she made.

Then her hands were on him, on his chest, under his shirt. She clumsily unbuttoned it while they kissed, her slender fingers finding their way. When it gaped open she broke the kiss and laid her lips on his chest and made hot paths of nips and licks.

She looked up and her warm breath flowed over him and into him.

"You are cold now," she said. "Share this." She opened the blanket and embraced him with it.

He felt no cold. He never would again. He joined her within the blanket anyway, so he could feel her body near his, and caress her through the thin cloth of her dress. His fingers sensed no stays beneath the dress. No anything. He kissed her again, on the mouth and neck, on the soft skin of her chest, while he teased himself by slowly unlacing the front of her dress.

He felt too good. Strong and firm and confident, he handled her like the man he was, a man not given to false flatteries or pretty words, a man born for command and decision. He made her feel young and small and fragile and safe. So safe. She yearned to stay forever in the shelter of his body and desire.

Slowly, slowly he unlaced her dress. She had to grit her teeth against what it did to her. Her breasts swelled against the fabric, waiting. She swallowed her cries of frustration.

Done, finally. The rest of the fastenings confounded him, so he did not bother with them. He pushed the dress down, off her shoulders and arms so she was naked to the waist. An unexpectedly gentle touch glossed over her. Her tips had turned hard and that soft touch sent a sharp pleasure down her body that made her gasp. His head dipped. He kissed the swell, the softness, then shocked the tip again and again. Hard arms lifted and swung her onto his lap so his mouth had better purchase. His hand caressed one breast while his teeth and tongue tortured the other. She held his head to her and smothered her whimpers against his hair.

She could hardly bear the sensations. They filled her until her hold on herself strained. Delicious and horrible and sweet and cruel, the pleasure awed her but left her hungry with a compelling need that grew and grew until it conquered even the pleasure itself. Tipping into abandon, she squirmed against his thighs to relieve the vacant pulse between her legs. She reached down between their bodies and closed her hand on the hard bulge in his breeches pressing her leg.

He lifted her to her feet and pushed the dress down to her feet until she stood naked in front of him. His eyes blazed while he slid his fingertips all over her and watched his hands move. Along her shoulders and down her arms, over her stomach and to her thighs. Lightly, surely, to that vacant ache. She clutched his shoulders while he stroked. He maddened her worse by sucking on her breast. She wept then. Her body did and her essence too, as desperate pleasure unhinged her mind.

He lifted the blanket and it flew around her and settled on her shoulders like a cape. Firm rough hands circled her waist and he buried his face against her body as if he sought to inhale her essence.

"What do you want, Marielle? Tell me."

She took hold of his head and kissed his mouth as hard as she could, so he would know.

"Say it. Tell me what you want."

"You. Now."

"Then come here." He drew her forward, back onto his lap, facing him, so that her knees flanked his hips. He loosened his garments and moved her hips closer.

She gasped when she felt him pressing her. Cried out at the hardness both satisfying her need and bruising her body. He stopped, then moved more slowly when he pressed further. He stretched her. Somehow her body accommodated him. She felt him in her in ways she had not thought possible. For a moment the need subsided.

Then he moved. Holding her hips firmly, he withdrew and entered again. And again, and again. The vacancy returned, and the pulse and the need. It all unfolded inside her, down where they joined. Wanting and demanding and crying again. It grew and grew and she moved too, urging more, smiling when he took less care. He thrust deeply and hard and she met him each time and swiveled her hips to beg for yet more.

He pounded into her in the end. He held her body down to his while the consummation tremors shuddered through him.

She collapsed in his arms, against his chest, still joined, still feeling him. He tucked the blanket around her closer and silently held her in the sweet night.

"We must go back inside now."

His words startled her. She had fallen asleep in his embrace. Perhaps he had too.

"It will be dawn soon." He lifted her to her feet and held her there until her limbs unstiffened. He grabbed her dress and held it so she could step into it.

They dressed, such as the dressing went. He made sure she wrapped the blanket snugly. "Dawn's chill is the worst."

Together they walked back through the garden. Far in the east the first gray light began to seep through the dark.

No one stood at the door. "I wonder where he went," she said.

"I sent him to bed."

She looked at him. "You knew when you came out that you intended to seduce me. That is why you sent him away."

He walked on, guiding her through the house to the stairs. He nodded, not one bit chagrined by her accusation. "Out there or in here. Either way, I knew I did not need guards at the doors, because I would be with you." He glanced over. "You were warned not to wander through the house and to stay in your chamber."

"I thought you said that because you were concerned I would steal something."

"You were wrong."

He appeared pleased with himself. Quite content. She debated whether to broach her need to return to London now, or in the morning. There was much to recommend asking a favor when a man had just taken his pleasure. He would find it very calculating, however. Much more than in reality any part of the night had been.

On the level with her chamber he pointed to large double doors as they passed. "My chambers are in there. You may visit whenever you like."

How thoughtful. Lord Kendale was not such a hard man it seemed. He did not shy away from the intimacy now between them. Pleased by his romantic gesture, she kissed him.

At her door he took his leave of her. She smiled up at him. "You may visit when you like too."

"That is generous of you, but I cannot."

"I can go there, but you cannot come here? I do not understand."

He rested his fingertips on her lips and looked in her eyes. "You are my prisoner. If I came to this door, you might feel an obligation. I am not that kind of man."

His prisoner. Still.

"You were that kind of man tonight. You even came out into the garden intending to be."

"I intended to have you. I did not intend to impose on you or obligate you."

"You are walking some very fine lines."

"You have no idea just how fine the lines with you have been, Marielle. As for tonight — you kissed me, remember? You said you wanted me."

Tell me what you want.

Damn him. Even at the height of passion he had remembered to trick her into all but begging for him first. His notions of honor had not been violated. One of them would sleep the slumber of the righteous.

She opened the door, entered, and slammed it shut on him. What kind of a man was he, to let her give herself to him like that, and still speak of her as a prisoner? He was not supposed to be thinking like a gaoler now. He was supposed to be wet clay in her hands.

CHAPTER 12

Mr. Pottsward arrived just after noon the next day. He ceremoniously set a wrapped bundle on the divan in the dressing room. "Her woman put this together for me. I was not present. I cannot vouch for what it contains."

Packages from Marielle's servant were all fine and good, but more important matters needed to be settled first. "Did you see the solicitor about the property I wrote to you about?"

"I did. He assured me that the deed will be ready for signing when you next come to town. He advised against buying a pleasure craft unless you intend to use it on the river, however. Anything of more substance is in danger of being requisitioned by the naval service."

"Spoken like a lawyer. They never account for fun. One wonders if they were ever children."

"He also itemized the costs of maintaining such a vessel. On which point, I feel I must mention that we really do not have room for a private navy, sir. I toured the cellars and attics before coming here, and as it is —"

"Don't worry. I'll not have sailors here. The lads are eager to try their hands at it themselves. How hard can it be?"

"No harder than hitting a target dead-on with a musket from two hundred paces, I suspect."

Kendale laughed. Mr. Pottsward was just being Pottsward. He turned his attention to the package. That old woman would not tuck a pistol in there, would she? He picked it up and gave it a few squeezes.

"They are not pleased at that house," Pottsward reported while he set about hanging clothes strewn about. "Those women, I mean. Odd place, sir. Not a man in sight. Not natural, if you ask me."

"I suppose they find men inconvenient in some way."

"I cannot imagine what way that would be. Any woman with sense would want a man around for protection if nothing else. They need not marry if they have radical notions on that subject. It need only be a servant, just so the world knows they are not vulnerable."

"I do not think they are without any protection." Indeed, Marielle and Dominique and the women who worked there had enjoyed some of the best protection to be had. That of agents of the Home Office. That of Lord Kendale and his men.

She claimed she was not a spy. If not, why had she not taken steps to remove the suspicions? Why allow them to stand all this time? Marielle had not done anything to kill the rumors. She had realized he followed her and never confronted him but allowed it to continue.

Perhaps she did like having men around for the protection they afforded. That attack on her, and the intrusion in her house, suggested she needed protection from something.

Then again, perhaps she could not kill the rumors because they were true. The prints she sent to France might contain information, hidden in ways only her allies would decipher. The engraver might be part of her network.

He should not forget that possibility. He must not allow last night to addle his brain. The tendency to make excuses for her had already led him to some bad judgments. He would have to be vigilant in the future, especially now that he had succumbed to his hunger for her.

He picked up the bundle and walked down to her chamber door. She opened it and looked at him with a low-lidded expression that did not bode well for the day. He handed over the parcel, thinking it would be wise for her to change into another dress. He could not see this one without remembering it sliding down her body to reveal her nakedness.

"My valet will go to the village and see about bringing a woman here to serve you." He said it on impulse, so the door would not close too quickly.

"That is a lot of trouble for what will only be a few days. I can do for myself a short while. Who knows what disruption yet another woman would wreck on this house. I am not sure your men would know how to behave."

"They would behave with the discipline of soldiers."

"I have seen what the discipline of soldiers is worth. Better if you leave the village women in their homes." She looked down at the bundle. "How long will I be here? Until you decide what to do with me, you said. How long will that be? I have a business in London. Those women depend on me."

"A few days." Perhaps a week. Maybe longer. He would know soon. "You do not have to remain here during the day. You can go on the grounds or elsewhere in the house."

"You are no longer concerned that I will run away?"

"I think you know that I would find you before you got far, so you will not bother to try."

A challenge entered her eyes. A small smile played on her lips. She nodded in agreement while she slowly closed the door.

Late that afternoon a commotion entered the house. It began in the drive and rolled through the door. Men's voices cascaded up the stairs.

Marielle left her chamber and listened. Some of Kendale's men had returned from some journey. She would not have thought this estate needed more servants. How many did he maintain?

Angus came running up the stairs. He stopped when he saw her, made a quick bow, then turned and ran to Kendale's chambers. Then Angus ran back and flew down the stairs.

Kendale emerged. He noticed her while he strode to the stairs. He paused, his hand on the balustrade and one boot already descending.

"Supper will be brought to you," he said. "You should make yourself scarce this evening."

She did not mind obeying. She liked her chamber. Old Pete brought up food late in the evening and set in on the table she had placed near the window. Noise from below made its way in when she opened it.

"It sounds like a party," she said.

"It is just the lads having some beer."

"How many lads live here? A good number from the sounds."

Old Pete rubbed his chin while he thought. "Hard to say. Here proper, there's maybe two dozen. Then there's the ones who come by like today. Maybe another dozen of them? Only milord knows the total, I guess."

"Why would there be servants who only come by on occasion? What use are they if they are not here?"

"Oh, you want to know how many *servants* there are. Well, now, there's me and the cook and Mr. Pottsward and —"

"If the others are not servants, what are they? Angus, for example."

"Angus? He is a soldier. A man-at-arms. No one better with a sword. I was a soldier too once, before I got old." He finished setting out the food and left.

She ate with the window open, listening to the male camaraderie below. Soldiers, Pete called them, but they wore no uniform of the British army. And Lord Kendale had given up his commission when he inherited the title.

He had a private army. That was the answer, she was sure. He had called these men soldiers, but she had not understood he meant it literally. This was the fort from which he sent sorties out to do — who knew what? *I have had others follow you instead.* She thought he had hired one of those men who investigate for pay, not that he assigned some of his private men-at-arms to do it.

Was this allowed in England? Were private armies common? She could not see how any government would welcome such a thing. In ancient times a lord had his own knights and fighting men, but this was not then.

Down below these soldiers ate in their mess. Soon they would retire to their barracks. No wonder there were no women here. No wonder he thought he could imprison her when he lacked any authority to do so. No wonder she could not find the portal on the garden's back wall.

Old Pete had provided a trifle for her meal's end. She dipped a spoon in the sweet custard. While she ate it, the thought entered her mind that perhaps Lord Kendale was mad. Utterly mad.

The safe return of comrades from a mission is always a cause for celebration. Kendale did not deny the men their boisterous joy, their beer and gin, or even their pranks. He sat with them for the long evening meal and listened to all of the stories about derring-do. He offered a few foulmouthed toasts along with the others.

Long after midnight, as one by one heads nodded or consciousness slipped a man's grasp, he faced one of the last men standing across a plank table in the cellar. He poured the short, glassy-eyed, balding Mr. Drummond more gin.

Drummond lifted his glass in salute.

"Before you drink that, Drummond, and fall under this table for the night, would you explain in more detail about Mr. Travis. Twelve left and only eleven came back, yet none of you appear concerned with his absence."

"He is sure to make it back, sir."

"That is what you have all been saying.

Did you lose him across the water, or in England itself? If in England, then most likely he is sure to make it back. If it was in France, that becomes less likely."

Drummond glanced to his left and right, looking for one of the others. They were all gone. "Um. He wasn't on the boat, so it must have been over there."

. "Was he captured?"

"Not to my knowing of it. No, sir."

"Eventually you will all have to tell me what happened. Tonight, while I am at least half-drunk, might be your best opportunity."

"He wouldn't come with us," another voice said.

Kendale turned his head. Sean, Angus's older cousin, walked over and slammed his hand on the table. "We had the information. We were back on the coast. We are all getting on the damned boat, and that fool held back. Said he was going to find out if the Colonel had been posted in Brest or Dieppe, since we had heard both given. Said he would return in a week or so with the right port. I ordered him to get on the fucking boat, but he just turned and walked away. It was either shoot him or let him go, sir."

"Sean here told him you would be most displeased," Drummond hastened to say.

235

"He said he had more right to see it through than we did, seeing as how he was at Toulon with you. Said he would find out where the bastard is or die trying."

"Hell and damnation," Kendale swore. "*Hell and damnation.* Why didn't you pick him up and throw him over your shoulder, Sean? You must be twice his size."

"He had his pistol out and ready. I had mine too, of course. Like I said, it was shoot him or let him walk. Should I have shot him?"

Kendale fought his way to common sense through the foggy fury. "No."

"Is possible he will find out," Drummond said cheerily. "That would be a good thing, right? It would save time."

More likely Mr. Travis would do something rash and heroic and get himself killed or captured. Kendale understood the man's determination to find some justice for that carnage in Toulon, but Travis could not control himself. They were not in the army any longer, however. He could not shoot a deserter from a troop of volunteers with no real duty to the mission.

"We must wait, it appears," he said. "We will give him three weeks, maybe four. But no more."

Kendale wiped his brow and lifted his sword again. Angus gave him a skeptical look.

"You sure you want to go on?"

"My weapon is raised, isn't it?"

"It has been on to two hours. Normally we do this an hour thereabouts."

"Are you tired? Have I worn you down?"

"Not tired. Just working harder than normal and wondering why." His expression cleared as if a thought had struck like lightning. "Ohhh." He looked over his shoulder at the house, then smirked.

"You are younger than me and stronger so another hour should not even make you sweat," Kendale said, not liking that smirk at all.

"Another hour?" He spit on his hands and grasped his sword, mumbling.

"What was that, Angus? Did I hear you say something about a woman arriving and ruining me?"

"You must admit you have been in rare form today. Riding out at dawn, ordering the stables cleaned, rousing the men who were sleeping off last night's celebration. If she is not the reason, it makes me wonder what is."

"There are things to do. Discipline here has been lacking."

Angus muttered something else. It sounded like, *That woman in your bed is what has been lacking.*

Kendale attacked. Steel met steel as they continued their dangerous dance.

Kendale did not lie to himself that he was winning at this exercise. At twenty-five, Angus had a good seven years on him, not to mention an inch in height and perhaps twenty pounds in weight. Fighting with swords was the kind of activity where such things mattered and there could be no equal skill as a result.

He threw himself into it and avoided calling a halt. If he stopped moving, stopped occupying his mind and body, he would get angry about Mr. Travis again. He would also become too aware of the presence in the house that filled the air he breathed. Even now, despite his own sweat, the vague scent of lavender entered his head.

She had not left her chamber since he told her to make herself scarce the day before. She certainly had not arrived at his chamber door last night. He knew she would not, but he had waited anyway, picturing her wrapped in a blanket that she dropped to reveal her body to him. He had her in his

238

dreams, which did not make for a restful sleep.

Angus was right. That woman was ruining him.

Something caught Angus's eye and he stepped back, lowering his weapon. Retreating as well, Kendale saw Old Pete walking across the field where they sparred north of the garden wall.

"Letters, sir," Pete called. "One looks to be in Jacob's hand. The other — well, I thought you should see it at once."

He stabbed his sword into the ground and took the letters. Angus lay down on the ground and sucked in deep breaths. He enjoyed a moment of smug pride that his younger opponent had tired first. But then Angus did not have this hunger making him too restless to stand still, giving him energy that had no release.

He broke the seal of Jacob's letter. From his chambers across from Marielle's home, Jacob wrote that there was a man taking an interest in the house. He came and went, but he passed slowly at least four times a day. Should one of them follow to learn more?

The second letter also came from London. It bore a seal he had not seen in over a year on any missive to him. He read its message.

The Duke of Penthurst had just invited himself to visit. That he dangled a gift and a good excuse did not make the notion sit any better.

Cursing, he walked toward the house to write responses to both.

Marielle did not find the note until she shook out the second petticoat in the bundle of garments. It had been buried inside the white cotton cloth and it fell to the floor like a leaf. She snatched it up and unfolded it. She should have guessed Dominique would hide a letter in the garments. She should have unfolded each one yesterday and looked for this, and not merely hung out the dresses.

There's men watching. Some across the way who never leave. Another who walks the lane and thinks he is sly in how he watches, but I noticed him three days ago. I don't think they are together. I hope one of them is a friend.

As for your visit with the viscount, I remind you that an English lord's protection is not to be refused lightly in these times, especially with what you might now face, and with what I suspect you plan to do. Other women have the luxury of standing on their virtue in ways we do not. I'd ensure his help myself if I were younger, but those days are past me now.

The women keep coming and I went and brought back engravings from Monsieur Ackerman. There is work, at least, and no one will starve.

Dominique's attempt at discretion amused her. Better to have saved the ink and just written, *Use your body to forge an alliance with this lord.*

She could not muster any indignation at the advice. Ever since the attack in the alley, a tight cold fear had twisted beneath her heart. It seemed every day since she had learned things that only made it clench more. The news that Lamberte had left the manor near Savenay. The sight of Éduard and Luc, beaten cruelly before being killed. The intrusion on her house and now, according to Dominique, unwelcome interest from strangers who watched and waited.

For what? Her, perhaps.

She tried to explain it all away. An argument could be made that her friend out of fear now saw men watching who merely walked the lane to go about their business. Dominique would never feel really safe again. She carried a knife at all times, didn't she?

The intruders might have been a coincidence, and only men who hoped to steal something of value. Éduard and Luc could have fallen victim to smugglers that they crossed, perhaps even Garrett himself.

Her mind wanted to nod after each explanation. Her soul heard none of it. She knew as surely as she breathed that the danger was real. Ever since those men grabbed her in the alley, she had known.

The only respite from nervous vigilance had been when she was with Lord Kendale. The only peace had come while he embraced her in the night garden.

She looked around her pretty chamber. If not for her long-awaited duty, she might gladly stay in this prison forever. It was time to leave it, before its safety sapped her of all her strength. She might follow Dominique's advice and arrange for Lord Kendale to protect her, but she could not stay here.

He had said he would not go to her, and he wouldn't. He approached her door only as a message bearer.

He could have sent Old Pete, of course. Even Angus, or one of the others. He didn't.

She answered his knock and faced him in

the shadows. Three candles on a far table gave enough light so he saw her clearly enough, limned in golden glows that turned her hair into spun bronze. She wore a dress he had not seen before, a light purple one with a tiny pattern of something flicking it. He assumed it was one of the dresses brought up from London.

She cocked her head, curious. "Do you want something of me?"

Despite her coolness he heard it as a taunt. Hell, yes, he wanted something of her. He burned from what he wanted.

"There will be visitors tomorrow. One will be a countryman of yours. I would like you to come down and meet them."

"Visitors? How interesting. I had heard that you never entertain, and rarely partake of others' entertainments graciously."

The information probably came from Emma, Lady Southwaite. The reference to lack of grace probably came from Cassandra, Lady Ambury.

"I am not entertaining. These men will be coming for other purposes. I would like your thoughts on the Frenchman, so I want you to meet him."

She stepped closer and looked in his eyes, searching. "Do you want my thoughts on him, or his on me?"

Damn, she was a suspicious woman. Shrewd too. "The other visitor will be a duke. Penthurst. They are traveling together. It can only help you to meet such an important man." He did not play society's games much, but after a lifetime watching he could not help but know the rules.

The duke's arrival intrigued her. "You may not entertain often, but you are very successful in your guests when you do. Is he a friend?"

"He has been a friend, yes."

"A strange way to respond." The oddity did not hold her interest. She turned and strolled into her chamber, then turned again. "A duke. Perhaps he will ask me to be his mistress if I provide what little amusement he is likely to enjoy tomorrow."

Another taunt. His head almost exploded. "That is not likely."

"I am not pretty enough? Not fashionable enough?"

"You are pretty enough, and you know it. It is still not likely." *Because I will kill him first.*

She considered that, her arm crossed over her body and her other arm rested on it so she could cup her own chin in thought. "Is it not likely because he will assume I am your mistress if I am here?"

"No." *Yes.* "He already has a mistress to whom he is currently devoted. He is not looking for another one right now." The lie came out too easily. He'd be damned if he allowed Penthurst to even entertain the notion of making Marielle a mistress, or let Marielle think she could achieve such a victory.

"That is too bad."

She smiled at him, her eyes glittering the way they did when she found something amusing. That did nothing for his temper. She knew what he was thinking. She saw the desire in him. Smelled it. Women like her were never ignorant of their effects on men.

He still stood on the threshold. He had not placed even one foot inside the chamber. Her gaze dared him to take the step.

Instead he took a deep breath. He was being the worst ass. How often had he mocked men for this? Hadn't he seen how lust often made men jokes, and sometimes victims?

He turned, not even taking his leave, and forced himself to walk away.

To his astonishment she followed.

Damnation, the woman had no sense. He refused to acknowledge her step behind him. If he looked at her, he —

He threw open his chamber door and

strode in.

"You lied," she said.

He turned then. He had to. Blood pounded in his head and his whole body seemed taut as a stretched bow. She was the one now standing right outside the door, looking in.

"What lie?" There had been a few.

"When I asked if you wanted something of me, you did not answer truthfully."

"I did."

"I do not think so. One of the others could have told me about these visitors. You came yourself." She looked down at her feet and the doorway. Slowly, elegantly, she toed at the invisible line with her soiled, silk slipper.

His whole being urged her to cross that line. He did not give a damn that it might compromise his honor, or make him one of those jokes.

She watched her foot trace her debate on the board. Then she stepped inside and closed the door. She walked over to him. "What do you want of me, m'sieur?"

He looked down at her, ridiculously elated and relieved and instantly as hard as he had ever been.

"Say it, Lord Kendale. What do you want?"

He pulled her forward and lifted her in an embrace. "You," he muttered. "You."

It did not take him long to get her clothes off her. She managed to avoid him ripping her dress to shreds in the process.

They tumbled onto the bed together. She knew how it would be if she did not take matters in hand. She found his impatience charming and his hard passion exciting, but there were times when one preferred more finesse.

She plucked at his neckpiece while she kissed him. "Perhaps you can remove this. And the boots."

He stopped and looked down at her. Then turned his head and looked down his own body toward those boots. He sat up and had them off in a flash.

She knelt behind him, circling his neck with her arms. She slid off his coat and reached around to unbutton his waistcoat and shirt. "You do not mind, do you? If I see you as you see me?"

"Of course not."

"After all, I too would like to kiss skin and not wool and linen."

She fell back on the bed while he undressed. He did it like the soldier he had been, methodically, neatly, quickly. He never took his eyes off her either, so she taunted him a bit, crossing her arms behind her head so her breasts rose, raising her leg to caress his chest with her foot while he finished with his lower garments.

Finally he was done. He joined her, lowering into her arms. An entwining embrace brought them close, touching everywhere in warmth, surrounded by sensual, physical scents. He kissed her furiously, his mouth claiming and devouring. She felt the explosive passion in him.

She pushed at his chest. Eventually he noticed and rose up so she was not pinned down. She pushed again, turning her body so he lay on his back. She straddled him, sat back, and admired what she saw.

Bending forward, she kissed a line across his chest. "You want me, and I want you. It is good, no? Tonight let us have each other in a special way. Let us enjoy this as if we know we will never know pleasure again with anyone, ever." She smiled at him. "It will be as if we are drinking the very best wine. Slowly savoring each drop."

She showed him what she meant by caressing him in long, careful strokes that let her feel him inch by inch. She closed her eyes so the sensations filled her awareness and created memories of touch and scent.

She leaned forward and kissed him deeply, slowly. Her breasts barely touched his chest, teasing her.

His arms surrounded her. He rolled so she was on her back. "Like wine, you say. That is all about taste." He kissed her mouth, his tongue tasting and moving, creating thrills. He moved to her neck in a slow exploration of other tastes, finding the spots that made her sigh. She explored too, her fingertips learning the details of his shoulders and back. She discovered ridges, long lines of scars. They felt like the one forming on her hip, only worse. Wounds, she guessed. Officers do not only dress up in nice uniforms. This one at least clearly had not.

His mouth moved lower, to her breasts. More tasting with lips and tongue. Gently at first. He created a luscious excitement that made her want to purr. She could not control it long, however. The pleasure built and changed and began denying her contentment. The arousal spread low in her body and into her head until she could not bear how good it felt. He palmed the tips lightly, then firmly, learning what made her cry out and moan.

He savored, the way she had asked. He took forever. When his kisses lowered yet again, to her stomach and hips, her whole body reacted. The anticipation almost unhinged her.

New kisses, high on her thighs. He tasted the soft flesh there. Higher yet, so that his breath flowed over her mound, making her tremble. Then he spread her legs wide and truly tasted until she groaned. Her sense abandoned her and she cried out each time the pleasure increased, sharpened, astonished. The most profound tremor began deep inside her then began contracting, getting tighter and tighter until she feared she would die. Then in an exquisite instant it snapped and unwound all through her, carrying the most perfect release all through her body.

He came up over her and bent one of her legs. He entered her, holding her thigh to his hip so he went deeply. He stayed there a moment, tension hardening his shoulders and back. Then he moved in slow, deep thrusts, as if he really did believe he would never know pleasure again and needed to savor the sensation now in order to remember it forever.

Eventually the pleasure conquered him too. It ended as it had almost begun, powerfully, hard, and with command. He took and she let him until finally the release cracked his control and shuddered through them both. She wrapped her legs around him and held him to her so they would remain joined in the aftermath.

CHAPTER 13

He watched her eating her breakfast. She took little bites that barely needed chewing, but ate more than he would have expected.

Her tumble of hair had been brushed but still appeared that of a woman in bed. Her old-fashioned dress hung on her, as if she had once weighed a bit more, or perhaps the woman who used to own it before her had been bigger.

He tried to decide if Penthurst would find her suitably shabby and beneath his interest, or be intrigued and want to buy her the latest fashions. His own reaction had been close to the latter option, but that did not mean another man's would be too. Still, as the hour wore on, he considered if having Marielle look this much a waif would be in his own best interests.

"Are you finished?" he asked when she set down her cup. "Come with me."

He led her to the stairs. She skipped up

beside him. "Have you no manners, Lord Kendale? To impose on me again so soon after a night of imposition is considered a little rude." She giggled even as she said it, and gave him an impish glance.

"Don't tempt me," he said. "We aren't going back to bed." His mind started calculating if they could and still be presentable at one in the afternoon.

"Then what?"

"Here, I'll show you." He opened the chamber nearest to his. Her eyes widened on seeing its appointments.

"This was the apartment of my brother's wife."

She drifted around, sliding her hand over the furniture and fingering the silk drapery. "She enjoyed fine things."

"They meant the whole world to her." Acquiring luxuries had consumed Caroline, if truth be told. He had never understood how any person could have such a single-minded pursuit of objects. For years he disliked her for what seemed an unhealthy avarice. Eventually he concluded that in some way her luxuries substituted for something else she could never have. Perhaps the affection of his brother, who treated her as little more than another piece of expensive furniture herself.

He walked into the dressing room. "I hope that you will not be insulted if I offer you the use of her things." He pointed to the wardrobes. "With a duke coming, I thought you might like to change into a different dress."

She threw open one of the wardrobes. "*Mon dieu!* Look at these gowns. I do not suppose this duke will stay for dinner and require me to wear one of these?"

"I believe he will not stay that long." Damn, he hoped not.

She pouted, and passed the gowns and pulled out a dress instead. She held it to her body and looked down to see how it might fit. "Why would I be insulted?"

"You might think I did not consider your appearance suitable as it is now."

She laughed. "*Of course* it is not suitable. I thought you were mad to consider having me meet a duke, looking like this, instead of telling me to hide in my chamber. Your scullery maid, if you had any maids here, would appear less poor." She peered into the wardrobe again. She pulled out another dress. This one had a very recent look to it. That made her joy dim.

"She passed not so long ago, if this was her dress."

"Two years. They both were in a carriage

accident."

"Perhaps I should not —"

"I want you to. She would too. There is no reason to leave them here to rot. I should have removed them long ago, but —" It was the apartment of the Viscountess Kendale. There was no such woman now, so the door could be closed and its contents ignored while he threw himself into other things.

Excited, she bent and gazed in the looking glass atop the dressing table. She fingered some pins strewn on the table's surface. "It is not inappropriate? You are sure?"

"I am sure. I will leave you to it. Make use of whatever you want."

Penthurst arrived in early afternoon. Kendale went out to the drive to greet them and to call off the dogs. The duke stepped out of his coach and made no attempt to hide his interest in the property. His gaze scanned the building and grounds while he and Kendale passed pleasantries.

His companion, Monsieur Calvet, did not impress with his person. Of average height, and slightly built the way the French could be, his dark hair already had thinned despite his not looking older than Kendale and Penthurst. Intelligence marked his eyes. They struck Kendale as the eyes of a man who sees clearly. Such a man, if he were a writer, would be dangerous to any government if he indulged inclinations to describe the world he saw.

While the duke examined the property, Monsieur Calvet examined his host.

"We finally meet, Lord Kendale," he said. "His Grace informed me of your interest in our introduction. It is rare that I am useful to anyone these days, let alone a lord of England. I would be delighted to find I am not completely irrelevant now."

"I asked for the introduction because I have some questions about France that you can perhaps answer. I would have called on you in London, however. You did not have to come here."

"His Grace concluded that your return to London might take some time. He had cause to travel past this place, and decided I should journey with him." He glanced at Penthurst. "I would not think there were questions your government does not know the answers to already."

"They are not the kinds of questions the ministers care about. There is also someone I want you to meet. Her name is Marielle Lyon. Have you heard of her?"

"She is well-known among us, by reputation. I have not met her, however. What do you want me to learn from her? Are you trying to discover the truth about her history? Whether she is a charlatan as some claim, or a noble orphan as she does?"

His determination to unmask her felt a betrayal now. He kept one eye on Penthurst, who had delayed their entry into the house by stopping to peer inexplicably at the small windows that gave into the cellars of the building. "I do not seek to discover anything in particular about her. However, if you have anything notable to say about Miss Lyon after you meet her, please wait to tell me until I arrange for us to speak privately."

Calvet glanced at Penthurst, then made the vaguest nod.

Kendale called for Penthurst to join them while he brought Calvet into the house. And thus he found himself not only entertaining, but offering hospitality to a man whose society he had avoided. No doubt Penthurst felt free to call because of that dinner at Ambury's. Ambury had a lot to answer for if that surprise had led to this.

He noted with relief that the footmen who rode the steps of the coach did not bring in baggage. His own footman, in the person of Angus, who had been once more forced into both the role and the necessary coats, opened the door to the library with a good deal of flourish.

"Please have Miss Lyon informed that our guests are here," Kendale said as he passed.

Calvet made himself comfortable in a chair. Penthurst continued to peer around, checking the prospects from windows and examining appointments. Perhaps he thought that if he appeared distracted, Kendale would ask the questions he had for Calvet in his presence. If so, he was much mistaken.

"You have been missed," he finally said, taking a chair for himself. His deep-set eyes gazed over expectantly. "Southwaite said he thought you had gone to the coast. I thought perhaps you had left the country."

"I would not leave the country without informing someone."

"Well, now, we both know that is not true. However, I was relieved to receive your return letter, indicating my own had found you here."

Mr. Calvet glanced from Kendale to Penthurst, and back again. He proved he possessed the intelligence his eyes had suggested by keeping silent.

"Relieved? I am touched that you worry for me."

"Not relieved for you. For myself. Pitt received word that some of our army entered France via the southeastern coast. Since no such action had been authorized, he quizzed me very closely regarding those of my friends who are known to sometimes act independently. Southwaite and Ambury are in London and absolved of suspicion. That left you."

"You should tell him that you are not responsible for the decisions of your acquaintances. However, if our correspondence will allow the Prime Minister to sleep better, I can only be happy."

"Regrettably, it did not entirely appease him. He began asking awkward questions about your household."

"Is that why you are here? To examine my domestic condition?"

"I am here to facilitate your meeting with Mr. Calvet. When I was called to one of my properties, I realized I would pass within a few miles of Ravenswood. Mr. Calvet was good enough to see the sense of accompanying me so the two of you could meet."

"Of course I am grateful you did, Mr. Calvet." Kendale moved the conversation to his true guest. "I understand that your decision to become a guest of England was precipitous."

Mr. Calvet described his career prior to his flight. He had supported the revolution in its birth, and did not quarrel that a few heads had rolled. "I survived the worst of it by disappearing. I returned to my family's village and became a farmer like my father. Let us say that it is fortunate better skills than mine feed the people. My pen proved more lucrative, as I published under a nom de plume. My old friends knew where to find me, and I remained informed, so always had foibles and disgraces upon which to comment. There is great freedom in being anonymous."

"Yet you had to flee all the same."

"Ah, yes. One of those friends chose to reveal my nom de plume right after I published a booklet that he believed criticized him. I learned that it did, but had no idea he was involved in the matter I exposed."

"It sounds like a dangerous profession."

"In France currently, yes. With the ambitious Corsican gaining influence, perhaps I will remain in England for some years, unfortunately."

"He is perfecting his English, so he can do for us what he did for them," Penthurst said dryly.

Kendale debated how to remove the duke from the conversation. Penthurst already knew he wanted to ask Calvet about minor political figures in France, but it would not be convenient for Penthurst to hear the details of either the questions or the answers.

A message passed to Angus at the door obviated the necessity for the time being. Angus came over and bent to his ear. "Miss Lyon is coming down."

"Send her in."

With a subtle drama, Angus opened both doors at once, then stood aside. Marielle Lyon stepped in.

Three men stood. Kendale all but stopped breathing. So did his guests. Stillness fell while they all stared at how a decent dress and a bit of jewelry could enhance Marielle's beauty.

She appeared taller. The column of green fabric emphasized her willowy form. The high waist showcased her perfect, round breasts. She had put up her hair and donned a simple pearl necklace and pearl earbobs, emphasizing the snowy curve of her neck. Self-possessed and stunning, she bowed to Penthurst during the introductions.

Kendale had to tear his gaze away. She had been lovely in her rags, but this was different. She wore these garments as naturally as she wore her skin. They did not awe her. They did not merely decorate her. They completed her.

Within minutes, Mr. Calvet had engaged her in conversation. They sat head-to-head, speaking rapidly in French. Marielle's joy in having one of her own people present could be seen in her face. Their attention focused on each other, and their laughter turned familiar.

Which left Kendale to entertain the Duke of Penthurst.

"You displayed an inordinate interest in the façade of this house when you arrived," he said.

"I do not know it well. I think I only came here once before. A house party that your brother and his wife held. You were in the army then."

"I did not realize you had developed an avocation for architecture. Have you taken to drawing plans?"

Penthurst looked right at him. He looked right back.

"I was not measuring walls. I was looking for *them.*"

"Who would *them* be?"

"The men who do your bidding."

"The servants do not hang from the cornices. They are where servants always are."

"I do not mean servants. Knowing you, there are damned few of that kind of *them*

262

here." He angled forward, rested his arms on his knees, placed one hand on top the other, and looked up. "Did you send men into France last week? Was that army about which the French complained your army?"

"No man who obeys me is in France."

"That is not what I asked." He sighed, and leaned back in his chair. Over on the divan, Marielle and Mr. Calvet chattered on, their speech sounding like a long, lilting melody. "A man has gone missing. An innocent, simple draper with no government position. He is believed dead."

"No man who obeys me would kill an innocent, simple draper."

"Well, you can imagine the suspicion. There are rumors of English in the region, then a man disappears. The letter to Pitt accused us of a vendetta against those involved in the Toulon situation."

"And this draper was involved. He does not sound so innocent to me."

"It is known you are bitter about that experience. That you blame our government for neither acting decisively nor demanding any justice. It is known that your unit was all but massacred as you found yourselves outmanned and surrounded while you tried to escape. A good deal of patience has already been spent on your refusal to see the bigger picture. If you are now seeking your own justice, it will not be tolerated."

"Were you sent here to threaten me? That is bold. A not so innocent draper disappears, and there are rumors that some English soldiers were lurking about his town, and the result is I am expected to pay heed to scolds sent secondhand from Pitt? He is a fool if he believes I will give a damn."

"Not threats. Not a scold. Nor did he send me to you. I wanted you to know that assumptions are forming about this, and about you. If you have indeed embarked on a campaign of revenge, be careful that you do not find yourself facing our army instead of theirs, that is all."

"*Mon dieu,* we have been impolite." Marielle's voice rose, and immediately shifted their attention off each other and on her. "Forgive me, please, Your Grace. I was so pleasantly surprised to find my countryman in your party, that I have indulged too much in the chance to speak my language at length."

"No apologies are needed from you, Miss Lyon. Mr. Calvet has much to answer for, however, for taking up all of your time and depriving Kendale and I of your charm." Penthurst stood. "I must demand my fair share. Perhaps you would take a turn with

264

me? As I remember it, there is a walled garden behind this house. You can continue speaking French if you like. I am told I have a fair facility with it."

Flattered and pleased, Marielle allowed Penthurst to take her hand and raise her up. "Your memory about the garden is correct, Your Grace. I would be honored to show you."

Without saying a word to the effect, Penthurst made it clear that in demanding Marielle's company, he desired no one else's. As they left the library together, she laughed at something he said.

Kendale watched them go, fighting a spike in jealousy. Penthurst not only was a duke, but a handsome, accomplished, gracious, duke sought after by hostesses for his wit and ministers for his counsel. He was a damned paragon. He most definitely was not anything at all like Gavin Norwood, Viscount Kendale.

"Lord Kendale." The voice jolted him out of his simmering thoughts. He turned to Mr. Calvet.

"You asked me to mention anything that I found odd, in private. And I did find several things about Mam'selle Lyon *pas normal.*"

"Explain yourself."

Calvet closed the door, then retook his

seat on the divan. Kendale remained standing. One of the library windows overlooked the garden. He considered telling Calvet to save his insights for another day.

"Her French is excellent. She is well educated. She is well bred."

"She is the niece of a comte, so none of that is a surprise."

"Yes, and no. Her speech is Parisian when she is careful, but localized when surprised or at ease. It was a common thing with our elite. They learned to lose the local accents so they were not seen as too country, and unfashionable. In times of emotion, the language of their youth emerges." He paused. "While we spoke, several times that happened with her. Little slips. A change in the accent, or a regional word not common everywhere."

"It is the same here. When boys go away to school, the ones from counties with strong local accents learn to lose them fast because they are teased. There is nothing notable about it with her."

Calvet made a tent with his fingertips in front of his mouth while he thought. "If there is indeed something notable, do you want to know? You said you did, but —"

"Of course."

"*Bien.* She says she is the niece of the

Comte de Vence. His province is in the south, near the sea. If she lived nearby, that should be the local accent she speaks when at ease."

"Yet that is not what you heard. Is it?"

"No. I heard a young woman from the west. Not Breton, that is clear. But — the Loire region perhaps." He shrugged again. "Perhaps her family lived there, and she claims a closer relationship with her uncle to make her way. So she says she lived not far away, and visited. For some who judge, that contact and proximity is as important as the blood connection."

Kendale wandered away while he considered Calvet's revelation. When Madame Peltier had made the same observation, he had given it little weight. As a writer and pamphleteer Calvet had traveled widely, however. And those who questioned Marielle — she would be very sure not to be at ease with them. Not to slip into any local way of speaking.

He found himself near a window, the one that overlooked the garden. Below Marielle and Penthurst strolled the paths. She looked exquisitely beautiful. Her distinctive way of walking suited her dress and made her appear regal. If she were who she claimed to be, she need not aspire to be a duke's mistress. She could dare hope to be his wife.

"Then there is the other oddity," Calvet said. "I do not know what to make of it."

He turned. "What other oddity?"

"Again it is her speaking. Only not her French. It is her English. It is too good, Lord Kendale. It is better than mine, and I have spoken English since I was a boy. Hear my voice, then think of hers. I do not believe you will find such English spoken elsewhere among the émigrés. Her accent is very light, but that is not the oddity. She does not struggle with how the sentences form like most of us. Either her powers of imitation are very good, or she had the most excellent tutors."

"She said that those who do not learn the proper accent are lazy. She said she makes a special effort."

"The effort is obvious, and has led to surprising success. Along with her command of the words and patterns she is unusually fluent."

Unusually fluent. *Je suis désolée. I am sorry I failed you.* So fluent that she thought in both languages at the moment of death. And other times. *You, I want you.* Not *vous* or *tu,* but *you.*

Was it evidence that she had been superbly trained, as he first suspected? Could she actually pass as English if a mission required it?

He hated how his mind started slicing the evidence, looking for its meaning. He had wanted very badly to unmask this woman. Now, with Calvet handing him reasons to believe his judgment of her had been correct, he did not want to accept their implications.

Below in the garden, Penthurst made some gesture. He must have also said something clever, because Marielle laughed. She turned her face toward the duke and her eyes glistened with humor. Penthurst was not easily bedazzled, but Kendale could not imagine him being immune. *Do not be too at ease, Marielle. Do not let your language slip if he practices his French with you. He is the sort to notice.*

He forced himself away from the window and returned to Mr. Calvet. "Thank you for your careful attention to my request where she is concerned. What you have told me is fascinating."

"Well, she is a fascinating woman, is she not, Lord Kendale?"

"To broach the matter on which I wanted to meet. Penthurst said that you know the politics of your country very well. Not only the ministers and national leaders, but those of importance in the provinces."

"My occupation depended on always keeping my ears and eyes open. I have a more thorough knowledge of my country than most, perhaps."

"Does the name Lamberte mean anything to you?"

Calvet turned up his face, curious. "May I ask how you came to know that name?"

"I overheard it mentioned by someone."

Calvet folded his arms and thought before speaking. "Antoine Lamberte is currently an important member of the governing body in the Vendée region. Perhaps the most important in terms of influence. He has ambitions and will most likely be given a position in Paris eventually."

"Speaking of him appears to make you uncomfortable."

"I am usually at ill ease when talking about a man who threatened to kill me, Lord Kendale. It was after that region resisted the revolution and rose up. Lamberte is the illegitimate son of a baron. He was educated by his father, and even given a position in the family household as a steward when his half brother inherited. He joined the revolution, however, and was put out. The fighting in his family's area, near Savenay, was ugly. There was chaos. And when it ended, Lamberte's brother was dead. Not an execution. Just dead in the riots that engulfed the land. Within six months Lamberte lived in that château, much as his half brother had, only now as a representative of the new government."

"Why did he threaten to kill you?"

"I made the mistake of asking questions about the baron's death. I went to the Vendée to write about this sorry episode in our great undertaking, and heard of this death among so many. His own servants killed him, some said. On seeing all was lost, he killed himself and his mistress, others claimed. I confess that I thought I would write a novel about this man. It was an interesting story to me."

"Lamberte had other ideas on that, I assume."

"He called me to him. He might have been a baron, the way he sat and examined me. Then he let me know it would be a wise decision to leave Savenay." He held up his hands. "I left. But I watched him from afar. Because of the trouble there, he has more power than he might otherwise. None gainsay his decisions. He has kept the opposing faction down, at times by executing those who present problems. There is always a trial of sorts, of course."

"Your dislike is apparent. Does no one else find him troubling? Is he favored by all the ministers?"

"Not all. There are some who think he cannot be trusted. Some who think he only seeks his own gain. Criticism of how he lives — too much like his father in his taste for luxury, it is said. I trust that these saner minds will prevail in the end where he is concerned, but one can never be sure of that."

No, one could never be sure. "If you wrote your novel, how would the last baron have died? The suicide?"

Calvet shook his head. "Such a disheartening end that would be. In my novel, he would be killed by someone taking advantage of the chaos to hide a murder that has nothing to do with politics or the people's cause. Like most murders, it would be about envy and greed, and long-held hatred. It would be a human story, not a political one."

Chatter sounded near the house, coming in the window. Doors opened and it grew louder. Penthurst was speaking lowly, in French. Kendale tried to hear what he said.

"He speaks it well," Calvet said softly.

Of course he did. He was a damned duke. A damned duke who now flirted in French spoken too softly and quickly for Kendale to decipher.

"He is telling her that she must stay in London during the upcoming Season, so she does not miss the amusements to be had."

She did not have a wardrobe for the Season. If she explained that, Penthurst would probably offer to buy her one.

They entered the library, both bright-eyed and smiling. Kendale found the grace to invite Penthurst and Calvet to share a meal before they left and they all moved to the dining room.

Calvet regaled them with stories about the foibles of the French government and the new shining military star named Napoleon. Penthurst quizzed him a bit. Kendale just let them talk. Marielle looked lovely and more interested than most women would be, but then it was her lost country being described.

Finally it was over. Marielle excused herself to much flattery and deep bowing. It was all Kendale could do not to push his guests out of the house then. As they took their leave, Calvet trailed behind. He stopped outside the door.

"Lord Kendale, a word, please."

Kendale paused. Penthurst walked on and

stepped into his coach.

"I have been thinking for two hours now, trying to decide if telling you something would violate a confidence. I have concluded it would not."

"What is that?"

"Your mention of Lamberte surprised me. It was one more oddity. You see, while Mam'selle and I spoke alone, she asked after the very same man."

He walked away and stepped into the carriage. As it rolled down the drive, Angus emerged from the house and watched. "The duke looked the house over while he was in the garden like he planned to paint a picture of it."

"I expect so."

"I think he was quizzing her, about who was here and such."

"Perhaps." He would find out soon. "Go and tell the men they can come out of the cellars now."

She peered down the stairs while the guests left. Angus came in first, striding to the back of the house. Kendale entered a short while later.

He noticed her standing partway up. He paused below and looked up at her.

"You were flirting with him."

"I was amusing him. There is a difference."

"Is there now?"

"Of course. Everyone knows that. If you spent more time with people while they took their leisure you would know it too."

He strode over and came up toward her. His expression almost caused her to back up.

He took her hand and kept striding. She had to scamper to avoid being dragged.

He opened her door and swung her inside. To her astonishment he followed and slammed the door behind him. "Get on the bed."

She did back up this time, but then dug in her heels and stood her ground. "Are you *asking* me to *please* get on the bed, Lord Kendale?" She narrowed her eyes on him. "Are you *asking me* if I would like to play the role of your lover right now?"

That checked him. He glared at her, however, not pleased to be given this lesson today. His jaw firmed and dangerous amusement glinted in his eyes. "*Please* get on the bed, Marielle."

It seemed a waste to perhaps ruin this nice dress because of his odd humor. All the same she sat on the bed, then lay back. To her shock he lifted and flipped her so she hugged the coverlet. Another shock stunned her when he lifted her hips until she knelt, handling her like a doll, positioning her to his liking.

She felt her skirt rise. He pushed it high until it bunched at her shoulders and cool air touched her legs and bottom. Flushed now, and more aroused than she would admit to him, she looked over her shoulder. Hot with desire and who knew what else today, he unfastened his pantaloons.

She looked away and waited for him to thrust into her. She expected no preliminaries. So he astonished her again when he stroked her with unexpected care. That caress affected her deeply. Her whole body shuddered from a pleasure that eddied through her core. Again and again he touched, finally playing at the spot where it was most intense. The sensation became unbearable and she could not control her reactions. Burying her cries in the coverlet she raised her hips more and moved on that touch as thrills shot through her.

She felt a kiss on the small of her back. "Yes, like that, Marielle. Show me how you need me."

A new caress, testing, discovering, making it worse. Her whole body cried and begged. Her breaths became a series of gasps of astonishment rising higher and higher until pure and complete release shattered her. He thrust in then, finally, over and over, so hard and deeply that she thought she would feel him for days.

"The duke asked me if I would like to ride back to London with him and Monsieur Calvet," Marielle said that night after debating with herself whether to speak at all.

Tonight's passion contained little of the gentleness of the last one. He had claimed her, unmistakably so, from the moment he took her hand and pulled her up the stairs. Perhaps the dress had caused it, or else their visitors. She had not missed how Penthurst's presence darkened Kendale's mood.

He had mostly moved off her, but he still held her closely. She only mentioned Penthurst's offer because now, held like this, she did not know any fear, least of all of this man's anger.

"He was not propositioning me, either. I think he suspects you have imprisoned me."

He rose up on his forearms and looked at her. "What did you say?"

"I said that I would stay a few more days."

His gaze warmed. "It is not much of a prison if you choose to stay. I could not have stopped you from leaving."

"I will admit I was tempted, but . . . I did not want it known that you kidnapped women and forced them to live in this house. It could be badly misunderstood."

"I am not much of a gaoler if you worry about my reputation." He kissed her shoulder, as if acknowledging that prisoner and gaoler no longer described them or this odd visit.

"Did he say anything else interesting? Ask about the household here?"

She might have known he had guessed. "He noticed there were no women, or many servants at all and thought that odd. I told him I had not expected to be the guest of such a monk, but there had been comforts enough to sustain me for a short while."

"A monk? This is surely not a monastery. As for comforts enough . . ." His hand closed on her breast and stayed there. The sweet warmth touched her, and brought more comfort than he would know.

"He was not sure about us. I thought I would leave him to wonder." She stretched her arms until they crossed behind his neck. "Why was he here? So full of questions. Too curious for a mere guest. I thought he was a friend."

"He was a friend once. Perhaps he still thinks he is. I haven't decided that part yet.

However, he came, I think, so others would not."

"What others?"

"The kind of others who follow pretty Frenchwomen who have ambiguous histories."

That agents of the government might be curious about Kendale alarmed her. That he still spoke so easily about her questionable purposes made her sad.

She scolded herself for feeling hurt. What had she expected? That a few nights of pleasure would turn him into the stupid man she had first dubbed him? The comfort he spoke of was very different from what she felt. A good meal probably made him just as contented.

"Have you done something wrong? You hid most of these men today. From the duke?"

He rolled onto his back, releasing her. She waited for his arm to draw her close again. She would nest her head within his embrace like last night, and perhaps experience that timeless peace again. To her disappointment he remained still and alone, his profile firmly set.

"I have done nothing wrong. Nothing dishonorable. I have simply mapped a path to justice and walked the first few miles."

"Do you not have courts for that here? I thought the English had many of them. More than most countries need."

He smiled, but shook his head. "None of our courts will see to this."

"What good is being a lord if you cannot have justice in a court? I would think even corrupt judges would be careful to be fair in your case."

"You misunderstood. Our courts are useless because it is not an English matter."

He said nothing more. The subject distracted him. She sensed his mind turning in on itself to dwell on this map and journey he referred to, and its final goal.

She had become an intrusion in this bed. She pushed back the sheet and reached for her clothes. His hand closed on her wrist. He pulled her to him and tucked her alongside. She rested her head on his shoulder, and her soul sighed as she set aside the weapons she always carried, just in case.

"Do you know about the Siege of Toulon?" he asked, the quiet question floating in the silence.

"Of course." He spoke of an uprising against the revolutionary government six years earlier, one of many that ended in victory for the republicans. English troops and the English navy had been involved, supporting the royalists. It was on many lips now because this Napoleon who had risen so fast had one of his early shining moments there.

"I was at Toulon, assigned to O'Hara," he said. "After he was defeated and arrested, after it all fell apart, we needed to get out. A group of us hid in a house owned by a woman whom one of my fellow officers had befriended."

"They were lovers?"

"He thought they were. God knows that he thought he loved her at least. He planned to bring her with him and would not hear anyone's argument that it would be too dangerous. Feversham was not a man to be sentimental about women, so his view of her received more respect than if he had enjoyed a long string of mistresses."

A man a little like you, she thought.

"It did not hurt that she was very beautiful, I suppose. All of the men were a little envious of Feversham. This woman helped fifteen of us hide for a week. She brought back information on the deployment of republican forces in the town, and news of the executions. There were a lot of those."

There always were when insurrections were put down. Thousands died as the new government tightened its grip and enforced its authority in regions less inclined to accept the new order. Six years ago France had been a country where one either hid, or died, or fled.

"She found ways to buy enough food without it being obvious she fed so many. She tended two men who had received wounds. When she came back one day and told us that the troops guarding the road north had been called to another town and the way would be clear that night, we took the opportunity to make our escape."

A thickness formed below her heart. She thought she knew what would come next.

"The road was clear. For a mile we moved easily. Then suddenly they were all around us, coming from every direction. We were outnumbered and surrounded and fighting for our lives. Feversham's lover had indeed come with him, but when he tried to protect her she broke away and ran to the soldiers. They let her through their ranks and she disappeared. Then we all knew she had betrayed him and led us there to die." He paused for a long count, then sighed. "And die we did, most of us. I never thought to see such carnage."

"Feversham?"

"He was cut down but I dragged him with me when I fought my way through. He died on the way, though. Only four of us made it back."

His confidences had charged the air with intimacy, as if he shared a secret. Only it was not a secret. The whole world knew about Toulon. But his memories had evoked her own from the place where she kept them and they met in the silence. She came close, very close, to telling him that she understood better than he would ever guess.

"Is your justice about this woman?"

Another pause, then he shook his head. "I learned that a colonel took credit for this rout. Her brother, a tradesman, profited handsomely with some kind of reward. I think she confided in him, and he went to the colonel."

But she had brought them to that road. She had been the betrayer. "You did not answer my question. Do you seek to punish this woman?"

A much longer pause, as if he debated the question. "I do not kill women."

A startling answer. His justice would be in blood, it appeared. "And that colonel? Who was he?"

He moved again, so that he covered her and their bodies sealed together. He gazed in her eyes and she saw the pain that these memories had brought. She saw something else too. A man looking at a Frenchwoman of ambiguous history, cautiously.

His caress ensured she would not think about that now. He buried the doubt in pleasure. When he had her crying from it, wanting him so much she did not care about his justice or hers, or about trust or faith, he clasped her hands together above her head and held her like that, submissive and powerless, while he thrust into her. He made her his prisoner in truth for a while, but for all of his command and control of her, he could not obliterate the restlessness and stream of raw emotion that she had always sensed in him. Only now she understood why it was there.

Chapter 14

It was time. Past time. Kendale decided that while he rode beside Marielle the next afternoon.

She had little experience on horses and it showed. They had saddled the oldest, calmest mount in the stables for her, but now they paced through the field slowly so she would not be alarmed. She wore one of the riding habits owned by the last viscountess, a deep blue one cut and decorated to look like a military uniform. That struck him as typical of the nonsense women's fashions could embrace. Still, she appeared very pretty, even if she did not hold the reins correctly no matter how many times he showed her.

"We can return to London tomorrow," he said.

She did not smile. Her eyes did not glitter. He wanted to think she regretted the end of this sojourn.

"That would be wise. Dominique is probably concerned for me, and I am needed
there."

"It only requires that we finally have that
conversation that is long overdue now."

She cast him a sidelong glance. "The
unfinished business must be finished, you
mean. Do you not worry that having enjoyed
the luxury of this house, and the wardrobe
of a lady, I will refuse to finish the business
in order to stay?"

"No." She would not stay. She could not.
She had something to do. He just did not
know what it was.

"Then let me make quick work of this,
milord. I am not a spy. I swear it on the
souls of my parents. There, all finished."
She looked over, belligerently. "Do you
believe me?"

Did he? If he did not, he would have taken
her to the Home Office agent in Dover. He
wanted to believe he had not found excuses
not to, in order to get her into bed.

"Yes. Although you have taken pains to
send items to France. You even sought out
Garrett on your own when your messengers
ceased to help you. I would like to know
why."

"I told you that I help send over engravings that satirize the worst of the leaders

there. If you agree I am not a spy, what concern is any of this of yours? Are you now fighting smuggling as well as the French?"

"People smuggle goods each way to make money. You paid Garrett. He did not hand money to you. You appeared to be paying for a service."

She groaned with impatience. "I thank you for your interest in my affairs, but you have even less authority on this matter than on the other. Now, since that part of our unfinished business is settled, tell me when we leave. In the morning?"

He would not mind putting it off until later. Much later. Weeks later. He doubted this liaison would survive the return to town. She had her world there, and he his, and they both had duties that did not include the other. He could be excused for calculating how late it would be practical to leave, but delay only put off the inevitable.

"Yes, in the morning."

He thought she might not come to him that night. The pending end of their tryst shadowed the day, much like an approaching storm ruined a summer outing. It was just there, dampening the mood in the house, shading every glance they shared while the last hours of light passed. That evening he distracted himself by tending to estate business at the library desk. She read a book while reclining on the divan.

When they went above he kissed her as they parted, too aware it might be the last kiss ever. Then he went to his chambers, stripped off his coats, and opened a window so the breeze might refresh the nostalgia-laden air.

When a half hour passed, he knew for certain she had chosen to avoid the awkwardness of trying to pretend this passion might last beyond this house.

He threw himself into a chair, closed his eyes, and tried to list the steps he needed to take before his next journey. The dangers and pitfalls finally distracted him enough that he did not hear any sounds disturb the silence. Instead he felt her presence all of a sudden, and opened his eyes to see her standing ten feet away.

"Thank goodness. I thought you might be asleep," she said. "Or did I wake you?"

"I was not sleeping." He took in the sight of her, astonished at how grateful he was that she had come after all. "You are painfully beautiful tonight."

She tossed her hair over one shoulder and looked down at herself. "It is one of the ball gowns. I had to wear one before I left. I never have before. It took me a long time to decide which one to put on."

She had settled on one the color of champagne. Its low neckline revealed a lot of the top swells of her pretty breasts. A good deal of beading and lace and other things decorated the bottom of the skirt.

"You can have it. Take it with you."

She smiled but shook her head. "I have no use for it. Perhaps, however, the one I wore yesterday, I will take that. It would be nice to have something more à la mode when I go to parties or visit Emma or Cassandra."

Her reference to the wives of his friends reminded him that she passed through his world on occasion. He would see her still. He was not sure that would be a good thing.

"I am glad you came here tonight, Marielle. I did not think you would."

"A sensible woman might not, but I had to. I thought, however, that perhaps — not that I think so, but one never knows — you thought there has been much of a prisoner seeking the lord's favor in my agreeability. If so, tonight that is no longer a possibility. Nor an excuse."

She walked toward him, the satin fabric rippling like water and her long curls ablaze with a thousand flicks of gold from the candlelight. If he lived to be eighty, he would never forget the way she looked tonight.

Her impish smile played on her lips, but she tried to appear very sophisticated as befit that gown. "Also, I had to come because there is still some unfinished business. Only part was settled while we rode."

It took a moment for him to realize what she might mean. He waited, hoping he was correct. The mere thought made him harder.

Elegantly, smoothly, she lowered herself to her knees in front of him. Once again her gaze held the promise of untold pleasure while her fingers went to work on his lower garments. This time they worked more efficiently. Soon she held his arousal in her hands. Her fingers began to move.

Normally when she did this he could ride the pleasure and enjoy it for itself. Tonight he could not. Her gaze and position promised more and these caresses became taunts that deliberately, ruthlessly drove him insane with anticipation.

She looked at him, enjoying her power over him. Her thumb circled the tip of his cock and he swelled even more. She leaned forward until the top swells of her breast faced him. Her head dipped. Her tongue flicked. The tease sent a coil of delicious tension through his loins. She repositioned herself slightly and warmth enclosed him.

He gritted his teeth against the overwhelming sensations but soon they owned him, all of him, and he completely surrendered to the pleasure of Marielle's parting gift.

"Where were you? You were missed at sessions," Southwaite said. "The Whigs kept looking for you to add your voice to their insistence that there be no negotiations with France. There is nothing like someone who has fought on French soil to add gravitas to the argument."

"I was at Ravenswood. I doubt I missed anything during sessions. I never do. The debates are all of a type, and minds are rarely changed."

They chatted while playing lazy hands of vingt-et-une at a polite gaming hall run by Mrs. Burton. At the next table Southwaite's sister, Lydia, and Ambury's wife, Cassandra, gambled at the same game. As best Kendale could determine, Cassandra had come to keep an eye on Lydia, who had taken to gaming with dangerous enthusiasm. Ambury had in turn come to keep an eye on Cassandra, who had been known to lose big herself. Southwaite, who was not a man given to delegating his duties, had also come to watch his sister.

Kendale was here because he needed distraction from thinking about Marielle. Thus far neither of his friends had provided it.

"I have a question, Ambury," he said while he collected the winnings on the most recent hand. "You can answer too, Southwaite. When you would have liaisons with women, how long did they disrupt your attention and life?"

The question caught Southwaite in the process of asking for a card. His hand hovered in midair while his blue eyes reflected astonishment. He looked at Ambury.

"He has been asking such questions of late," Ambury explained. "Kendale, being Kendale, cannot simply pursue a woman, bed her, fall in love if Eros so desires, tire of her, and part from her. Prior to any sortie in this special war, he insists on nailing down the rules of engagement."

"Is he contemplating marriage?"

"Not marriage. He keeps asking about liaisons. Not whores either. He knows all about them. The middle ground. Mistresses."

"That is interesting. Rather sudden too."

"It had to happen eventually."

"Hell, I am standing right between the two of you."

Ambury clamped a hand on his shoulder. "I'll be damned, you are right here, aren't you. Now, to your question. It depended on the woman and what I discovered once things became intimate. This may shock you, but they are not all that they seem at times. Some of the clever ones become more dim-witted with each encounter. Some of the kind ones become cruel. It is very hard to keep a mask on during an affair."

"Let us assume that you concluded it would be best to end it, but you had not become so disillusioned. How long would she distract you?"

"You mean be in your head all the time? Interfering with normal occupations?" Southwaite asked.

"Yes. That happens at times, doesn't it?"

"Indeed it does. Has it happened to you?"

"Me? Don't be ridiculous. I am just curious."

"He is just *curious,*" Ambury repeated, catching Southwaite's eye.

"So what did you do when it happened, Southwaite?" Kendale said, swallowing the impulse to thrash Ambury.

"I tried to be good, but I usually bedded her unless it would be very dishonorable to do that."

"And that solved the distraction?"

"It usually was the beginning of the end."

"He wants to know what we did when it did not end," Ambury said.

"Yes. That was my question."

"Well, that only happened once," South-waite said.

"So what in hell did you do?"

"I married her."

Kendale threw down his cards in disgust. "Neither one of you is any help at all. For years I have had to listen to long, boring tales of your triumphs with women. Of your seductions and your mistresses, but it sounds as if you learned nothing from the battles. Each time you ventured forth as green as a new recruit."

His outburst garnered their attention rather too thoroughly. He had to suffer a few moments of them glancing meaning-fully at each other. He hated when they did that.

"Kendale, have you become entangled with some woman and can't see how to extract yourself?" Southwaite asked, his voice too much like an understanding vic-ar's.

"Is it Madame Peltier?" Ambury asked. "If so, all you need to do is cut off the gifts and she will be rid of you in a blink."

"I have not become entangled with Madame Peltier. I did not say I was entangled with anyone. I merely asked how long it takes for a woman who has been distracting you to cease to do so if you avoid her."

"Who is she?" Ambury said firmly. "You are far too curious of a sudden and there is some woman at the bottom of this. I insist you tell us who she is. You may think we acted as new recruits, but if *you* ever venture onto the field without our strategic advice, you may as well have a target painted on your chest."

"Damnation. I ask a simple question out of idle curiosity and end up insulted." He collected his winnings and took his leave. "Southwaite, you might look to your left. Your sister is winning big again. She should find tomorrow's lecture on the perils of gambling very amusing."

Marielle slowly turned the copper plate on its cushion while her hand guided the burin. She carefully carved the outline of a pleasure craft on a river that she had already engraved. She needed to make a few of her views to earn some extra money. The prints she sent to France earned nothing. They cost more than she normally could afford.

Nor would they alone solve her predicament. She needed to act, which meant she needed money. She doubted she had saved enough despite the deprivations of the last years.

A letter rested on the side of the table. It had come in the mail but she had not opened it. She thought it was from Kendale. It bore no special seal that said so, and she had never seen his hand before, but the paper had a quality that suggested it was his, and the penmanship reflected a confident, masculine writer.

She had not seen him since she climbed into his coach the morning she left Ravenswood a week ago. He had not even ridden back with her, but chosen to go on horseback. Just as well. That long journey would have been too sad if they shared it. They both knew things would be different in town. He would be going to parties with the best of society, and she would be in this house, listening for intruders, wondering if Lamberte would send more men to learn about her, worrying that the past was catching up with her before she had adequately prepared to meet it.

She turned her attention again to the burin. While she did the door opened. Dominique came in, walked over, and sat down. She lifted the letter and held it to the sunlight coming in the window.

"Are you going to open and read this or not?"

"Later."

"Is it from him?"

"Possibly."

"You have been so quiet and unhappy since returning, I would think you would want to know if it is, and what he writes."

She put her tool down and took the letter. She gazed down at it. "What if it is some dull, polite apology? That would break my heart. What if in hindsight he decided we had been rash and bad? Or worse, only I had been rash and bad?"

"He might have written a love letter. Did you consider that? He may have written that he cannot live without you."

She tried to imagine Kendale writing a love letter. The effort amused her so much that she laughed for the first time in a week. "I think it is safe to say it is not a love letter."

Dominique wagged her finger. "You read that now or I will open and read it for you."

With some trepidation, she broke the seal and smoothed out the paper.

It was not a love letter. Of course not. His words made her smile anyway. Or at least the ones that did not make her worried did.

My dear Marielle,

I have resisted the impulse to call on you to explain what I write here. I keep telling myself that decision is a wise one.

I want you to know that you are still being watched. Perhaps you noticed. There are men across the lane in an apartment that looks over the street. There is also a man who passes your house several times a day.

The men in the apartment are mine. I am inclined to leave them there until whatever intrigue you are pursuing is over. The man who walks by is not mine, however. He has been followed, but his various destinations shed no light on his intentions. Perhaps I worry for naught. Take care, nonetheless.

Should you have need of my men, the dark-haired one is Jacob and the fair one is Pratt. They will send for me if you ask, or you can yourself should that be necessary.

In a fortnight or so I may be gone for a while. Ambury thinks highly of you for helping his wife, and I am confident that any request of aid from him will be honored.

Your servant,
Kendale

Dominique took it out of her hand and read it. "He invites you to send for him."

"If I am in danger."

"Which you are."

"We do not know that."

"Don't we? Then send for him merely to enjoy his company. He will not care what the reason is. That is the letter of a man who has not turned a page where you are concerned."

Her heart wanted to agree. She imagined the joy of seeing him. Just the fantasy brought her happiness.

"I dare not."

"Why?" Dominique cried in exasperation.

She took Dominique's hand. "Because he will try to stop me. And when this man tries such a thing, he normally succeeds."

Dominique's fingers tightened around Marielle's. "Stop you? From what? My God, what have you been thinking this last week while you walked these boards so long into the night? Yes, I have heard you. Tell me now, so I can prepare myself."

"It is time. It is past time. If I wait longer, and discover a faster return would have made a difference, I will never forgive myself. Already it may be too late."

"Lamberte —"

"That is why it is time now. I do not know

if he came here in the hopes of finding me, or if he has gone to Paris to ingratiate himself. All I know is I am told he is not in Savenay. I may never have such a chance again."

Dominique shook her head over and over. "Your father does not expect you to come for him. He does not want you to risk yourself to free him. No father would want that. I have told you this for six years, Marielle."

"Perhaps he does not. It is my decision, however, not his. I do not only do this for him."

Dominique rose and paced, throwing up her hands while she muttered. She turned, fresh worry creasing her brow. "He will know it was you, of course. If you go there, and succeed, he will know you are alive for certain. Who else would help that particular prisoner escape?"

Marielle picked up the burin and carefully filed its tip on a sharpening stone. "I expect that is true. He will probably realize it was I and that I made it out alive."

"He will guess you have those records. The ones in the little book that you hide in the wall."

"Perhaps." She blew the tiny shreds of metal off the stone, then continued filing the burin.

"He will surely come here then, if he has not already."

"If he does, he will be one more poor émigré. He will have no power, no army. He will be in a strange land with no friends and many, many enemies." She turned back to the copper plate. "Let him come."

CHAPTER 15

It turned out, as Kendale learned to his annoyance, that avoiding a woman who distracted you did nothing to resolve the distraction itself. Rather the opposite.

He spent the next days planning for the journey he would take soon, but even that did not hold his attention the way it should. He would pore over maps and plot routes but suddenly the lines and papers would disappear while his mind wandered to memories of Marielle at Ravenswood. Not all of the images were erotic. A laugh, a smile, a taunt — he dwelled for long stretches of time on details that had entranced him.

He took to spending his afternoons boxing and fencing and riding hard through the parks, trusting the activity would help him sleep. And every night he lay abed for hours, too conscious of a void in himself where he never realized one existed before.

Three more days of this torture led him to a decision. Actually Mr. Pottsward led him to it. The valet had a talent for making one see the obvious.

He was examining a map of the coastal waters when Pottsward brought in his morning coffee. After pouring and laying down linen and spoon, Pottsward glanced at the map, then the papers strewn over the table.

"Will you be consulting your solicitor before you go, sir?"

"Why would I do that?"

"I thought you would need to leave instructions of what to do in the event you do not return. Is that not expected of peers? That matters of inheritance and such be clarified?"

Not return. The notion, while not welcomed, could hardly be called preposterous. All the planning in the world, and all the bravery, could not account for all eventualities. In a truly fair world he would definitely return, but he knew better than most that he could not count on it.

"I suppose I should meet with him."

"If you want, I will arrange a meeting tomorrow for you. Shall we say three hours? That will allow you time to alter your will if you choose. That last one was written in such haste and with such little care on your part that you may conclude it requires alteration. Should you want to provide for longtime retainers, for example."

"Are you deliberately being morbid, Pottsward? Is it your way of saying you do not approve of this?"

Pottsward made efforts to tidy the papers. "It is not for me to approve or disapprove. If it is the only way to finally resolve your anger over the loss of your comrades, perhaps it is for the best. Better like this than if you were still in uniform, acting recklessly in battles. I merely remind you that righteousness does not make a man immortal or invincible and that even the virtuous fail sometimes. It is the sort of thing one thinks about as one gets older."

He did not expect to fail. He certainly did not intend to die. He had not ignored the possibility that he might, but he had not dwelled on it either. Now he did, thanks to his valet.

He considered what he might lose and what he might regret. He viewed his plans and decisions from a new prospect. The only thought that made him pause, and the only moments that evoked a wistful sense of true loss, were when his mind turned to Marielle.

He perused his mail in a sober mood. Invitations had begun to arrive daily as the Season got underway. He glanced at each and made two stacks — a big one for balls and parties he would not attend, and a very small one of those that might have guest lists that included people whose company he did not find tedious.

One in particular caught his attention. Taking the letter, he had Pottsward call for his horse.

A short time later he tied up his mount on Albemarle Street and entered Fairbourne's auction house. Men moved through the large exhibition hall, cleaning and sweeping and hanging paintings. The manager, Mr. Nightingale, noticed him and hurried over.

"Lord Kendale, you honor us. How can we be of service?"

"I am hoping that Lady Southwaite is here."

"Lady Southwaite? Here?" He frowned in puzzlement at the question, as if it had been asked in Chinese.

The lady in question appeared in the office doorway at the rear of the chamber. With a warm smile she walked over. "Lord Kendale, how pleasant to see you. Do not be alarmed, Mr. Nightingale. Lord Kendale is a dear friend who knows all. He will be discreet about my continued involvement here."

She invited him back to the office. "We are very cluttered now. The days we hang are busy and unsuitable for visitors."

"My apologies for intruding then."

"Do not apologize. Please. I am always happy to see you."

She moved a small bronze statue of a nude woman from a chair so he could sit beside the desk. She perched on her own chair nearby.

He liked Lady Southwaite. He had liked her before she married and still did. Forthright and not given to the affectations of society women, she had proven herself to be as honest a person as he knew. They had shared at least one experience of the type that forged a bond between people. He expected that to make this conversation easier, although it would be one he had never had the likes of before.

He set the invitation that he carried on the desk. "Thank you for inviting me to your first grand preview of the Season."

She was not a beautiful woman in the normal way, but her direct gaze could compel one's attention. It had captivated Southwaite, and now captured him. "I hope that you will come."

"I would like to, thank you. However, I am curious to know if someone is on your guest list. I thought perhaps you would tell me."

"Someone you want to avoid?"

"Not necessarily. Have you invited Marielle Lyon?"

Her gaze cooled. "I always invite her. She does not come, however. I know you mean well, and that you believe her to be dubious at best, but I count her as a friend and am sure the rumors about her are untrue. If you think to warn me off associating with her, please do not."

"I did not come here to warn you off. I came to learn if indeed you counted her as a friend." He chose his next words carefully. "I was wondering if you would receive her here, or in your home."

"Her blood is better than mine, Lord Kendale. She is amusing, even fascinating. Why would a hostess not receive her?" She leaned forward conspiratorially. "The real question is whether they would receive *you,* sir."

He laughed. It was the damned truth, he supposed. Few besides Emma Fairbourne would say it outright, however. "Since you say that I am not sought after, my next question must be rephrased from how I had planned it. Would I be more acceptable or less acceptable if my name were linked with hers?"

Astonishment. Even shock, perhaps. Her mouth gaped a fraction. She stared at him. "Do you mean what I think you mean, when you say linked?"

"I believe so. There is no way to know for certain without being indelicate."

"Indelicate? Oh, my." She tapped her fingertips on the desktop, nervously. "Does Darius know? Does Ambury?" A thought made her frown. "Does *Marielle*? Forgive me. That sounds odd, I know, only I just realized that perhaps she was not aware that you had *indelicate* intentions."

"She knows of my interest in her, Lady Southwaite. I think she has known longer than I have. As for my intentions, I hope to formalize those soon. The matter of discretion needed to be addressed. With the world at large, of course there must be much of it. With my close friends, keeping a liaison a secret would be nigh impossible, and very awkward. I would not want to cause her to be insulted, however. So I am trying to determine if you, and perhaps Lady Ambury, would receive her and remain friends with her if you knew."

"How thoughtful of you. Truly. I assure you that I am the last person to cut a woman for this. I cannot speak for Cassandra, but I do not believe she would be cruel to Marielle for any reason."

"Thank you." He stood. "I will remove myself from what appears to be a busy day for you."

He opened the door.

"Lord Kendale, one moment."

He turned to her.

"Lord Kendale, have you . . ." she stammered, but collected herself. "Have you ever done this before?"

He just looked at her. She flushed deeply all the way up to her hairline.

"I refer to the *formalizing* that you mentioned, sir. Have you experience in it? I would not like to see her insulted anymore than you would."

"I have no experience at all, but I expect I will manage." He bowed and left, wondering how long he had to settle this before Ambury showed up to give him lessons.

Not long enough, as it happened. Ambury charged into his apartment just as Mr. Pottsward was brushing the coat he would wear that afternoon.

Ambury halted his stride right at the dressing room door. "Damnation. All those curious questions. *Marielle Lyon?* I thought you believed she was a spy."

Pottsward's brush paused a moment, then brushed on more purposefully. "You did not tell me you were calling on a lady, sir. I wish you had before I chose the coats."

"Does it matter?"

Pottsward sighed. He shot Ambury a glance. Hell, it was as bad as having Southwaite here.

Ambury stepped in and considered the coats. "He will have to do, Pottsward. Just a less formal knot in the cravat, perhaps, and a patterned waistcoat —"

"He has no patterned waistcoats, sir." Pottsward plucked at the cravat's tie and loosened it, then reached for a fresh linen. "I have told him repeatedly that he should have some made, but, well . . ."

"Yes, yes, I understand."

They fussed around him like two tutors preparing a pupil for his first public recitation. Kendale suffered it.

"There, that will do. Thank you, Mr. Pottsward," Ambury said.

Kendale checked his watch. "You just dismissed *my* valet, Ambury. Did you forget once again that I am in the chamber?"

"It would not do for him to hear us as we review your strategy."

"You have convinced me that you employ no worthwhile strategies. I am therefore on my own."

"What are you bringing with you? What jewels?"

"I am bringing no jewels."

Ambury grimaced. "See, that is why I came. You are ill equipped to do this on your own. It is customary, especially when a man broaches the topic you intend to broach, to bring a very nice gift."

"She can have gifts aplenty. Whatever she wants. But I will not bribe her today."

Ambury groaned. "It is not a bribe. It is a *gift*. As for her having whatever she wants, do not say that, whatever you do. She could ruin you if you make a promise like that."

"She will not ruin me. More likely she will refuse everything." Even him. Since he had never pursued a woman, he had never been rejected by one. He steeled himself for that possibility. It would probably be unpleasant in the least.

Ambury crossed his arms. "What are your plans, then? You must know before you go. Will you offer a house? An allowance? Do you intend to bring her here? Go to her home? Rendezvous out of town? Does she get a new wardrobe? A coach? A —"

"A wardrobe. Yes, I think she would like that."

"And the rest?"

"She and I will talk about it and decide, I expect." He took his gloves off the table.

"Where will you be meeting her? You are not going to call at her house, are you? A coach like yours will attract the attention of the entire neighborhood. Do you want her shredded by gossip?" Ambury pointed to the table. "Put down those gloves, and write what I tell you. You will ask her to meet you in the park during the fashionable hour."

He dutifully sat and wrote what Ambury dictated. Satisfied that he had shown his pupil the proper approach, Ambury departed, proffering tidbits of advice all the way out.

As soon as he was gone, Kendale crumbled the letter in his hand, picked up his gloves, and went down to his carriage.

Marielle noted the time and hurried to the front of the drawing room. Behind her the women chattered. A new stack of engravings had arrived, so the tables had filled with willing hands, some now rough from months of color soaking them when they dabbed the rags into the basins of thin paint.

She positioned herself so she could look

out on the street but not be obvious herself to passersby. Unless something had changed, and she hoped it had, the mystery man would stroll past within the next fifteen minutes.

Kendale said he had been followed, so she had never followed herself. If he did not slow as he passed her windows, if he did not always study the façade and alley, if his dark eyes did not remind her of a hawk's, she might believe he lived nearby, or had his employment in the neighborhood, and walked this route with regularity due to his day's occupations.

She spied him at the end of the block, taking his time, ambling like a man with nothing else to do. She watched him come, memorizing again his countenance and form. Was he French? Perhaps so. She wished she knew for certain.

Noise came from the other direction. The racket of a carriage rumbled louder. She turned her head to see it stop right in front of her house. It bore no escutcheon, but it looked much finer than any carriage to roll on this lane. The matched pair of bays did it proud.

Everyone noticed. Children emerged out of nowhere to circle the horses. Neighbors appeared at windows. People walking by slowed their pace. Even her mystery man appeared curious as he approached.

The gathering talk outside attracted Madame LaTour to the window. She peered at the coach and nodded with approval. "Very handsome. My God, look who it is. That lord who visited before. He has come to call on you yet again, Marielle."

Indeed he had. Dressed like a man of the highest society making calls on important people, Kendale stood near the door of the carriage after he stepped out. He turned and said something to his coachman. While he did, her mystery man began passing between the coach and the house.

At just that moment Lord Kendale stepped toward the door, right into the hawk-eyed man's path. They both stopped and looked at each other. She could see Kendale's face, but not the other. He gave the other man a glare that could cut stone. He made no attempts to move.

He said something. The other man hunched his shoulders, darted around, and continued walking with more deliberation. Kendale approached the door.

Madame LaTour made shooing gestures at Marielle with her paint-stained hands. "Go, go. Go up and fix your hair and change your dress, Marielle. We will visit with him until you come down."

Kendale sat in a little chamber in the back of the house, making small talk with the formidable Madame LaTour. The moments ticked by slowly. Painfully. He admitted that his dislike of such social situations was not what made it excruciating. He waited too hard, with too much anticipation, to see Marielle again.

Searching for a topic that might pass the time with less effort on his part, he asked about Madame Peltier. Madame LaTour had a lot to say about that lady. She chattered on, sharing tidbits of whispered scandal. His own mind wandered, but he thought he heard mention of Ambury in passing.

Finally Madame LaTour broke off her river of gossip in midsentence. Gazing past him, she smiled with approval at whatever she saw.

He turned his head, then stood at once. Marielle had entered in her small-stepped, silent way. She wore the dress she had taken from Ravenswood beneath the dark patterned shawl that had not been sliced in the alley. She looked beautiful, and would have even in her poorest garments.

Madame LaTour retreated to the other

side of the chamber. Marielle and he sat facing each other on two chairs.

"Is she to be your chaperone?" he asked, glancing to their company.

"Perhaps she thinks you will be shocked if I do not have one." She smiled at him so warmly that the last ten days might not have existed. "I am glad that you called, Lord Kendale. Is there a particular reason that we are so honored?"

"I thought it would be useful if that man who walks by knows you are not unprotected, should he have any ideas regarding either you or this house."

"That was kind of you. He appeared to take whatever you said to heart."

There were not many men who could hear a threat of evisceration with equanimity. He decided she did not need to know the details. "I would like to speak with you about something important to me," he said. "But not here." He glanced at Madame La-Tour.

"The garden?"

"I would prefer if you agreed to ride in the park with me."

"The park will be crowded. Your people have come to town for the parties and balls."

"We can go out of the city, if you prefer, and walk in the country."

"That might be wiser, no?"

Probably. He wanted to show her off, however. He wanted the world to know she was his.

Of course, she wasn't yet. The conversation to be held might indeed be wiser on a country lane.

She walked over to Madame LaTour. Much whispered French passed between them, with darting glances in his direction. Finally Marielle tsked her tongue with exasperation and strode away. "Come, let us go."

As soon as the carriage left her lane he could not restrain himself. He took her hand in his, and savored her soft, delicate skin. Then he lowered his head to kiss her palm and to inhale the scent of her.

Marielle never thought to see Lord Kendale humble himself in any way. Yet his head bowed over her hand while he held and kissed it, as if grateful for this small part of her. She raked her fingers through his hair and pressed her own kiss to his crown.

He released her and sat back. "I had to see you. I hope you are not annoyed."

"Not at all. I am delighted."

"I was warned there would be talk if I called on you."

"I do not care about that."

"Madame LaTour —"

"Madame LaTour only is concerned that I am not playing a game well, in a way to win best. She has no objections to the goal of the game, and assumes that your intentions toward me are not entirely honorable."

He waited until they were in the country, heading west before speaking again. In the interim she told him that Jacob had come over and introduced himself. She thanked him for troubling himself with her safety.

Her gratitude unaccountably irritated him. "How could you think that your safety would be a trouble to me? I would think that I have some responsibilities toward you after what happened at Ravenswood."

"No, you do not. No responsibilities at all. And no rights, Lord Kendale."

He scowled at that. She almost laughed. Now that was the face of the Kendale she knew.

He helped her down when they stopped. A rustic vista stretched in front of them, of a large field dotted with wildflowers and surrounded by trees and shrubberies. She could make out some roofs of houses in the distance here and there.

"This is Hampstead Heath. Have you been here before?"

318

"No. It is not far from my lane, yet it is another world."

"Walk with me. We will go to the hill. You can see the City from it, and St. Paul's dome."

They left the carriage and coachman behind and strolled down the lane.

"We did not speak when we parted about what had happened between us," he said. "I have regretted that."

There would be a dull, polite apology after all. Better in a letter if it had to come at all. "You should not regret anything. I do not."

"Don't you? That is good to know. What I meant to say was that we did not speak about whether there would be a future. I would like to talk about that now."

She laughed, and gave his side a little poke. "Did I become a bad habit so quickly? One that you find it hard to break now?"

Smiling, he caught her in his arm and held her to his side while they walked. "A most enjoyable habit. One that I do not want to break, and that I miss badly, rather like a man fond of drink who wakes to find he must sustain himself on coffee."

She looked up at him and admired his strong profile and the way the breeze tousled his dark hair. "You do not want to speak of marriage, I think."

He looked in her eyes warmly. Kindly. "No."

"I did not think so."

"It is not for the reasons you may believe, Marielle. It is not that you are not good enough, or not virtuous enough, or not English enough."

"You must admit those are three good reasons."

"They are the ones my dead father and brother would have given me, but they are not mine. Nor is it a lack of affection, although — I confess I am not sure how much is enough of that."

"For a man who does not speak much, or worry about his words, you can be most eloquent when you choose. That is perhaps the best way I have ever heard to express doubts about one's affection, and the cause and constancy of it."

He flushed. "I did not mean to —"

She stretched up and kissed his cheek. "Do not allow my teasing to dismay you. I understood you well enough."

"I do not think you understood me at all." He stopped walking and faced her, holding her hands. "If my mind went that way at all, it did not go far. You have told me you are not a spy, but you have not told me what you are instead. I have chosen to believe

320

your declaration, but I am not so blinded that I do not notice what you do not say as well as what you do. Only a soldier who is a fool chooses an ally who might be fighting on a secret front, Marielle. A peer of the realm definitely does not wed a mystery."

She understood. She also heard the rest that was not said. He would allow himself to know her for pleasure thoroughly and friendship partially. He would give her affection, but nothing deeper. Unless she were honest with him. Totally honest. Then she might have everything.

It tempted her. It would any woman. But telling him everything would surely make her unsuitable to be his wife, and maybe even his lover. He possibly already guessed as much.

"What does this soldier and peer propose instead, Kendale?"

"A different kind of alliance. We will do it with as much discretion as you want, although with our mutual friends I would prefer not to pretend. Tell me what it will take for you to agree."

"I do not think a formal arrangement would be to my liking. I am not sure that planning a lengthy liaison in advance is necessary either."

"Two weeks. We will try it that long. If

you do not want it, if you want me to call on you every time I need to see your face, so be it." He paused. "If you prefer I stop seeing you at all, we will do that too."

Two weeks. A brief trial. It was an ideal proposal, since any time longer might be impossible.

She considered her response while they walked up the hill. From the top she could see the rooftops of the City, and the high dome of St. Paul's. With the hilly terrain between this spot and its view, the church appeared surprisingly close even though it had to be several miles away.

He stood behind her and held her while they watched the low sun paint the dome in orange and blue. He turned his head and kissed her temple. His hand cupped her breast beneath the shawl. "Two weeks, Marielle. Say you will be mine at least that long."

"I will want a carriage available to me. It can be hired. I want to be able to move around the town quickly if I am to have rendezvous with you. And I do not want to visit you in your chambers where your valet serves you, or at my home where all those women will gossip."

"We passed cottages on our way here. They are close to where you are in town. I will let one. Will that do?"

"Yes. I think so."

He held her to his body closely. His hand still softly caressed her. She luxuriated in the way it made her sensuality purr.

"You require nothing else?"

"Madame LaTour will lecture when she learns that I did not demand property and jewels, even for two weeks. I do not want such things from you, however. I prefer this be an affair, not an arrangement."

He turned her in his arms, then took her face in his hands. He kissed her furiously. Her own passion soared at once.

They could not return to the carriage like that, biting and clutching and devouring each other, giving in to a primal fire stoked by long denial. Still entwined they stumbled to a tree. He turned her and she grasped at bark to steady her balance. He lifted her skirt impatiently.

A hard entry. Their sharp intakes of breath sounded in a harmony of relief. He withdrew with excruciating slowness. He thrust again. "Finally," he groaned.

Again he moved. He cursed, but it sounded more like a prayer.

She heard little after that except her own breath and cries. She did not know if anyone saw them mating under that tree. She did not care.

CHAPTER 16

Her carriage waited in a line of much finer ones that inched forward on Albemarle. Roll, stop. Roll, stop. She stuck her head to the window and judged the time left. Three ahead of her. Right now the Duke of Penthurst was stepping out of a very fine coach indeed, alone it seemed. He probably would not stay long, and was on his way elsewhere, but Fairbourne's would benefit from his attendance.

Finally the door of the auction house faced her through the window. A man at the door saw her and whispered to another who hurried off. The first man approached, opened the door, set out the steps, and handed her down. He took a good amount of time doing it.

She did not mind. This was a debut for her. She had never before attended a party hosted or attended by the best society of England. There were some émigrés who had patrons among the aristocrats here who helped them gain entry, but she was not one of them.

She nervously felt the silk of her dress, and the fine, soft wool of her mantle. The garments had arrived yesterday, delivered to her house wrapped in muslin. They came from Ravenswood, and were among the nicer items in that wardrobe. Even so she had not known which would be appropriate, and had exchanged several letters with Emma to get her advice.

The doorman escorted her in, but immediately released her. Another man took his place. Not a doorman or a servant. Kendale fell into step at her side.

"I told them to let me know when you arrived." He patted her hand. "You look beautiful, Marielle."

"Thank you for sending for the dresses."

"There was not enough time to have new ones made, I realized."

He had just promised a new wardrobe. Dominique would be pleased. Madame La-Tour had scolded about the property and jewels, but Dominique had only pointed out that she could not be on a peer's arm with the clothing she possessed. Of course she had not expected to be on his arm or at his side in this way. If she had not been so preoccupied with her own contentment when they climbed back into the carriage at Hampstead Heath, she might have had the presence of mind to reject his suggestion that they attend Emma's grand preview together.

The exhibition hall proved crowded. A small orchestra played music and servants passed wine. They took some, and she pointed out the objects displayed that she had brought to Emma from the émigrés, so they could turn luxuries into silver.

"Where is Lady Southwaite?" Kendale asked, looking around. "Ah, there she is near that wall, with her husband."

Marielle spotted them. Emma carried the catalogue sheets just like everyone else examining the works for sale. She and Southwaite discussed a landscape just like others who debated the value and attractiveness of the consignments. No one would guess, looking at her, that this abundant and impressive collection had been organized for sale by Emma herself. The man they believed really responsible stood at the head of the chamber, accepting all the credit from the guests who passed by.

"There you are. Well, well, *well."*

Marielle turned, startled by the low laugh near her ear. Cassandra and Ambury had come up behind them. Cassandra's blue eyes looked drunk with curiosity. Her very dark hair tumbled around her head and shoulders in a most artistic manner. She squeezed Marielle's hand tightly then kept it in her grasp. She gave Kendale her full attention.

"Lord Kendale, you seem well," she said. "Does he not appear well, Ambury? More rested than normal. More . . . something. Give me a moment. I am sure that I will understand the change in him."

"Cassandra," Ambury muttered in admonishment.

"Oh, no, do not scold. Do not dare. Lord Kendale does not mind if I tease him. Do you, sir?" She narrowed her eyes on him.

Kendale's expression remained bland. "Not at all. I might even say that your teasing is not only expected, but possibly deserved."

"Possibly? You have fallen off a very high horse, sir, and I intend to enjoy every minute of it." She laughed and wagged her finger at him. "I suffered from your prejudgment too often to allow you to escape easily now. We will have your reckoning later, however. Tonight, I am more interested in having fun with the lady who favors you with her company." She pulled Marielle by the hand. "Come with me, mam'selle."

Tripping after Cassandra, apologizing to Kendale with her eyes, Marielle was pulled through the hall. When they passed Emma, Cassandra gave her a firm poke in the back and kept walking.

They passed into the office in back. Cassandra closed the door and finally released Marielle's hand. Almost at once the door opened again and Emma slipped in.

Cassandra crossed her arms over her silver silk dress and ample bosom. She nailed Marielle in place with a glare. "How, please to heavens explain to us, did you find yourself romantically entangled with that rude, arrogant, hopelessly insufferable man?"

"They have been in there a good while," Kendale said.

"It has only been a quarter hour," Southwaite observed.

"What do you think they are doing?"

Southwaite and Ambury burst out laughing.

"Nothing much," Southwaite said, strangling to catch his breath. "Talking. Chatting the way women do. About . . . this and that." He barely got the last word out before laughing again.

"They are talking about me, you mean."

"Oh, yes," Ambury said. "I think so."

"I don't think that would take long, or even be very interesting."

Southwaite rested a hand on his shoulder. "Kendale, in your family's library, do they have one of those anatomy books? The kind with plates that show all the organs and veins one would see upon dissecting a human body?"

"Of course. My tutor would use it. He made me memorize the name of every bone. Perhaps he thought I was only fit to become a surgeon."

"Well, you are the body, and they are the surgeons, and right about now Ambury's wife is going for your liver."

"Or more likely your bum," Ambury mused. "I think that once she saw it, so she might feel compelled to comment on that."

"She *did*?" Southwaite asked, astonished. "How did I miss this?"

Kendale glared at Ambury. Ambury bit his lip, no doubt remembering that Southwaite had not been regaled with the episode because Cassandra had not been the only woman there.

"So it is a physical dissection that is underway," Kendale said. "It is interesting to learn women do that. Ambury suggested as much once, but I did not believe him. Do you think it will take much longer?"

"I am joking. More likely it is your character being discussed. Do not worry. Emma will defend you, as will Miss Lyon, surely," Southwaite said. "Our wives will express concern and curiosity like good friends, but in truth they are dying to know how this came about. It is, you must admit, an unexpected development that piques the imagination."

Kendale wanted to think Marielle would defend him, or at least not be swayed by Cassandra's obvious prejudice. As long as that did not happen, the ladies could talk about him all they wanted.

The door opened. The ladies emerged. Two went to their husbands. Marielle came to him. They returned to previewing the paintings.

"What did they want?" he asked.

Marielle pursed her lips while she examined a history painting showing a Roman matron and her children. "They wanted to make sure that you are not taking advantage of me, and that I am not under any illusions regarding your intentions. I was polite because they are my friends, but, really, do they think I am stupid? They explained life to me as if I had just come in from a farm on the back of a cart."

She did not appear vexed, just a little insulted.

"I expect that was annoying."

"Very annoying. I am not a child. I have seen more of the bad in people than they will ever see, I hope to God for their sakes. And they do not understand you at all, Kendale. You have, I think, been too reserved with them. They do not know the man you are. I had to tell Cassandra that you are not — well, as she said."

She *had* defended him. He pictured it and smiled, both amused and touched. He tilted his head near hers. "Do you know that you are the most beautiful woman in this entire assembly?"

She brightened, pleased with the flattery. Not a false flattery, though, such as that spewing from so many other mouths here tonight. Look as he might, he really could not see another woman to equal her.

He wanted to take her away then. He wanted to ride to that house he had let and see if it suited her. He wanted to have her alone, where they did not have to be discreet. Mostly he just wanted her.

They stayed another hour. Marielle enjoyed herself enough that he did not want to interfere with her foray into society. He bade his time and dug up some pleasantries to mumble when acquaintances stopped to talk. When it was over he admitted to himself that it had not been as tiresome a night as he normally found such events. Perhaps that had been because he saw how it gave her pleasure.

Marielle did not walk to her meeting with the new messengers. She rode in the carriage Kendale had hired to be at her disposal when she needed it. She had insisted that he hire one with a French coachman so that one of the émigrés would earn some coin.

As she stepped out she wondered if his men followed her. She could see him doing that for her safety now, much as he kept Jacob across the way. Her reassurances that she was not in danger had fallen on deaf ears.

They did not speak of his questions, and the ones she never answered. She did not even know if he still suspected her of being a spy. He might have convinced himself she was not one, but that did not mean that he did not still consider it a possibility.

The thought of Kendale made her pause beside the carriage. This afternoon, this carriage would take her to the cottage. Kendale would ride in a while later. They would send the carriage away, to return in the morning. Most of the time between would be spent in bed. But not all of it.

Twice now they had visitors. It had surprised her when, two days ago, a man arrived at their door. Kendale went outside with him, and held a serious, private discussion. She had not recognized the man as one from Ravenswood, but she guessed he was part of the private army.

Steeling her spine and her bravery, she put thoughts of Kendale aside and entered the alley just enough so her eyes would adjust to the dim light in it. She had no intention of walking into it deeply. Never again would she be that careless.

She waited, making herself visible. Eventually a shadow moved and a man stepped into the light. He assessed her, and came forward. Only then did she walk another twenty feet. No more.

"Farmen sent me," he said, naming the stationer in Dover. He spoke English. Monsieur Farmen had indicated he thought English would be better in the future.

"I have only this." She handed over a letter and the fee. "It is to go to Monsieur Garrett directly. Carry it yourself. Do not leave it with Monsieur Farmen."

He looked at it. "That is a lot of money

for posting a letter that the regular service will carry for pennies."

"I do not know how to post a letter to Monsieur Garrett. I do not know if that is even his real name."

"Does he know how to post a response to you, or will you be waiting three weeks for me to bring one?"

"That is not your concern. Just take that to him after you give Monsieur Farmen his fee to ensure he remains a friend."

He chuckled. "Friend. As good a word for it as any, I guess." He tapped his hat with the letter by way of farewell.

She returned to the carriage. Her coachman, André, made a skeptical face at her. "Perhaps I should explain to his lord that you meet strange men in alleys."

"Did he tell you to report my movements?"

He shook his head. "Perhaps he would prefer I did anyway."

"He would think you did not know your place if you told him such a thing." She fished in her reticule while she spoke. Clumsy things. Her old pockets had served her with more subtlety. "Here. Take this. Not as a bribe, and certainly not as blackmail such as you foolishly attempted. Rather for keeping watch so carefully, so I would be safe."

André pocketed the coins. He opened the carriage door and turned down the steps smartly. From his expression, she knew they had reached an understanding.

He trusted her as much as a man could trust a woman who insisted on remaining more than half a mystery. Which meant that as much as he wanted to make decisions based on trust, there were some he could not.

Before making one decision in particular, Kendale called on Ambury at his home on Berkeley Square. He was received in the library. Ambury had been writing some letters. Cassandra's aunt sat in one of the chairs near the fireplace, reading a book.

Ambury greeted him, pointedly noted the muslin roll he carried under his arm, and suggested they go to his study.

"If you want privacy, you should just ask for it, Ambury," Lady Sophie said, setting her book aside. "You were here first. I was the one to intrude. I did not realize you expected a visitor."

"There is no need for you to leave. We will do as well elsewhere."

"Tosh. I will stroll in the garden. I could use some air." She gripped the chair arm to support her rise to her feet. After arranging herself upright, she took the time to notice just who the visitor happened to be. Her eyes lit with delight. "Kendale. Oh, my, it is delicious to see you."

Delicious seemed an odd compliment, but then this was an odd woman. "Thank you. The joy is mutual."

Rather spry suddenly, she advanced on him, giving him a thorough scrutiny from head to toe. "I always said there was more to you than others gave you credit for."

"Thank you again. I think." He looked at Ambury, wondering if he was among those others, or only his wife. Ambury opened his hands in a gesture of perplexed confusion.

"But a Frenchwoman?" Lady Sophie said. "With your lack of experience, do you think it is wise?"

He found himself at a loss for words.

"I understand the appeal," she continued. "Such a lovely language, for one thing. Even base matters sound elegant in French. *Merde,* for example. How much nicer that sounds than sh—"

"Aunt Sophie, I do not think Kendale's head gets turned by the sound of a language."

"Nonsense. Everyone loves the French language and is lured by it. Goodness, my

337

head was turned by a Frenchman who had nothing else to speak for him except the sound of his voice. I only acknowledge his limitations in hindsight, of course. At the time I was madly in love for a good fortnight." She caught herself, and smiled apologetically. "I did not mean to imply that your current affair will only last a fortnight, Lord Kendale. I am sure it will see you through the Season."

"It is reassuring to know that you believe I will have enough time as that."

"You will have time if you make time and you take time, sir. Too many men do not comprehend that *l'amour* and impatience are not compatible. You appear puzzled. I would be happy to explain. If you have taken up with a Frenchwoman it would not do to have you ignorant. For the pride of England you must acquit yourself well." She looked around, seeking a chair on which to perch so the conversation could continue.

"The garden, Aunt Sophie. I believe you said you wanted some air," Ambury interrupted.

"I did? Well, it is a fine idea, so I will embrace it. Farewell, Lord Kendale. Call whenever you need advice. You will find none better than mine."

"My apologies," Ambury muttered while

she walked to the garden doors. "She has lost all notions of discretion."

"She could not be indiscreet with me unless others first were with her. I am glad my suitability to maintaining an affair with Miss Lyon is providing the entertainment in drawing rooms this week."

"Hell, what did you expect? You accompanied her to Fairbourne's grand preview. The whole world saw you leave together too. Do not let it annoy you. The scandal sheets will move on to others soon enough."

He had no idea he had been in the scandal sheets. He never read them and right now, even if he normally did, he did not have the time for such frivolities.

"What is that there?" Ambury pointed at the roll covered in muslin.

"A conundrum. You are going to help me see my way clear out of it." He set the roll on the desk, untied the string holding the muslin in place, and allowed the whole of it to unroll.

Ambury bent his head to the engraving on the top. "Interesting. These are being made either for the French market, or to sell to the émigrés here. I would think the former. Who is he?" He pointed to Lamberte.

"A government lackey in one of the provinces."

"Well, someone is accusing him of the sort of embezzlement that gets heads lopped off over there."

"I was more curious whether you see anything at all on that image that might be other than it appears. A message, for example, that only the initiated would see and understand."

"Do you mean a code?" Ambury peered hard at the image, then at the words engraved all over it. "Would have to be a very short message if it is among those sentences. I can see nothing to suggest such a thing. Can you?" He lifted the top image and held the paper to the window's light.

"No. However, I wanted another opinion, and another pair of eyes." Satisfied, he began to roll the prints again. Half of his conundrum had been solved. He trusted Ambury to give good advice on the other half.

The door opened then, and Lady Ambury entered. She looked around the library, and sighed with exasperation. "Where has she gone? I told her to wait *here.* Ambury, did you see Aunt Sophie?"

"She has gone to the garden."

"Oh, *no.* How could you allow that? We

are to make calls together. Now she will be covered in mud and —" She noticed the engravings. She came over, curious. "What have you there? Ah, she has turned her scorn on French fools, I see. That is understandable, but I will miss how she skewered our English ones so neatly."

"What do you mean, *she*?" Ambury asked.

"Why, Marielle. This is her work, I am sure. Did you not tell him, Kendale?"

"No, he did not, although one of his questions makes more sense now."

Lady Ambury lifted the top print to reveal an identical one below. "Why, these are new. She has not sold any of them yet. I hope that you have not scolded about this, Kendale. Those views of hers are much more artistic, but they do not sell nearly as well as her satires."

"I do not think I have seen her views," Ambury said.

"Nor I," Kendale said.

"They are lovely. Scenes of the river, mostly. She would not show them to you. I am surprised she did with these. She would fear that you would be scandalized that she plied a burin on copper, just as the women who dab that paint never admit to others that they labor for pay in that house." She stilled suddenly, as the last words emerged.

341

She flushed. "She did not show these to you either, did she? You discovered them on your own somehow, and I have revealed something she would not want you to know."

"Do not castigate yourself over it," Ambury said. "Kendale here understands that Miss Lyon must earn her bread. He has seen that house. These can hardly shock him."

"They do not shock me at all. I am glad to know she made them." He could not decide if that would make what he had to do easier or harder.

"Her desire to remain anonymous would explain why there is no credit taken or any address, I suppose," Ambury said. "I merely thought them unfinished."

"They are unfinished, I believe," Cassandra said, bending over the print. Her dark hair dangled in long tendrils that brushed against the paper. "I was once shown a satire she did and it had a name and address. All fictional. Her views will have her address, but not her name. She uses male names instead."

"So the engravings being colored in that house are made by her," Kendale said.

"Some of them. Mostly she brings in others from printers. If you asked, I am sure she would explain it all to you. Now, I must find my aunt before she pulls out half the garden. Please excuse me."

After Cassandra left, he finished rolling the prints.

"Your question, about the code," Ambury said. "You are still not sure of her."

"I am sure of her. I was not sure about these."

"Yet she makes them. So . . ." Ambury shrugged. "If we are all wrong, she is unlikely to do anything with you in her life. She would not have much chance for it, would she? Nor would she get away with it. I trust you have not embarked on this affair for that purpose, Kendale. To keep watch on her and her movements, that is. You risk far too much if you have."

"I came here to be convinced that I was not making excuses and refusing to see what I did not want to see. Also, to ask for advice. She does not know that I have these. She thinks they were lost. I allowed her to believe that."

"You lied to her."

"At the time I believed I was lying to a spy. I would like to return them to her now, and explain."

"You would like to rectify that lie so it might not stand between you in the future."

"Exactly. How to achieve that has puzzled

me. I thought you might help."

"Let me see if I can provide you with the words. *My darling, at a time when I did not yet enjoy your favors and we were not as one, I discovered these images and kept them, unbeknownst to you, because I believed them to be evidence that I could use one day to have you hanged.*"

"I can be that clumsy all on my own. You are supposed to find a better way to say it, so I do not appear a scoundrel to her."

"*My dearest, I have been in possession of some of your property for some weeks now, and thought it best if I returned it to you. My only excuse for my deception is that at the time I believed you to be the worst fraud, and entirely untrustworthy.*"

"That is hardly better."

"Kendale, there is no good way to say it. It can't be prettied up with eloquence. Better to say it in your Kendale way and hope she has enough affection for you to understand."

He left Ambury's house even less contented than when he had entered. By now the mystery of Marielle should be unwinding. Instead it only seemed to deepen. Ambury's questions did not sit well either.

He *had* toyed with the idea that an affair would keep Marielle close, so he could eas-

344

ily keep watch over her. It had been one possible excuse that he considered for doing what he wanted to do, during her first days at Ravenswood. She had convinced him she was not one, however. He did not want to think that had merely been lust making him blind after all.

This was not a time he wanted to be doubting her. Soon, too soon, he would embark on a mission that held risk and danger, and he wanted to spend the remaining time enjoying the rare contentment he experienced with her. Instead the last hour had him wondering if that contentment had turned him into the worst idiot, the kind he had sworn he would never be — a woman's fool.

He did not think she had used her wiles to obscure his thinking, but . . . An engraver, now. In England the daughters of the aristocracy might draw or do watercolors, but engraving? He thought it unlikely that the niece of a comte would have been taught this skill. Men in England served apprenticeships for such work. Using a burin on copper did not lend itself to dabblers. Cassandra had said that the other prints, the views, were lovely too. An expert engraver, then.

He wondered how many people knew she

possessed this skill. The rumors she was a charlatan could have emerged from people learning about it.

He could no longer pretend that the rumors were wrong.

CHAPTER 17

Marielle loved the cottage. She enjoyed looking out the windows and watching buds and shoots emerge in the rustic garden outside. She found the low-beamed ceilings cozy and the big hearth domestic. She noted how, whenever André pulled up outside and she emerged from the carriage, it seemed she had stepped into another world.

A fantasy world, perhaps. One where no dangerous quest waited and no dangers lurked. One where, for a while, Kendale was not a viscount and lord, but just the man whom she embraced in peace and passion.

She had taken to arriving at the cottage early, so she would have a few hours to play at being a simple country woman with nary a care in the world. Today she sent André off with instructions to come back for her in the morning, and eagerly entered the house. She carried a basket of food that she had cooked in the kitchen of her house, darting in to stir the stew and knead the bread between dealing with the new engravings, some to be colored.

She set the bucket of stew near the hearth and stirred in embers she had brought in a firepot, so that there would be some warmth for both food and the night. She put the bread on the table and admired the fine job she had done with its form and baking.

The cook had found her intrusions into the kitchen odd and annoying, and even seemed surprised that she knew how to form a loaf. Marielle Lyon should not. It had given her joy to do it, however, and to know that Kendale would eat food made with her own hands. Quite a bit of nostalgia had filled those private moments too, and memories of doing this for her father.

Not a sound interfered with her hour in the cottage, other than those of nature outside. She savored the calm, and her happiness. Thoughts of Kendale's arrival brought poignancy to her heart, and also a stirring anticipation.

Two weeks he had said. The fortnight was almost over. She sat near the window and watched a mouse nose its way through some ivy in the garden while she clung to the joy that would certainly end soon. She would have to end it, wouldn't she, if she were to do what she had to do?

The sounds of another carriage worked its way up the lane. That would be Kendale. He too had one bring him here, so he would not have to deal with his horse on a property ill suited to maintaining one. She knew the sounds of all of his carriages now, and recognized the fine one that had called on her when their estrangement ended. Its wheels gave out that particular cry as they stopped.

He entered, his hair mussed from the breeze and his high boots dirty from a day of riding. He carried a long fat cylinder covered in muslin that he set on a chair, then came over and gave her a kiss.

"All is well at your house?" he asked.

She stood and linked her arms around his neck. "Very well. That man who was walking by still has not returned. Jacob and Pratt still watch out their window. The women are busy with a new stack of engravings sent by a book publisher. And Madame LaTour has been most helpful so that I can steal away to visit this little cottage."

"You come early, so she must be very helpful." He embraced her, but looked around the humble sitting room. "I was concerned you would find this too poor. It was all that was available immediately, however."

"I find its simplicity charming."

He looked down at her warmly, but she sensed a distraction in him. Not one that removed her from his attention. Rather it centered on her, and caused him to concentrate on her too thoroughly. She waited for words that she saw in his eyes and felt in the air.

Instead he kissed her. A mere brushing of his lips at first, then more fully. His arousal changed the kisses even more. It appeared the stew and bread would not be eaten for a while.

The kisses turned hard, devouring. His embrace encompassed her tightly. She recognized the signs of impatience. When he picked her up and carried her to the small bedchamber, she wondered if he would even bother to undress.

He surprised her, as he could at times. Instead of throwing her on the bed he set her on her feet and set about disrobing her. Suddenly he was taking his time, a lot of it, carefully unlacing her dress and working the hooks on the back. Reverently folding each garment and setting it on the chair. And always, each time he looked at her, that concentration.

Her own arousal teased and played at her. Her body waited and her thoughts blurred. When she was naked, however, he traced the curve of her form from shoulder to thigh in a slow, careful line drawn by two finger-tips. The way he looked at her then, that deep consideration, caused a note of worry in the melody of her bliss.

She stopped his hand by clasping his wrist. He had to look up at her then. "You look at me as if you are memorizing me," she said. "Are you leaving?"

"My journey is not for a few days yet, at worst."

She had not only meant that journey that he planned. Relief sighed through her heart when he only heard that question, however.

He laid her down then undressed himself. Instead of impatience he took infinite care in how he handled her. The pleasure was as slow and sweet as that night at Ravenswood, when she forced him to admit he wanted her. This time it affected her differently. He might not be leaving, but she could not ignore that he would be soon, and she would be too, and this fortnight of happiness had almost ended.

She clung to him as a result. She held him as closely as she could. She did memorize him while she caressed, and listened to his breaths and noticed every detail of his touch. Soon, very soon, the pleasure sank low in her and every kiss, every tease, deepened it so she was ready much sooner than he.

It maddened her to wait. Another day she might have demanded he join with her. But she sensed this slowness was not for her sake, but his. He did not lack desire. The evidence of that was undeniable and prominent. Rather that concentration distracted him still, and she guessed he was noting every touch as much as she did.

He could tell how much she wanted and needed him. She did not know how to hide it. He indulged himself a while longer anyway, carefully closing his teeth on one of her breast's tips while he flicked the other with his thumb. She cried out at what it did to her, and on impulse grasped his hand and tried to move it lower.

Instead he rolled and brought her above him. "Take what you want, Marielle. This way I can still admire you."

Almost frantic now, she grasped him and rose up. She lowered herself and all of her gave a silent moan when he filled her.

She sat back, absorbing him and enjoying the welcomed fullness. Dusk gathered outside, and shadows grew in the chamber.

No candles had been lit, so the light had turned gray and soft.

She enjoyed looking at him like this, at his handsome face and intense eyes. She reached out and caressed his hard shoulders and chest, moving down until her fingers touched the new scar, still somewhat red, from the wound he received in the alley. That made her look at her own body and the fine line on her hip.

She rose up and lowered herself again and watched his reaction.

"Slowly," he said. "So it is a new revelation each time."

She did it how he wanted. "That is almost poetic."

He smiled in amusement at her description. It was the first smile of the day, she realized. He reached out and drew his fingertips along that welt on her hip. "I do not think this is the first time you have been hurt, Marielle. There are no other scars, but not all wounds leave them on the body. That is especially true for women."

She stopped moving.

"There are things I have not thought much about," he said while he caressed her slowly. "I chose not to, because one thing leads to another and they would all lead back to the mystery of Miss Lyon. But you were a girl when you came here, and you came alone. Unprotected. Were you hurt as you made your way through the hell that was France then?"

She leaned forward until her face hovered mere inches above his. She slammed shut the door in her heart that his words had nudged open, before too much sorrow could escape. "First poetry, then a cruel question guaranteed to ruin my pleasure. I expect you to make amends, my lord."

"Of course. My social skills still need much work."

He did make amends. He kept her in that position with kisses while his hands devastated her by teasing at her breasts. Each touch and flick made her tremble where they joined. He moved her forward so he could use his mouth and that made it wonderfully worse, especially since they barely remained connected then so the teasing created powerful shivers of pleasure. He finally released her when she had grown crazed, and she rose up on her arms and slammed her hips down hard so he filled her again.

She took what she wanted then, as he had said to. She moved this way and that, finding relief that also made the marvelous sensations of release begin. He grasped her hips and took over, and no longer was it slow and sweet, but almost violent in how he thrust into her. She came twice before he was done, and again at the end when, limp and exhausted, she accepted the last of his turmoil.

Night had fallen. He did not sleep. Marielle did not either. He could tell, even though she did not move in his arms. She rested in the crook of one, with her head on his chest. Her palm lay flat on him over his heart.

His reluctance to leave the bed came from many things. The comfort of holding her. The new questions that would not leave his head. The roll of muslin out in the sitting room.

"I was not hurt as such," she said into the silence.

"Do not speak of it if you do not want to. It was churlish of me to say anything." It had been an impulse, a thought spoken aloud as he looked at that knife wound and thought about Marielle the mystery and how much he had assumed that had probably been very wrong.

She did not respond, so he assumed she did not want to. But she shifted in his embrace and, it seemed to him, huddled closer.

"You said you were at Toulon, so you saw how it could be when rebellions against the new government were put down. It was the same elsewhere. France was as bloody after the revolution as during. There was much killing."

Especially in the west. *She does not speak like a person from Provence, but from the west.* Two people had told him that.

"I expect the entire country was not safe," he said. For a girl to travel alone — He did not want to imagine the kinds of danger she would have seen.

"Not safe at all. Every man loses a part of his humanity in such a world. I saw enough to know how it might be when I fled. So, as I left, I arranged to be protected."

Of course she had. It had been the smart thing to do, and she was very smart. "Were you hurt?"

"Not the way I think you mean. He was someone I knew, not a stranger. I understood the bargain as I took it. I was not forced, if that is your question."

That she assumed it was gave him some relief. If Marielle did not know how some men hurt women as part of pleasure, he would leave her with that small corner of innocence.

"It was as if it were happening to someone

else," she said. "That was my only memory of it, in truth. Other emotions, bigger ones, occupied me. I was glad to have a man with a pistol and some bravery guiding me to the coast and helping me find a boat. But, of course, I would never be an innocent again. I had lost so much of my childhood from what I had seen, it seemed a small loss in comparison, however."

It touched him, how matter-of-fact she spoke of it. He debated anew whether he really needed to know anything else about her. Perhaps all the rest really did not matter.

He laughed at himself, but not happily. Here he was again, finding reasons to avoid learning the truth. He could only hope she did not realize what an idiot he had become because of her. For her. It was a hell of a thing to find yourself counting on the good character of a person you had sworn could not be trusted.

"I expect that you learned to live with fear during that time," he said.

"It was my constant companion." She turned and looked down at him. "It is interesting how that changed people. I have noticed that some of us live in fear still. It will not go away now no matter how safe we are. Others of us learned that one must move forward even when afraid."

"Which are you?"

"I was the latter, but — I have learned that it does not take much for it to own me again."

He almost wished it owned her, if it meant she did not move forward on whatever scheme she had in mind. She did have one. Those engravings and that visit to the coast said as much. If she was not a spy — and his heart said she was not no matter how often his brain debated it still — then she schemed in some other way. Probably a dangerous one.

He caressed her face until his fingertips found her mouth. They rested there, on their softness. His eyes could not see her face, but his mind could. She had worn many masks with him in the past, but he guessed that now, in the dark, as they held each other, she did not.

"It does not have to own you. If you ever need protection, I will give it to you. Even if we are no longer lying together like this, I will keep you safe if you allow it."

She opened her lips and caught his finger between them. Then she pressed them to his chest. She sat up, and gave him a little poke. "You may not have a stomach, but I do. There is food waiting."

■ ■ ■ ■

They ate her stew on the little table, both in dishabille. He wore pantaloons and a shirt, and she her chemise and her shawl. He built up the fire some so the night would not make them cold in such undress.

"This is good bread," he said, breaking off another piece. "You have a better baker than I do at Ravenswood."

She nibbled on her own, secretly pleased at the compliment. From where she sat she could see that roll of muslin that he had brought. She wondered what it was. Not a gift for her, from the looks of it. Perhaps one of those men would visit tomorrow and take it away.

"You said that you would not be leaving on your journey for several days at least," she said. "Or perhaps not at all?"

He used some bread to sop up the sauce from the stew, which also gave her pleasure. "I am committed to go at some time. I await some information first, so the exact day is not clear."

"But it will be soon?"

"Yes, I think so."

She had assumed that his suggestion that they try this affair for two weeks had something to do with this journey's start. She had made her own plans accordingly. Now she wondered how she would make changes if his own departure were delayed.

Her brain began calculations but her heart hoped he would be delayed forever. If so she would not be able to execute any plans, and be free of them for a while, and instead continue this idyll of pleasure and safety. How quickly this cottage lulled her into forgetting the world that waited back in London, and in France.

"Where are you going?" The question emerged without her choosing to speak. Her heart gave it voice, not her head.

He said nothing.

"I am sorry. You would have spoken of it if you wanted to. Of course you cannot tell me."

"Why do you think I cannot?"

A good deal of joy instantly vanished from the little chamber. Rather suddenly he appeared very much an army officer again. "You cannot because you do not know who I am, as you once said. I am a mystery and might yet be the spy you suspected."

He reached for her hand and held it firmly. "Why do you think a spy would have interest in this journey? I could be planning a circuit of the family properties."

"I suppose I thought — that is, I assumed that — your discretion on it alone suggested it was something more." She stammered, uncomfortable now, and guessing each word she said only made it worse. "And those men, the ones who come here to talk to you —"

He smiled, much to her relief. "You may not be a spy but you would make a good one." He lifted her hand and kissed it, which relieved her even more. "To speak of it would only spoil our time together, and perhaps cause you unnecessary concern."

Just the mention of concern caused her some. She had assumed he was going to conduct some surveillance somewhere, of some other possible spy, or of the southern coast, or whatever it was he did. "Are you up to something dangerous? Is this about that colonel and what happened at Toulon?"

"Let us not talk about it. I am trying to spare you *unnecessary* concern, remember?"

He did not say it would not be dangerous, however. So while her *unnecessary* concern dimmed, it did not go away.

She cleared the remnants of the meal. As she did, that odd cylinder of muslin kept distracting her. When she was finished she pointed to it. "What is that?"

He turned his head and looked at it over his shoulder. He gazed its way a long time. One might think he had forgotten he had brought it with him. With resolute abruptness, he stood and walked over and picked it up. "It is something for you."

He carried it over and untied the muslin. As soon as he did the fabric fell apart and a roll of paper unfurled on the table.

It was a stack of her own engravings. The ones she had lost in the alley. Only they had not been lost, since he now had them.

She fought the urge to scold him for lying to her. She wondered why he had taken this long to return them. She stared at them, fighting anger and disappointment, telling herself that of course he had lied to her. He thought they were secret documents that day. Perhaps he even wondered if she hid information among the figures and words.

He sat, and rested his fingers on the edge of the top print. "They are not colored. They are more of the ones you send to France."

She nodded.

"I am told you make them yourself. Not only ink the plate and pull the print, but use the burin to carve the lines."

"Who told you that?"

"Is it true?"

Perhaps Emma had told him. That was how Emma found her in the first place. Or maybe Cassandra. Or even Madame La-Tour, who was too impressed with the visits from a viscount to remain discreet. Or someone else might have revealed it. She had kept this skill and work a secret as best she could, but eventually people figure some things out when they have nothing else to do.

"It is true." She did not look at him. She did not want to see how he regarded her. A few minutes ago she was at least possibly the niece of a comte. Now, unless he truly was Handsome Stupid Man, he knew she was not. It changed everything. Everything.

"Who taught you? It is not a skill one learns on one's own."

Her heart weighed heavily in her chest. She wished they had never left the bed because whether he intended it or not, he was at long last interrogating her the way he had initially planned that day they first spoke.

She considered what to say and whether to speak at all. She could refuse, and wait the long hours before André arrived pretending to sleep in one of the chairs.

"My father taught me. It was his skill and trade." There, now he knew. Her birth was far below his. She was not a woman to whom such a man as he gave affection. If he took a woman like her, it was not a romantic liaison, but something baser.

She did not think she could lie with him ever again now. She would not want to see if it made a difference in how he treated her, or kissed her. She would know if it did with the first touch.

"How did you know how to —" He caught himself and stopped.

She finally looked at him. Instead of a new scorn she mostly saw intense curiosity. "How did I know how to act like a lady? Is that your question? How was my birth not obvious every time I spoke or took a step? My mother worked in the household of a baron. I would visit her there, and see the ladies and how they moved and spoke and carried themselves. So much is in the carriage. Even more is in the mind. It was not hard to imitate. Even as a child I had started doing so, although there were those who thought me bold to dare such airs."

"I was not going to ask that. I was going to ask how you know so much about the comte with whom you claimed a relationship."

"Ahh. Well, you see, while I was a low-born woman pretending to be a lord's niece, someone else was a lord's sister pretending to be a lowborn woman. Dominique is the true relative of the comte, and filled me with the descriptions and information I needed. She hides in her caps and simple clothes and unpainted face. She never wants her true birth known and none have questioned or guessed. She came very close to being killed and has never felt safe since. She is one for whom the terror never ended, so you must promise to keep the secret."

"Of course I will keep the secret."

Curiosity still burned in him. She waited to see if he would swallow it, or interrogate her further. She was not sure there was much more she could say that would not spur yet more questions, some of which she must not answer.

His fingers moved, until they rested on the image of Lamberte. Her heart beat harder. There were many ways to ask about the image of Lamberte. Some of them would require her to lie, unless she wanted to tell him everything.

Did she? Perhaps now that he knew her true history, or at least some of it, he would no longer care what she did. Maybe he would leave her alone to do as she wanted. Even his promise tonight to protect her — it had been given to Marielle Lyon, niece of the Comte de Vence, not the daughter of an engraver.

"That is a man named Antoine Lamberte," she said before he could choose his words. "He is one of many who rose in the revolutionary government, but who did not care about the ideals. Lamberte only cares about himself, and his own power and wealth. He committed many crimes. Such men should not be allowed to act without sanctions, or be free from justice."

"So you make these images and send them to France to denounce such as he. So you explained before. Do you have particular knowledge of his sins?"

She shrugged and hoped she appeared indifferent to the question. In reality her nape prickled. "His excesses are well-known."

"Not this one that you accuse him of. Stealing from the government itself. If that were well-known, his head would not still be attached to his body."

"Perhaps it is not. I would not know."

He reached over and lifted her chin with his hand so she had to look at him. "Do not treat me like a fool, Marielle. I have warned you about that before."

"I am not. I am simply tired of all your questions. Why do you care about any of this?" She swept her hand across the image.

"I care because you have gone to great trouble and expense to accuse this man of a crime that could cause him more trouble than a hundred murders committed during the years of unrest. If he knows about your prints, he cannot like them. Everyone knows the power of both the pen and the burin. I think he sent men to track those engravings back to their source, much as I have tracked them from you to the coast, only in reverse. The men who tried to kill you in the alley came from him, didn't they?"

"Perhaps. I do not know."

He raked his hair with his hand, exasperated. "Don't you? They beat two men to death to learn how to find you." He tapped Lamberte's bearded face. "He is as bold as you, and more dangerous, if he sent killers to stop the denunciations in these satires. And even knowing that, you do not stop making them. Do you? Hell, you will probably send these over now that you have them back."

She could not sit still while he browbeat her about the prints. She stood and paced away and tried to calm the indignation rising in her. "If I do not do what I can to stop such men, who will?"

"Someone else. *Not you.*"

"Why not me? Because I am a woman? You said you seek justice for what happened in Toulon. I would think you would understand."

"That is different. That is personal. Let someone else bring this man down."

She swung around and faced him. "Who? A soldier? They are all on his side now. The people? After the massacres in his region, there are none left brave enough to speak against him. The government in Paris? Not unless they are given a reason to look at him suspiciously, instead of being grateful such a tyrant keeps the rebellions from reoccurring." She slammed her hand down on the print. "Such as this helped destroy a monarchy in France. If I have the skill to help bring this man to justice, I will do it."

"No, you will not. Turn your attention to another if you must. This one is too sly, and too dangerous, and too close already."

I do not want to turn my attention to another. There is no other who matters like he does. She almost yelled it at him. She barely caught the words before they spilled.

"You have no right to tell me what to do," she yelled in frustration.

He rose and strode to her and grasped her shoulders. "I took the right when I took *you.* I'll be damned before I let you get yourself killed over these. Find another crusade. Seek justice elsewhere."

She jerked free of his hold and turned away so he would not see the tears filming her eyes. She had known he would try to interfere if he guessed any of it. He was that kind of man. She wiped her eyes with the back of her hand and fought for composure. Thank God she had not allowed their intimacy to lure her into confiding in him.

He took hold of her shoulders again, much more gently this time. His hands slid down and caressed her upper arms. She felt a kiss pressed to her crown.

"Promise me that you will not try to send these to France, Marielle."

She looked at the table and the print showing Lamberte on his throne made of oppressed people. "I promise that these prints will not go to France."

He turned her, and lifted her chin with his crooked finger. "Do not be angry. I only demand this to protect you."

She knew that. She also realized that his touch did not feel different after all. Nor did he look at her any differently. "Are you not angry that I hid the truth of my birth from you?"

"I always knew you were not whom you claimed. The only mystery was who you were instead." He backed up toward the bedroom, leading her by the hand.

There was no passion when they went to bed. Not of the sexual kind, at least. They lay together and slept. During the night she awoke, and looked into the dark while she inhaled the scent of him and listened to him breathe, and wondered what he really thought about discovering that she was no lady.

In the morning two carriages arrived. Kendale climbed into his and it headed west. André helped her into hers and they rolled in the opposite direction.

There was much she had to think about, but try as she might she could not remove her thoughts from that cottage and the emotions of the prior night. She had deceived him since the moment they met, but it had never felt wrong before. She had been able to tell herself there was no choice, that he pursued her for his own reasons and she would use his interest for hers. It was different now, in ways that confused her mind and hurt her heart.

Love was weakening her, perhaps. Distracting her. Consuming her so that she forgot that she had promises to keep and larger concerns than whether her lover was happy with her. Deceptions in the name of duty were not so bad, were they? He had lied about having the prints for that reason, hadn't he?

Too often as she lay in his embrace last night she had been tempted to waken him and tell him everything about herself, her history, about Lamberte and the prints and the way she had very particular knowledge of his crimes. If she explained about her father, would that make a difference? Would he stand aside and let her do what she had to do? More likely he would lock her away so she never had the chance to even try, if he thought she might come to harm.

She lost sense of time while debating it all. So it startled her when the carriage stopped. She looked out the window, expecting to see a blue door. Instead she saw only trees.

The little door between the cabin and André opened. "The way is blocked, mam'selle. Another carriage is ahead and it does not move."

She scooted over and stuck her head out the window. The carriage up ahead was a big coach with footmen in livery. She peered into the trees. Perhaps the occupant had needed to relieve himself and the delay would be brief.

One of the footmen walked to the coach's side, then turned and strode toward her carriage. His powdered wig indicated the coach was owned by someone wealthy, even if the size of the equipage had not made that clear enough. The tax on powder for wigs was so high that it had ended that style forever in England. To spend it on servants —

That wig appeared outside her window. The young man wearing it bowed. "My lord requests that you ride with him, Miss Lyon." He opened the door and set down the stairs, as if her compliance could not be questioned.

Since her own carriage could not move unless she agreed, she stepped out and walked to the big coach. The profile of a man showed in the window. She recognized the straight nose and deep-set dark eyes of the Duke of Penthurst.

Upon seeing her, he moved to the seat behind the coachman. The footman handed her in, set up the stairs, and closed the door. The grand coach moved. She trusted André would follow.

"Did you block this lane for long while you waited for me?" she asked.

"I have been here only an hour."

"I am flattered, Your Grace. Also disconcerted that you knew I would be traveling this way."

"Discretion is not one of Kendale's preoc-cupations. Perhaps he finds it as tedious as he does other social requirements. It was not hard to learn about that cottage."

"I cannot imagine why you would care to learn about it, let alone waylay me as I left it this morning."

"Can't you?"

The way he said that, and the way he looked at her, told her much. This was not a man interested in her as a woman, that much was certain. This was no silly little abduction as a romantic game, by a duke trying to steal her from a viscount. Rather this man regarded her with a frankness that both worried her and flattered her. *We are both intelligent people,* those eyes said. *Let us save time and avoid dissembling.*

"No, I can't," she said finally, although it did not sound convincing to her own ears.

"You sound cautious. You have nothing to fear from me."

Of course she did. For all of his grace right now, he struck her as a dangerous man. She had some experience in knowing them when she saw them.

"Kendale accepts you are not a spy," he said.

"You trust his judgment so completely?"

373

"In the least I accept that if you managed to convince him, you would probably convince me as well. I can think of no man less likely to be swayed, no matter how pretty and charming the liar."

She wondered what this duke wanted. He had inconvenienced himself to have a conversation with her, but about what? He would tell her soon, so she did not ask.

"That cottage," he said. "As I said, he is not famous for discretion and it is most discreet in location. I wonder if that is only to create privacy for your rendezvous."

"I demanded little except privacy."

"How generous of you. Still, have there been any visitors?"

"No."

He eyed her. She gazed back impassively.

"As you can see, I have some questions, Miss Lyon, but they are not about you."

"You must think very little of me if you believe I will take well an interrogation about him."

"I think that you are a woman who has learned to be practical. Kendale believes you are not a spy and I am inclined to as well. However, the opinion is not unanimous. Should you ever find yourself in the hands of those who still wonder, my friendship will be very useful."

A bribe more than a threat, but a shiver ran through her anyway.

"Has he ever mentioned Toulon to you?"

Her mind raced to decide her response. To claim ignorance would imply a lack of intimacy with Kendale, and call into question his opinion of her. To tell this duke everything that had been shared would be perhaps a betrayal. Would half a loaf do?

"He said he was there, at the siege. He has some scars from it. He does not speak of it with me, however."

He nodded vaguely. She had responded correctly.

"Has he spoken to you of a mission or a journey that he is planning?"

The question alarmed her. It would not have been asked unless this man already knew something. "He spoke of visiting his properties sometime, perhaps in summer. I think he believes he has neglected them."

"No other journey? One more imminent?"

She shook her head and widened her eyes, innocently. "He would have told me if such a thing were going to happen soon, I think. He would not want me to arrive at that cottage only to find myself alone for the night."

Such a scrutiny she received then. She was well practiced in being interrogated, however, and even a duke's examination did not fluster her.

"He said you and he were friends not so long ago," she added, to direct this elsewhere. "After you visited Ravenswood, that is what he said." He had also said that Penthurst might have come to prevent others from coming. Did this duke seek to expose Kendale with all his questions at Ravenswood and now? Or to protect him? And expose what? Protect from what?

"That is true," he said.

"And yet you are no longer?"

"He holds something against me. I cannot blame him, since I have never explained it." He rapped on the wall of the coach, and it slowed and stopped. "I will return you to your carriage now."

The footman set down the stairs, but it was the duke who handed her out. He strolled beside her as they walked back to André. Partway there, he stopped.

"Miss Lyon, I must say something. Forgive me in advance for the words and the implications if they are misplaced."

She faced him. He smiled, but she sensed a dark intensity at work in him below his amiable surface.

"You should know that despite the estrangement, I still count Kendale as a friend. And I still value his judgment where you are concerned. However, if he is wrong about you and if you do anything to cause harm to come to him because of confidences he has made to you, I will see that you are imprisoned until you are a very old woman."

With that, he continued escorting her to her carriage.

After the door had closed and Penthurst had walked back to his own coach, André bent and spoke through the little door. "Another lord?"

"Yes. A duke."

"The first lord will not be happy to know you met the second one."

"That is true. It would be best if you did not tell him about this."

"He would expect me to. I was instructed to let him know if anyone interfered with you."

Rolling her eyes, she opened her reticule and plucked out some coins. André's hand was already waiting at the little opening.

CHAPTER 18

Two mornings later, Dominique entered Marielle's bedchamber while she washed for the day. "Two letters came early," she said, waving them. "Both are very fine paper. One is from him, I am sure."

Marielle kept her back to Dominique while she closed her eyes and hid her reaction. She had not expected to hear from Kendale again. He would provide the protection he had promised, but the rest — between her deception and her true history — she believed he would now drift away from her.

She finished washing while Dominique sat on the bed holding the letters, impatient to learn what they contained. Finally she reached for them and sat next to her old friend. She broke the seal on Kendale's first.

My dear Marielle,
I expect that journey to happen soon.

Within a few days. Preparations have occupied me. I would like to see you before I depart.

You should be receiving an invitation to an event hosted by Ambury's parents, the Duke and Duchess of Highburton. It is as much a celebration of his father's better health as it is one of the Season. Ambury arranged for this invitation when I said I would like to attend with you. I hope you do not find the lateness of its arrival too impolite, and will forgive my interference if you do.

Mr. Pottsward has arranged for the gowns from Ravenswood to be brought up and delivered to you. They should arrive tomorrow. I feel neglectful for not having bought you a new wardrobe as I had planned. Would you have accepted one?

I will call for you at ten that night, unless I receive a letter saying you decline.

Your servant,
Kendale

She lifted the other letter. The paper proved so thick one could cut cold butter with it. Dominique bent over it and examined the seal.

"It is from a duke," Marielle said while

she slid her finger under that impressive seal. "Whoever thought I would receive letters from one?"

Even Dominique, who had known fine papers and seals in her day, was impressed. The secretary's elegant hand flowed over the paper, requesting Marielle's attendance.

"It is a ball," Dominique said. "And you say Lord Kendale learned the truth of your blood? Perhaps he did not understand."

"He understood." Was it possible it did not matter? If so, she should give him a new name. Peculiar Man.

"You must have won his heart, if he wants you at his side at such an affair even knowing your parentage. It is not a place where a lord normally brings the daughter of an engraver."

"No one else will know I am the daughter of an engraver. Perhaps that makes a difference."

"It is good that he is sending the gowns. I told you that you needed a better wardrobe now."

Word spread in the house that she was attending a ball. Dominique, who normally kept her own counsel, confided in Madame LaTour. Madame confided in her two best friends. They passed the news to others. By noon all the women knew and it was the talk of the studio.

They all peppered her with advice. The next day a larger than normal number of ladies came to work. When the gowns arrived all painting stopped while Madame LaTour held up the likely choices so all could comment and give opinions.

Consensus settled on an ivory satin gown with silver threaded embroidery all around the lower part of the skirt. One of the ladies removed some silk flowers from another gown and proceeded to fashion a headdress.

No one went home that evening. Some helped her bathe. Others helped her dress. Still others hovered while discreet, artful painting enhanced her eyes and lips. Marielle felt like a bride being prepared for her wedding with all these handmaidens chattering around, laughing and increasing the excitement.

Finally, all was done. She stood to a group evaluation. Most of the eyes glinted with joy. A few did not, notably the ones owned by Madame LaTour.

"No jewels. Surely someone has something we can use." She patted her upper chest which, on Marielle, displayed nothing but skin. "You are so lovely many will not care, but the vacancy will be noted."

"Will this do?" Dominique asked. She

held out a little box.

Madame LaTour opened it. Her eyes widened. "Is this yours, Madame Beltrand? It is very fine."

"I wish it were mine. It was delivered today, while Marielle bathed. A footman came with it."

"Ah, it is from him, Marielle. Look, look." Madame LaTour held up the necklace of finely worked gold. From the delicate chain a pendant hung with diamonds set in a gold filigree field. She came over and clasped it around Marielle's neck.

Marielle looked down on the jewel. Kendale had chosen well. This appeared costly without calling so much attention to itself as to be gauche.

The sounds of the coach arriving could be heard through the window, attended by the sounds of the lane reacting to its arrival. Dominique hurried down to the door.

Instinctively Marielle reached for her dark Venetian shawl.

"Not today, mam'selle," Madame LaTour scolded, snatching it away. She held out in its place a soft wrap of raw silk that had come with the other garments. A pale primrose, it added a nice splash of subdued color to her ensemble. All was complete when one of the women pulled a pair of silk slippers from a little sac she had brought.

Madame LaTour tweaked at her hair, pinched at her cheeks, rubbed at her lips while chanting instructions about comportment when meeting the duke and duchess. "Be proud, Marielle. Such people do not respect the demure and docile."

Marielle hugged her, then gazed at the sparkling eyes of the women who had helped her prepare. She was going to a ball and, in their minds, all of them were going with her.

"You are determined to be the subject of gossip, I see," Southwaite said while he looked to the clutch of women five feet away.

Kendale had just arrived, and Cassandra and Emma had taken Marielle aside to admire her and to point out various notables in the crowd. Feminine fingers aimed here and there while Cassandra whispered in Marielle's ear.

"Surely there is better gossip to be had than me." He found it hard to keep his eyes off Marielle. Her beauty astonished him tonight. He might have appeared normal when she walked down the stairs at her house, but inside he had been gawking the way the children did on the lane when his coach rolled up.

"Not much," Ambury said. "I warned you that it would be like this. No one thought you would ever pursue a woman, or have a liaison, so this is of great interest. I am only sorry that I did not lay down bets on the matter when I suspected something was afoot."

"Nor have you been especially discreet," Southwaite said.

"I have been very discreet. Not as discreet as you would have been, but far more so than Ambury here. It is not as if I was seen leaving her home in the middle of the night."

Southwaite enjoyed Ambury's discomfort on that. "Do not worry," he said. "Soon some young man will get caught doing something inappropriate with some girl, and you will be forgotten."

He shrugged. "If they gossip, I can't stop that. Nor do I care." He did not give a damn what anyone said. Let the gossip fly.

The two of them exchanged glances.

"That necklace looks expensive," Ambury said. "It suits her. Did you choose it yourself?"

"I did. Do you approve?"

"I think it is handsome," Southwaite said. "I am trying to picture it, however. You at a jeweler's shop, poring over baubles. Try as I might —" He shook his head.

"He probably did it in his Kendale way," Ambury said. "He visited the first jeweler he saw once he had made up his mind, peered at three or four items, picked one, and was out in five minutes."

"Do you think he had decided on a necklace before he went? Or just stumbled into it?"

"Stumbled. Jewelers know his sort. They aim high, assuming the gentleman will not bother to ask to see more in his haste to be done with the chore."

"Well it is much more attractive than I would have expected from him. Who would have guessed that Kendale had an eye for artistic design."

That continued on like that. He preened like an idiot at the evidence that he had not condemned Marielle to wearing jewelry that no woman would want. He had not done it in "his Kendale way" at all. It had taken him over an hour to choose that necklace while he suffered bouts of unaccustomed indecision.

The lights in her eyes when she thanked him had made it worth every minute and every shilling. Thus, he supposed, did the wrong kind of woman lead a man to ruin. He was damned lucky she was not that sort or he might be doomed.

"Excuse me," he said. "I think I will ask a lovely lady to dance."

They glanced at each other, then stared at him. Southwaite placed a politely restraining hand on his arm. "Do you know how to dance? I am aware that you have seen it often enough, and probably assume that through force of will and intellect alone you can imitate that which you have seen, but it is more difficult than it appears."

"Army officers dance all the time."

"In general they do. The question is whether *you* do. I have never once seen you dance, Kendale. Not once. Not even when we were of an age when dancing was the only way to touch a woman, and even that through two levels of gloves."

"That I did not choose to dance does not mean that I did not know how to dance."

"You cannot know how to dance if you never have danced. There is an element of practice. There are men who know how to shoot a gun but their aim is horrible and they are better off never shooting. It is much the same with dancing."

"It is embarrassing if you get the steps wrong," Ambury hastened to add. "Your spoken faux pas of the past will be nothing compared to the scene if you trip up a whole line of dancers by hopping right when you should hop back."

"I do not know what I would do without the two of you mothering me like I had hatched out of an egg yesterday. Now, excuse me."

He walked over to the ladies and asked Marielle to dance. The other ladies appeared shocked. Cassandra gestured for Ambury and mouthed something that might have been, *For goodness' sake, stop him.*

"Why are they so astonished?" Marielle asked, looking back over her shoulder while he led her to take a place in the line.

"I cannot imagine."

"Emma is twisting her hands together."

"It might be better if you pay attention to this rather than to her. I am told that precision matters. We do not want to knock anyone over."

She laughed. The sweet woman thought he had made a joke.

The music started. The steps unfolded. He trusted his mind to call up their order from the hours of enforced practice when he was a boy. Between that and keeping a close eye on the fellow next to him, he managed well enough with only a few, barely noticeable missteps.

When it was their turn to walk down the

line, Marielle favored him with one of her sparkling, coquettish smiles. "You do this very well, Lord Kendale. I would not have expected you to be a dancer."

"I have never called myself one, that is certain."

"You do not enjoy dancing?"

"I do tonight. Do you?"

"Very much."

That delighted him. He even enjoyed it himself a bit after that. The next time they passed together, her smile held less mockery and a good deal of warmth. "You do not normally dance, do you? You are doing this for me."

"Nonsense. I am euphoric with pleasure."

"When was the last time you danced?"

"A while ago. A few years." He had to laugh at her skeptical expression. "Twelve years."

The music ended. He bowed to her curtsy. Supporting her hand he returned her to the ladies. Cassandra could not leave well enough alone.

"You amaze us all, Lord Kendale. Who ever guessed that your refusal to conform to social niceties really did derive from scorn, rather than incompetence."

"Are you saying you feel bad that I never asked you to dance, Lady Ambury? I imagine that I could keep this up for one more turn, and make amends, if you like."

"Oh, dear, what a disappointment, Ambury has claims on the next one." She turned her head this way and that. "Where has he gone to?"

"I will find him and remind him of his obligation."

He set off to do just that, lest he find himself doing a country-dance under Cassandra's critical eye. Spying Ambury by the far wall, he made his way there.

Two other heads came into view as he neared. Southwaite and Penthurst. Whatever conversation they held did not appear a pleasant one. All three expressions looked stone serious.

Penthurst excused himself and walked away. Kendale joined his friends. Southwaite wore the smile that never boded well.

"Have we just been scolded, Ambury, or warned?" he said through a tight smile.

"I choose to think the latter, but I cannot disagree there was some scold in there too." Ambury moved slightly to accommodate Kendale's presence into what became a tight little group around which the crowd milled. "Be glad you chose to dance, Kendale. If you had been here, I worry there would have been fisticuffs in the garden by now."

"I can still challenge him and thrash him, if you want. Has there been a turn off the road to reconciliation?"

Southwaite looked around, then gestured for them to follow him. They strode out onto the terrace and down into the garden. Even after finding privacy within a boxwood-hemmed circle of benches, he spoke lowly.

"He informed us that we are the subject of suspicions in both the Home Office and the War Office."

"Surely they do not think you are disloyal."

Ambury threw up his hands in exasperation. "Hardly. What a mind you have. It is the opposite. There has always been discomfort with that network of watchers on the coast, and now they worry we are planning something more intrusive."

"How irrational of them."

"Not entirely, of course," Ambury said. "I told you, Southwaite, that our little excursion to France last year would not remain a secret. Now whenever there are whispers of other such missions, all eyes turn to us."

"That was a rescue mission," Southwaite said firmly. "Penthurst knows that. Hell, Pitt knows that. We were just accused of something quite different."

"As was Kendale here. Oh, yes, the warning was for you too."

Kendale just listened. He could think of nothing to add to the conversation.

"Absurd, of course," Southwaite said after a curse. "Bizarre! What possible motive would we have to invade France? Where would we find the army to do it? Hell, if I collected every man I could trust with such a thing it would not fill a pleasure yacht. And once there, what would we do? March ourselves twenty strong to Paris and liberate the city from the revolutionaries? I find it hard to believe anyone is taking this seriously."

"Strange," Kendale muttered. "Bizarre, as you say."

"Yet someone is," Ambury said. "Penthurst spoke as a friend, he said, but it was clear that he has been told more than theories. Someone has decided they have some kind of evidence on which to base these suspicions."

"Perhaps something happened on the coast of which we are not aware," Southwaite said. "You and I have not been there in months. Kendale here has always made the journey."

An odd quiet fell on the circle within the boxwood. Southwaite and Ambury looked at each other through the night, their expressions visible due to a party lamp hanging from a nearby tree. The whites of their eyes appeared to grow larger.

"He wouldn't," Ambury said.

"Wouldn't he?" Southwaite said.

"If Kendale were going to do such a thing, it is unlikely the ministers would find out."

"He cannot act alone. Others can be careless in ways he would never be."

Ambury frowned over that. "All those rides to the coast. We forced it on him, of course. But while there he could have put such a plan in place."

"And after last year, when we all went over, he would know quite a lot about how to do it. I daresay if this is afoot, it began then."

"Could he pull it off? Is he that good?"

"Damn, yes, he is that good. As to pulling it off, he had better or we will be on another rescue mission."

"I am standing right here," Kendale said.

"So you are," Southwaite said. "Standing there and saying not a damned word."

"I am not sure you would want to hear what I have to say."

"If it is that you are planning a visit to

France, you are right about that." Southwaite looked to the sky and uttered a curse
in a tone of astonishment and resignation.

"Our government will not stand for it,
Kendale. Hell, what if you are caught? Can
you imagine the implications? It will be assumed by the French that you are a spy.
They will execute you for sure, and make
the most of the show. It will demoralize our
own people, and delay any possible diplomacy between the two countries," Ambury
said.

His scold sat there in the air, waiting for a
response that Kendale had no intention of
giving.

Exasperated, Southwaite kicked one of the
stone benches. "Hell and damnation, he is
not denying it, Ambury. Whatever you are
plotting you had best call off, Kendale. If
Penthurst suspects, others do too. An army
may be waiting for you when you make your
move. Maybe ours. Maybe theirs. It is not
worth it, whatever the scheme might be."

"That is an odd advice and judgment
coming from you, of all men, Southwaite,"
he said. "You do not know what the scheme
might be, if there is one, but you are sure it
is not worth it. Not worth as much as the
last time, I assume you mean. Not worth as
much as rescuing the ne'er-do-well relative

of your lover. Did I refuse to join you on that foolhardy mission, or harp on the price to our necks and England's diplomacy if it failed?"

Southwaite's posture lost its rigidity. He gazed at the ground between them for a long pause, then spoke with calm thoughtfulness. "No, you did not. Nor would we have succeeded without your leading us. My worry for you obscured my memory of that debt. I must seem an inconstant friend compared to your loyalty. Instead of expressing annoyance, I should be asking instead if you need my help now in return." He looked up. "Do you?"

Not long ago he might have invited their help. Not now. Both of them had too much to lose now, and he doubted they would be effective comrades on any such adventure as a result. Besides, he needed soldiers, not gentlemen who debated honor at every turn.

"If I now planned another foolhardy mission, I would be sure to call the debt. Since I do not, your help is not needed. As for Penthurst, he is too interested in me these days. Perhaps he resents that I have not held out the olive branch as quickly as the two of you, and conjures up reasons to blame me for that instead of himself. Now, we are neglecting the ladies. Yours will not mind, since she has many friends in that ballroom. Mine, however, might need my attendance."

He stepped out of the grass circle and turned to the house.

"This is about Toulon, isn't it?" Ambury said. "You have cooked up some scheme of revenge, haven't you?"

He did not answer, and walked away.

Angus was waiting outside the duke's house when she and Kendale emerged. He stood next to her carriage as if he were a footman, but his expression revealed he had come for some other purpose.

He waited until she had been handed in before whispering to Kendale. Whatever he had to say did not take more than a few words. Kendale did not react at all. He merely said, "A horse." Then he climbed up and joined her in the carriage cabin.

"Did you enjoy the ball?" he asked.

"It was different from what I had imagined. Busier. Crowded. The music was heavenly, as was the dancing." She stretched to give him a kiss. "Thank you for that. For dancing with me."

"It was my pleasure, as is so much where you are concerned, Marielle." He moved beside her, so he could embrace her with one arm. The streets grew silent as they rode through town.

She had packed a valise to take to the cottage, and his boot rested against it. He seemed very aware of that boot and what it touched. Several times she found him looking down at it.

André pulled up at the cottage in Hampstead. While André helped her out and carried the valise into the cottage, Kendale untied a horse from the back of the carriage and led it around to the back of the building. André built up the fire in the hearth in order to banish the spring's damp and the stone's cold. He was gone by the time Kendale entered the cottage himself, carrying his frock coat. There was a small stable beyond the garden and she assumed he had dealt with the horse despite his formal attire.

"Do you intend to ride back in the morning?" she asked. "In hose and pumps?"

He took her hand and bid her rise, then swung her around to the hearth. "Just stand here near the light so I can look at you. I barely had the chance in that crush and had to be satisfied with glimpses."

He sat down and she struck a series of poses in front of him. First she tried to appear demure. Then sophisticated. Then naughty. Finally she pretended to be one of the ladies who always appeared very critical of all she saw, and never in good ways.

Her game amused him. He reached out and pulled her onto his lap. "I like this one the best. Just Marielle, being Marielle."

The night had given her such joy that she could hardly contain it. It spilled out in the way she held him and the smiles that formed under his kisses. She slid off his lap and took his hand. "Come to bed with me."

She made love to him that night, in a way she never had before. She bid him lie there and accept the pleasure she gave him. She did everything she could think of to make him crazed, using her hands and mouth to delight him.

"Your coachman will return in an hour," he said. "I must ride off soon, and I did not want you to remain here alone so I told him to come back."

"Are you going to Ravenswood? Have you been called there?"

"I will be going there eventually. First I must go somewhere else." He turned on his side. "That journey beckons a little sooner than I had expected. I will lose two days from my fortnight, I fear. Can I claim them when I return, or will you hold me to the letter of the agreement?"

Her voice caught in her throat. She wished she knew when this return would be. It would be unkind, and ungrateful, to tell him he could have those days if she would not be here to give them. "If you still want them when you see me again, they are yours."

Did she imagine that he noticed the way she phrased that? More likely the heaviness in her heart had her sensing what did not exist.

"We must buy you a wardrobe then," he said. "Ask Emma and Cassandra which dressmakers to use. I do not want you in faded cloth and tattered lace again. If you favor those long shawls, you must have new ones."

"I will be as fashionable as Madame Peltier," she teased. "Perhaps one or two dresses would be enough. Not a whole wardrobe." She was not even sure what a whole wardrobe consisted of in his mind. For a woman of style, it meant many ensembles. It would be like him never to have noticed how often women of fashion changed their clothes.

"You must be more fashionable than Madame Peltier, if you want." His thoughts seemed to drift away. He fell silent. He did not sleep, however. She felt his alertness to her, the chamber, the time.

"I want you to stay at your house while I am gone, Marielle. Do not come here. Do not venture far on your own. I still worry for your safety. I have told Jacob and Pratt to follow you if you go out into the City. Do not be offended and do not argue. I need to know you are safe."

It touched her that he worried, and tried to ensure her safety. She would lose his men's surveillance when she had to, of course, especially now that she knew to look for it.

She did not sleep at all. She heard the carriage arrive. André did not enter the cottage but waited in the night.

The arm embracing her tightened. She looked over her shoulder, right into Kendale's eyes. He said nothing, but kissed her neck below her ear, closed his eyes, and inhaled deeply.

Then he was gone, up from the bed, pulling on his garments. She sat with the bedclothes pulled around her and watched him dress. When he was done he looked down at her.

"Wrap yourself in the blanket and see me off after I saddle the horse, Marielle."

He strode off to do that chore. She pulled the blanket off the bed and swaddled herself in it, much as she had that first time she spoke to him in his chambers.

She waited in the sitting room. She could not sit. The ache inside her would not permit it. This parting made her want to cry for what had been and hadn't, and for what probably never would be again. She tried to take solace in knowing she only intended to do her duty to her father and her family, but it did not dim the pain much at all.

The first vague light of dawn was leaking onto the horizon when he returned to the cottage. He would indeed be riding in his ballroom clothes, but she guessed Angus was not far away with boots and more practical garments.

He ran his fingertips around the edge of the blanket near her neck. "I should only be gone a week. When I return, I will come to see you right away. There are things I need to say to you. Perhaps while I am gone I will find the words."

She already knew the words *she* wanted to say. It would be cruel and selfish to do so, however. She might find contentment that she had spoken, but a woman scheming and deceiving should not indulge herself by speaking her heart's thoughts.

"Be safe," she said. It was a common farewell but today, perhaps, it meant more than usual.

"I will be safe. This is not a dangerous journey." He kissed her again, then left.

She listened for his horse's gallop until its sound disappeared. She went into the bed-chamber, found the valise, and donned one of her old dresses. She carefully folded up the ball gown fit for a comte's niece. Numb with sadness, she made the bed. On impulse she lifted the pillow where his head had lain and inhaled deeply. It reminded her how he had done that while he held her, as if he too wanted to remember the mere scent of her.

After packing the rest of the ball ensemble into her valise, she picked up the gown and went out to André. "Take me home," she said. "Then get some sleep, and return this afternoon. I need to explain how I will need your services in the days ahead."

CHAPTER 19

"There be no mistaking it, Lord Kendale. The soldiers claim to be here for training the local militia as is their way sometimes, but there are too many of them and they ride out a lot. They are looking for something. Or someone."

The report came to Kendale informally while he sat in a library north of Dover, drinking the fine port his host had poured. Mr. Percy Ryan was one of the watchers in the network on the coast that he, Ambury, and Southwaite had set up in order to reinforce what had been a very loose net two years ago. Mr. Ryan, a hearty, thick man of middle years, had warmed to the duty and employed a variety of devices to monitor the movements of nonlocals in the five miles north and south of his handsome manor. Since the soldiers were not local, he had kept an eye on them.

Kendale always made it a point to call on

Mr. Ryan because Mr. Ryan liked to talk. A wealthy gentry squire, he especially liked to talk to the peers who had invited him into their circle. He often proved a font of useful information. If Ryan suspected the extra soldiers in Dover had ulterior interests besides the abilities of the local citizen militias, Kendale was inclined to give that opinion weight.

"How long have they been here?"

"Some for a week. More came two days ago. There may be others who have been here longer, but I did not notice them. A few extra red coats do not stand out. Thirty extra do, especially when they file their horses along that road down there."

"Has anything happened to create concerns that would draw them here? Something I do not know about, that perhaps did not seem significant enough to report?"

Mr. Ryan flushed to his fair hairline. "We report everything, sir. At least I do. I cannot speak for my counterparts up coast or down." He sipped his port, then set it aside. "I was thinking you knew what was up. The officer with these soldiers, Colonel Horace Watson, indicated he knows you."

"He does. We met during our early years in uniform. Did he ask after me in some way? Or did you ask if he knew me?"

"He mentioned he knew you. He seemed to assume I did too."

Kendale looked around the library while he thought. Almost every book had the same brown binding. He wondered if Mr. Ryan ever read any of these books, or only owned them so they could line the shelves in their expensive, unblemished leather.

"Between the soldiers and Colonel Watson — a colonel, mind you, but with only about twenty men — I wondered if someone is coming over, Lord Kendale. Someone important. Or maybe someone is coming back, as it were." He glanced over with a sly, inviting smile.

"I have heard of no notable person intending to come over. As for coming back — what do you mean?"

Ryan chortled. "Nothing, nothing. However, between the two of us — we watch here for Frenchmen sneaking onto our coast to gather information, don't we? So it is normal to wonder if some of our people don't sneak onto theirs. If our army sent a few of its men to do that, it might want to welcome them back in a manner that ensures no one interferes or learns of it."

"By no one interfering, you mean us."

"Could be awkward, no? For such as us to be counting French noses as they get off

404

a boat, only to realize they are actually all English noses. Hard to keep secrets that way."

It would be very hard to keep such secrets. That was why those English noses never landed on the coast in boats when they returned. The naval service picked them up at sea and saw to their safe return instead. Which meant the army had no reason to move a unit here for that purpose. Unless the goal was not to welcome a returning party, but to prevent a departing one.

Damnation. Penthurst had indicated that suspicions were in the air that someone was planning some independent action. Someone wanted to stop that badly enough to create a little show of force.

He rode back to the farmhouse fifteen miles inland, where he had left Angus and six other men, including Harry Travis, who had been waiting for them here when they rode in yesterday. Travis had indeed made it back two days ago, and immediately sent word that he had seen the colonel in Brest.

Mr. Pottsward had come along, and stood by the fireplace stirring a pot while the other men lounged on chairs, bored and impatient.

"Did you learn anything, sir?" Angus

asked as soon as Kendale entered the simple cottage.

He threw his hat and gloves down, and shed his frock coat. He stuck his nose to the pot and its fragrant lamb stew, then straddled a chair. "The army sent someone to stop us. They think they know the what of it and may have even guessed the why of it. Whitehall does not want the trouble."

"Fuck them," Travis snarled.

"It may be best to wait."

"You can wait if you want. I didn't stay there risking my neck to make sure of his location only to lose the chance to finish this now."

The other men said nothing. If he announced they would not move, not a one would complain. Travis was different. Kendale could not totally control him because this was personal for him. He had been at Toulon, and he too had barely made it out alive.

Their gazes locked not so much in a challenge as in a mutual acknowledgment of that experience, and the long wait to rectify it. "If I decide it is too rash to move, we will not."

Travis's eyes narrowed. "It is always rash to move. Nothing new there. Hell, it was rash to go over two months ago and rash to stay when the others came back. I'll follow where you lead, as long as it is not in retreat."

"I did not speak of retreat."

"You suggested we wait. Same thing. I've waited long enough. I thought you had too."

The rest of the men watched silently.

The impulse to be rational that had begun this conversation fell away as Travis's words ripped at him. They *had* waited a long time, seething under the humiliation of the worst kind of retreat, swallowing the rage of watching comrades cut down left and right. The French had been ordered to kill, to obliterate, and not merely to capture and stop. He had fought like a madman even after the sword sliced his back because he had known if he fell, he would be finished.

Now the bastard who had arranged that betrayal and that trap and that slaughter had a name, and was within reach. Three months hence he could be in Paris instead, or even halfway across the Continent.

The hunger for revenge swelled in him, the way it did at night sometimes. This plan had hatched out of that craving. He would fulfill his promise to Feversham, but he would also even a bloody score the only way he knew how.

He gazed around at the others. Then he

looked down on Travis's hot determination. "These others did not agree to walk into a trap. If I think there is danger of that, I will delay our plans or even end them. If I do, you will obey me."

"Or what? If I'd done what you said last time, we would not know what we know."

"If you had done what I said, the coast would not now be crawling with soldiers."

"It is a big coast. A few more soldiers don't scare me." He grinned, and picked up his cup to down some ale.

The challenge was unmistakable. Every man in the farmhouse knew it had been made. If allowed to stand, this mission would descend into chaos and the unit into rabble.

He gazed at the man who had crawled across France with him not so long ago. In the army, there were ways to deal with this insubordination. Severe ways that ensured such challenges rarely occurred.

They no longer were in the army, however. Not an official one, at least.

He rose abruptly, overturning the table as he did. It crashed against Travis and slammed to the floor, its sound breaking the tense silence. He grabbed Travis by the front of his coat and swung him toward the door. He strode over, opened the door, threw Travis out, and followed.

Chickens scurried away. Travis collected himself. No longer smug, he looked across the dirt yard warily.

Kendale removed his coat and threw it aside. "I can't flog you and I can't have you shot, but I'll be damned before I let you endanger the others. Turn and run and be out of this for good, or defend yourself as best you can if you want to stay."

"I've more right to it than they have. You know that better than anyone."

"It is why I gave you a choice. But *you* know better than anyone that I cannot allow you to challenge my command and go unpunished."

Travis hesitated, then shed his own coats. Jaw hard and eyes burning, he paced back and forth like an animal preparing to charge.

He rushed forward, fists at the ready. Kendale parried his blow with one arm and landed a solid punch in his stomach with the other.

The sounds of fisticuffs brought the others outside. They formed a circle that left little option except a close fight. Within that circle, under the eyes of their comrades, they settled the question of leadership in the most primitive way known to man or beast.

■ ■ ■ ■

"What am I to do if he writes to you?"

Marielle folded a dress and pressed it into the valise. "I do not think he will write. It is not his way."

"What if he comes here, looking for you?" Dominique sat on the bed, her round face creased with worry, while she watched the preparations.

"He will not come until I am well gone." *If he comes at all.* At some point Kendale would step back from the passion and assess this affair from the viewpoint of his position and birth. He knew enough about her history now to conclude that their liaison was most irregular for an English lord, in several crucial ways. It was only a matter of how long it would be before the expectations of his world would dim his ardor. This journey he had taken would give him plenty of time for that to happen.

She allowed herself a few moments of nostalgia and sorrow. The loss would be inevitable, of course. She deprived herself of little by executing this plan. She could not allow her own happiness in that affair to interfere anyway, but knowing that at worst she gave up only a little more time

410

with him made it easier to do what she had to do.

Reaching into a drawer in her dressing table, she sought the little sack that held her money. She had removed it from the hidden cupboard last night and counted it out. Now she did so again, to reassure herself that she probably had enough.

Memories of Kendale kept intruding into her head no matter how hard she tried to block them. She finally resorted to other images in an effort to concentrate on the tasks at hand. She pictured her father, as she had last seen him, ordering her to run and take her chances in the town while he diverted Lamberte and his men. He had known he would be captured. He had sacrificed himself so that she would get away.

How intently he had looked at her while he explained his plan and stuffed that little account book in her pocket. How firmly he had embraced her before pushing her away. She saw it and felt it with a raw reality, as if it had just happened. No, not captured. He expected to be killed just as her mother had been killed — so no one would remain alive who had witnessed Lamberte murder his own half brother.

"Dominique, if I do not come back —"

"Do not say that!" Dominique crossed herself three times. "To even think it is —"

"If I do not come back, you are to give Lord Kendale that little book that is hidden in the cupboard downstairs."

"What should I say to him when I do?"

"I do not know." Kendale could do nothing with that little book. No one in England could. She had to give it to someone, however. It could not sit in that cupboard forever. And if she failed, it could be dangerous for Dominique and Madame LaTour to have it.

"Say it was Lamberte's, taken from him to prove how he stole. Say it was why I made those prints that accused him of that. It was why he sent men to that alley that day. He wondered if whoever made those prints might have the proof of it." At least Kendale would have some answers then. The interrogation that he had planned that day would finally yield something.

"Take the plates for yourself. The views are still good for printing and you can make some money that way. The others can be sold for the copper at least. You and Madame LaTour can continue the work here, of course. The lease is paid for until Michaelmas."

Dominique frowned at these instructions.

The softness left her. "Are you finished?"

Was she? She checked the valise. She forced a calm on herself while she examined her mind to be sure she had given all the messages and instructions that the last sleepless nights had presented to her. "Oh, if you can, tell Emma and Cassandra who I really am. Or ask Lord Kendale to do so. There are few with whom my deception felt wrong, but with them it did. You can tell Madame LaTour too, although she is unlikely to appreciate knowing the truth."

"Are you finished *now*?" Dominique stood and came over to her. "If so, you will listen to *me.*" She poked through the valise. "As I thought. Money for bribes, but nothing for protection. Do you think to procure it the same way as before?" She fished in her deep pocket and withdrew her knife. "You will take this. You keep it on you, as I do. And if you need to, Marielle, you will use it."

She looked down at the knife. Not a dagger as such, its thin blade still had little purpose besides stabbing at things.

Dominique grasped her shoulders and looked at her directly. "He will be much changed. He will not be the man you remember, just as you will not be the girl he last saw. Do not expect it to be like before."

"I will not."

"Do nothing to draw attention to yourself. You must shed the airs behind which you hid here. You must speak the local way."

"I will, although I will not mingle with people much. I am going in the way my prints did, and will get help from the bookseller who took them. I will know the château better than the servants who live there now, since I played in it as a child. Do not worry for me too much, Dominique. No one is loyal to a man like Lamberte, and if he is not there my bribes will open the doors I need to pass through."

"And if he is there?"

They looked at each other a long moment. "I will be left to my wits, I suppose. It is a good thing that you taught me how to use them well, dear friend."

Dominique collected her into an embrace. She sank into the older woman's softness, grateful as she had so often been that this sister of a comte had bothered to love and protect the daughter of an engraver.

"I will not watch you go in the morning," Dominique said, her voice thick and low. "My fears for you should not be the last thing you see."

She understood. Her own fears would conquer her if Dominique wept and worried in the morning. She needed them to

414

remain where they were, in the pit of her stomach, heavy and sour.

Kendale was grateful for the fair evening as he rode north along the coast. The night would be clear. With any luck, tomorrow night would be too.

He was well away from Dover before dusk turned to night. He knew the road well, and kept his mount at a canter to make good time.

Halfway to Deal he passed a lane snaking up the cliff. In the half moon's light he could make out the cottage that belonged to the Fairbournes. A little farther on another lane aimed west to the village of Ringswold. Just past that he turned toward the coast, riding cross-country to the cliff path that followed the top of the rise and overlooked the sea.

It began dipping down toward the sea soon. Just before it leveled off, he pulled his horse right. On its own it found the rocky path that angled steeply down toward the water against the cliff wall.

Fifty feet from the rough beach below, he stopped, dismounted, and tied his horse to a young tree. He made his way along a ledge of stone. One of the deep shadows gaped wider than the others, leaking faint light and smoke into the night.

He stepped into the cave. The low fire said he was expected, but no one could be seen. Hand on his pistol, he walked in ten more feet.

A shadow suddenly appeared on the far wall. It moved toward him. A man stepped into the light. Casual garments hung on his slender frame and a dark beard and mustache moved as he smiled.

Kendale relaxed his guard. "Were you expecting someone else, Tarrington? This can't be a very good smuggler's lair if you need to hide whenever someone arrives."

Tarrington helped the network of watchers on occasion, which was how Kendale had come to know him. His usefulness caused them to turn a blind eye on his illegal trade, which he controlled on this section of coast almost all the way down to Dover. In one of the coves nearby he kept a little flotilla of boats and small ships. The galleys were used for quick crossings of the channel. The ships ventured farther, sometimes as far as Amsterdam.

"That I'll be needing a new lair is for certain," Tarrington said. "There has been some indiscretion about the location of this one, I think."

He slid his eyes to the right. Kendale did

not miss the warning. He moved to the left and pulled out his pistol.

Another shadow appeared. Kendale guessed who it was even before its owner emerged from the cave's far recess.

"It is good to know that you are as battle ready as ever, Kendale, but it would be very awkward if you shot me," Penthurst said.

With a curse he set the pistol down. "What are you doing here?"

"I decided to call on Mr. Tarrington, to thank him for his distinctive aid to his country."

"Did Southwaite tell you about his aid?"

"No. Another did. Who does not matter." Penthurst strolled over to a rough table where a very fine decanter rested. He opened the decanter and sniffed. "French claret."

"Very old claret, Your Grace," Tarrington said. "Bought by my father a long time ago. Have some, please."

The duke poured some and tasted. "It is good to know it was not recently brought over. I would hate to have to report that."

"No need, Your Grace. No need, I assure you."

Penthurst set the glass down. "Would you excuse us, Mr. Tarrington?"

Tarrington was only too glad to leave.

Once he had, Kendale allowed his annoyance to show. "My old tutor was less intrusive than you, Penthurst. What the hell do you want?"

"I am here to tell you that you must give up your plans. I tried to warn you in every way I knew that your intentions were suspected. They have been guessed, and provisions made to stop you. I came tonight to deliver the news that if you make any attempt to cross over, the men with you will be arrested. The army is waiting. So is the naval service."

"Neither impresses me."

"I did not think either would. Thus I have impressed on Mr. Tarrington that if he uses his boats to take you anywhere near the French coast, he too will be arrested and tried as the smuggler he is. He *was* impressed."

Kendale wanted to thrash him. Penthurst must have seen it in him, because he took the pistol and set it on the table, out of reach.

"I do not expect you to believe me, but I have had no role in this other than informing you that others had suspicions, and now of warning you off. If you had gotten away with it, and found your own justice, I would not have cared. I might have even cheered."

Kendale helped himself to some of the claret. It helped the anger ease and resignation to begin finding a place in his head.

Penthurst sat down on the bench beside the table and leaned against the stone wall. "Were you really going to kill that woman?"

Penthurst knew the story, of course, just as Southwaite and Ambury did. It had happened before that duel and before this duke had killed one of their circle. Kendale wished he had not been so indiscreet. He did not want Penthurst, of all men, judging him.

"I don't kill women. Do you?"

"I have never had cause to. *We* do, all the time, however. Three women went to the gallows in the last month, I believe. Justice does not spare them, and it was justice you sought, so do not be insulted by my question."

"I am not insulted. I do not give a damn what you think."

"Of course not. So you were not going over for her. That means you know who was behind it. A government official? No? Army then." He acted as if he had only to look over to know the answers. The arrogance of that had Kendale's mind splitting with rage. That Penthurst was guessing correctly only made it worse.

"That you did not invite me on this adventure is understandable," Penthurst said. "That you kept it from the others . . ."

He did not finish. The implications, such as they were, floated in the air, unspoken.

"It was too dangerous."

"How like you, to risk your life without a second thought to help your friends, and to show loyalty even after death, but to deny your friends the privilege of doing the same for you. It speaks to a selfish streak in you, Kendale, and more than a little conceit. I will not let them know how inconsiderate you have been."

"That is good of you," he said. "I hope that you are finished. It is not my plan to be your entertainment all night."

Penthurst stood. "I will leave you to whatever it is that you plan instead. As long as it is not being rowed to France to kill a French officer, I doubt anyone will interfere with you."

Kendale just wanted the man gone. He needed to decide whether to give weight to this warning. If he did, and canceled the crossing, he needed to decide how to manage Travis's disappointment.

Halfway to the cave opening, Penthurst turned. "On learning who I was yesterday, Mr. Tarrington proved most cooperative. I daresay he told me everything he knows about any crossings that have happened in the last year or two. Then he babbled something regarding a Mr. Garrett. You might ask him what that was about."

The night outside swallowed Penthurst. Almost immediately Tarrington appeared as if the dark spit him into the cave's opening. He advanced, looking defensive, chagrined, and careful.

"There was nothing I could do. When he cornered me at the tavern in Ringswold yesterday and handed me his card, it was clear we would never go over tomorrow night. He knew more than half already, so don't be accusing me of betrayal."

"I am not going to accuse you of betrayal."

Tarrington appeared relieved. "It is a hell of a thing. Tell a duke what he wants to know and a viscount will nail your tail to the wall. Don't tell him, and the duke will have your hide instead. Not fair, really. Not much choice, seems to me."

"No choice at all." He poured the claret into another of the fine crystal glasses on the table. "If you want to save that tail now, sit down, and tell me everything that you told him. You will not leave out anything if you are wise."

Tarrington downed the wine, then began

his tale. Being loquacious, his description of that conversation with Penthurst probably took longer that the conversation actually had. There could be no doubt that too much had been known by Penthurst before one word was spoken.

Finished, Tarrington held out his hands in hopeful resignation. "I trust that you won't be feeling the urge to get even by laying down information about anything that you may have seen during our prior adventures together."

"I haven't decided. You left something out. You did not tell me everything."

Tarrington objected, then frowned, then his expression cleared. "You mean the business with Garrett? Doesn't signify, does it? It is another matter entirely, not connected to you."

"Who is this Garrett?"

"A partner in trade."

"Another smuggler, you mean."

Tarrington rolled his eyes. "I so dislike that word. However, if you insist, yes. He established himself to the south a ways. An interloper. He and I had some . . . disagreements. He saw the error of his ways and this partnership formed."

"So he works for you now."

"It is a partnership."

"What did you say to Penthurst about him?"

"Let me see, what did I say? I did not realize I had said anything, but when a duke is quizzing you, it is wise to keep talking and I may have —"

Kendale lifted the pistol. Tarrington's eyes widened. He began talking again, long and fast.

CHAPTER 20

Marielle could only pray that everything had been arranged. She had not received a letter either begging off or describing delays, but that did not mean she could count on success.

That messenger might have taken her money and never delivered the letter. Or the recipient of the letter might have read it, laughed, and ignored its detailed instructions. Since he would want the money that would come with compliance, she assumed he had not done that. She would learn the truth one way or another soon, however.

She slipped out of the inn in Dover where she had spent the last two nights, and made her way down the lane. Carrying a valise felt conspicuous, but the people she passed did not appear to notice or care.

She kept her other hand on her skirt, atop the bulge in her pocket. Her money was there, and the knife. She hoped the former would be enough after all these years of saving and denying herself the most basic comforts. She had no idea if the latter would be needed, but she had to admit it gave her a little more courage.

The May morning air smelled sweet as she made her way to the house that Mr. Garrett used on the outskirts of the town. A small open carriage waited outside. Her messenger sat at the ribbons. He hopped down when he saw her, took her valise, and set it on the floor of the gig. He handed her in.

"It won't take long to get there," he said. "Garrett asked me to meet you. He has preparations to make. There's army everywhere, and two naval frigates on the sea, so he is setting up a distraction for them."

She had noticed a lot of army uniforms in Dover and its environs. If she had been the spy everyone thought, she would have known they would be here, and perhaps chosen another time.

"How long will it take?" she asked.

"To go over? I don't know." He laughed. "Depends on where you go, I guess. Boulogne ain't far. There are good galleys that can row there and back in a day if it is fair. Or so I'm told. Never do it myself. Scared of the sea, I am."

She had no idea if she were scared of the sea. The last time she had been on it, so much else had scared her that she doubted the sea itself had made any difference. Nor was she going to Boulogne. This would not be a one-day journey, no matter how fair the day.

A mixture of excitement and fear built as the gig left Dover behind and took a road north. The sun burned brightly as it kept ascending to her right over the edge of the cliffs. After two hours of silent riding, her messenger turned toward the sea.

A large manor house could be glimpsed to the south as they approached the crest of a rise. Her messenger pointed to it. "That there is Crownhill Hall, the Earl of South-waite's seat."

She stared at the roof and chimneys in shock. If that was Crownhill, they now rode over Southwaite's property. She turned and scrutinized the man delivering her to her embarkation. For all she knew he could be part of that network of watchers, and her plans had been betrayed.

"Is the earl in residence?" she asked.

"Nah. This time of year those types are in London, aren't they? Going to balls and such while others do their planting. Though I hear one of his prize stallions got a mare with foal, so he may come down for that when she is due next month."

Talk of Southwaite added nostalgia to her alarm. She would have liked to see Emma before she left. Cassandra and Lady Sophie too. They had been better friends to her than she had been to them. Confiding would have been impossible, but a silent farewell and kiss — She scolded herself for sentimentality. The last time they had known anything about her movements, Kendale had learned of it and followed her to the coast.

If either Emma or Cassandra suspected anything, if she revealed with her manner that she indulged her emotions in seeing them, she did not think they would keep silent. Nor would they ever approve of her plans. Still, it would have been nice to be Marielle Lyon with them one more time, in ways she never would be again if she were successful.

The gig stopped. Jarred out of her reverie, she looked around. A hill faced them, one too steep for this carriage. Crownhill could no longer be seen.

"We have to walk now." Her escort hopped out, handed her down, and grabbed her valise.

Up that hill they trudged. She wished

someone had told her to wear low boots or some other more practical shoes. She slipped on some stones, and after that he held on to her arm to steady her, all but pushing her up ahead of him.

At the top she stopped and caught her breath while he joined her. Then she saw why they had climbed that hill.

Below her stretched a wide cove protected by a thin arm of land circling into the sea. A small ship sat at anchor behind that arm, its square sails being unfurled while she watched.

"Impressive, eh?" he said, admiration in his tone.

Very impressive. Mr. Garrett must be a very successful smuggler. She had chosen well. She had expected a galley that would take a week to reach the Vendée while it followed the French coast west, then south. She had assumed she would sleep on the ground at night, or on the bottom of the boat, clutching her knife. Instead Mr. Garrett had provided what looked to be a private yacht.

"We have to go down the way we came up. Might be best if you hold on to my shoulder or arm. It is hard not to slide."

Slide they did, their feet sending down showers of stones while they fought the urge to hurtle forward. Twice she went down on her rump to avoid falling and just rolling down to the small, rocky beach.

The last hundred feet the ground all but shot them forward. Giving in, she released him and let herself run, hoping she landed upright at the bottom. When finally her feet stopped, she bent over, gasping for breath, more exhausted than she had been going up the other side.

Mr. Garrett appeared from a spit of the rocks behind them. "I would have sent a horse, but I am told you do not ride. Horses take that better than people." He stuck his thumb over his shoulder at the steep, tall hill.

She brushed off her skirt, then her sleeves, and finally her face. It was a good thing she was not a vain woman. "As long as I am here in one piece, that is all that matters. When do we leave?"

Garrett pointed to the top of the arm of land. "See that fellow up there? When he signals, we can sail out."

"How long before he signals?"

"That is up to His Majesty's Navy. We don't want to be interfering with their frigates."

"Perhaps we should wait for nightfall."

"That is hardly necessary, and unwise in a

429

waning moon, I'm told. 'Course, if I had my way, I would not be doing this at all."

And yet he would be. What an honorable man, to follow through on his implied commitment, and even to arrange such splendid transportation, after having failed to inform her that he did not want the duty.

Over on the ship, men continued with the sails. Two others climbed down into a small boat. One began rowing it toward the narrow beach where she and Mr. Garrett stood.

The sun turned the boat and its occupants into silhouettes. She squinted. Something about one of them . . . "Who is that?"

"That is the ship's master, and he who owns the yacht and pays the crew."

"It isn't yours?"

Garrett laughed. He thought the question hilarious. She turned on him, vexed at the realization that he had involved someone else in her plans. "What did you say to obtain their agreement to use their ship? I wrote that I need to go over to bring back something of great value, but you have misunderstood. I can hardly afford such as that, and I am in no position to explain my intentions or purpose. You should have never taken such a step without sending word to me, so that I could —"

"Is she burning your ears, Mr. Garrett?" a

voice called.

"That she is, sir. Interesting how it sounds sweeter with that accent, though."

Stunned, she pivoted toward the sun and the men crossing the beach. The one in front walked right up to her and looked down.

Kendale's green eyes reflected amusement at the sight of her gaping at him.

Her heart glistened with joy, then sank as she realized what his presence meant. The little ship was not for her. She would not be going anywhere.

For a few seconds Marielle appeared happy to see him.

Then other emotions showed in her eyes.

He took her hand. "Come with me."

He led her behind an outcropping of rock, so they would have some privacy. She sank to the ground and sat with her back against the hard, chilled wall. With her legs stretched out and her body slumped, she reminded him of that day in the alley, when he wondered if she even lived.

He sat down beside her.

"I did not know you had a yacht," she said in a dull voice.

"It is a recent acquisition."

"So you are going over in style then, and

by sea all the way to your destination. Do you not worry that you will be too visible? Smugglers' galleys are not ideal for longer voyages, but they do not herald themselves with sails either, or depend upon the winds."

"You sound as if you have weighed the alternatives carefully."

She laughed to herself, sadly. "I have had six years to do so."

"As it happens, I will not be taking the journey I had planned, Marielle. Those naval frigates are there to stop me. The soldiers in Dover and along the coast will detain me on sight. The government suspects my plans and has decided I am too dangerous to their own."

"They did not learn of it from me," she said. "Penthurst asked, but I did not tell him even though I had guessed. I said you intended to visit your properties, which you had neglected too long."

"I know you did not tell him."

"You cannot be sure. Just as you know I am not a spy, but you cannot be sure."

Except he did know for sure. Not only because the evidence said so. Penthurst, in his own way, had been trying to act as a friend through all of this. If he had learned anything from Marielle, if she had been disloyal, he would have let it be known, again in his own way.

"I am sure, of both things. My head says it is so. More important, my heart does."

She looked straight ahead, not reacting. Then she wiped her eyes with her hand. "You can still do it. You can go over on your own, one man, maybe two, at night. If you stay off the roads and avoid the towns, you can make your way overland, much as you made your way back that time."

"I considered it." For a few minutes, after Penthurst had left that cave, the plans had taken form. "I have chosen to put it off for now. Perhaps forever."

She struggled valiantly against the tears that tried to conquer her composure. "I cannot do that. Put it off forever. I ask that you not force me to."

He gathered her into his arms. Within the billows of her skirt he felt the hard lump of a purse filled with coin, then the long shape of what might be a dagger in its sheath.

"What is the treasure that you need to bring back? Garrett said that you wrote of something of value."

"Mr. Garrett is a poor excuse for a man if he revealed what I wrote in a private letter."

"He is a smuggler. He cannot be expected to follow the social niceties on such questions."

She looked up at him, her eyes glistening from unshed tears. "Did you threaten him? That was wrong of you, especially since it was only to pry and satisfy your own curiosity about something not your concern."

"Listen to me carefully, woman. Your safety *is* my concern. I have told you so before. You do not have a say in that, Marielle. I did not threaten Garrett, but if learning the truth required it, I would have held a pistol to his temple. Now, why are you so determined to risk everything to go back? Tell me."

She sank against his chest. The rebellion seeped out of her and she stayed there, limp and unhappy. "I may as well. I never did before because you would stop me. Since you have stopped me anyway — It is not a treasure, the way men like Garrett mean. I am going back to get my father. He stayed behind so I could get away."

"Where is he?"

"Near the town of Savenay."

This did not sound very difficult.

"He is in a château there," she continued. "In its donjon, I would guess."

"He is a prisoner?"

She nodded. "Not an official one. There was no trial. Lamberte captured him, and that château where Lamberte lives has a

434

donjon, so he was put there. If he is alive, that is."

Her goal had changed from not very difficult to almost impossible with a few short sentences.

He thought of that dagger in her long pocket. "Was it your intention to kill this Lamberte?"

She took some time to respond, which perhaps was an answer in itself. "That château belonged to his half brother who was a baron. Lamberte is a bastard of their father. When I was very young, my mother became the lover of the baron, and went to live there. I would visit her, and came to know the château and its people well."

"Was her lover killed during the revolution?"

She shook her head. "He survived. The Vendée was not very enamored of the revolution, however. Even so, the baron did not join the uprising against the new government when it came six years ago. He remained out of it, isolated in his château. While the army was crushing the rebellion and killing so many, my father and I took refuge there. We were there the day that Lamberte marched in with twenty-five men. His brother went to greet him and Lamberte shot him dead. Just like that. No accusations. No trial. No guilt. It was brother murdering brother, for reasons that were not political, I have realized. In the hell that existed then in that region, however, it was only one more death among many." She took a deep breath. "And then he killed my mother too. And their closest servants."

"Did you see it?"

"Yes."

It pained him that she had witnessed such carnage. As much as he had, maybe more. Only he had been a man and a soldier, and she had been a girl of perhaps fifteen years. Had her youth made it harder to overcome the memories, or easier?

"She had hidden me, and given me this little book, like a journal, to take to Papa. It had been brought to the baron secretly, and it contained Lamberte's own accounts of the money he collected in taxes. It shows his thievery. He must have learned his brother had it, and simply killed anyone who might be aware of it. I hid while he tore apart their chambers looking for it. When he left, I ran to my father, who got me out."

"If he sacrificed himself to do so, he would not want you to come back for him and risk undoing that."

She pushed out of his embrace, and

scrambled to stand. "I knew you would say that. This is not about what he wants. It is about what *I want.*"

He grasped her arm and held her in place. "Do you think to enter the château without this man knowing? Will you walk up to him and use that dagger that you have in your pocket? It is harder to kill than you may think, Marielle."

"If I did kill him, I would be justified. However, he is not in there now. Or he was not a few weeks ago, and I hope he has not returned but is currying favor in Paris."

"How do you know this?"

"I ask. I speak to the new arrivals and find out what I can of the region, and of Lamberte. Why do you think I became the niece of a comte? So they will talk to me as an equal, who has suffered the same losses. They would never confide in the daughter of an engraver. Such as I filled the courts, calling for their heads."

She jerked her arm out of his hold, stood, and brushed off her skirt. "Now you have ruined everything, Lord Kendale. Mr. Garrett is probably afraid of you, and the trouble you can make for him. It will be years before I find another like him. I can only hope you forget about me by then, and do not ruin it once more."

He stood. "How did you plan to get your father free?"

"I have money for bribes. I have been saving since I arrived."

Whatever she had, it would not overcome a man's fear of someone like this Lamberte.

She stepped away from him and the wall, into the sun. She eyed that high hill she had just come down. With a sigh, she walked toward it.

"I will take you there."

She stopped, then turned. He walked over to her.

"I will take you there, Marielle, and try to rescue him. However, you must obey me, and do what I say, without argument or question. If I conclude it is hopeless, you must accept that and leave with me when I say so."

She looked at the yacht. "Will the navy not —"

"Leave that to me. Do you understand how this must be done? Do you give your word that you will obey my commands?"

Her expression brightened. Her eyes took on the impish sparks that had entranced him from the beginning. "All your commands? I do not know, Lord Kendale. It might be improper for a lady to agree to some things."

He hardened at once. His mind began romping through all kinds of improper commands. "Damnation, Marielle, stop that. Do you give your word?"

She stepped so closely that their bodies almost touched. She smiled coquettishly. "Of course, m'sieur le vicomte."

Up on the top of the cove's outer crust, Garrett's man waved his arms in a signal.

He took Marielle's hand and hurried her to the water and the waiting boat. It had been a hell of a time for her to flirt with him, let alone allude to *those* kinds of commands.

And God help him, he loved her for it.

"It is too big for you, but it was the best I could do at the last minute."

Marielle looked down at the yellow dress that Kendale referred to. It had been waiting on the yacht for her to put on. She sat beside him under an awning, with a neatly dressed Angus across on another chair. They might be merely three fashionable people sailing out to enjoy a fine day along the coast.

Mr. Stanton, the yacht's master, called orders to his crew to work the sails this way and that. They all kept an eye on the frigate a mile away up the coast. Presumably the frigate watched them as well. Back and forth they sailed, meandering without destination or purpose.

Kendale held his pocket watch in his hand. "Soon, Mr. Stanton," he called.

Angus stood and gazed to the north, past the frigate. He squinted, and shielded his eyes from the sun with his hand. "Tarrington is on the move, sir."

"Be ready, Stanton."

"What is happening?" she asked.

"We have it on good authority that a smugglers galley will make a run right about now. The frigate will probably assume I am on the boat, and move to stop them," Kendale explained.

Mr. Stanton peered north. Marielle did too. She could barely see a thick, dark, low line moving on the horizon. The frigate began turning toward it.

Mr. Stanton called orders and a burst of activity bustled on the yacht. Sails moved. The yacht took a decided turn, so abrupt that the entire vessel dipped sideways.

"While the frigate is busy chasing the galley up there, we will sail east down here," Kendale said.

"Will the galley be caught?"

"After giving a good chase, it will be. The naval captain will find he has taken a boat

440

of suspicious use with fifteen men aboard, but no contraband, and no trained fighters."

"And no you." Those trained fighters lounged in the hold of the yacht, out of sight. It would be close quarters for everyone the next few days.

Wind caught the sails smartly. The yacht sped forward through the sea. Mr. Stanton kept his gaze on that frigate. "Mr. Tarrington is providing excellent diversion, Lord Kendale. I do not think anyone on His Majesty's Ship has noticed what we are doing yet."

"Can we outrun them if we have to?" Marielle asked.

"That is questionable. Frigates are fast, as is this yacht. It need not catch us to matter. It only has to get within firing range, and Mr. Stanton will be forced to lower the sails. The real danger is when we turn south. If it follows, the frigate can cut across at an angle. Do not worry, however. The men on that galley will dodge it for at least a half hour."

She did worry, however. She could not take her eyes off the sails of the frigate, no matter how small they became in the distance.

"You knew last night that you were going

to take me over," she said while staring north. "This dress says you did. Why did you not say so at once when I saw you?"

"I only knew I *might* take you over. I needed to know the goal, and the reasons. And I had to obtain your agreement to my rules."

Rules. Command. Obedience. Kendale was acting and thinking like an officer. Perhaps he always did, at least with these men he now led. He appeared to consider her one of them on this mission. There had been little warmth from him since they left the beach. Not even a stolen kiss or secret embrace. Instead he had explained the yacht's organization and hierarchy, as if she had signed on as cabin boy.

They lost sight of land, and even the sails of the frigate. Nothing but water surrounded them. The yacht turned south and began a long, slow curve.

Kendale stood and offered his hand to help her rise. "Come with me."

He led her into the owner's cabin. The privacy delighted her. It had been hard to spend hours pretending that he only saw her as a lady in distress whom he was helping.

She waited for him to embrace her. Instead he sat her down at the small table, and placed a sheet of paper and an inkwell before her. He took a small knife and sharpened a quill. "I want you to draw out the plan of the château, as best you can remember. I'll not have these men going in blind and caught in a maze if one of them becomes separated from the rest."

"You can't think to bring them all, surely. Twenty Englishmen filing through the countryside will be noticed. We must go alone, with perhaps one or two others at most."

"I promise that I will give your advice on military tactics all the weight it deserves, Marielle." He handed her the quill. "Now, please draw the plan."

She grabbed the quill, dipped, and pictured the château's ground floor in her head. Her concentration did not entirely obliterate her annoyance that he would assume her advice deserved no consideration at all. Nor did his manner make her happy. They were alone now, and he might show her at least a little affection.

She outlined the building, then divided out the public rooms. She took some time and great care in placing the stairwells correctly. "Have I offended you in some way?" she asked while she pictured the back servant stairs in her head, and the kitchen and services rooms to which they led. "Or does being a soldier just naturally bring out the coldness in you?"

He stood beside her and leaned over her shoulder to watch the plan take form. "You are already a distraction. If I gave into my inclinations, it would only be worse. Should I do that anyway, and take you here? If I do, every man on the deck will hear it, and every one below."

"I was thinking more in terms of a kiss, so that I know you are not so angry with my deceptions that you have grown indifferent."

She felt the warmth of his lips on her temple. "I could never be indifferent, Marielle. Do not pretend that you are ignorant of the way you have thoroughly entangled me. As for your deceptions, both those revealed and perhaps those still to be known, that is for another day. Unless it bears directly on our chances for success, leave any surprises for then."

He left her to finish her drawing. She wished he had not. Better if he had thrown her on the berth even if it meant the whole ship heard and knew. Now, with him gone, she could not avoid the rest of this duty he had given her.

Steeling her composure, she turned the

paper, and dipped the quill. Then she
outlined yet another level of the château,
and filled in the one chamber up there that
she remembered — the baron's bedchamber, where her mother had died.

CHAPTER 21

With its sails down, the yacht did not call much attention to itself. Low and long, and obscured by the inlet's reeds and overhanging tree branches, its profile would be missed by passing boats unless they deliberately looked for it. Kendale counted on no one doing that.

He paced its deck, waiting. He had been here since the hour before dawn and every passing minute increased his concern. It had perhaps been a mistake to put Mr. Travis in charge of the scouting party. Once on French soil, he might abandon them to go off on his own again, to seek his own justice. He had the most experience, however, and he had given his word as a gentleman to fulfill this mission. Since he still bore the signs of that thrashing he had received, and since he had not left them after regaining consciousness, Kendale believed him.

Shutters were drawn on the two cabins

above deck, one fore and one aft. Stanton slept in one, but would be up very soon. Marielle slept in the other.

He had resisted the urge to go to her there. He stayed below with the men, spending the nights on a hammock strung below the floor of her cabin. He judged his nose to be no more than four feet from her back and he could hear her turn in her sleep. On two nights he had listened to her soft footfalls as she paced the boards.

She had not upbraided him again for lack of affection. If she chafed at there being no more than the rare embrace or kiss, she did not display resentment. He did it in the name of discretion and because he needed to concentrate on the task at hand, but he admitted that he also did not need any of these men accusing him of having his judgment twisted by the kind of intense lust that turned many men into idiots.

So he suffered it. She knew he did. She would catch him watching her while she looked at the sea, and her eyes said she knew what he had been thinking. He hoped that she suffered too. It would be a hell of a thing if denial only affected him.

Morning desire was always the worst, and now it taunted him, urging him to stride to that cabin even though it was already too late to do so. He had no choice except to burn with hunger while he looked at the trees into which Travis and the others had disappeared the last evening.

It appeared the lowest tree branches moved. Either that or the fading night created an illusion. He moved and looked harder. While he did a blond head charged into view, followed by four more men at a run. Travis came last.

They waded into the water with muskets and pistols held high and sloshed toward the rowboat that had brought them to the shore. While they climbed in and began rowing, Mr. Stanton emerged from his cabin as if he sensed their arrival. He lowered a rope ladder. He called other men, who came to help the party board.

Travis handed up his pistol, then climbed the ropes. He drank some of the ale being passed, then presented himself to Kendale.

"Was farther than she said," he explained. "That manor is a good three miles north of the town, not one. We circled through the country coming back. There's army on the roads. We were hugging ditches twice as they passed."

"Could you find your way back without using the roads?"

Travis shrugged. "Young Angus there

stayed alert to landmarks. Maybe we could do it."

Maybe was not what he wanted to hear. "And the château itself. How many soldiers guard it?"

"There are guards, but not army as such, and not many that we saw. Two at the entrance. None on the roof. There's a walk up there and if an army was lodged there I'd expect to see some on watch up there, armies liking to keep men busy and all. It appears to be a private residence, though. The army is in the town."

This part of the report was better than he had hoped. This château served as the home of a tax collector, not an army colonel. It could be hard to bribe soldiers. Servants were another matter.

"Get some food and some rest. We will leave at five, and take our positions before sundown."

Travis left him. Angus sidled over and looked at the cabin at the other end of the deck. "Have you told her yet?"

Kendale looked over his shoulder. The shutters of one small window had opened. Marielle's pale face looked out. "I will now."

"She is not going to like it."

"She will obey me anyway. I hope you are not doubting my ability to command one

449

small woman."

"Not at all, sir."

Kendale left the men to their business and strode to the cabin. As he let himself in, he heard the shutters closing.

Marielle stood, wrapped in a blanket. The commotion of the party's return had woken her and pulled her out of bed.

He told her the information that the scouting party had brought back, while he tried to ignore how that blanket conjured up memories, many of them erotic.

"So, we will go soon?" she asked. "We will do this today?"

"This evening."

She sat on the edge of the narrow bed. "It is hard for me to believe that finally — it feels odd, and unreal. To know it will happen, but to have to wait all day — I will go mad."

"We will need to prepare most of that time." Most of the preparation would be so the men did not go mad too. Waiting for action affected one's nerves. It was best to keep busy.

"So you will be with the men, and I will be pacing these boards. I have no guns to clean. Perhaps I will sharpen my knife, then decide which of my clothes makes me look most like a woman of the Vendée."

"Do you mean a blanket will not do?"

She looked down at her current garment and laughed. "Perhaps I should spend the day washing clothes. I did not bring enough."

Relieved to see her humor improve, he took his leave and went to the door. He had other things to explain to her, but decided it would not hurt to wait until later in the day.

"Do not go yet."

Her words reached him as he pressed the latch. He looked back at her.

"Lock the door." She opened the blanket and let it fall around her hips. Her nakedness glowed in the pale light finding its way into the cabin. "We will have no time before this danger today. Lock the door and come here. Please. I won't make a sound. If they know what we are doing anyway, I do not care."

Her outstretched hand coaxed him. He secured the door and went to her.

She wrapped him with her arms and pressed her cheek against his stomach. Then she looked up at him with a naughty smile. "If anyone suspects, they will think Mademoiselle Lyon is showing her gratitude to Lord Kendale. They will not be wrong."

When her fingers went to work on the buttons of his pantaloons, any lingering considerations of discretion vanished. The day was long. There would be enough time to prepare for evening.

She took his cock in her hands, surrounding him in warmth. She stroked with her fingertips and his arousal roared in his head. He watched her hands move, then closed his eyes and let the sensations do their worst. Moist heat surrounded him. He looked down while she used her mouth to create unbearable pleasure.

"No." He did not know how he managed to say it. His body already felt release within reach.

She looked up, confused and surprised. He pushed her back and lifted her legs. "Not this time. Not now."

Her back barely fit across the narrow bed. Her shoulders and head rested on the wall. He bent her legs so her feet were on the bed too, and pushed her knees apart.

She was beautiful. All of her, but especially the soft, delicate part of her that only he knew. He caressed carefully, watching how her whole body reacted. She struggled to swallow her cries, and finally covered her mouth with her hand. He lifted her hips, bent, and used his tongue along the soft folds, and finally circling the sensitive nub.

She became frantic. Tremors shook her and wetness flowed. She clawed at the bedclothes, the mattress, his hair. His mind narrowed to a single, sharp awareness of only wanting to claim her.

He flipped her so she knelt. She raised her bottom high and parted her legs. Barely audible pleas floated on her short breaths. He entered her slowly and somehow found the control not to come at once.

Sensations more profound than mere pleasure owned him. A primitive contentment with utter possession joined the sublime pleasure. He brought her to a convulsive climax, then found his own while he ravished her.

Voices. Bootsteps. Men moved all around the outside of the cabin. Marielle lay on her side, sated and dazed. Kendale sat beside her with his back against the wall. He looked to be sleeping.

An argument of some kind broke out down the deck. His eyes opened and he listened. He swung off the bed, fixed his garments, and raked his hair with his fingers. He looked down at her with a warmth that meant more to her than any pleasure or any words. He hooked his finger into the blanket and dragged it over her nakedness.

"I must go. There are things to do."

"Of course. I need to prepare too."

He sat again, and leaned on one arm, hovering over her. "You do not have to do anything. It might be best if you stayed here, out of the way."

"I need to at least dress properly. We will be walking some distance. I brought some low boots, and a warm wrap. The nights are cool near the coast here even now."

He watched his hand as he pushed some errant strands of hair away from her face. "You will not be walking. You are not coming."

She peered at him, to see if he meant it. He met her gaze. He did mean it.

She sat up. "I have to come. You will not know where to go. What if you are stopped? None of you speaks French well enough to fool anyone. You all sound like the Englishmen you are."

"All that will save us in not being stopped in the first place. That will be easier if you do not come."

She scrambled off the bed. "This is a bad decision and I do not accept it. You are being sentimental. I am not one of your delicate ladies. I crawled my way out and I can find my way back, and I have planned and saved for this for years, and *I am going*."

"No, Marielle, you are not."

He said it so calmly. So confidently. He had decided, and that was that. She wanted to hit him. She turned away while she lined up her furious thoughts, looking for one that would sway him.

"Marielle, all that you remember of the château is in your drawings. You are not needed. We will do it without you. I will find him, I will bring him back, we will sail away, and you will not be endangered unnecessarily." He embraced her from behind. "You gave your word to obey me and now you must."

"And if I do not?"

"I will see that you do."

She glared at him over her shoulder. She thought her head would burst from the rage building in it.

"The drawing I made is rough and incomplete. When I enter that château, I will remember more than I do now. I will remember all of it."

"The drawing will be sufficient."

"You are impossible! Without me to speak the local language, those who guard it will kill some of you as soon as you utter one word. Is protecting me worth that blood, if it might be done another way if I am there?"

"At least if someone dies, it will be a man and a soldier."

"They are not real soldiers. They are a private army and this is a private war. Only you forget that it is *my* war." She turned and faced him. "You were willing to have a woman guide you once before, and if it were anyone but me, you would be again. You must forget I am your lover when you consider which way has the better chance of success."

He released her and walked to the door. "I have already considered and decided. I will let you know when we are leaving. Stay here until then."

A thought came to her in a rush, slicing through her frustration and anger, stunning her. "This is not only about protecting me, is it? It is also about her."

He turned, exasperated. "You are not making sense."

"Aren't I? You let a woman guide you before and she led you into a trap." Astonished and hurt, she walked over to him and looked in his eyes, searching for signs that she was wrong. "You are not really sure that I will not do the same thing, are you? You are still not completely sure of me at all."

He cupped her face with his hands. "That

456

is not true. I trust you totally."

"Then let me come. I have a right to. You know I do. And you know that you need me there. Gavin Norwood, the army officer, knows it, even if Viscount Kendale, the protector of Marielle Lyon, does not."

His expression hardened. His eyes burned. He walked away and left, the door crashing open and closed with his departure.

She pulled out her valise, to find her half boots.

Mr. Stanton had the crew lower the small rowboat into the water again. One by one, the men went down the rope ladder. Kendale watched Travis descend, then four others. The rest would stay here. There was no point in having a dozen walk into trouble if it was waiting.

They were as ready as they would ever be. He doubted that anything mattered more than the gold coins he had on him. Gold spoke to men as nothing else did. Despite what Marielle said, it was the only language that might make a difference tonight.

Marielle emerged from her cabin, wearing boots and her faded fawn dress and a long knit shawl. She had braided her hair into a long plait and donned a white cap edged in a frill.

Angus stood beside him, and watched her approach them. "You will have to explain to me again how easy it is to command a small woman, sir. I am trying to learn all I can from you, see, and you went into that cabin of one mind, with orders to give her, and emerged of another and with no such orders given."

"I explained all of that to all of you an hour ago, Angus."

"You did, sir. The change in strategy part at least. Even Mr. Travis came around on that. What I am longing to learn, in a student sort of way, is how one small woman changed your thinking so fast."

"The clarity of her argument could not be dismissed."

"It was logic then, was it? The two of you had a long, enlightened conversation on the question?"

"Absolutely. Now, I advise you stop smirking."

"Yes, sir."

Marielle went to the rail and looked down. "They do not appear too English, I am relieved to see."

"I am glad you approve."

Her eyebrows rose at his tight tone. "Won't all the weapons draw attention?"

"We will not all walk together on the

458

roads. We do know what we are about, Marielle."

"Of course. Well, should we join them in the boat?"

"Not just yet." He drew her aside. "I am of half a mind to still make you stay here. Should you join us, you will do nothing on your own initiative. Nothing at all. Do you understand?"

"Yes, sir." She said it in the clipped way Angus and the other men did. He chose not to hear it as mockery.

"I am charging Angus with protecting you. He will fight to the death doing so, so do not make that necessary if it can be avoided."

"Why Angus? Won't you be there?"

"I may be otherwise engaged at times."

"Do we go now?" she asked impatiently.

He brought her over to the rail and showed her how to climb down the ladder. She still did not do it correctly, it being her first time. Angus reached up and grabbed her lest she fall into the water. She sat down on one of the plank seats.

Kendale began his own descent, wishing like hell that Marielle were still in that cabin.

"This road will circle around to the west, then there is another that joins it and goes northeast." Mr. Travis explained the round-about route while drawing with a stick in the crossroad's dirt. Marielle frowned down on the X that marked her town of Savenay, and the other showing the château to the north. "It is longer, of course, but avoids the town completely."

"Much longer," Kendale said. "Hours longer."

Other than Kendale, no one else watched. Angus and the other four men were keeping their eyes on the four roads that joined here, in order to warn if anyone approached.

"We can go across country," Mr. Travis said. "No roads at all then."

No roads and no light and slow going, Marielle thought. She looked to the northeast, and a forest in the distance beyond the farmland. She allowed memories to come to her. Some of them she had avoided for six years.

She picked through them until she arrived at the ugly night she had fled to the coast, going the opposite way of what they now attempted. Her guide had known the region well.

"There is a faster way." She took the stick from Mr. Travis. Retracing her flight the night her mother died, she drew a wavy line through the forest, from the road near the château, then across farmland to that road which they had just walked, only inland a bit more. She pointed to what she had just drawn. "When I left, I came this way. It is not a proper road, just a rough broad path used by these farms along it."

Mr. Travis scowled at her wavy line. "You are sure of that?"

"As sure as I can be."

"That is not sure enough for me."

"I was running for my life. It is not a night I will forget."

Mr. Travis did not mask his skepticism. "No telling what is in that forest, sir. It could be like Feversham described it was in America, being picked off by muskets firing out of the trees."

"There is no reason for any muskets to be in this forest," Kendale said. "There is no way for anyone to know we are here."

"And if that path is not well marked? It will be dark by the time we get there."

"If it is used by farmers, their carts and livestock would keep it clear enough for us to follow it."

Mr. Travis began to say something but a hushed call from twenty feet away cut him off. The man watching east raised his arm in warning. Men flew into ditches and ducked behind brush. Kendale obliterated the drawing with his boot, then grabbed her arm and dragged her off the road and down into the high grasses that edged a stream along the road.

She waited for the telltale signs of horse hooves or bootsteps that said members of the army approached. She knew exactly how they would sound. Another memory flashed through her head, of hiding in the brush before, so terrified of those horses and boots that she silently wept.

The sounds never came. She parted the grass and peered through. A cart rolled into view, pulled by one ox. A man walked alongside the animal. He looked like a young farmer. No one else walked with him or followed.

She scrambled to her feet. Kendale reached out, grabbed her arm, and pulled her down again. "What do you think you are doing?" he whispered angrily.

"I am going to find out if that path is how I remember. You stay here. There is no danger from this man. He will only see a woman from this region, which is what I am."

He hesitated, then released her, muttering a curse. She looked back once while she walked up to the road. She saw he had his pistol at the ready, just in case.

■ ■ ■ ■

Marielle walked down the road toward the cart, hailing the farmer in her native dialect. Kendale heard the cart stop, then start again. Now as it approached the patter of conversation accompanied it.

While they passed within several feet of his head, the farmer said something to her that caused her to snap a terse response. The fellow laughed and muttered what Kendale translated to "you cannot blame a man for trying." Marielle rattled off a response so rapidly that he could not make it out. He trusted she put the farmer in his place, but he readied himself for fast movement if necessary.

The cart kept going. The conversation did not. When he heard nothing more, he ventured a look. The cart could be seen in the distance, heading to the coast. Marielle came skipping down the road.

"He says it is as I remembered," she said.

Mr. Travis, Angus, and the other men joined them on the road.

"The little lane breaks away just around that bend." She pointed east. "Then it crosses through the fields and snakes through the forest."

"Did he not think it odd that you needed directions if you live here?" Mr. Travis asked.

"I told him I am on my way to visit my sister, who is in service at the château, and she told me of this faster way but I could not find the road. I told him I am from a farm a day's walk south of here." She began walking west. "Perhaps we can be through the forest before nightfall."

The men looked at him. Kendale nodded. "Let us go. Hopefully we can not only avoid curious travelers but also save hours from our mission." He strode toward Marielle.

She paused and waited for him, then fell into step alongside. A quarter mile beyond the bend they found the unmistakable start of a broad path. It split through the field. Crops rose on either side, and hoofprints and wheel ruts marked the uneven, rough dirt.

Marielle wrapped her knit shawl around her like an ermine cloak, and stepped onto that path as if it were covered in red velvet. She glanced back at him, her eyes alight with triumph. "I told you that you needed me on this mission. Oh, the farmer told me something else. Lamberte is indeed not at the château. That is good news, no?"

"It is, assuming the gossip this farmer

heard is not two months old."

Her expression fell. "I suppose we will not be sure until we enter the gate."

"That is the unfortunate sum of it. In the meantime, I will hope for the best, and prepare for the worst."

"Mark this spot, gentlemen." Kendale stood in the deepening twilight on a low rise of land several hundred yards behind the road that passed the château. From up here they could see that manor house. Its high-pitched roofs marked its French pedigree, as did its fine-boned classical details mixed with medieval turrets and long windows. English country houses did not look like this.

Marielle stood near the crest of the hill, out of hearing distance. She gazed at the château as if it were not quite real. He wondered what thoughts and memories worked in her mind. From the dull lights in her eyes, he guessed they were not good ones.

Angus and the others studied the terrain, noting landmarks that only each one would notice or remember.

"I have it," Angus said. The others nodded.

"If we are separated, this is where we

465

meet. If things go badly, you get out and come here if you can. Wait one hour at most, then go back. Make your way to the coast and the ship. Mr. Stanton has orders to sail at dawn, no matter who is or is not there, so do not delay."

Mr. Travis looked down at the château. "How do you plan to get in there? I see no subtle approach. We have to walk up that lane and there are two men at the end of it. They are sure to see us coming."

Kendale looked over at Marielle. He hated to admit it, but she had been right. They did need her. "The lady will help us to get in. You will keep the others beyond the lane, out of sight. Angus and I will accompany Miss Lyon to the door."

Mr. Travis laughed and shook his head. "Did you bring your calling cards?"

"Just be watching, Travis. When those two men are gone, bring the others up." He left the men and joined Marielle. "We will go down shortly. It will be as we planned while we walked here. Are you ready?"

She did not respond at first. Then she shook off her reverie. "Of course."

He slid his arm around her back and pulled her to his side. "Are you sure?"

She nodded. "To be here again. To see that building. It all comes back, very clearly."

She paused. "Everything."

He wished he could erase the worst of the everything. He wondered if tonight would at least allow it to dim again.

"Thank you for allowing me to come," she said. "Thank you for allowing me to do what I could."

He could think of nothing to say to that. He took her hand. "Let us go."

Mr. Travis kept the men hidden in the night beyond the lamps that lit the lane. Kendale and Marielle began the long walk to the door, with Angus in their wake like a servant.

He looked over at her. She did not hide the airs that her girlhood hours in this château had given her. She walked with the elegance that had long ago become second nature. She had released her hair from its plait and removed the cap so her hair fell in fashionable abandon. The knit shawl might have been made out of silk from the way it fell around her lithe form and flowed with her steps.

The two men saw them coming. On alert at once, but curious, they came together and walked down the steps of the château and into the circle where carriages would stop. The flames in the lamps around that circle showed their consternation that three strangers approached so boldly in the late evening hours.

Marielle walked right up to them. She gave each a good, long look, then smiled one of her devastating smiles. Both men immediately appeared taken aback. She spoke in French to them. Parisian French.

"I am Marielle de Lyon. I must see Monsieur Lamberte on a matter of great importance to him. Take me to him at once."

"He is not here. You must leave, madame."

"He is here. He must be. I have traveled a great distance in very rude circumstances. Send word to him that I am here. I promise you that he will want to see me."

They looked at each other, confused by her insistence. One, presumably the leader, sighed with exasperation and explained yet again that Lamberte was not at the château.

"Then let me in so I can leave something for him. It is a document most important that he will certainly want to have."

"That is impossible. We cannot allow a stranger —"

"I am not a stranger. He knows me well. I can see, however, that you will not help me to help him unless —" She held out her hand to Kendale. He placed four gold coins in her palm. Their value probably exceeded what these men earned guarding this door in a year.

She held it out. "Allow me in. A half hour at most, and I will be gone. I only need to leave the document where I know he will find it, but others will not."

The second man only had eyes for the gold. The leader also gazed at it longingly. While both men contemplated their duty, Angus moved until he stood by Marielle's other shoulder.

"No," the leader said gruffly, shaking his hand and all but pushing the gold away. "You must go now. Leave, madame, before I wonder too much why you are even here."

"Now, sir?" Angus asked Kendale.

"Yes."

In one instant the guards were peering at gold and lovely Marielle. In the next they were peering into the ends of Angus's two pistols. Angus made sure those ends were very close to the spots between their eyes.

"You should have taken the gold," Marielle said while Kendale relieved both men of their own weapons.

Angus stepped forward. The guards stepped back. They kept at that until they were out of the light in the carriage drive and under the eaves of the entrance. Angus placed the pistol right on the forehead of the second guard. "Ask him how many like him are inside."

Marielle translated. The leader cursed at his comrade to keep silent, but the pistol spoke louder. Two more guards manned the donjon, they were told.

The shuffles and sounds of boots grew louder on the lane as Travis and the others hurried forward. They set about tying the guards up.

"Went sweetly, sir," Angus said. "Not a shot and barely a sound. There's light above, but no one looked out."

Marielle came over to him. The excitement in her eyes glinted like stars in the night. "Only two more, too. That should not be hard."

"So he says. He could have lied."

"Do you think he did?"

"I think there are more than two of Lamberte's men in this house. Perhaps not guards. They could be footmen or retainers or even relatives, but they will not allow an invasion without a fight. I do not anticipate strolling in and out without being challenged."

The guards now sat on the ground, trussed and gagged. With a gesture Kendale told Angus to move them out of sight and away from the entrance.

When all was secured, he gathered them all in the shadows. "You two will stand here as they did. If anyone in the house looks out, let him see two men at their posts. Mr. Travis, you and the others will come with me. Angus, I want you to take Miss Lyon back to that hill. Remember my orders. You wait one hour, then you go."

Marielle froze. When Angus went over to her, she slapped his guiding hand away. Angus turned to him, none too pleased to be the object of her displeasure.

Kendale went to her. "I do not have time for this now. You will go with Angus. I am grateful for your help thus far, but you are not going inside where we do not know what we will face. There will be no arguments now. No persuasion. Do you understand?"

She hesitated, then nodded, her face hard with anger and worry.

"After one hour, Angus, you leave. Carry her if she resists. Do not wait if we have not returned."

"I expect to see you before that, sir."

"And I you. However . . ."

Angus nodded.

He turned to Marielle again. "You know I am right to do it this way. In your heart you do. Let us not part in anger."

Her expression broke. "No. Not in anger. I want to come so I know you are safe, not wait on that hill wondering."

"I will be safe."

She looked past him to where his men waited. "Can I kiss you?"

"I do not believe anyone will be surprised, after this morning."

She rose on her toes to give him the kiss. "May God go with you. Know that my love does too."

He resisted the urge to kiss her long and deeply then. He walked over to the others while Angus led her back toward the circular drive.

He realized he had forgotten something, and strode after them. "Marielle, what is his name? It would not do to bring you the wrong man."

"John. His name is John."

"Jean Lyon. Very good."

"No. *John.* And not John Lyon. His name is John Neville." She waved and followed Angus into the shadows that flanked the lane.

John Neville?

Damnation. Her father was English.

CHAPTER 22

They paused inside the reception hall and listened. Muffled sounds from above drifted down the grand staircase. Sharper ones came from below.

Kendale gestured for the others to follow him. Pistol at the ready, he walked down the passageway to the stairs that would take them below. The chateau might appear a manor house, but its foundations had been constructed for defense. The stone stairway wound tightly between thick stone walls. They filed down its spiraling curve. He went first, and the curve of the stairs left him blind to what lay ahead.

A loud shout from in front of him made him freeze. A laugh responded to the shout, and two male voices began talking. Other sounds, of doors closing and boots walking and metal scraping indicated they had found the servants quarters, just as Marielle had remembered. If her map was correct, the kitchen was at the far end of this lower level, and the donjon lay one floor below.

Slowly, with soft footfalls, they continued down the stairs. No lamps illuminated the way now, although a dim glow eked up from below. Dampness on the walls indicated they were underground now.

At the bottom of the stairs, Travis stepped down beside him. The other men pressed close. Kendale looked around the stair wall. Two men sat on stools flanking a crude table in the long, dark passage stretching to the right. One lamp hung on the wall near them. They spoke in low voices to each other.

"Too much to hope they would be asleep," Travis muttered.

"We are left to pray that they are cowards," Kendale whispered. He raised both of his pistols and took the last step so he could see the guards clearly. Aiming one pistol at each man, he claimed their attention by telling them in French not to move.

The man farthest away was having none of it. He overturned the table and dropped below its shield. While his comrade scrambled to join him, he fired his own weapon. Mr. Travis answered in kind. Lead balls started flying.

They took turns on the bottom step, moving back up while reloading. The two guards took turns too, from behind their table.

"Sir! From above." The sharp warning came right when Kendale fired. He switched positions with the man who uttered it, and proceeded to reload. This time he stayed in place and waited for the boots coming slowly down the stairs.

A head peered around the curve of the wall. Kendale made sure the eyes saw his gun. *"Allez,"* he said. He fingered a gold coin out of his pocket and threw it around the curve. It clattered against the stone, out of sight. *"Plus d'apres."* He was not sure he said it correctly, but he assumed the message would be understood. When the boots started trudging up, not down, he knew it had been.

"I just wounded one," Travis said while he pulled out his powder. "The other can't do this alone without cover while he reloads. He will give up soon."

In fact he gave up immediately. The blasts stopped and the donjon became a silent cave. Kendale stepped out of the stairwell and around the stone wall. One of the guards stood behind the overturned table, with his weapon balanced atop its edge. The other sat next to him, holding his shoulder with bloody fingers.

"Have someone tend the wounded one, but tie up the other," Kendale told Travis. He reached out for the keys that hung on the wall near the lamp. He looked the standing guard in the eyes and gestured to the doors. "English?"

The guard pointed to the door nearest the stairs, then reached over and pointed to the correct key.

Kendale set the key in the lock and swung the door wide. Inside a thin, white-haired man looked up in surprise from where he sat on a cot.

"John Neville?"

"That be me. Are you English? I could have sworn I heard my mother tongue coming through this door."

"You did hear English."

"What in hell are you doing here? Is the war over?"

"We are here for you, Mr. Neville. I am Viscount Kendale and these are my colleagues. We were sent by your daughter."

"My daughter?" He stood and walked to the door and looked out at Travis and the others. He shook his head, then smiled. "Well, I'll be damned."

John Neville trudged beside Kendale along the path in the forest. Other than a request for reassurance that his daughter fared well, he had not spoken a word since they left the donjon.

A thin man of middle height and years, his hair and beard had grown while in that donjon. Kendale worried that his sight had failed too, which was common, but the man walked like he could see where he was going. A bath was in order, soon, but on the whole Mr. Neville's appearance probably would not shock Marielle too much.

He trusted they would find her with Mr. Stanton on the yacht. With the very first shot fired he had thanked God that he had not allowed Marielle to enter that house.

The adventure had taken longer than anticipated, due to the unexpected tenacity of the guards. They had left both of them locked in Mr. Neville's cell. With luck the gold would buy the servants' indifference until daybreak, but they could not count on that. Every man understood that they needed to return to the inlet as quickly as possible.

"You must think I am an ungrateful man, not saying much like I am," Neville said.

"I expect you are too surprised to have much to say," Kendale replied.

"Isn't that. I'm trying to accommodate the ironies of the situation."

"Take your time. I do not require conversation."

"Don't you now? Good of you, sir. Viscount Kendale, I believe you said you were." He sighed. "In all my living days, I never thought to be rescued by the likes of you."

The last words were not spoken with admiration.

"The likes of me were all that was available. Would you have preferred not to be rescued at all?"

"No, no. I'm not saying that. Just it is an irony. But then my life has been full of them. I mean, I've spent my life devoted to getting rid of your kind, haven't I?"

"Have you?" That was something else Marielle had neglected to mention.

"Hell, yes. Why do you think I'm here? Came over to lend my skills to the great cause of equality. Of course I did not expect they would go and kill you all. Just get rid of the titles and such. Spread the wealth around more. That sort of thing."

"Great causes often get out of control. I suppose finding yourself a prisoner of one of the revolutionaries was one of the ironies?"

"One of them, but far from the first. I mean, how would you feel if you were me, plying your skills in the cause of eliminating the aristocracy, and your own wife goes and becomes the mistress of the local leading aristocrat? That was a hard irony, let me tell you. It helped that the man was likeable, but that was sort of ironic too."

"You sound philosophical about it, however."

"Had no choice, did I? He was good to my daughter too. Let her come to that château and stay with her mother. Of course, that influenced her and not to the good. She would come back home and be talking funny and walking funny — like a damned aristocrat, I realized. Hell, I'm in my workshop making prints calling for their downfall and my daughter was turning into one in front of my eyes." He sighed again.

"She has grown up to be a beautiful young woman, as you will soon see. She does still talk and walk a little funny, however."

Neville turned his head. "Did she whore for you? Is that why you did this? No, don't tell me. I don't want to know. I am still accommodating that you are a viscount. I owe you my freedom and maybe my life, and I don't even think viscounts should exist. It's a hell of a thing to digest."

Kendale left him to swallow what he could during the rest of the walk back. When they emerged from the woods that edged the inlet, he could see that figures waited on the deck.

"We are here, Mr. Neville. Marielle is waiting for you as soon as you get on board."

Neville peered at the yacht. "Who?"

"Marielle. Your daughter."

Neville chuckled as he climbed into the boat. "Is that what she is calling herself these days? Well, if it got a viscount to come get me out of that bastard Lamberte's clutches, I would be a fool to complain."

Marielle watched the little band emerge from the trees, her emotions swinging between elation and dread. Travis and the other men came out first, gesturing and calling to the ship to announce their success. Kendale showed last. He escorted a white-haired man with long hair and a beard.

Papa had never worn a beard. Surely he had been taller too. This man looked like a stranger.

They all waded to the rowboat and got in, then aimed toward the ship with their oars. Mr. Stanton began giving orders to prepare to sail.

One by one those men climbed up the rope ladder. She looked over the railing, staring at the white hair, seeking some recognizable detail so she would know it was Papa for certain.

It was his turn to climb. He refused help and took it slowly, with Kendale coming right behind him. Finally he stood on the deck, looking around at the ship and sails and all the men who had made the journey. He appeared confused, and even afraid.

His gaze came to rest on her. Squinting hard at her face, he approached her. "I'm told by this viscount this was all your doing."

She nodded, too moved to say more. Not a stranger now. Not at all. Those were Papa's eyes and that was Papa's voice. She looked down at the hands that she had seen so often holding a burin. Strong hands. Careful ones too.

He kept peering at her, as if she were a stranger too.

"Don't you recognize me at all?" she asked. "Have I changed so much?"

He shook his head slowly. His eyes filmed with tears. "I would recognize you anywhere, my girl. I am just astonished at how much you look like your mother now." He spread his arms. She flew into his embrace and they wept with joy together.

"Marianne," she said. "My given name was Marianne."

They sat on the deck with their backs against the wall of the cabin, bundled in a blanket. Mr. Neville slept inside. The reunion had been a little awkward, but very heartwarming. Every man on the yacht now enjoyed the satisfaction of having successfully executed a good deed.

"I could not keep the name once I ran from the château that night. I needed Lamberte to believe I had perished. It would not do for him to hear that Marianne Neville, who had witnessed his murders, thrived in London."

That made sense. Everything she had done made sense. Her history also explained away many inconsistencies, such as her thin accent when speaking English, and her comfort with the language. *Je suis désolée. I am sorry that I failed you.* One apology to her French mother, and one to her English father.

"Marianne Neville." He tried out the sound of it. Not as lyrical as Marielle Lyon, but he supposed he could get used to it.

"I have not been Marianne Neville for six years. I have not thought of myself that way for almost as long. I am not sure I can become accustomed to the name again. I suppose I will have to try, however."

"You can use any name you like."

"The Frenchwomen probably will not want to work in my studio if I am Marianne Neville. It helped that they believed I was one of them. Not only French, but an aristocrat too."

"It probably did. Your father would say that our kind have a natural prejudice against those who are not our kind."

She did not say anything, but he guessed what she was thinking. Her father would say that because it was true.

"You will have to show him your prints, Marianne. He will be proud that you learned well from him, and used your skill as he would have."

She huddled closer under his arm, and pressed her eyes to his shoulder. "Yes, of course. He *will* be proud, I suppose. Only — Please do not address me like that. Not tonight. Not yet. Let me be Marielle Lyon with you for a while longer. Until we reach England, perhaps, but at least tonight."

He drew her closer yet, so that they formed one shape within the blanket. Her limbs and breath warmed him beneath the stars while the sea smacked in rhythms against the ship's hull. He lifted her chin so that he could kiss her. "It is only a name. I want you no matter what you are called."

She nodded and nestled in, but he knew, he just knew, she did not believe him.

CHAPTER 23

Two weeks later Kendale entered Brooks's. Southwaite spied him and called him over.

"Where have you been? I know you do not care for the Season, but you have never played the hermit during one before."

He shrugged. "I was at Ravenswood, and some other properties."

It was not a lie, although he had become perhaps too smooth of late with the half-truths. He *had* been at Ravenswood the last fortnight, first while Marielle — the name she decided to use for now — negotiated Mr. Neville's future, then with Marielle alone after her father had been established in a house up in Newcastle. John Neville, after reading every paper and journal that Marielle could buy between the coast and London, had concluded his future lay with the workers of the new industries emerging in the north.

As for the other properties, he could not

be blamed if Southwaite assumed he meant properties owned by the Viscount Kendale.

"Will you remain in town now?" Ambury asked. "There is to be a first-rate sale at Tattersall's on Friday."

"Perhaps. For a few days at least." He had finally, reluctantly, brought Marielle back to London and her life behind that blue door. He pictured her in the studio, showing some recent French émigré how to dab color on an engraving.

The two of them continued their conversation, which unfortunately had to do with a report from Mr. Ryan that Southwaite had brought with him. He read a paragraph describing the sudden appearance, then disappearance, of too many red coats in Dover two weeks earlier.

"He believes it had something to do with an attempt by Tarrington to row over to France in broad daylight," Southwaite explained. "A naval frigate gave chase, and the galley dodged and maneuvered for a good hour before surrendering."

"Odd for Tarrington to risk that," Ambury said. "Normally all he wants is the light of a half moon."

"Odd and unwise. According to Ryan, he was questioned for days but insisted he had only been practicing for —" Southwaite read on and laughed. "This is rich, and it sounds just like him — *For the annual galley rowing competition held south of Deal every summer.*"

"I had no idea there was such a race."

"I daresay there will be one this year." Southwaite read on, scanning the letter for news to share. His gaze halted in the middle of the back of the sheet. "In conclusion Mr. Ryan expresses regret in not seeing me on my recent visit, and warns me that the whole coast is talking about my new yacht and will be imposing themselves in the hopes of sailing in it with me." He glanced sharply in Ambury's direction. "His last sentence reads, *Please tell Lord Kendale that I enjoyed our conversation when he visited, and hope that my service to the two of you continues to be useful.*"

Ambury turned a smile on Kendale, one of amiable curiosity. "Kendale, was one of the properties you visited Southwaite's property?"

"I usually ride across it when I go to the coast to deal with the watchers. It is hard to avoid Crownhill's lands." He called for a servant and ordered some wine.

"He was there," Ambury said to Southwaite. "He is going to pretend that Ryan was not clear as to when they met, but he

487

was there recently. Probably when Tarrington played his odd game with the frigate."

"Perhaps he merely enjoyed a day sailing on the new yacht that I do not own."

"We can but hope. More likely he has been up to something with his band of merry men. If we were not told, it was either dangerous or illegal."

"Do you think he finally did it? Went over and —" Southwaite replaced the rest with a meaningful stare at Ambury.

The wine came. He drank some while they eyed him.

"Damnation," Ambury muttered. "He had an adventure and did not include me."

Southwaite frowned. "Did you kill someone, Kendale?"

He put down his glass. "No, but the day is still young."

That checked them. With only three or four more glances exchanged, they began a forced discussion of that sale at Tattersall's.

"I am wondering," he said, interrupting. "When you buy your ladies jewelry, which jeweler do you use?"

"Is this more of your idle, unaccountable curiosity about women? Or do you plan to purchase such a gift?" Ambury asked.

"I am considering another purchase."

"Are you speaking of a little bauble, or a very good piece of jewelry that will become a family heirloom?"

"The latter, I expect."

"Is this for Miss Lyon?" Southwaite asked.

"It is."

A slow smile broke on Ambury's face. "Oh, how the mighty fall. Has she completely vanquished you, Kendale?"

It was a hell of a thing to ask a man, and in the grand salon of Brooks's at that. Yet it seemed to him that only a coward would ignore the challenge.

"She has."

Never in his life had he seen either of them look more astonished.

"I trust you are not going to faint, Ambury."

"No. Of course not. No." Ambury collected his wits, then his limbs. He stood. "I will take you to several very fine jewelers and help you pick. Do not argue with me. Like everything else in the matter at hand, you are ill equipped to act without advice. Luck smiled on you the last time with that necklace, but is unlikely to do so again."

"I will come too," Southwaite said, rising. "Ambury's taste can be too dramatic at times. A restraining opinion may be needed."

There was no way out of it. He joined his tutors. They bickered about Ambury's taste in jewels all the way out to the street.

There were times when valor required humility. Kendale reminded himself of that as he approached the very fine house on Grosvenor Square. He did not expect this call to be a comfortable one. Unlike Southwaite and Ambury, he was not yet ready to absolve the man within of all guilt. That made being in his debt all the more galling.

The servant took his card, and returned quickly to escort him to the library. Penthurst looked over quizzically as he entered.

"I am glad that I found you alone," Kendale said.

"I expect that you are. Sit with me, Kendale. Bend that rigid, uncompromising spine of yours for a few minutes."

He sat. He did not bend much. "I have come to thank you for the warning."

"I am glad you heeded it. I was not sure that you would."

"There were others involved. I would have only faced scandal, of course. They might have been transported."

"I believe Whitehall was thinking more in terms of the hulks for them. If it is any consolation, I have heard that the man you

490

sought has been just posted to some obscure spot in the Pyrenees. The new military star in France has some questions about your colonel's fitness for his rank. Too many retreats, it is said."

"You think that you know who he is, do you?"

"I believe that I have known longer than you have."

A slow burn started in his head. It would not take much for it to explode into a conflagration. "Damnation. Why did you not tell me? You knew that I —"

"I did not tell you because you would do something rash and brave and diplomatically disastrous in the name of a promise given to comfort a bitter, dying comrade. Besides, for the last year we were not talking at all. Remember?"

He smothered the heat through a sheer force of will. He sought humility again. "I also want to thank you for pointing me in the direction of Garrett."

"I will not ask what you did with the information, although I have reason to think it would be a fine story. Since you are here, hale and fit, I assume you saw success."

"In the matter of the day, yes. Not entirely, however." He reached in his coat, and removed a small, thin, leather bound book.

"Do you have any friends who have diplomatic ties in Paris? Who know like-minded men on the other side who are principled and honest?"

Penthurst gazed at the little book. "I may."

"Can you get this to someone over there who would find it useful?" He handed over the book.

Penthurst examined its pages. "Ah, Monsieur Lamberte has been a bad boy. At least he shared with his friends. These pages back here appear to be his bribes. The conspirators were good enough to initial them, so he had proof. That is a very good way to ensure friendship." He paged to the end, paused, and looked up. "Your colonel is here. From right after Toulon, when he was posted in Nantes."

"Is he? I'll be damned."

"Convenient for you."

Very convenient. Marielle had no idea what a gift she had given him when she placed that book in his hands and asked him to do what he thought best with it.

With a vague smile, Penthurst returned to examining the book. "Does this Lamberte know you have this?"

"He may have deduced that it is in England. He would not guess that I have it."

"It is dangerous for anyone to have it. He

knows he will not survive this if it is used against him."

"He is a thief and a murderer. If I could be sure he would come for it himself, I would let him know it is in my possession, and meet him on the field of honor and take care of it privately. However, he might not come himself, but send others. Therefore I will leave it to France, and hope I hear of an execution soon."

"I cannot promise that you will."

"Such men as that always have more enemies than friends. Even now he is making more of them as he tries to rise. Given the chance, those enemies will have his head."

Penthurst set the book aside. "Then we will do what we can to give them that chance. Enough talk of politics and war. Tell me, are you enjoying your new yacht?"

The coach attracted attention on the lane as it always did. Marielle heard it arriving when it was a block away.

Dominique peered out the window, then closed her eyes and placed a hand on her chest, calming herself. "He has come. I feared that — well, knowing everything, that he would not."

Marielle had not feared it. She had been

sure of it.

It had not helped that her father had refused to show Kendale any particular respect, and spoken freely about the irrelevance of lords in a modern age of free men. It had been very hard to be Marielle Lyon when her own father made sure all who heard him remembered she was Marianne Neville.

Their last days together after returning from Newcastle had been passionate and poignant. She had grabbed all that she could while she could. She had abandoned herself to loving as freely as her heart chose, so much and so intensely that she ached from the experience. As a result, ever since they left Ravenswood and she entered this house, she had grieved the loss.

Now he had come to call on her again, as he had said he would and she had believed he would not after giving the liaison serious thought. He had come in his state coach with the escutcheon on the side. Four, not two, horses pulled it.

He stepped out of the coach. He appeared magnificent, and every inch the lord he was. His expensive coats and doe-skin breeches flattered his form. His fashionably cropped hair brought attention to his green eyes. He appeared serious. So serious that her joy fell.

It would be just like him to feel an obligation to explain why the liaison had to end. Other men might simply let it fade away, but not Viscount Kendale.

He came to the door and she and Dominique pulled back from the window.

She looked down at her old dress. The paint on her hands would never come off in time.

"I wish he had let me know he would call, so that I had time to prepare, and look my best." Since he knew she was not an impoverished aristocrat, she would merely appear poor and tattered now.

Dominique walked toward the door to answer his knock. "He has seen you at your worst and your best. Did it ever make a difference? Run to the sitting room. I will bring him there."

She hurried past Dominique and darted into the sitting room. She untied the rag that bound her hair at her neck and stuffed it under a chair after trying in vain to rub off the blue paint.

Her heart rose to her throat when she heard his bootsteps approaching. Perhaps he had not come to regretfully end their liaison. Maybe he wanted it to continue awhile the way it had, meeting in that cottage. Should she do it? That would be different too now, wouldn't it? There could not even be a pretense that they came together as equals anymore. Her father had lectured long and hard on that when they had privacy, in case she had not realized how Kendale's view had to change.

He entered the chamber and for a bedazzled moment she forgot about all of those worries. Seeing him brought too much happiness for such as that.

He appeared happy too. That gave her heart. He smiled and came over, bent, and kissed her. Then he sat beside her. "Will we be left alone, or will Madame LaTour take up her post near the window?"

"She is not here today, and Dominique will see no one intrudes."

He embraced her and kissed her more fully. "I brought you something." He reached in his coat and took out a little box.

She opened it. Two perfect pearls dangled below two tasteful emeralds on a pair of earrings. The pearls alone were priceless. She heard Madame LaTour's admonition. *Property and jewels.*

"They are beautiful." She picked one up and fitted it, turning the tiny screw behind her lobe. When she had them both on, she faced him. "How do they look?"

"Elegant, just as you are."

That was a sweet thing to say. She kissed him and set the little box aside. She could not resist moving her head so that she felt the pearls tap her skin.

"Are they a parting gift, Gavin?"

His expression fell. "Of course not. Why would you think that?"

She shrugged. She should not have to humble herself by putting it into words.

"Of course, if you want to part — I must accept that. However, I had hoped we would not," he said. "If we do, I will curse myself even more for allowing pride and anger to interfere with the fortnight you allowed me."

"I am fortunate that you did, however. I am in your debt."

He took her hand and pressed a kiss on it. "I do not want you in my debt. I do not want it to be like that."

She turned her body toward his so she could look in his eyes. So serious he appeared. And, perhaps, a little confounded. It would be cruel to make him wonder, especially when her heart almost burst from relief and emotion.

Stretching her fingers into his hair, she drew him closer. To her surprise he rested his head on her breast. She kissed his crown. "It could never be like that. Only debt. I love you too much to think of you that way, even though I will always be grateful that you did not lose faith in me after all the deceptions. The rest of the fortnight is yours, and however longer you want."

He straightened and looked at her. He did not appear nearly as joyous as she had hoped. In fact, he frowned.

She had misunderstood. Erred somehow. She began to speak again but his fingers came to rest on her lips, silencing her. "No, do not speak. Allow me. Here is the thing —" He paused forever, chewing over just what the thing was.

Finally, she took pity on him. "You do not have to declare yourself too. You have proven your affection in ways few women ever know."

"Yes, I must. It would be cowardly if I do not. I lack practice, that is all." He cleared his throat, collected himself, and his face found its confident, hard angles. "You cannot know how happy I am to hear you say you love me. I am not a man it is easy to love, I suspect. I am no great prize and am appealing to women mostly for the accidental inheritance of title and estate. I do not dance attendance well, and am hopeless when it comes to the flatteries and dissembling expected by society."

"You are most appealing, sir, in ways that have nothing to do with your title or —"

Again those fingers silenced her lips. "You must let me speak. Please."

She nodded meekly.

"I wanted you for months before we ever spoke. You were correct about that. You knew. I still want you. I always will. If you will give me as long as I want, we are speaking of a lifetime, darling. You need to know that. It is not mere desire that makes me want you now, or affection, but love. I have been a long time coming to know that emotion. I do not love easily. I do not think I stop loving easily either. This will not pass, ever."

He astonished her. Had any man ever said this better? Or as honestly? She only had to look at him to know he meant every word.

He took her hand. "You are in my heart all the time. In my head too. When a man feels like this — The earrings were not a parting gift, Marielle. Nor baubles for a mistress. They are a gift to my lady, so that she might look favorably upon my proposal of marriage."

Marriage. She startled enough that the pearls tapped her again. "I am not Marielle. I am Marianne. Do you think to let others continue believing I am the niece of a comte? If the truth comes out —"

"Of course it will come out. We have no reason to lie, and it would not be honorable for me to present you as other than you are. As for your name, you will always be Marielle to me but you can use any name you want. I already told you that."

Emotions jumbled inside her. Love and worry and a poignant regret. "I do not think you have carefully considered this. Even Southwaite did better in his match with Emma. I will love you forever, and all the more for offering this, but —"

"I am not a man who speaks rashly. And no one, no man, will do better than I if you agree, Marielle."

He believed that. She could see that he did. She also saw indescribable warmth in his gaze, and some astonishment at himself and this love.

"Of course, I agree, Gavin. I would be honored to marry you."

He embraced her fully, encompassing her in his possessive arms. He gave her a deep kiss full of desire and love.

She nestled against him, listening to his heart, enjoying the protective, caring closure of his arms. Happiness moved her so much she wanted to cry from it.

"Will Ravenswood be our home when we are not in town?" she asked, picturing the chambers and imagining some improvements they should make.

"Of course."

"Will I be allowed to have my female friends visit?"

A pause. A good ten-count passed. She bit back a laugh. Lord Kendale had perhaps not thought everything through as thoroughly as he believed.

"Certainly," he said. "I will even sit in the drawing room and listen to the gossip and such."

"That will not be necessary. You can go off hunting and riding with the others. You do not have to change. I would be a poor wife if I did not accept your Kendale ways."

"If you insist," he murmured against her hair. He sounded very relieved.

They shared the excitement and contentment in silence a little longer.

"Will I be allowed to have some female servants at Ravenswood?"

He stilled. A statue in stone would move more.

"I expect you will need some."

"Old Pete can hardly dress my hair."

"Of course not." He kissed her temple. "How many is 'some'?"

"I think six would do."

"Six?"

"It would help even things out there a bit."

He sighed. "I suppose it would."

She giggled, and turned so she could face him. "I am joking, darling. A lady's maid, and Dominique as a companion are all I really need."

He brightened. "That would be fine. That is, whatever you want will be fine."

"I promise not to ruin everything. You can still have a barracks in the cellars, and send men off on suspicious missions. I won't ask about them or interfere in any way."

"You can ask. They think of you as one of them, after France. It is another reason why you are the perfect wife for me."

No one else would think her the perfect wife for him, but if he did, that was all that mattered. "No one will ever love you more or be more loyal, I promise you that, Gavin."

He took her face in his hands, in that caring way he had. "I know. I am sure of it. I am sure of you. And I am so glad that I felt compelled to solve the mystery of Marielle Lyon."

ABOUT THE AUTHOR

Madeline Hunter has published twenty-three critically acclaimed historical romances. Her books regularly appear on the *New York Times* and *USA Today* bestseller lists. More than six million copies of her books are in print, and her books have been translated into twelve languages. She has won two RITA awards and is a seven-time RITA finalist. Madeline holds a PhD in art history, which she teaches at the university level. She loves to hear from readers and can be contacted through her website: www .madelinehunter.com. You can also follow her at MadelineHunter on Twitter, Facebook, and Goodreads.

The employees of Thorndike Press hope you have enjoyed this Large Print book. All our Thorndike, Wheeler, and Kennebec Large Print titles are designed for easy reading, and all our books are made to last. Other Thorndike Press Large Print books are available at your library, through selected bookstores, or directly from us.

For information about titles, please call:
  (800) 223-1244

or visit our Web site at:
  http://gale.cengage.com/thorndike

To share your comments, please write:
  Publisher
  Thorndike Press
  10 Water St., Suite 310
  Waterville, ME 04901